BEYOND THE CRESCENT SKY

THE BALKAN LEGENDS

OTHER BOOKS BY A. L. SOWARDS

BEYOND THE
CRESCENT SKY

THE BALKAN LEGENDS

A. L. SOWARDS

SHADOW
MOUNTAIN
PUBLISHING

Library of Congress Cataloging-in-Publication Data
Names: Sowards, A. L., author. | Sowards, A. L. Balkan legends ; book 2.
Title: Beyond the crescent sky / A. L. Sowards.
Description: [Salt Lake City] : Shadow Mountain Publishing, [2025] | Series: The Balkan legends ; 2 | Summary: "In 1383, in the midst of conflict between Serbs and Greeks, Serbian soldier Ivan is captured and becomes a pawn in a dangerous power struggle. Helena, a Greek healer, is tasked with caring for him, but as they grow closer, their budding romance risks her life and his freedom. Facing the Ottoman threat, they must choose between loyalty and love."—Provided by publisher.
Identifiers: LCCN 2024021845 (print) | LCCN 2024021846 (ebook) | ISBN 9781639933006 (hardback) | ISBN 9781649333063 (ebook)
Subjects: LCSH: Healers—Greece—Fiction. | Soldiers—Serbia—Fiction. | Serbia—History— To 1456—Fiction. | Turkey—History—Ottoman Empire, 1288–1918—Fiction. | BISAC: FICTION / Historical / Medieval | FICTION / Romance / Historical / Medieval | LCGFT: Historical fiction. | Romance fiction. | Novels.
Classification: LCC PS3619.0945 B49 2025 (print) | LCC PS3619.0945 (ebook) | DDC 813/.6— dc23/eng/20240617
LC record available at https://lccn.loc.gov/2024021845
LC ebook record available at https://lccn.loc.gov/2024021846

Printed in Canada
PubLitho

10   9   8   7   6   5   4   3   2   1

For Samantha Millburn

Friend, editor, sounding board, muse, and advocate.
Thank you for believing in my work and making it better.

Map by Heather Willis

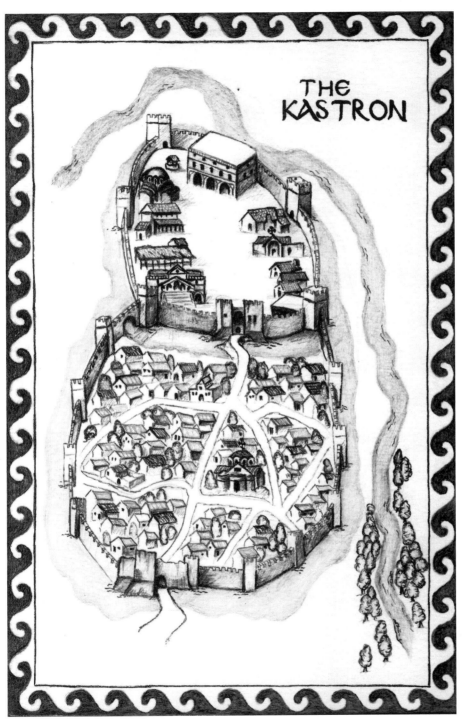

THE KASTRON

Graphic by Heather Willis

GLOSSARY AND
HISTORICAL BACKGROUND

Acropolis: The heavily fortified portion of a kastron.

Akincis: Ottoman irregular, light cavalry, often serving as scouts or a vanguard to the regular army.

Bey: Originally a term for a Turkish tribal chieftain but also used as an Ottoman title for a local representative of the sultan's authority.

Byzantine Empire: The Byzantine Empire was the eastern half of the Roman Empire, though contemporaries did not use the term. The Byzantines referred to themselves as Romans, and their neighbors often referred to them as Greeks. Their capital was Constantinople. For centuries, the Byzantine Empire controlled the Mediterranean world, but by the time of this novel, their borders had shrunk significantly. The empire still included much of Thrace, the Peloponnese, and lands around Thessaloniki. Though their military and political power was on the wane, their cultural influence remained strong. Their religion was Orthodox Christian.

Corselet: A piece of armor meant to protect the torso. It was normally hip length, with or without sleeves. Often made of lamellar in this novel's setting.

Courser: A warhorse, known for strength and speed.

Dalmatica: A garment with wide, three-quarters-length sleeves and a roughly knee-length skirt, generally layered over a tunic. Could be worn by men or women.

Dama: Term of respect for a Serbian noblewoman.

Destrier: The most valuable type of warhorse, trained for battle and tournaments.

Effendi: Turkish title of respect.

Ghazi: For the purposes of this novel, the term refers to an Ottoman raider who depended on plunder for his pay. The word has a more expansive definition outside the setting of the fourteenth-century Balkan Peninsula, but the more limited definition is used for clarity and accuracy in this book's historical setting.

Grad: A fortified Slavic town.

Great Mortality: The term contemporary people used to refer to the plague now known as the Black Death, which swept through Europe, peaking in the late 1340s and early 1350s.

Grody: A fortified area of a Slavic town or village.

Greek Fire: A Byzantine weapon similar to napalm.

Gusle: A single-stringed musical instrument held in the lap and played with a bow.

Hauberk: A shirt of mail armor, usually with sleeves and reaching to the midthigh.

Hyperpyron: A gold coin minted by the Byzantine Empire. (plural: *hyperpyra*)

Imam: Muslim religious leader.

Janissaries: Elite Ottoman infantry. Until the seventeenth century, they were formed largely of Christian children taken from their homes and forcibly converted to Islam.

Kastron: A fortified Byzantine town.

Kastrophylax: Kephale's assistant for maintaining a kastron's defenses.

Kataphraktoi: Heavily armored Byzantine cavalry.

Kephale: Byzantine commander in charge of a town's military and civil functions.

Kispet: Leather trousers worn during oil wrestling.

Knez: Serbian term for a prince.

Kral: Serbian term for a king.

Kyria: Term of respect for a Greek noblewoman.

Kyrios: Term of respect for a Greek nobleman.

Lamellar: A type of body armor made from laced plates of leather, horn, or metal.

Manjaniq: A Turkish siege weapon used for slinging rocks.

Meroph: A Serbian serf. Merophs owed labor, tribute, or both to their feudal lord and to the church.

Narthex: The entrance area, antechamber, or court of an Orthodox church.

Nave: The main part of an Orthodox church between the narthex and the sanctuary.

Ottoman Empire: A Turkish empire established in Asia Minor, then expanded into Europe. Murad I, the founder's grandson, is sultan during this story. In the 1380s, many Balkan Christian rulers were vassals to the Ottomans, but Turkish control was not yet complete. The Ottomans were Muslims. They saw Europe as a new frontier—a land of opportunity and destiny.

Palfrey: A horse valued for its smooth gait, ideal for riding long distances.

Palaiologoi: A dynasty that ruled the Byzantine Empire from the mid-thirteenth century until the empire's fall.

Paroikos: Greek tenant farmer. (plural: *paroikoi*)

Pasha: Ottoman title for a high-ranking military or civic leader.

Pehlivan: Contestant in an oil-wrestling match.

Petrobola: A beam-sling weapon used to hurl rocks or other items. (plural: *petroboloi*)

Pronoia: Land granted by the Byzantine emperor in exchange for military service.

Rumelia: Ottoman term for Europe.

Saracen: Originally a term for Muslim Arabs, but by the time of this story, it was used by Christians to mean any Muslim.

Satnik: Serbian official, subordinate to the župan, with military and civil responsibilities.

Scimitar: A sword with a curved blade.

Semantron: A percussion instrument played with a mallet, often used at Orthodox monasteries.

Serbian Empire: The Medieval Serbian Empire reached its zenith in the middle of the fourteenth century and included much of the Balkan Peninsula. It suffered serious setbacks with the death of Emperor Stefan Dušan in 1355 and a devastating loss at the Battle of Maritsa in 1371. The Serb religion was Christian Orthodox, and their culture was heavily affected by both Byzantine and Italian influences.

Shahada: Muslim profession of faith.

Sipahis: Ottoman cavalry, compensated by salary or land grant.

Spathion: Type of sword common in the late Byzantine era, about three feet long with a double-edged blade.

Timar: An Ottoman feudal estate, granted by the sultan.

Tzaousios: Byzantine garrison commander or similar military leader.

Varangians: An elite Byzantine guard unit, originally composed of Viking warriors. By the fourteenth century, it relied heavily on Anglo-Saxon recruits.

Vlach: An ethnic group in the Balkans, often shepherds during the Middle Ages.

Župa: A geographic area ruled by a župan.

Župan: Serb lord, comparable to a count.

CHARACTER LIST

IVAN'S FAMILY

Ivan Miroslavević: Serb nobleman to inherit the župa of Sivi Gora

Danilo Darrasević: Ivan's cousin

Župan Konstantin Miroslavević: Župan of Rivak, Ivan's older brother

Dama Suzana: Konstantin's wife

Marko: Konstantin and Suzana's eldest son

Pavle: Konstantin and Suzana's second son

Župan Miroslav: Župan of Rivak until his death in 1371, father of Konstantin, Lidija, Ivan, and two daughters who did not survive childhood

Dama Lidija: Miroslav's daughter, Ivan and Konstantin's sister, Decimir's wife

Dama Zorica: Miroslav's sister, Danilo's mother, Ivan and Konstantin's aunt

SERBS FROM RIVAK

Miladin: Member of the Rivak garrison

Bojan: Member of the Rivak garrison

Kuzman: Member of the Rivak garrison

Zoran: Member of the Rivak garrison

Father Vlatko: Priest at Rivak

SERBS FROM SIVI GORA

Župan Đurad Lukarević: Župan of Sivi Gora, Ivan and Konstantin's maternal grandfather

Goran: Member of the Sivi Gora garrison

Cyril: Member of the Sivi Gora garrison

OTHER SERBS

Župan Dragomir: Župan in lands near Rivak

Decimir: Župan Dragomir's grandson, Lidija's husband

Knez Lazar: Serbian prince and leader

Miloš Obilić: Serb noble, Lazar's son-in-law

Tatjana: Danilo's intended

HELENA'S FAMILY

Kyria Helena: A Greek midwife in Byzia

Kyria Euphrosyne: Helena's sister, Leo's wife

Leo: Euphrosyne's husband, Basil's nephew

GREEKS WHO LIVE OR WORK IN THE ACROPOLIS

Kyrios Basil Kameteros: Byzia's kephale (civic leader)

Andronicus: Basil's eldest son

Alexius: Basil's youngest son

Kyria Domnica: Alexius's wife

Gregoras: Byzia's tzaousios (garrison commander)

Demetrios: Member of Byzia's garrison, Gregoras's son

Radomir: Byzia's kastrophylax (commander of defenses), a native Serb, Župan Dragomir's estranged brother

Callinicus: Member of Byzia's garrison, Helena's intended prior to his death

Matthias: Member of Byzia's garrison

Niketas: Member of Byzia's garrison

Paulus: Member of Byzia's garrison

Petros: Surgeon in Byzia

Philippos: Stableboy at the acropolis

Pasara: Servant at the acropolis

OTHER GREEKS

Father Symeon: Priest in Byzia

Christophoros: Paroikos, reserve member of the garrison, Ithamar's husband

Ithamar: Paroikos woman, Christophoros's wife

Theodora: Christophoros and Ithamar's oldest daughter

Zöe: Christophoros and Ithamar's younger daughter

Anna: Midwife who trained Helena

Antonina: Paroikos woman

Constantina: Paroikos woman, Antonina's mother

Bardas: Paroikos, reserve member of the garrison

Himerius: Paroikos, reserve member of the garrison

Isaakios: Paroikos, reserve member of the garrison

Maria: The blacksmith's wife

Martina: A woman in the kastron

OTTOMAN GHAZIS

Iskandar bin Abdullah: Ghazi spy and raider, Abdullah bin Isa's son

Abdullah bin Isa: Leader of a ghazi band, father of Nasuh, Saruca, and Iskandar

Nasuh: Abdullah's son and Iskandar's half brother

Hasan: Ghazi raider

Ahmed: Ghazi raider

Ali: Ghazi raider

KASIM'S FAMILY AND RETAINERS

Kasim bin Yazid: Ottoman military leader

Bahar: Kasim's first wife

Saruca: Kasim's second wife, Abdullah's daughter, Iskandar's half sister

Evhad: Kasim and Saruca's son

Desislava: Kasim's third wife, a Bulgarian

Cemal bin Salih: Soldier working for Kasim

SULTAN MURAD AND HIS COURT

Sultan Murad: Ottoman sultan from 1362 to 1389

Bayezid: Sultan Murad's son

Yakub: Sultan Murad's son

Savcı: Sultan Murad's son

Çandarlı Halil Pasha: Sultan Murad's vizier

Lala Şahin Pasha: Ottoman military leader

CHAPTER ONE
OFF TO WANDER

The Balkans, 1383

IVAN LIFTED HIS THREE-YEAR-OLD NEPHEW from the back of a dappled gray pony. The hem of Marko's short tunic fluttered around his small trousers as Ivan placed him on the straw-strewn floor of the stable. "We'd like to take you with us, but if we took you away for an entire fortnight, your mother would kill us."

"And if your mother kills us, there will be no one to help you snitch pastries from the kitchen." Danilo, Ivan's cousin, winked, then plucked the boy up, tossed him in the air, and caught him again.

Marko squealed in delight and patted Danilo's beard. It was dark and full, and Ivan, a year younger than his cousin, tried very hard not to be envious of it. "But you'll be away too long!" Marko stuck out his bottom lip.

Ivan took the saddle off the pony and put it on a post. "It will be shorter than my last trip. You'll remember me when we return, won't you?" Ivan had been gone most of the summer, off in his grandfather's lands, where he was heir. But it was here in Rivak where he'd grown up and where the people most dear to him lived. It had taken little Marko dozens of pony rides, a score of stolen pastries, and a full week to once more grow comfortable with Ivan upon his return. Leaving so soon meant he might fade from Marko's memory again.

Marko squirmed in Danilo's arms. "But I want to see my father."

"So do I." Ivan pulled a few pieces of dry grass from the pony's coat, then set about doing a thorough brushing despite their hurry. Based on the news they'd received from a passing monk, the army Ivan's brother led was somewhere in Macedonia, still some distance from Rivak, but Konstantin's brotherly lectures over the years had stuck in Ivan's head—there were no shortcuts in the care of horses or ponies. Ivan and Danilo had taken Marko out for a ride, so it was their responsibility to care for the animal afterward, especially when most of the grooms traveled with the army.

"We'll make sure your father comes home safely." Danilo set Marko down and saddled two coursers. Though kinsmen, Ivan and Danilo looked nothing alike. Ivan's aunt said he took after his father, her brother, the former župan of Rivak, and Danilo took after her husband, the Turkish refugee who'd served Župan Miroslav until their deaths at the Battle of Maritsa. Ivan had to take her word for it because the battle had been twelve years in the past. He had been five. He remembered his father only a little and his uncle even less.

"Why are you taking so many swords?" Marko poked at Ivan's sheaths as Ivan fastened them to the saddle.

"The saber is for fighting on horseback. The spathion is for fighting on foot." Ivan took the swords out to show the boy. "See how the saber has a curved blade so it's less likely to get stuck? And the spathion is sharp on both sides. But we won't need either. Your father leads a mighty army. And we'll be in friendly lands all the way there."

"Mostly friendly." Danilo's lips twisted into a half smile.

Ivan adjusted his horse's bit. "Mostly friendly." Travel in the remnants of the Serb and Roman Empires always involved risk. The monk had made it unmolested, but few brigands would see him as a tempting target. Men traveling with warhorses and pack mules might not be so lucky. Ivan should have known better than to tempt fate. He'd seen illness, death, and disaster befall his family often enough that caution should have been his constant companion. Yet standing in the familiar stables, warmed by the early autumn sun, it was hard to feel anything other than excitement at the prospect of a journey with his cousin.

Danilo took his horse's reins in one hand and Marko's fingers in the other. "Come on, we best turn you over to your mother before we ride off."

Ivan expected to find Suzana in the chapel or in the keep, but she stood just outside the stables, arms crossed as she studied the two laden mules Ivan and Danilo had left near the palisade wall of Rivakgrad's fortified grody.

"Where are you two going?" Her brown eyes hadn't lost their normal warmth, but they were narrowed in suspicion.

"To find your husband." Ivan glanced around the bailey to make sure his aunt wasn't nearby. He didn't think they would get away with leaving if both women were set against it.

"Your brother isn't lost. And you're needed here—you can't ride off during harvest. It's bad enough that Kostya and most of the garrison are gone."

Ivan checked the ropes on his pack mule. "The merophs will manage the crops, as they always do. We'll be back in time to help with everything else."

Suzana frowned, probably because Ivan was right. There was work for them if they stayed but nothing that couldn't wait until their return.

"Don't be angry, Suzana." Danilo's lips made a charming sort of pout. "We'll pester him with tales of your sweetness and beauty and speed his return to you."

"Kostya will do what is most practical for the army regardless of his wishes to see me again." Her voice was stern, but the frown had softened.

"Marko was saying how much he'd like to ride with us. You'll let him come, won't you?" Ivan knew the answer would be no. Marko wasn't the first child born to Konstantin and Suzana, but he was the first to survive infancy. Everyone felt a keen need to protect the boy, including Ivan and Danilo. But if they agreed to leave Marko behind, despite never intending to take him anyway, Suzana might feel that she'd won a concession from them.

She took Marko's hand and pulled him to her side. "That's not funny, Ivan. Marko isn't going, and you aren't either. There may be brigands or ghazis, and there are only two of you. It's simply not safe."

"I'll keep my bow strung just in case we run into trouble." Danilo pulled his bow out and wedged it between his feet to string it.

Ivan suspected he would unstring it again as soon as they were out of sight because Danilo was meticulous with his bows, and leaving it strung too often would stretch the string or warp the limbs.

"You're still boys. You may not go," Suzana said.

Ivan mounted his horse. "Nearly eighteen is hardly a boy. And Danilo is nineteen. We should have gone with the army in the spring."

Suzana walked to Ivan's horse. "Kostya had you stay because he wanted you safe."

"And I need to see that he is safe." Not only had Ivan and Konstantin lost their father, but they'd also lost their mother and all three of their sisters over the years. They still had Aunt Zorica and Danilo and Suzana and Marko, but as much as Ivan loved each of them, no one could replace his brother.

Suzana glanced at Danilo. "What did your mother say?"

Danilo fiddled with his horse's bridle. "I wrote her a loving letter explaining our intentions and asked one of the grooms to deliver it." Ivan had overheard his cousin tell the groom not to deliver it until they were out of Rivakgrad, but neither of them told Suzana that.

"I really think you should stay." Suzana crossed her arms again.

Danilo finished adjusting the straps. "I think you're jealous. You want to come. I'll saddle your mare for you."

Suzana sighed. "I know my place. It is here, managing my husband's lands when his overlord calls him away to war."

"And our place is at our župan's side," Ivan said.

"Kostya won't be your župan for long, Ivan. You know your place."

"Which is why I must go to Kostya now. It's one of my last chances to show him my loyalty." Come spring, Ivan would live with his grandfather in Sivi Gora permanently, and then he would see his brother but seldom. "Our days together are numbered. Can you blame me for wanting an extra week with him?"

"I understand why you wish to go." Suzana ran her fingers through Marko's fluffy brown hair. "But what if something happens to you?"

"We're armed. I'll sleep in my armor if it will ease your worry." Ivan hoped she wouldn't make the request, because the mail hauberk was heavy and uncomfortable. He intended to leave it on the pack mule unless they spotted bandits.

Suzana shook her head. "Don't be too proud of your skill with the sword. It can't protect you from everything, and it's easy to outnumber a party of two."

"But Danilo has his bow, and he's the best archer in all of Rivak. It's unlikely he'll let anyone get close enough for me to test my blade, should we encounter anyone hostile, which we won't."

Suzana looked over their equipment. They both had bows, quivers, multiple swords and daggers, lances, and maces. "I've sent enough people off to war this year, haven't I? Will you make me send you off as well?"

"You're not sending us to war. The weapons are mostly for hunting. We're bound to grow tired of salted fish and biscuits." Danilo managed to say everything with a straight face. Ivan had to reach down and pretend to adjust his stirrup to hide threatening laughter. He supposed it was possible to hunt wild boars with a mace, but he couldn't see why anyone would try. He and Danilo intended to ride, not hunt. The weapons were for defense, should they be attacked.

"Please, Suzana?" Ivan asked when laughter was no longer imminent. "You can't blame us for loving Kostya."

She groaned in frustration. "You'll keep arguing with me until I agree, won't you? Or ride off the moment I'm distracted?"

Ivan and Danilo both nodded.

Suzana looked to the eastern horizon, then back at them. "It seems I can't really stop you, but do try to stay out of trouble."

"Danilo excels at keeping me out of trouble."

"He also excels at getting you into trouble." Suzana chuckled. "God speed you on your way. And give my love to Kostya."

Danilo gave Marko a final goodbye and then tossed Ivan the lead ropes for the pack mules. He mounted, and the two of them left before Suzana could change her mind.

CHAPTER TWO
CAUSE OF WAR

LIES WERE POWERFUL. ISKANDAR BIN Abdullah had told a handful the day before, and as a result, he'd drawn out seventy Greek warriors. They stood before him now, arrayed in a mix of mail and scaled lamellar, half on horses, prepared to attack a passing Serb army. If the Christians fought each other, they'd be less able to resist Ottoman raiders such as the band of ghazis Iskandar's father led. Once weakened, they would be easy to conquer, and once conquered, they would no longer impede the growth of the Ottoman Empire. Iskandar yearned to see the arrogant Greeks put in their place almost as much as he wished to earn his father's approval. He had never been his father's favorite, but not even Iskandar's half brother, the beloved son of their father's cherished first wife, had provoked a war. Iskandar hadn't either—yet. But he was close, and his actions would earn his father's gratitude.

Iskandar laced his voice with respect as he spoke to the Greek kephale. "If you attack when they reach the river, the bridge will slow their escape. You'll be avenged, and they'll be dead."

Basil Kameteros seemed tempted but cautious. The Christian emperor wouldn't have appointed him kephale of Byzia if Basil hadn't learned to think before he attacked, so though the thoughtful restraint irritated Iskandar, it didn't surprise him.

"You say there are twenty of them?" Basil asked. Sunlight and shadow alternated across his lean, bearded face as the wind made the surrounding tree branches dance and sway.

"Yes, lord, but most are not as well-armed or well-trained as your men." Iskandar bowed from his waist. Greek lords weren't so different from Ottoman lords. They expected subservience from men dressed as shepherds, as

Iskandar was. The gesture had the added benefit of hiding his face should it somehow betray him. The Serb column, in truth, contained closer to fifty, and all were experienced warriors, clothed in mail hauberks and armed with lance and mace, axe and sword.

When Iskandar straightened, the kephale's eldest son looked at him through narrowed eyes. "Can a Vlach shepherd count so high?" Andronicus was near Iskandar's age, twenty and nine, but his pride seemed a great deal older. Arrogance like Andronicus's was one more reason Iskandar was determined to lure the Greeks into battle against the Serbs. The remains of the Roman Empire had shrunk so much that it was hardly worthy of the title, but the Christians of Rumelia still acted as though they ruled from Iberia to the borders of Persia.

"My flock was once the size of the Serb column," Iskandar lied. "But my liege lord gathers excessive taxes. Now our sheep are few. And my lord is among the Serbs."

One end of Andronicus's lips curved up in an amused smile, and blood lust shone in his eyes. "So you wish us to punish him for you?"

"I cannot punish him myself. I am but a humble shepherd, without even a dagger."

"How do you fight off wolves without a blade?" Basil asked.

Iskandar bowed again. "I have only a simple sling, lord. Its rocks protect sheep but are unlikely to slay Serb nobility."

"You mentioned plunder?" Basil appeared relaxed as he spoke, but Iskandar and another ghazi, Ali, had spent a fortnight learning all they could of Basil's lands. Byzia would welcome riches taken in battle.

Plunder was the key to Iskandar's lie. He expected greed for it to drive Basil's decision. But it was also the least plausible element of his tale. The Serb column was returning from war in Anatolia, where they had fought for their Ottoman overlord, Sultan Murad, in his campaigns to subjugate rival Turkoman tribes. On their journey there, they had carried with them the required tribute. The sultan would not allow Christians to plunder Muslims, so going home, the Serbs had little more than food and bedding. But the Greeks wouldn't know Murad's policies on pillage. "They took much gold and silver."

"Uncle," Leo, Basil's nephew, stepped around his cousin to stand near the kephale. "We have no quarrel with the Serbs. Their war was not against us. They fought Muslims, not Christians."

Addressing a noble without leave was dangerous, but Iskandar risked it. "Kyrios Leo, did they not pass through your lands?"

"Yes," Leo admitted.

"Did they plead permission?"

Basil frowned. "No."

"I saw burned fields yesterday. Surely their army is responsible."

Basil nodded.

Leo did not. "Our paroikoi reported fire, but they didn't see who burned their crops."

Iskandar bit his lips, hatred for Leo burning sharply in his stomach. He'd watched Leo. He had a beautiful young wife and a thriving wool business, so perhaps the kephale's nephew didn't wish to risk his contented life for questionable glory. But Leo's calm reluctance threatened Iskandar's plans. Leo's cousin Andronicus, in contrast, seemed eager for battle, despite his probing questions. It was in his smirk, in the confident lay of his shoulders, in the way his fingers played with the hilt of his sword. Others must have felt the same, or Basil wouldn't have led seventy men to this clearing in the forest. They were ready to attack. They needed only a small push to fall on the Serbs.

"Gregoras?" Basil called.

The garrison commander handed his reins and his lance to a nearby soldier and dismounted, joining the kephale's family and Iskandar in the center of the clearing. "Yes, lord?" The tzaousios's deep voice matched his broad build. His beard was fair—almost golden. Perhaps he descended from Varangians.

"How long would it take you to organize scouts?"

"They could be back with their report by the sixth hour."

"See to it."

Scouts would discover no treasure wagons and fifty men rather than twenty. The Greeks would still outnumber the Serbs, but only just. Basil might not risk attack if he knew the truth, and inaction would foil Iskandar's ploy. He'd promised his father he would weaken his enemies, and he did not intend to fail. "Lord, by then, the column will be across the river."

"Are all Vlach shepherds as impertinent as this one?" Andronicus spoke to Gregoras.

Iskandar acted as if he hadn't heard.

"Perhaps we should withdraw," Leo said. "To attack without proper intelligence is folly, and once they cross the river, the landscape will work to their advantage."

Basil seemed about to agree.

Iskandar's scheme balanced on the edge of failure, so he tried another tactic. "Forgive my eagerness, lord. I do indeed wish to see my liege lord punished. But if you fear to engage them, it's not my place to encourage you. I had thought your men could easily vanquish a group as small as the Serbs. But I'm not a warrior. Perhaps I was mistaken."

Andronicus drew his sword and extended the point toward Iskandar's throat until the steel blade pressed into the skin. It didn't draw blood, but Iskandar regretted his last remark. He meant to spur them to action against the Serbs, not against himself.

"Andronicus."

The tall heir lowered his sword at Basil's warning.

"Gregoras, prepare the men. We ride for the river."

Iskandar backed into the shade of a beechwood and watched them organize themselves. Staying out of the way was easy. Hiding his satisfaction was more difficult.

The Serbian Empire was shattered and the Roman Empire shrunken. The more they fought each other, the easier it would be for Iskandar's people to take the lands waiting for them here. That was their destiny—to take these lands and forge them into a new empire, one devoted to Allah. Iskandar looked forward to making his report as much as the haughty Andronicus seemed to crave slaughtering a weak foe. Iskandar would finally have a chance to outshine his half brother and throw off the stigma that constantly shadowed him because his mother had been only a second wife, born Christian rather than Muslim.

Iskandar had provoked a war. His father would surely take notice and finally give his youngest son the honor he'd earned.

CHAPTER THREE
SKIRMISH BY THE RIVER

SUNLIGHT DANCED ACROSS WARM LEAVES of crimson and ocher as Ivan and Danilo dismounted to rest their horses and pack mules. Midday approached, warming Ivan through his wool clothing. He rolled up his cloak and put it in his saddlebag as the animals drank from a creek. Then he tried to walk out some of the stiffness in his thighs. After seven days on the road, soreness pulled at his muscles, but they had to be getting closer to his brother's army, and then all the aches would be worth it.

Danilo peered into the distance and straightened. "I think that's them."

Ivan followed Danilo's gaze. The figures taking shape looked like an army. No turbans, so probably a Christian army. But whose? Eagerness to see his brother urged him forward, but caution held him back. "Do you recognize anyone?"

"Yes. There's Kostya." Danilo pointed to a rider near the middle of the column.

At that distance, the man's bearded face looked no bigger than Ivan's thumb. He was dressed much like the fifty men surrounding him, in a mail hauberk and iron helmet, with an almond-shaped shield on his back. How could his cousin see so far? "I think you're part eagle."

Danilo let out a two-syllable laugh. "Who else would be riding a giant palfrey and leading two magnificent destriers?"

"Another warhorse? If he keeps it up, we'll have to build larger stables."

"We'd already have larger stables if we didn't have to pay tribute to the sultan."

Cursed Turks. Could anything be more humiliating than vassalage to the men who slew their fathers? "That's one thing I won't miss when I leave Rivak."

Danilo quirked an eyebrow. "The Hungarians will give you almost as much trouble."

"Perhaps." Konstantin had an Ottoman overlord who demanded tribute and men for military service. Ivan would have Hungarian neighbors greedy for more land. Enemies surrounded his family, and his family had few allies.

Ivan and Danilo mounted and headed toward Konstantin.

"You know he's going to scold us," Danilo said, keeping his horse next to Ivan's.

"Of course he will. Duty demands it. But he'll forgive us with the next breath." Ivan adjusted his grip on the reins. "Anyway, it's too late to turn back now."

They rode through tall grass with sun-dried tips and a sharp scent, keeping a sedate pace so they wouldn't alarm anyone by galloping toward the group before they were recognized. Konstantin raised his hand as they drew near, and Ivan couldn't contain a grin. Every time his brother rode off to war, Ivan feared he wouldn't return, but Konstantin appeared strong and regal as he rode toward them. If he was surprised to see them, it didn't show in his calm expression.

"What are you two doing here?" Konstantin said by way of greeting.

Ivan guided his horse next to his brother's. "A monk returning from pilgrimage said you were coming home. He saw you in Thessaloniki when you bought supplies. But he had no news of the campaign. How went the battles?"

"We won, and our losses were slight."

"Good news, then," Danilo said.

Konstantin frowned. "Sometimes, I'm not so sure. If Sultan Murad defeats or makes peace with his enemies in Anatolia, he can move more men here. I doubt he'll honor his promises to us when they no longer suit him."

Their Turkish yoke had chafed at Konstantin especially hard since the battle of Dubravnica, when Knez Lazar had defeated an Ottoman army. Other Serb nobles were standing up to the Turks, but Konstantin's clan wasn't yet strong enough for that. And if they continued to pay tribute and lose men in the sultan's battles, they might never be strong enough.

Konstantin led them back into the column. "The two of you shouldn't have come alone. You might have run into brigands."

"The most dangerous thing we ran into was a few snow flurries in the mountains," Ivan said. "And even if we had seen someone hostile, we're armed, and we ride good horses. Between my sword and Danilo's bow, I wouldn't worry about a few outlaws."

"What if you ran into more than a few? What if it were a score against the two of you?" Konstantin turned his gray eyes on Ivan, one eyebrow raised in disapproval.

Ivan knew exactly how to change the subject. "It was to be three."

"Oh?"

"Marko wished to join us." Mention of Marko softened the normally stern lines of Konstantin's face, so Ivan continued. "But his mother feared it would interfere too much with the future župan's naps. And anyway, his pony could not keep up with our horses."

Konstantin's lips pulled into a smile. "How is Suzana?"

"She is well and sends her love. As does Marko."

"I'm surprised she didn't dissuade you from coming."

Danilo choked back a laugh on the other side of Konstantin.

"She tried, didn't she?" Konstantin asked.

"She didn't have much of a chance," Danilo said. "We were already saddled when we told her."

"And Aunt Zorica? What did she say?"

Neither Danilo nor Ivan answered.

"You did tell her, didn't you?" Konstantin turned in the saddle to look Ivan fully in the face. "Ivan?"

Ivan avoided eye contact. "We sent a groom with the message."

"Ivan! How could you scare her like that?"

"We're out of danger now, aren't we? Besides, I had to come. I had to know you were safe."

Konstantin opened his mouth as if to speak. Ivan braced for the expected scolding, but Konstantin stayed silent.

No lecture? Ivan hurried to change the subject before his brother changed his mind. "And Decimir. I wish to see him safe as well. Is he riding with his grandfather?" Ivan wouldn't have been surprised to find their late sister's husband riding with Konstantin, but he was more likely to ride with his grandfather, Župan Dragomir, their clan's most trusted ally. When called to fight for the sultan, the two armies usually traveled close enough to support each other, so maybe they could visit Decimir after both groups made camp for the night.

Konstantin clenched his jaw and looked away. "He fell."

The whispered words struck Ivan like a warhorse. "But you said our losses were slight!"

"Rivak's losses were. None dead, only a few wounded, most of the wounds already healed. Župan Dragomir's loss was more devastating."

"How?"

"Decimir had little desire to live. That made it easy for him to die."

They rode in silence. The last year had been hard on their family. First Lidija and the baby. Now Decimir. Ivan tried to be as stoic as Konstantin, but he'd always had a difficult time hiding his emotions. On the day they received word of their father's death, Ivan had wept in his sister's arms until he'd fallen asleep. Konstantin, seventeen and suddenly the župan, had taken his favorite palfrey and galloped away alone. If he'd grieved, he'd done it then. When he'd returned hours later, he'd appeared calm, and Ivan had never seen him cry in the twelve years since.

Ivan fiddled with his reins. "Do you suppose they're together now, Decimir and Lidija?"

Konstantin granted Ivan a rare smile, even if there was grief behind it. "Yes. That is what I believe. And I think that is what he wanted. But enough talk of sadness. I have good news for Danilo. I've found you a bride."

An expression of curiosity pursed Danilo's lips and widened his dark eyes. "Who?"

A hint of excitement touched Konstantin's voice. "Relatives of Knez Lazar. There are five brothers, then Tatjana. They're marvelous warriors. A wonderful family to have ties with. And they say their sister is pretty and pious."

"Pretty, according to the brothers." Ivan clucked his tongue. "I don't know that a brother would be the best judge on a matter such as that. And pious . . . No doubt she spends all her day in prayer and won't have time to entertain a husband."

"Don't laugh too hard, Ivan," Konstantin said. "You're next. Father Vlatko told me years ago I should find you both brides, and I intend to before next summer."

Ivan struggled to keep his face calm. He didn't mind the idea of marriage, but being assigned a bride—that made him a little nervous. "It will be a challenging task for you, finding someone I'm not related to. And someone Grandfather will approve of." Their maternal grandfather, župan of Sivi Gora, expected Ivan to marry well.

Konstantin gritted his teeth. "The task is giving me a headache already. Don't make it harder than it needs to be, or I'll hand the whole matter off to Grandfather, and I doubt he'll consider your preferences as much as I will."

Ivan grimaced. Grandfather had selected Suzana for Konstantin, and it had been a good match. But that spring, Grandfather had contemplated marrying Ivan to a widowed Hungarian noblewoman. Ivan had been horrified that the prospective bride had been double his age. Danilo had been dismayed that she had been Catholic instead of Orthodox. But it was Konstantin's pointing out that a woman barren to her first husband was unlikely to provide her second husband with an heir that had finally convinced Župan Đurađ Lukarević that the match was not in the family's best interests, even if it would have given Sivi Gora a friendlier border.

"Do I get to meet her?" Danilo asked. "Before it's settled?"

Konstantin nodded. "After we get back to Rivak, we'll arrange a visit. If you like her, I'll pursue the matter further. We can have the betrothal ceremony before the Nativity Fast. And if you don't like her, I'll keep searching."

"How old is she?"

"Fifteen or sixteen, I think."

"Fifteen or sixteen." Danilo considered it for a moment. "That's not too young, is it?"

"Only a little younger than my mother or my wife were when they became brides."

Ivan scoffed. "Yes, but mother's family was devastated by the plague, so she was eager for a new start. And Suzana didn't think you would hit her as often as her father did."

"I've never hit Suzana!" Konstantin looked hurt that Ivan would even suggest it.

"But she didn't know that when you met. You were strangers." She'd told Ivan about it once, how pleased she'd been to discover that a man could be fierce with his enemies and gentle with his wife.

The column slowed as the men in front of them moved into single file to cross a narrow bridge over the river. Ivan maneuvered his horse behind Danilo's and ahead of Konstantin's. Someone near the end of the column shouted. Ivan looked back as an arrow struck Konstantin's palfrey in the hindquarters. The horse collapsed and knocked Konstantin from the saddle.

"Kostya!" Ivan reined his horse in and jumped to the ground.

Konstantin stood and gripped his sword hilt but winced as he put weight on his left foot. "Get your shield, Ivan!"

Ivan grabbed it from the pack mule just before the next salvo of arrows whistled through the air and thumped into his shield and both of Konstantin's destriers. They'd flown from a row of thick trees to the road's south. Enemy horsemen moved among the archers sixty paces away, marshaling themselves into ranks for a charge.

Differing emotions tugged at Ivan—elation at a chance to prove himself against so vast an enemy and terror at what might happen. He'd seen battle on his grandfather's lands, but nothing involving so many men and never when so outnumbered. "Who are they?"

"Greek kataphraktoi." Danilo finished stringing his bow. He nocked an arrow, drew, and let it fly, striking down a man atop a bay charger.

"Why are they attacking us?" Ivan's people and the Greeks were not enemies.

"Shall I ask them? Or shoot them?" Danilo caught Ivan's eye for a moment, then loosed another arrow.

Konstantin shouted commands to the men around them. "Bojan, ride to Župan Dragomir for aid. The rest of you mount! Prepare to charge!" The early salvos had injured a score of horses, but Bojan's was uninjured, and most of the other men had more than one.

Ivan slipped his foot into the stirrup, but Konstantin stopped him. "Not you, Ivan. You and Danilo are too young, and you're not in armor. Stay here. Use your arrows, but if they break through, head for the river."

"But I've been fighting brigands for years!"

"These are not mere brigands, and we don't have time to argue." The Greeks were charging now. "Besides, I need your horse." Two of Konstantin's still stood, but arrows pierced their coats, and they'd be difficult to control while injured. The third—Konstantin's favorite warhorse, Veles—lay on the ground, thrashing about dangerously as it bled from a pair of arrow wounds in its neck.

Ivan handed over his reins but kept his weapons.

Konstantin organized the line from the center. Miladin, Konstantin's satnik, ordered from the right. The group formed a tight, even row and pushed their mounts forward. They didn't have enough time to reach a full gallop, so when the Serb line met the Greek charge, the Greeks had the advantage in speed. The clash of iron echoed across the small plain, punctuated by the screams of horses and men.

Ivan wedged one end of his bow between his right foot and left leg to string it. He shot and took down a Greek rider. Danilo took down two. After that, the groups were too mixed for safe aim.

"Left behind like children." Ivan squinted, then shot a dismounted Greek soldier who had broken from the main group. When Konstantin was Ivan's age, he'd become a župan. When he was only a bit older than Danilo, he'd led an army.

"He's just trying to protect you." One of Danilo's arrows sliced through an enemy soldier's neck. The bow was Danilo's weapon of choice, so he wouldn't find their orders quite so bitter.

Ivan grunted, waiting for a clean shot. He wasn't a fragile child anymore. His hands itched to grab his sword and run into the melee, where all the real action was taking place. His people were bleeding, and all he could do was launch an occasional arrow. "We're outnumbered. Adding in the two of us would help the odds."

"Marginally." Danilo aimed his bow again. "We're helping from here."

"You are. I'm not as fast a shot as you."

The area around them was strangely calm, other than the struggles of the wounded horses. All the men from Rivak, besides Ivan and Danilo, fought in the main battle some twenty paces away. In the center of the skirmish, Konstantin disarmed a man only to have two more Greeks attack him.

Ivan didn't like his brother's chances. "Stay here and see if you can pick anyone else off." Ivan untied his quiver and thrust it at Danilo. "Kostya needs help."

"He told us to stay."

"I'm not going to stand by and watch my last sibling be slaughtered."

"All right. But I'm coming with you."

Ivan grinned and plucked an abandoned shield from the ground. Then the two of them dashed into the fray.

The battle lines had mixed and shifted. Kicked-up dust obscured men and horses. Where was Konstantin? A dismounted Greek warrior ran at Ivan with a sword. Ivan blocked the thrust. The Greek spathion glanced off his own, and the man's momentum carried him past Ivan, who swung his sword round and sliced into the man's back. The blow cut through a seam in the lamellar armor of scaled leather.

Ivan looked back for Danilo, who was near Miladin, sparring with Greek foot soldiers. The two of them would watch out for each other while Ivan found Konstantin.

A Greek man-at-arms ran at Ivan and tried to skewer him with a javelin. Ivan dodged, then thrust his spathion through the man's stomach. His opponent fell, ending that threat, but Ivan had to drop and roll to avoid a horseman charging at him with a lance.

Before he could regain his feet, another enemy attacked him. Ivan whipped his shield around to block the downward thrust. His adversary, still on his feet, had the advantage, but Ivan kicked at him, connecting with the man's knees and shoving him back long enough to hop upright. The man took his time as he planned the next strike, stepping to the side. Ivan stepped with him, then rushed him, aiming for the man's throat. The Greek brought his shield up in time to stop Ivan's blow. He met Ivan's next thrust and the one after that as well. But Ivan's fourth strike drew blood when it sliced into the man's left arm. The man cursed him. Ivan swung his sword round. The blade pushed through his opponent's parry, then bit into the man's neck. The man cried out and dropped to the ground.

Men shouted and grunted all around him. The field was strewn with discarded weapons and dead and wounded men. Ivan had seen death before, many times. He'd even slain brigands in Sivi Gora. But he'd never been in anything like this. He gasped for breath and stepped around the flaying legs of a disemboweled horse. Though dying, it was panicked enough to break bones with each kick.

Five paces away, Konstantin clashed with two Greeks. One drew back, wounded by Konstantin's sword, but the other, a giant of a man, pressed closer. As Konstantin fought him off, the wounded man sprang forward and stabbed Konstantin in the thigh. Konstantin yelled in pain and stumbled back, barely keeping on his feet. Konstantin finished off the man who'd injured him, but his tall opponent showed no sign of easing the attack.

The two fought on, but Konstantin's wound left him vulnerable. Ivan ran closer as the Greek warrior knocked Konstantin's sword aside and rammed his face with his shield. Konstantin's sword slipped from his hand, and his opponent kicked his wounded leg and shoved him to the ground. The Greek lifted his sword to deliver Konstantin's deathblow. Ivan charged forward and threw up his sword to block the strike. When it hit, the force of the Greek sword sent tremors up Ivan's arms and into his chest.

The Greek scowled down at him. "I seek not to fight children. Retire to the bridge, and I shall let you reach manhood."

Ivan understood the Greek words, thanks to Father Vlatko's tutoring, and he answered in the same language. "Manhood is defined by action, not by age."

"Noble words. But I expect they shall be your last." The Greek warrior swung his sword round, and the battle between them began.

Ivan parried each stroke and blocked each swing. His lack of armor left him exposed, but it also left him agile. He ducked away from the man's thrusts, then pounced forward to deliver his own. Their blades connected and clashed and then separated over and over again as they parried and riposted. His opponent had skill, but he was tiring.

A Greek warrior fighting a different duel tumbled back and jostled Ivan off-balance. The one who'd almost killed Konstantin seized his chance and lunged forward. Ivan threw his shield up to block the blow but had to twist away from the next thrust.

The man kept his sword in his right hand and picked up a mace with his left. He swung the new weapon into Ivan's shield with such force that the wood cracked as it smashed back into Ivan's shoulder. Next, he swung at Ivan's legs. Ivan jumped out of the way, but the man barreled into him and shoved him backward.

Ivan dodged one strike, then another, trying to avoid not only the man's blows but also the bodies littering the ground as he was forced back a step at a time. With a final, desperate parry, Ivan swung his sword upward. His sword sliced into the man's forearm, and the Greek warrior screamed in pain. Ivan kicked the man's left arm, and his mace tumbled across the field. Ivan struck again, pummeling the man's helmet with the flat of his sword and knocking him to the ground.

Ivan stomped on the Greek blade so the man couldn't use it, then with lungs burning for air, he managed to say, "Do you yield?"

The man nodded.

"Ivan?"

He recognized Konstantin's voice and glanced behind him. A bandage wrapped his brother's thigh, and another injured Serb supported him. "Yes?"

"We're outnumbered. It's time to withdraw." Konstantin scrutinized the prisoner. "You, what are you called?"

"Leo Kameteros."

Konstantin pursed his lips. "Son of Basil Kameteros, the local kephale?"

"Nephew."

"I'll wager you'll still fetch a good ransom." Konstantin switched from Greek to Slavonic and gave orders to his injured man. "Zoran, tie him up behind the supply wagon."

The two left. Leo didn't resist. Zoran had his sword ready to run him through if he did.

"Come, Ivan. You've proved yourself a warrior. Now it is time to prove yourself wise. We can win nothing here. Best to leave the field before we lose any more strength."

As Konstantin spoke, the Greeks still on horseback regrouped for another charge. Most of the Serbs were now on foot. Ivan pulled his brother's arm around his shoulders because Konstantin could put almost no weight on his injured leg and helped him back to a cart with the other injured men. Danilo was among them, letting Father Vlatko wrap a gash in his arm.

"Is it bad?" The wound was covered, so Ivan couldn't see it.

"Just a scratch," was the reply, but Danilo wouldn't have held still long enough for the priest's ministrations if it weren't serious enough to hamper his archery.

Konstantin shouted orders to the men still standing, telling them to form a rear guard. "Not you, Ivan."

"But I'm not wounded, and I'm good with the sword." Ivan took a helmet from one of the injured men and stuck it on his head.

"Stay with me."

"If I were anyone but your brother, you would have me fight. Admit it."

The wagons crawled toward the bridge. Konstantin's lips formed a hard, thin line on his pale face. "I admit it, but that doesn't change my mind. Stay with me."

The Greek line of horsemen hit the thin Serb rear guard and pushed it back. Men on both sides fell amid grunts and cries, but the Serbs were still outnumbered.

"If you gave good counsel, I'd listen. But you're letting your heart dictate military tactics, and that's a certain way to lose battles." Ivan ran to join the rear guard, ignoring his brother's demands that he return.

Ivan met the enemy with calm resolve. He knew what to do. They would allow the Greeks to push them back slowly, conserving their numbers with solid defensive actions. Once the wounded were across the river, they would retreat more quickly. When the last Serb made it across the bridge, they would destroy it to prevent the Greeks from following. No doubt Konstantin or Miladin already had men assigned to the task.

A Greek foot soldier charged at Ivan, and he finished him quickly, jabbing his sword through the armor shielding the man's abdomen, then running the blade into the side of the man's neck.

The next man was more of a challenge. He looked the warrior—broad, with close-fitting scale armor and a massive sword. Yellow Beard was elusive, drawing Ivan in, then retreating, pulling Ivan away from the rear guard. Ivan wounded him in the arm, but it decreased the force of his blows only a little. Finally, Ivan's better judgment took hold. His mission was to protect the retreat. The next time the man darted back, Ivan let him go.

A mounted man rode past him, swinging downward as he galloped by. Ivan blocked the sword, diverting it from his neck, but it bit into his unprotected shoulder. The cut wasn't deep, but his flesh howled with pain. The Greek rider twisted his charger around and came back. Ivan stood his ground. As the man rode past, Ivan met the rider's sword with his own, deflected it, and then sliced his blade at the horse's hind legs. The horse crashed to the earth, and the rider sprang to his feet. He was tall, with arrogant brown eyes. Blood stained his armor, and Ivan suspected it was the blood of his friends and kinsmen.

Ivan charged, hacking through the man's arm to the bone. The Greek shouted in rage, and a comrade ran to his aid. He looked just like him, only his eyes contained less conceit. Nor did he wield his sword with as much skill. Ivan's fourth slash sliced into the man's side, and he dropped in a cry of pain.

"No!" the other Greek warrior yelled. He charged again at Ivan, his eyes wild now instead of haughty. Ivan risked a quick slash and cut into the warrior's belly. His bellow of rage changed to a cry of pain as he collapsed to the ground.

Ivan had a feeling he'd struck down brothers. He didn't check to see if they lived—that was unimportant. What mattered was that they couldn't hurt him or his people anymore.

The last few opponents had pulled Ivan away from his comrades. He was about to run back when two Greek horsemen charged him at the same time. He couldn't outrun them, so he raised his sword to defend himself. The one on the left was slightly ahead of the man on the right. The horses' hooves tore into the field as they approached, sending up clumps of dirt and weed and making the ground beneath Ivan's feet vibrate. He met the first blade and threw the rider off-balance, but Ivan couldn't escape the iron-tipped lance plowing toward him an instant later. It ripped into his abdomen and a cry of pain escaped his lips as the horses thundered past him.

His body shook, and waves of agony threatened to knock him to the ground. The clash of battle sounded less heavy in his ears, and the figures on the edge of his vision blurred. The riders circled around for another strike. The next charge would finish him.

Ivan could barely stand. The horses galloped closer and closer. Leather bands protected the horses' necks and rumps, but the lamellar didn't extend to cover their chests. Perhaps loss of blood affected his vision, but the horsemen seemed less synchronized now. He summoned every last bit of strength and bolstered it with anger that the Greeks had attacked without provocation. Ivan plucked a broken lance end from the ground, and as the first horse drew near, he hurled it like a javelin at the black hair of the horse's chest. The weapon struck its mark, the horse swerved and tumbled, and Ivan was crushed beneath its falling body.

CHAPTER FOUR
THE MIDWIFE OF BYZIA

THERE WAS SOMETHING SACRED IN an infant's first cry.

Helena cradled the wiggly, wet babe as he kicked and wailed. She swallowed back the catch in her throat. "You have a son!"

Tears of joy streamed down the mother's cheeks. "Is he healthy?"

"He's perfect." Helena placed the baby on his mother's abdomen and dried him with a clean cloth.

Ithamar gently handled her son, looking at each finger, touching his plump cheeks and wet hair. "Welcome, little one."

Ithamar's gray-haired mother gazed at her newest grandchild with adoration before glancing up at Helena. "Thank you."

"You're welcome." Helena's work that day had been easy. It was Ithamar's fifth delivery, and there had been no complications. The birth pains had been fierce, but their intensity had shortened the period of labor. Helena glanced at the window. The curtains were pulled open to let in the breeze, and judging by the sun's position, it was perhaps the ninth hour. She'd been summoned at the third. Helena only wished there'd been a similar outcome during Ithamar's fourth delivery. There had been complications then, and the baby had not lived an hour.

Helena dealt with the afterbirth when it emerged. The red and purple mass of flesh seemed whole, so Helena tied the cord near the organ and then three fingers' width from the baby. She cut them apart with a small knife. Then she helped position the wailing infant so his mother could offer the baby her breast. On his third attempt, he latched on and began to suck.

He was so different from the brother who'd been born a year ago. That baby's skin had been more blue than red, his cry more a whimper than a wail. Helena and Anna, the midwife Helena had trained under, had done all they could, but the baby had come before its time. A healthy new babe was like a salve, easing the pain of the prior loss.

Helena wiped her hands and crossed the room. She went to her knees and looked under the uneven trestle table. Two small, tear-stained faces peered back at her. "Theodora? Zöe? Would you like to meet your brother?"

The small faces nodded.

"Is my mother going to die?" Theodora asked.

Helena held out a hand to the seven-year-old girl. "No. Your mother is strong. She'll need your help as she recovers, but all is well."

"Will the baby die?"

"Not this time." Helena pulled Theodora, then Zöe out from under the table and prayed her words would prove true. She had seen enough infants die before they'd taken their first step to know her promise was uncertain. But Theodora had been frightened by her mother's pain. She needed comfort, and the baby did indeed look healthy. Zöe was younger, three. Her fear would soon fade. The girls' grandmother held out her arms, and Zöe climbed onto her lap.

"Why is he so red?" Theodora asked.

"Because it is hard to be born," Helena said. "For the mother and for the child."

"What is that?" Theodora pointed at the afterbirth.

Helena opened her mouth to explain, but before she spoke a single syllable, the cottage door swung open.

"Kyria Helena?" The bright sunshine behind him obscured the speaker's face, but she recognized the voice of Demetrios, the garrison commander's son.

"Yes?"

Demetrios seemed hesitant to speak in front of the others. Helena went to the doorway and took in his tall stature, curly golden hair, and beard that had only fully come in that summer. Normally, his face portrayed confidence. Today, concern and sadness showed in the lines of his lips and the cast of his eyes. Dried blood clung to his armor, but he seemed uninjured.

"The Serb contingent was stronger than we were led to believe."

"Were you defeated?" Fear of what that might mean—and of who might have been killed—snaked through her chest.

"No. They fled the field. But our losses were significant. I've been sent to fetch you. We need your help with the wounded."

"My help?" Helena glanced back at the newborn. Her work here wasn't finished. "Surely Petros would be of more use than me. I am only an apprentice midwife."

"Petros has fallen, my lady."

Helena felt cold. The old surgeon had been her mentor, especially since Anna had died. Would she never again see his bushy gray eyebrows scrunch together as they discussed treatments? Never again watch his kind eyes twinkle as he read one of his medical codices?

"What of Christophoros?" Ithamar asked.

Helena held her breath, hoping Demetrios wasn't about to report the death of the new baby's father. Yet Christophoros was more farmer than warrior. If the Serbs were stronger than expected, casualties would fall hardest among the paroikoi.

"He is well," Demetrios said. "He's assisting the wounded."

Helena unrolled the sleeves of her tunic and began gathering her things. She didn't like leaving so soon after the birth, but Ithamar and her mother had experience caring for newborns, and it seemed Helena was needed elsewhere. "Are there many wounded?"

"Andronicus. Alexius. Others as well."

The kephale's sons. But what of his nephew? "And Leo?"

Demetrios looked away.

Helena wouldn't normally press a man, but she had to know what had become of her sister's husband. "What happened to Leo?"

"He was taken prisoner."

She knew little about the Serbs the men had fought and even less about how they would treat prisoners. She prayed they would be kind. "And Kyrios Basil?"

"He is safe."

That was some good news. Helena went to the baby, sleeping now in his mother's arms. "I am sorry to leave so quickly."

Ithamar's mother touched her granddaughter's shoulder. "Theodora, go help with Kyria Helena's horse." Then the woman turned to Helena, inclining her head in respect. "I can care for them now. I had seven babies of my own, and this isn't my first grandchild. They will be well."

"Thank you." Helena would have rather stayed longer to be certain Ithamar and the baby were well, but she was leaving them in experienced hands.

Demetrios cleared his throat. "Kyria, you are needed at once."

Helena turned for a final view of the new baby, then followed Demetrios outside. They had a half hour's ride ahead of them. Theodora had already brought Helena's gray mare around, and Demetrios saddled it for her. Christophoros and Ithamar's home was new and only half completed. Helena used the pile of rocks that would eventually form a wall to mount Cleopatra, and soon she and Demetrios left the cottage and its baby far behind.

"Kyria Helena, there is something else you should know."

"Yes?"

"Callinicus is fallen."

Callinicus. Petros's nephew. She should have felt more emotion to learn that her intended was dead, even if he hadn't been her choice. She'd been avoiding him since the day after their betrothal ceremony but had hoped they would settle into a pleasant marriage. Now she would never know.

She would mourn Callinicus later. At the present, care for the wounded was her primary task.

The injured soldiers waited in the surgeon's house within the acropolis walls. Two dozen men with minor wounds sat either on the floor or on wooden benches set along the stone walls of Petros's front chamber, where he had done his work. Seven men with grievous wounds lay on straw-stuffed pallets in the back chamber, where the surgeon had slept. Three looked at Helena with hope when she stepped into the backroom. Three were unconscious. One was dead.

The deceased one was Andronicus, eldest son of the kephale. Christophoros, Ithamar's husband, stood as she approached. "He died right after Demetrios left."

Amid the grief, Helena held to her memory of hope. "Your wife is delivered. You have a healthy son."

Christophoros nodded his gratitude, then excused himself so the small chamber wouldn't be so crowded.

Helena went to the unconscious men. Two she didn't recognize. The other was Kyrios Basil's second son, Alexius. Given his rank and the seriousness of his wound, she began with him.

"Can I help?" Demetrios asked.

"Yes. Take his armor off. All the clothing near his wounds as well. Same with the other men." Alexius was covered in so much blood that it was hard to tell where he was hurt. A bandage suggested an injury in his lower abdomen, but there might be others.

Helena's sister burst into the chamber. "Leo? Has Leo returned?" Euphrosyne's clothing was normally immaculate and her face usually calm, but today the veil over her curly black hair was crooked, her cloak was nowhere to be seen, and worry lines creased her forehead.

Helena wished Euphrosyne hadn't come. She loved her sister, but she couldn't spare time comforting her while there were injuries to tend. "Demetrios, you had best give her the news."

While Demetrios and Euphrosyne spoke, Helena picked out pieces of cloth and bits of plant from Alexius's wounded abdomen and washed it with wine. The cut went through his muscles into the intestines. It wasn't a part of the body she was familiar with. She had often sat with Petros while he'd spoken of past cases, but attempting surgery based on a few conversations was folly. Tears threatened to form because she was inadequate to the task. She didn't have the skill to heal a wound so grave, yet no one else did either. She would have to try.

"How dare they hold fellow Christians for ransom!" Emotion made Euphrosyne's voice shake. "What will they do to him if we cannot pay?"

Demetrios pointed to one of the other unconscious patients. "That one is a Serb. High born, we think. His boots are finer than Kyrios Basil's, and he fought like a lion. Perhaps we can trade. If he survives."

Was it safe to keep an enemy next to Alexius? Would he rouse himself and begin the battle anew? She glanced at him. No, he would not wake soon. She could worry about that later because there were sufficient problems to consume her at present. Helena cut out the injured portion of Alexius's intestines and stitched the remaining ends together with silk thread. She went to the front chamber and searched the cupboard where Petros kept his herbs. If a woman had a rupture during childbirth, she would sprinkle it with dried comfrey roots, cumin, and cinnamon. But according to Galen and Trotula, women were, by nature, cold and moist. Men were hot and dry. Would a treatment that worked for a woman work for a man? Alexius's skin was gray and his breathing labored. She needed to act quickly. She took the powders and sprinkled generous doses on the gash in Alexius's side.

"May I help?" Euphrosyne's skin, currently pale, was a testament to her easily nauseated stomach.

Helena glanced at the injured around her in the back chamber. She would see to them herself. The others were less likely to make Euphrosyne swoon, and their wounds didn't require skilled care. "Start with the men in the other room. Wash their wounds with water, then with wine. If the cuts are deep, I'll stitch them when I finish here."

Euphrosyne took a flagon of wine and went to the front of the house.

As Helena sewed Alexius's muscles back together, Kyrios Basil came into the chamber with several other men. Normally, Helena would bow to him, but Kyrios Basil lifted a hand. "Do not let me interrupt." He went to the body of his older son, Andronicus, and knelt in prayer.

After stitching Alexius's skin, Helena covered his wound in a layer of olive oil to protect it from dust. She glanced through the doorway and saw Euphrosyne hard at work. At twenty-one, she was three years older than Helena, taller, and a favorite in Kyrios Basil's court. And it seemed that for today, she was overcoming her natural squeamishness.

An unconscious man with a head injury came next. The wound, probably from a mace, had created a bloody mess behind his left ear. But the cut was shallow and the underlying bone felt sound. Of the other Greeks on pallets, one needed stitches in his arm, and the other needed stitches in his temple. She washed their wounds with wine and bandaged them when she finished sewing.

The last Greek had an injured shoulder. Demetrios had helped him remove his tunic. She assisted him into a sitting position and untied the makeshift sling to examine the arm more closely. It hung lower on the injured side, and in the back she could see a depression in the skin where the bone should have been. The man winced as she felt both shoulders to compare them. "Can you move it?"

He shook his head.

"Let me move it for you. Tell me when the pain worsens."

She gently raised his arm, and he gasped. She gave him some wine. "The arm has come out of place from where it joins the shoulder. We shall have to put it back in. The pain will be strong, but it will be short."

He nodded and used his functioning hand to lift the goblet and drain it.

She had him lie on his back, then she knelt beside him. She bent his arm at the elbow until it formed half a square. "Do your best to relax the muscles." Grasping his palm and his elbow, she smoothly guided the bent arm from his waist to above his head. She heard a pop, and the patient sighed with relief.

Helena felt the man's wrists, making sure his pulse was the same on both sides. "Put the sling back on, and rest it for a few days."

Kyrios Basil finished his prayer and turned to his younger son, Alexius. "Will he recover?"

Helena didn't want to answer, but Kyrios Basil's eyes met hers, and she had no choice. "I do not know, lord. I'm not a surgeon. And his wound is deep."

Kyrios Basil felt his son's forehead. "Do everything you can. I do not wish to be deprived of both my sons and my nephew all from the same foolish skirmish." He turned to his advisers. "Radomir, your Vlach shepherd proved false."

Helena peeked at the gray-haired kastrophylax, who was in charge of maintaining the kastron's defenses and setting the watchmen. She didn't know him well, but she'd heard rumors of a checkered past. Like the enemy, he was Serb.

Radomir bowed his head. "I apologize, lord. Perhaps he saw only part of the army? Or miscounted? But our lands were attacked. We couldn't let the raiders go unpunished."

Euphrosyne walked into the back chamber and set a handful of blood-stained cloths in a wooden bucket. The cuff of her fine silk tunic was spotted with red, as was the loose-sleeved dalmatica she wore over it. She came toward the kephale. "Kyrios Basil?"

Basil took Euphrosyne's hand. "Kyria Euphrosyne. You look pale. Perhaps you should rest."

"First, I would speak with you. Demetrios said my husband was captured."

As Helena poured fresh water into a bowl, she studied Basil. He seemed outwardly calm, but his grief had to be heavy. Basil called to Demetrios, who was in the other room, tending his father.

Demetrios finished Gregoras's bandage. "Yes, lord?"

"What did you see of Leo?"

Demetrios came to stand in the doorway. "I saw him at the Serb carts. I tried to reach him, but I couldn't get past their rear guard."

"Will they release him, hold him for ransom, or sell him?" Basil asked Radomir. It had once been customary to release coreligionists taken during war, but that tradition had weakened with desperate times and Latin influence.

"Hold him, I suspect."

"How much will they ask?"

Radomir glanced at Alexius. "It depends. If Leo becomes your heir, they will ask more."

Basil looked at his sons. One dead. One wounded so seriously that Helena feared he would not see another dawn.

"Lord?" Demetrios walked to the last unconscious man.

"Yes?"

"We found this man under a horse. I saw him during the battle. He fought well; they'll want him back. Perhaps we can exchange him for Leo. At least bargain with him to reduce the ransom."

Rumors of financial strain circulated the kastron and showed in the too-thin bodies of the paroikoi. Helena hoped Demetrios was right, because she wanted Leo to come home again, and she didn't want Byzia cast into poverty.

Basil's shrewd eyes examined the wounded Serb prisoner. "Do you recognize him, Radomir?"

Radomir drew closer and brushed the blood-matted hair from the wounded man's forehead. "I knew his father, and he looks just like him. You've captured Župan Konstantin Miroslavević. His mother's lands include a silver mine. You're likely to get Leo back and a generous amount for your treasury."

"He's young for a župan."

"His father died at Maritsa. I remember he was young." Radomir felt the unconscious man's cheek. "He must have been very young. I daresay he has yet to grow a beard."

Kyrios Basil turned to Helena. "What are his chances?"

"I'm not sure, lord. I've not yet examined him." Helena felt her face go hot. His wounds were serious, so she should have cared for him earlier, but she'd been reluctant to help an enemy before she tended the Greek casualties.

"Do so."

"Yes, lord." Greek men awaited her care in the other room, but she would not disobey Kyrios Basil. And she was beginning to understand. By helping the wounded Serb, she was helping her sister's husband.

Kyrios Basil and his advisers moved Andronicus's body to the chapel and left Helena to her work. The Serb's injury was much like Alexius's but not as deep. The muscles had been pierced but not the intestines.

Euphrosyne came to fetch more bandages and paused, watching Helena. "It's bad, isn't it?"

"Yes." Helena dabbed a needle and its silk thread with wine. She picked a splinter of wood from the wound, then gently pulled on a piece of cloth trapped amid the gore. It stuck. She tugged, and it came loose with a gush of blood.

Euphrosyne fainted.

"Demetrios, help her!" Helena couldn't stop to check on her sister, not if she wanted to save the prisoner and thereby save Leo. She gripped her threaded needle with sticky red fingers and searched for the source of the bleeding. It wasn't as bad as she'd first feared. The blood must have built up behind the wadded bit of fabric, but the flow subsided from a stream to a trickle as she pressed a clean cloth into the cut. She stitched the torn flesh, then washed it with wine and sprinkled it with the same powders she'd used on Alexius.

"How is my sister?" Helena risked a quick look over her shoulder. Demetrios had laid Euphrosyne on the pallet made empty when Andronicus's body had been moved. Her veil had come off, and disheveled hair and sky-blue silk swirled around her face.

"She'll be fine. And our prisoner?"

"I'm not sure yet." Helena bandaged the cut she'd stitched and examined the rest of his muscled body. A slash in his shoulder was deep enough that she would sew the skin together there as well. Bruises covered his chest and abdomen. She removed the torn tunic someone had draped over the man's legs and saw that the bruising extended to the thighs, along with another gash. She was unaccustomed to seeing a grown man without clothing and felt her face grow hot. Why couldn't his injuries have been on his arms instead? Or better yet, why couldn't he and his people have stayed in their own lands and left Byzia in peace? The prisoner was half-dead now, but what would happen if he recovered? It was like taking a sleeping bear inside and hoping it would behave when it awoke.

She laid the tunic back over the prisoner. She stitched his shoulder neatly, though she wasn't sure why. He was an enemy. If his face seemed pleasant, it was only because he was young. If his body was strong, it was only because he used it to wage war against her people. And if she felt any sympathy for his wounds, it was only because he was so utterly helpless. He was a devil. And only love of her sister and her sister's husband kept her fear in check.

CHAPTER FIVE
A SEARCH

As Iskandar wandered the battlefield, satisfaction grew in his chest. He had promised his father he would weaken their enemies, and he'd succeeded. The traditional way of hurting an enemy was terrorizing his peasants and ravaging his lands, causing destruction that would either drive a lord into reckless battle or leave him too poor to fight back. Drawing two enemies into battle against each other was vastly more effective. Greek and Serb would ruin each other, and the wealth of the land would remain unprotected, ready to be plucked up by his father's band of ghazis.

Because Iskandar traveled on foot, he'd missed the battle. He had arrived in time to see the Greeks collect their dead. They were gone, but Iskandar remained, trying to discover how badly each side had been beaten. He counted the bodies remaining on the field—nine, all of them Serb, and each of those deaths made his father's work less risky.

"Don't move!" The words were Greek.

Iskandar stayed perfectly still, cursing himself for his lack of caution. Had some of Kyrios Basil's men returned? Would they recognize him and punish him for his false report that drew them into battle? Yet when the speaker came into view, with an arrow nocked and his bow held ready, his armor was more Serb than Greek. Despite the clothing, Iskandar was confused. He didn't look like a Serb. His hair and skin were the same shade as Iskandar's.

The man's arm was bandaged, and he held a well-made composite bow with horn tips. It looked like he could loose an arrow at Iskandar as easily as he breathed. The man put his thumb and first finger in his mouth and issued a shrill whistle. "Did you watch the battle?"

"No. I arrived after it finished."

"What did you see?"

If he said he'd seen nothing, would the man let him go? Iskandar doubted it. But if he cooperated, perhaps he could draw out clues about the Serbs, information that might prove useful. "I saw the Greeks leave with their dead."

"How many?"

"Twenty." It had actually been twelve, but if the Serbs thought Byzia weak, perhaps they would fight again, magnifying the initial damage Iskandar had caused.

Four horsemen crested the hill. The whistle must have been a signal. They wouldn't know of his role in provoking the skirmish, but that didn't mean they'd be kind to a stranger, and Iskandar was no match for that many warriors, even if some of them were wounded. His fellow ghazi, Ali, was still in Byzia, much too distant to come to his aid, and his father's band was even farther away. Iskandar did his best to hide the fear that nibbled at him.

"You are a shepherd?" The man with the bow glanced over Iskandar's rough-spun tunic, felt cap, and leather leg bands.

"Yes." Iskandar didn't correct the man's assumption. He had, after all, been pretending to be a Vlach shepherd for the past fortnight.

"Where are your sheep?"

"Slaughtered by Kyrios Basil's men." It was as good a lie as any, and perhaps by telling them they had a common enemy, Iskandar could gain their trust.

The other men drew near and dismounted. There was no question here; they were Serb.

Five bodies lay nearby. The newcomers looked at them with sober faces.

"Gather the others and bury them," one of them said. Though no older than thirty, his voice carried authority. A bandage wrapped one of his legs, and the man put no weight on it.

"I couldn't find him," the first man said. They spoke Slavonic now. Iskandar pretended he didn't understand. In truth, languages came easily to him. He'd learned Vlach and rudimentary Slavonic from his mother, Turkish and bits of Arabic from his father, and a good deal of the vernacular Greek during his work in Byzia.

"Why would they bury him and leave the rest of our men uncovered?" The leader hobbled closer. "Have you looked everywhere?"

"You know I would leave no stone unturned for him, Kostya."

Kostya—no doubt his real name was Konstantin—motioned to Iskandar. "Who's this?"

"He was here when I arrived. Probably seeing if there's anything worth stealing from the bodies."

Iskandar almost laughed. He had much loftier plans than robbing dead soldiers.

Konstantin spoke to Iskandar next, in Greek. "Did the Greeks bury any of my men?"

Iskandar bowed. "They took their dead and wounded away in carts, lord. I've not seen any graves."

Konstantin frowned. "Miladin, tell me again what you saw."

"I saw him fall, lord," another fair-skinned Serb said. "He was attacked by two horsemen. It's unlikely he survived."

Konstantin studied the bodies of his slain comrades. "I have to know for sure." He bit his lip and shook his head. "He shouldn't have been here. You shouldn't have been here either, Danilo."

"He would have come without me had I told him to stay," the bowman said. "He was driven to find you."

Konstantin looked at the sun sinking into the horizon. "How can I have lost him?"

"Maybe . . ." Danilo started, then broke off.

Konstantin whipped his head around. "Maybe what?"

"Could they have taken him prisoner? For ransom? Or to sell as a slave?"

"I'll find out." Konstantin took a step toward his horse and almost stumbled.

"Župan Konstantin, you cannot go." Miladin brought the horse closer.

"Why not?"

Danilo spoke next. "Your injury. And you're needed back at the camp. You have to lead the army home. I'll go."

"You? So I can lose my brother and my cousin in the same day?"

"If the Greeks see me, they won't think me a Serb. That will work to my advantage. Besides, Rivak cannot lose its župan." Danilo looked again at Iskandar and switched to Greek. "The Greeks who fought here. Do you know where they live?"

"Yes. Byzia. I know it well."

"Could you lead me there? I'll pay you."

"I will happily be your guide." If Iskandar wished to defeat the Christians, he needed information about them, and traveling with one was bound to yield insight. He had planned to return to Byzia anyway to reunite with Ali. Now his journey would earn him coin as well.

When the Serbs finished burying their dead, they lent Iskandar a gelding. Konstantin handed Danilo a coin purse and part of a Greek uniform as he gave him his final instructions. "Shed no blood unless it be in defense of your life, or Ivan's. We don't want to provoke another ambush. Tomorrow we'll push on until we reach lands belonging to Miladin's kin. We'll be protected there while the wounded rest and we await your return. But the mountain passes won't be clear much longer. You have three days. That's all we can spare."

Danilo nodded and mounted his horse. He turned to Iskandar. "Ready?"

"Yes."

They rode through the first watch of the night. The moon lit their path, and the wind at their backs seemed to push them toward their goal. When they made camp and Danilo slept, Iskandar was tempted to cut the Serb's throat and steal the heavy-looking purse. But why steal a purse now when patience might yield a far more profitable reward?

When the Serb awoke, the questions began. "Byzia. What's it like?"

Iskandar and Ali had spent much of the last fortnight there, watching Kyrios Basil and his family. "It's an old kastron. Administrative offices and a garrison within a walled acropolis on a hill. A walled town at the foot of the hill with perhaps fifty families."

"How big is the garrison?"

"The barracks are large enough to hold two hundred, but there were only seventy when they set out to fight you."

Danilo nodded.

"Who is it you seek?" Iskandar asked.

"The župan's brother. We didn't see his body, so we hope he still lives." Danilo divided the rations equally and gave Iskandar his portion. "Tell me more of Byzia."

"Once, it prospered, but now the garrison is insufficiently manned and the lands underdeveloped and underpopulated."

"Where do you think they would take a wounded prisoner?"

Iskandar chewed on the dried barley biscuit he'd been given and decided to tell Danilo the truth. He could lie and send Danilo to his death, but he preferred earning the man's trust. Perhaps it would be useful later. "A surgeon lives in the acropolis. His home is between the chapel and the tzaousios's home."

"The tzaousios?"

"The garrison commander. There are also cells in the northwest tower and between the barracks and the stables." Iskandar plucked a stick from a nearby tree and drew a map in the dirt. "The kephale's keep is on the north. It's three levels high. Barracks, stables, and administrative offices on the west. The armory and the gatehouse to the south. Homes of the officials important enough to live in the acropolis to the east, along with a small chapel. A wall twenty cubits high with five towers surrounds it all."

Danilo studied the map and Iskandar's marks of where the tower, jail, and surgeon's home lay inside the fortress. "You have earned your pay well, my shepherd friend. What do you know about the night watch?"

Helena pulled her veil off and tied her curly hair back with a ribbon. She could barely keep her eyes open after working almost nonstop for a day, a night, and a day in the too-warm surgery. First Ithamar's baby, then the casualties from the battle. Weariness clung to her, piercing her to the bone, but perhaps the coming night would bring rest. Only Alexius and the Serb remained in Petros's old surgery.

Konstantin. That was what Radomir had called the young Serb prisoner. His body burned with fever, and mumbled words escaped his lips. She almost recognized some of them, but she didn't speak Slavonic. She'd spooned broth and water into his mouth, providing him nourishment, but he had yet to open his eyes.

Alexius was even worse. She prepared more cooling herbs—rose, violet, and malache—and mixed them with water. She spooned some in his mouth and rubbed more over his body with a cloth. Then she did the same for the Serb. She was still scared of him, but Gregoras had organized a guard for the front of the surgery, using his soldiers instead of ordinary watchmen from the villages. If the prisoner woke, and if he was hostile, help was only a few paces away.

Little had changed in Alexius or Konstantin since they'd been brought in, but both men were still alive, and she considered that no small accomplishment.

"Kyria Helena?"

Helena turned. "Yes?"

Pasara, a young serving girl, held a tray with seasoned chicken, lentils, bread, and wine. "Kyria Euphrosyne asked me to bring you this. It's supper time."

"Already?"

"Yes. Should I bring anything for them?" Pasara looked toward the injured men.

Helena sighed. "I wish they were well enough to eat. They haven't woken."

The Serb prisoner began mumbling again, more desperate this time.

"Do you understand him?" Helena asked.

"No, kyria." Pasara glanced at the Serb a final time and left.

Helena listened to the prisoner as she dipped her bread in olive oil and sipped her Muscat wine. It sounded as if he were reciting something, but what was he saying?

She repeated her ministrations with the cooling herbs, then retired shortly after the sun set. Her eyes itched with exhaustion, and her movements felt as if they were made in water. Niketas would wake her when he ended his watch and Matthias took his place. She would check on the patients again then. She climbed into Petros's bed, grateful it wasn't yet time for any of the women she cared for to be delivered. She craved sleep with an intensity that made closing her eyes and giving herself permission to stop fretting a rare pleasure.

She woke to the whisper of a breeze. A dying fire burned nearby, casting a glow around her and leaving the patients obscured. Had one of the embers cracked and woken her? Had a gust of wind stirred her blanket?

"Ivan?"

Helena barely picked out the soft word. She squinted at her patients and recognized a shadow bending over the prisoner. The next words were foreign, so she didn't understand them. Fear crawled across her skin and pinched her chest, making it hard to breathe. Who was next to her prisoner-patient, speaking Slavonic? And why?

The answer to her second question came quickly. The dark form lifted her patient across his shoulder, stood, and walked toward the window.

Helena watched, afraid to speak. But if the prisoner were rescued, would they ever get Leo back? And her patient wasn't stable enough for any kind of journey. "If you take him, he will die."

The shadow spun toward her. Firelight reflected off the edge of the knife he held, poised to throw.

She inhaled sharply. She shouldn't have been surprised. Of course the man would be armed. Firelight revealed a sword, quiver, and bow hanging from his belt.

"If I leave him, will he survive?" The words were Greek, though spoken with an accent.

Helena glanced at the door. It was closed. She hadn't shut it. She could yell for the guard, but the knife would reach her before Niketas did. Perhaps the intruder would miss. But what if he didn't?

"Your guard is drunk. If you call him, you might wake him, but I'll slay him quickly. I didn't come here to kill him, as much as your entire garrison deserves to be razed. Answer me. If I leave my friend, will he recover?"

Helena pulled her eyes from the door. Niketas wasn't normally a drunk, but he and Andronicus had been good friends, and he was taking the recent deaths hard. She suspected the man spoke truth about the guard's current state. The intruder claimed to be Konstantin's friend. Was he planning to take the injured man all the way back to Serbia? "I'm not sure. His wound is deep. And his fever is hot. But he has a better chance here than he does if you crawl through that window and ride off to your camp."

"Come here."

Helena stayed where she was.

"I won't hurt you. Obviously, you are helping with his care, and I want him to get better. But I prefer not to shout across the room at you."

He was hardly shouting, but she relented because she needed to check her patient's bandages. The friend laid him back on the pallet. Helena knelt to pull away the cloth on the patient's abdomen. That much jostling could have started him bleeding again, but nothing seeped from the wound.

"What will you do with him if I leave him?"

Helena stood and studied the man. He was younger than she'd first thought—about her age. He'd tucked his knife away, but one hand rested on the hilt of his sword, and the other rested on his bow. "You have a Turkish face, Greek armor, and, if I am not mistaken, a Serbian tongue."

"The armor is stolen. From one of your soldiers."

Helena stiffened. "What will you do with the men you took?"

"You attacked us without warning and without cause. We'll hold them as compensation. If you cannot ransom them, we'll find someone who can. Turkoman pirates, Genoese slave traders."

Without cause? "Of course we attacked you—you burned the fields of our paroikoi."

The man let out a sound the reminded her of a growl. "Someone burned your fields, but it wasn't us, and you have no proof that it was. Leo Kameteros admitted as much."

"You have Leo?"

"Yes."

"And the others?"

"Leo, Romanos, and three whose names I don't remember. I searched the field after the battle. Your side collected all your bodies, so it should be easy to determine who is missing."

She was glad for a confirmation that Leo lived, but immediately a new fear arose. "Are they well?"

"None are injured seriously. If they obey, that will remain true."

"I imagine Kyrios Basil will treat this prisoner the same. If he behaves, he will be cared for. And when he is well, we will trade him for the prisoners you took."

The shadow gave a short laugh. "One man for five? He is certainly worth five of your men when it comes to valor and courage, but you would be wise to prepare a better offer."

"But he is your župan, is he not? Župan Konstantin?"

His eyebrows drew together in surprise. "Who told you this was Konstantin?"

"Kyrios Radomir."

He drew his sword partway from its leather scabbard. "Radomir is here?"

Helena had begun to think she was safe with this man, but the calm vanished. She sensed danger in his words and took a step back.

"Is he?" His voice remained quiet, but there was iron in it.

"Yes. He's our kastrophylax. He said this man looked like his father."

He huffed. "Of course. The old župan's face probably haunts Radomir's dreams at night. Did he tell you that it was his betrayal that led to Župan Miroslav's death?"

"How?"

"Radomir went to the Turks and told them the location of the Serb camp along the Maritsa. Then he recalled the watchmen and did not set new sentries. The Turks attacked while my people were unprepared, and few in the Serb army survived. I would hunt Radomir down and murder him in his bed this very night if it were not for two things."

"What two things?" Helena took another step away, alarmed by the passion in the intruder's voice. She'd heard revenge was a virtue among the

Serbs, and this man didn't seem like someone who would let an apprentice midwife stall his vengeance.

"If I did that, you would call the guard. I could tie you up and cover your mouth, but if my friend needed you, you'd be unable to care for him. And Župan Konstantin told me to shed no blood, unless in self-defense."

Helena looked down at the prisoner. "How could Župan Konstantin give orders when he's been lying here unconscious since the battle?"

"This is not Miroslav's eldest son. He is Miroslav's second son, Ivan."

As if in response to his name, Ivan began to mumble again. The words were soft, run together, and foreign. Helena knelt to feel his hot forehead. "He's been doing that off and on all day. What is he saying?"

The Serb with a Turkish face listened for a time, then translated. "Lead us not into temptation, but deliver us from evil."

"He's reciting the Lord's prayer?" She had spent the last two days thinking of Ivan as her enemy. And that was still true, but it seemed he was also a penitent Christian.

"Yes. The priest who taught him that also taught him classical Greek. When he gets better, he'll understand you. But keep him away from Radomir while he recovers. That traitor is responsible for the death of both our fathers, and Ivan is unlikely to wait for full recovery if he sees the chance for revenge. Swear to me that you will take good care of him."

"I'll do my best." He seemed to want more, so Helena spoke again. "It's not in my nature to let another suffer when I might help him. And Leo is my sister's husband. We want him back, and a prisoner exchange is our best hope."

"Leo is your kin?"

"Yes."

"Then I have another request. You will tell none of your people that I was here. Not the guard, not your lord, not the Serb traitor living off the work of your paroikoi. And you'll not tell because if Basil sends a party after me and I don't return to my camp, Leo will end up in the hands of the cruelest slave traders in the known world. You will promise your silence?"

Helena swallowed, horrified to think of Leo as a slave. "Yes."

The man released the hilt of his sword and knelt to take Ivan's hand. He spoke into Ivan's ear words that Helena didn't understand. "Take good care of him," he repeated to her. "And if he doesn't recover, give him a proper Christian burial, because he is the best man I know."

Helena nodded. The man went to the window, hoisted himself out, and disappeared into the night. Helena stared after him, wondering if anything he had said was true.

Rage against Danilo burned in Iskandar's chest like a wildfire in the summer heat. He'd told the half-breed everything he wanted to know. And then, at sunset two nights before, Danilo had tied him up and said, "I'm sorry to do this, but I can't take you with me, and I can't risk you warning the kastron, so you'll have to stay here." Iskandar's wrists still bore marks from his struggles against the ropes.

Danilo had returned in the third watch of the night, alone. He'd paid Iskandar generously and cut him free, then left him with no horse. It had taken Iskandar all day to steal one and find Ali. But now, praise be to Allah, they had finally caught up to the Serb army as the Christians prepared to cross the mountain pass.

The group was smaller, to be sure. They moved slowly to accommodate wounded men and injured horses, but the battle hadn't beaten them as decisively as Iskandar had hoped. Their leaders had been wise, recognizing they were weaker and withdrawing in an organized, orderly manner. Pity their legendary stubbornness hadn't kept them on the field longer, until they and their enemy had suffered more serious losses.

Iskandar clicked his horse forward, following the army from a distance. Of the two groups, Greek and Serb, both were now weaker. But the Serbs were richer. He and Ali would follow them to their home. And when they had learned all they could, Iskandar would lead his father's ghazis to pillage and plunder. Iskandar's father had amassed a large group of followers. Their success the year before in Bulgaria had allowed them to live well for a time, but the men were restless and the treasure largely spent.

Now it was time to strike again.

And striking against the Serbs would bring Iskandar the added satisfaction of taking revenge on Danilo.

CHAPTER SIX
A DEATH AND AN INTERROGATION

ALEXIUS DIED THREE DAYS AFTER the shadowy Serb's visit. Helena closed his mouth and positioned his limbs so it looked as if he were sleeping. Exhaustion held her so tightly that she didn't cry at first. The tears came later as Basil, Euphrosyne, and the newly widowed Kyria Domnica came to mourn.

It wasn't Helena's fault—the wound had been too deep. But she couldn't shake the dreadful realization that despite her best efforts, she had failed.

Euphrosyne sat next to her on the bench in the surgeon's chamber when the others left to follow the body to the chapel. She took Helena's hand in her own. "You did a good job with him, you know."

Helena pulled her hand away. "I can't have done a good job, or he would have lived. I should have used different herbs or cut out more of his guts when I sewed them together."

"He was partially disemboweled. Have you ever seen anyone recover from that?"

"No. But until Petros was killed, I had seen few battle wounds."

"Precisely. We asked you to do a hard thing, something you had no training for. And when I see you sad like this, it makes me sorry we asked."

"But you had to ask me. There was no one else."

Euphrosyne took her hand again, and this time, Helena let her hold it. She studied the bright embroidery on the cuff of her sister's tunic. The shapes reminded her of enormous tears.

"Will he recover?" Euphrosyne gestured at the prisoner.

Helena wasn't sure. Ivan's fever hadn't broken, nor had she seen him wake. But the gash in his side wasn't swelling and festering the way Alexius's had. "Maybe."

"I hope so. For Leo's sake. And for yours. I hate to see you work so hard and not succeed."

Helena stood and walked to her patient to check his wounds again. The cut on his abdomen was by far the most serious, but it was improving. His shoulder was also healing, but the cut in his leg was growing worse. Helena took fresh water and put it above the fire so she could boil more malache. Once it cooked, she would drain it, mix it with oil, and put it on cabbage leaves over the wounds. It hadn't saved Alexius, but maybe it would help Ivan.

"Leo is the heir now. At least to the parts of the pronoia that are hereditary," Euphrosyne said.

Helena blinked in surprise. Grants of pronoia lands came with an obligation of service to the emperor, but they also came with a steady revenue for the kephale. If Leo was heir, Euphrosyne's future was secure. "Leo will be a good leader."

Euphrosyne watched steam rise from the pot. "Andronicus was not ready, but Alexius would have done well as kephale. I'm sad they're gone, and I mourn for Kyrios Basil. He is taking the deaths hard."

For a widower to lose both his sons within days of each other was a heavy blow indeed. "And Kyria Domnica?"

"I'm not sure. She does not confide in me."

"I imagine meals in the hall lack cheer lately." Helena hadn't eaten in the great hall since the battle, too busy taking care of her patients.

Euphrosyne stood. "They are strange. There was music yesterday but little mirth. Though there is little mirth here. Will you be all right?"

Helena nodded. "Yes. Returning this man to health will keep me busy." Helena approached Ivan again. His forehead felt cooler and his pulse stronger. His skin was a better color now, pale on his chest and tanned on his face. "And then we'll use him to get your husband back."

"Leo has to come back." Euphrosyne looked through the door to make sure the guard wasn't nearby, then lowered her voice to a whisper. "I'm carrying his child."

The chamber had contained sadness before, but Helena embraced her sister with genuine joy. "Why haven't you told me until now?" Leo and Euphrosyne had wed four years ago, and when no baby had come, her sister had feared she was barren.

"I wasn't sure until yesterday."

"Leo doesn't know?"

Euphrosyne shook her head. "I wish he were here. I would rather have him be part of it."

Helena glanced at Ivan, their surest hope of regaining Leo. "He'll be back before the baby comes."

Ivan lay on the edge of awareness. His body blistered in pain. He wanted to go back to the blackness that had consumed him so the agony in his side would go away. But the pain wouldn't release him. His eyelids were heavy, but eventually, he forced them open, and the chamber around him slowly came into focus. Stone walls, a large hearth, an icon of the Virgin Mary. He recognized nothing. Where was he?

He remembered riding off with Danilo to meet Konstantin's army. Snow in the mountains, sun in the plains. Images of Konstantin's horse pierced with arrows and Konstantin falling to the ground.

Ivan sat up on his pallet. The blanket fell from his torso, exposing a bandage across his stomach, and dizziness threatened to pull him down. The walls swirled around him and turned gray and then black briefly before coming into color again.

There had been a battle. A lance had nearly disemboweled him. A charging horse, a desperate throw . . . And then nothing. Had Danilo or Konstantin plucked him from the field? In good weather, the journey to Konstantin's grad took seven days, but some of the men Konstantin rode with had ties to estates nearer the border with Macedonia. Maybe they'd left Ivan with an ally to recover.

A tapestry with a man and a woman in regal robes hung near the fireplace. A royal couple? The man was clean-shaven, so he wasn't a Serb kral, nor a recent emperor from Constantinople. Perhaps an earlier emperor? Theodosius or Justinian? Intermarriage between Serb and Greek nobles was common enough. The hanging could belong to the home's Greek mistress. Or had Ivan been taken by the Greeks who'd attacked Konstantin?

A fire iron lay near the hearth. Ivan moved his legs off the mat and discovered he wore no clothes. He grabbed the blanket and held it about his waist. He tried to stand, but the dizziness returned, worse than before, so he crawled. His left leg hurt. He favored it, keeping most of his weight on the right one as he crept across the brightly woven rugs. He didn't remember injuring his leg. Had something punctured it as the horse had fallen on him? Or had an enemy pierced it when they'd discovered his body?

The massive oak door creaked open. Ivan made a lunge for the fire iron and grasped it firmly as he turned to meet whoever entered. If it was Danilo or a Serb physician, the improvised weapon would be unnecessary, something to joke about in a few days when Ivan's head stopped spinning. Instead, a graceful young woman stepped through the door. Her blue veil, tunic, and dalmatica were Greek in cut. A bronze brooch fastening her cloak was her only adornment.

Her brown eyes widened in surprise. Then a smile spread across her circular face. "You're awake."

Her words were Greek. That was warning enough, but the golden-haired guard who entered the chamber next wore the same style of armor as the Greek kataphraktoi. The soldier noticed Ivan's fire iron and drew his sword. Instant loathing spread across his face.

Ivan gripped the fire iron with both hands as he stood, then went back to a one-handed hold when he felt the blanket slipping. His enemy had a better weapon, but Ivan thought he could hold him off, if only his eyesight would stop fading in and out.

The woman motioned for the soldier to put his sword away. Then she took a step toward Ivan. "You're safe here. But you shouldn't be out of bed so soon. Will you give me the iron and lie down? I'd like to check your wound."

"And then you'll kill me?" Ivan had studied Greek with Father Vlatko since he'd been a boy, but the words sounded hoarse and unpracticed in his ears.

"No. I said you are safe, and I meant it."

"But you are the ones who attacked us?"

"Yes." The soldier's voice held both satisfaction and contempt. "We are the ones who defeated you."

"And I am your prisoner?"

"For the time being." The woman came closer.

Panic mixed with the nausea in his stomach. It felt as though chains were suddenly clutching his soul, and he was desperate to shake them off. "Are there other prisoners?"

"No."

That meant there was no reason for him to stay. Ivan used the wall to keep upright. He glanced at the window and stepped toward it. The shutter was open. Surely in another moment or two the pain wouldn't be so bad. Then he could disarm the soldier and make it outside. He didn't want to start a fight that might endanger the woman, but nor did he want to give up an opportunity to escape.

"Please," the woman said. "Put your weapon down and rest before you make yourself ill."

Ivan took another step toward the window. Beads of sweat ran down his neck, and he winced as the pain in his side flared, but he kept hold of the fire iron.

The soldier strode toward him, his sword raised. "You will obey Kyria Helena, or I will disarm you myself and cuff you firmly in the head so that you listen more quickly the next time."

"You can try to disarm me. You might not succeed."

The soldier laughed.

Helena gave the soldier a look that silenced him. "You're scaring him."

"He's trying to escape out the window."

Helena pursed her lips in disapproval. "Surely he's wise enough to recognize that as folly. He has no horse and no clothes. He is many days' ride from friends, he has had almost nothing to eat for a week, and even if he were to get away, his injuries would reopen under such exertion, and then he would die."

Ivan hadn't looked beneath the bandages. Was his body so fragile? Was the woman bluffing to keep him here, or was she telling the truth? His arm shook from holding the fire iron, though it wasn't heavy. He wasn't hungry, but he felt weak, as unwell as any time he could remember since childhood and the fever that had taken his mother and a sister and left him frail for years afterward.

Helena fingered a bowl and a pile of bandages. "Please sit down. It's time for me to check your injuries."

Escape would have to wait, because Ivan was near to falling over. He dropped back onto the pallet. He might as well sit with dignity before he lost consciousness. He kept the fire iron.

"Thank you," Helena told him. She glanced at the soldier. "You may go, Demetrios."

She moved toward Ivan, but Demetrios stopped her. "I'll not leave you with him while he's armed." He drew his sword and stepped forward, holding his hand out for the fire iron. "Give it here."

Ivan had a feeling that if he gave in to the guard now, he would be forced to endure more humiliations in the future. The Greeks may have surprised and driven Konstantin's men from the field, but Ivan wouldn't meekly submit to this man's domineering.

"Ivan, please."

Ivan met Helena's eyes. How did she know his name?

"Will you give me the iron?" she asked. "I am no danger to you. I'm trying to heal you."

"Have you been caring for me since the battle?"

"Yes."

"That is why your voice is familiar." His ears seemed to recognize her even if his eyes didn't. Perhaps he'd heard her while feverish.

"Will you give me the iron?" She stepped closer.

"If you will give me my clothes."

She smiled as if amused. "Most of your clothes are ruined, but I can arrange replacements." She pointed at the fire iron. "I need that now, and then I need your cooperation while I tend your wounds."

Ivan handed her the iron. Demetrios glared at him and strode from the chamber.

Helena knelt beside the mat and motioned for him to lie down. When she removed the bandages, Ivan lifted his head to glimpse at the puckered red skin that ran in a crooked line from rib to hip. She applied some sort of unguent to it.

"Your shoulder is nearly healed," she said. "It looked well when I checked it this morning. But your leg is infected, and the wound in your side still needs time. I ask that you stay in bed a while longer, until you regain your strength."

"Then what? Am I to be executed? Made a slave?"

"In the spring, you will be exchanged for the men your friends captured."

In the spring? "But I'm needed at home now. I've got to help store the harvest and prepare everything for winter." He and Danilo were still supposed to repair the weak spots in Rivakgrad's palisade wall. They had to gather fodder for animals and chop wood for winter fires. He couldn't stay until spring.

"If you were home now, you'd be in bed, not helping with the harvest." Helena applied a fresh bandage to his abdomen.

Perhaps he shouldn't have left Rivak after all. But if he hadn't been there to stop it, might Leo have killed Konstantin? That would be small comfort to his family if they thought Ivan dead. "Do they know I've been captured?"

"Yes."

"How?"

Helena didn't have a chance to answer. The door opened again, and Demetrios led in three men. Two wore rich robes, one wore armor over his tunic, and all had swords at their sides. The fair-haired soldier with a yellow beard was familiar. Ivan had wounded him in the arm during battle, after the man had drawn him far into the Greek line. He looked like an older version of Demetrios. The trio seemed too highborn for executioners, but their sober, angry faces made Ivan ill at ease.

Helena gave the men a graceful bow.

A man in a rich silk dalmatica with jeweled roundels stood at the foot of Ivan's mattress. "Do you know who I am?" he asked Ivan.

"No."

"I am Kyrios Basil, kephale of the pronoia your men attacked."

"What? You ambushed us!" The Greeks had attacked without provocation or warning.

Kyrios Basil huffed. "Only after you destroyed our fields. We were defending our paroikoi."

Ivan sensed a lie. "We had no quarrel with you. Why would Konstantin ravage your fields?" Konstantin might be stern, but he was fair and compassionate. He wouldn't have attacked defenseless Greek peasants.

One of the other men drew his sword and pressed the point into Ivan's chin. "One more lie and I'll cut out your tongue, young župan." The man's Greek was not as effortless as Helena's or Demetrios's, nor was his robe as extravagant at Kyrios Basil's.

"I'm not a župan yet. And I do not lie. Nor do I believe that Konstantin or his men pillaged your lands. They bought supplies in Thessaloniki. Why would they steal what they'd already purchased?"

Basil considered Ivan's words with hard eyes and downturned lips. "You bought supplies in Thessaloniki?"

"Konstantin did. I rode out to meet him and arrived shortly before your ambush."

The other man pressed his sword in, making Ivan tilt his head back so the blade wouldn't break the skin. "Your lie might work if you did not look so very much like your father."

Curiosity mixed with Ivan's anger. "You knew my father?"

"Yes, Konstantin. I knew your father. It appears you inherited his looks and his stubbornness."

"I'm not Konstantin."

The man pulled his sword back and slapped Ivan with the flat of it. It sent his head spinning. Helena flinched.

"Liar!" the man yelled. "You are Miroslav's son."

"Yes, I am." Ivan's head had ached before, and now it pounded. "But I'm not Konstantin. Kostya has nearly thirty winters. Do I look so old to you?"

Ivan thought the man would smack him with the sword again, but Kyrios Basil held out a hand. "You are Konstantin's brother?"

The man with an accent huffed. "Miroslav's second son died when the plague swept through the grad and took Miroslav's wife. He's lying. Perhaps he thinks that if we don't know the truth, we will strike a more favorable bargain when it comes time to exchange prisoners."

"It was camp fever, not plague. My mother and one of my sisters died. I fell ill, but I recovered."

"What convincing liars these Serbs from Rivak are. Don't be deceived, lord." The man glared at Ivan.

"Kyrios Basil?" Helena's soft voice broke through the anger.

"Yes?"

"He is Ivan, not Konstantin. I'm sure of it."

"How do you know?"

"His . . . He spoke when feverish. And he has been quite ill since the battle. If you question him too harshly, he may relapse. I humbly ask that you end the interview soon."

The man who'd threatened Ivan with his sword opened his mouth as if to speak, but Basil held out a hand, and he was silent.

"How soon before the battle did you arrive?" Basil asked.

"We barely had time to exchange news."

"You spoke with Župan Konstantin?"

Ivan nodded, and a sharp pain passed behind his forehead. Whatever information they sought, he didn't have it, and his head hurt. Why wouldn't they go away?

"Did he mention pillage?"

"No."

"What will he do with prisoners?"

"Ransom them, probably." Nausea twisted Ivan's stomach. He took a deep breath, trying to control it.

"Very well. We'll finish our questions later." Kyrios Basil turned, leading the older soldier and the man who'd thought he was Konstantin away. The younger soldier stayed, standing near the door.

Helena pressed a piece of bread into Ivan's hands when the kephale and his advisers disappeared from sight. "Eat this slowly." She placed a cushion behind his back so he could lean into it and handed him a goblet.

His throat was parched, but it took effort to keep his hand from shaking as he sipped his drink. "Your wine is different from ours."

"You've eaten almost nothing since the battle, so that is nine parts water and one part malmsey."

That explained the diluted taste, but it didn't explain the woman. Helena. She matched the picture Ivan had always had of Homer's Helen: beautiful—and capable of creating chaos. He'd never liked Helen of Troy. But this woman seemed gentle, and without her intervention, Kyrios Basil and the other men would still be questioning him. Ivan wasn't sure what to think of her, but he could describe how he felt about waking up weak and imprisoned. Horror at his condition made the wine bitter, the air oppressive, and the firelight cold. He'd woken up to a nightmare.

Ivan was dressed and sleeping when Helena brought boiled cereal a few hours later. His sleep seemed fitful. Had the fever returned? She felt his forehead, pushing back some of his messy brown hair. The temperature seemed normal. She hummed as she studied him. He had a small brown mark to the side of his left eye, as if someone had drawn in his eyelashes while he slept and had dropped a spot of ink just to the side of them. Otherwise, his complexion was clear and its color no longer so sickly. His eyes were a rare hazel. She hadn't noticed their color until he'd handed her the fire iron.

She glanced at it, by the fire again. He hadn't gone far to get it, but she was surprised he'd made it so soon after his injury. But it must have strained him, because his skin had turned gray while Kyrios Basil had questioned him and when the oaf Radomir had struck him with a sword. She couldn't have been more infuriated had the kastrophylax taken a vase she'd created and smashed it. Had he any idea how much effort she'd spent making their prisoner well and how much they needed him to ensure Leo's safe return? She hoped Radomir hadn't caused permanent damage.

Helena took the fire iron and placed it in the front chamber, where the prisoner wouldn't see it or take it to use as a weapon. When she returned, Ivan was watching her, his gaze so penetrating that it startled her. She paused for breath. "How do you feel, Ivan?"

"Were you humming?" he asked.

"Yes."

"Have you hummed that song before, around me?"

Helena thought back. The same pensive melody had been meandering through her mind since the day of the battle. "Probably. Do you know it?"

"No. But it sounds familiar." He scrutinized her. "How do you know my name?"

Helena checked the other room. Niketas and Paulus sat on the far side of the chamber, hunched over a game of Nine Men's Morris. "One of your friends came to take you the second night after the battle."

"What?" Devastation turned Ivan's lips and pinched his eyes. "Why did he leave me?"

"Because you were half-dead already, and death seemed certain if he took you from the kastron. But he saw I was caring for you. And they have prisoners, so you'll return eventually."

"Who came?"

"He didn't tell me his name, only your name, because I supposed you to be Konstantin."

"Why does everyone here think I'm Kostya?"

Helena hesitated. After seeing Ivan's attitude toward the fire iron, she worried he might try something reckless if she said Radomir had named him. "Your friend was most reluctant to leave you. He looked Turkish rather than Serbian."

Ivan glanced at the hearth. "Danilo. I don't think he's ever left me behind before."

"You wouldn't have survived the journey had he taken you."

Ivan was quiet for a moment, then met her eyes again. "Were you frightened of him?"

Helena eyed the window Danilo had climbed through. "A little. Of his blades."

"Danilo is good with the sword and even better with the bow. But he wouldn't use them to harm a woman. You were safe with him. And you are safe with me. I won't harm you, no matter what your guards think."

"Yes, I believe you."

A corner of Ivan's lips pulled up. It wasn't quite a smile, but it was at least friendly. "I'm glad someone here believes me. I'm not accustomed to being called a liar."

Helena gave him a full smile in return. They were enemies, but that didn't mean she couldn't tease him. "You were no doubt strong before your injury, but you've been in bed seven days, so that makes you considerably less frightening. And I heard you praying. I don't imagine a man who utters the Lord's Prayer with such frequency while feverish would intentionally harm someone trying to restore his health."

"You listened to my prayers?" There couldn't have been as much indignation in his voice if she had confessed to robbing a monastery.

"I didn't mean to. But you spoke them over and over again while I tended you."

The friendliness in his face disappeared, and he turned away from her. "You attack my people, rob me of my freedom, and take my clothes. And now you've violated the privacy of my soul."

The force of his resentment was almost tangible, but he wasn't being fair. "Don't be angry. I couldn't help hearing you."

He nodded, once. "No, I don't suppose you could." But he said nothing more the rest of the night.

Helena returned to the surgery the next morning, pulled by the need to change Ivan's bandages and by a growing curiosity about the man she'd healed. He looked up from his bowl of porridge when she entered.

"Has your appetite returned?" she asked.

"Some."

"Good. I'll send more throughout the day so you can rebuild your strength. Now I need to check your wounds."

He put his bowl down slowly and glanced up with wary eyes. "Do *you* always check them?"

"Yes."

"All of them?"

"Several times a day." Except the day before, when the kephale had interrupted one exam and Ivan's hostility had convinced Helena to forgo another that evening.

Ivan's face colored, and he put his hands down firmly on the edges of the blanket. He scooted away from her as best he could in his weakened state. "Perhaps you should just look at the one on my shoulder."

"The wound in your shoulder is the least worrisome. I have herbs for the others. And new bandages."

Ivan didn't answer. He had moved so far toward the edge of the pallet that he would soon be on the floor.

"Are all Serb men so shy?" she asked.

"Are all Greek women so brazen?"

Heat flooded Helena's face, a mix of ire and embarrassment. She had examined parts of the body normally covered with clothing but only with the intent to heal them.

"You just checked them yesterday," Ivan said.

"Yes, and the one on your left thigh was festering, and the one in your side received a great deal of jostling when you went for the fire iron." Helena folded her arms across her chest when he showed no sign of yielding. "If I don't keep them clean, they'll get worse, and you might die."

"I would think you glad to be rid of me after I captured Leo and injured the kephale's adviser."

Helena physically recoiled. "You captured Leo?"

"Yes."

"But you're more boy than man, and Leo and Gregoras are the best swordsmen in Byzia."

"Are you scared of me now? Or do you think I'm lying?"

Helena wasn't sure what she felt, but she didn't think he lied. She wanted to hate him for capturing her sister's husband, but she couldn't. She'd put too much effort into healing him. "I need to check your injuries now. I've invested too much time in your care to let a festering leg wound send you back to death's door. And I need you healthy so we can trade you for Leo."

Ivan shook his head.

"I've already seen everything." The instant the words escaped her mouth, Helena regretted them. Ivan looked absolutely humiliated. Was that the real problem? Shame from being captured? Embarrassment at being naked and at the mercy of his enemy? She tried again, forcing her voice to be more like honey and less like vinegar. "Please let me check them. I only need to see your leg. You can use the blanket to cover everything else."

He finally nodded. She turned away for a moment to let him arrange the blanket for privacy. Then she started at the bottom of the cut, applying an herbal paste to the wound. As she moved slowly up his leg, his muscles grew tense and his hands fisted. She kept her eyes mostly on her work, but on occasion, she peered at his face. He stared at the wall and wouldn't look at her. He stiffened again when she lifted his tunic to check the wound on his abdomen. She skipped checking his shoulder. The wound there had been healing without complications when she had last examined it.

When she finished, she left without a word. She would let someone else deliver his food and deal with his surly attitude for the rest of the day. He was no longer in danger of death, so she was going to give herself—and her patient—a little break.

CHAPTER SEVEN
BETWEEN HATRED AND FRIENDSHIP

THE NEXT THREE DAYS FORMED a pattern. Helena no longer had to argue with Ivan about checking his injuries, but he wouldn't meet her gaze and spoke only when answering questions. Even then, his answers never consisted of more than a few syllables. How did he receive the wound in his shoulder? A sword. The one in his side? A lance. The one in his leg? He wasn't sure.

Sometimes she wished he had stayed unconscious. He had to be lonely, but he showed no interest in friendship with her, giving instead only the barest of courtesy and utterly no warmth.

The fourth day was different.

"Good morning," she said as she brought Ivan's breakfast into the room.

She expected him to grunt, as he had the three previous days, but instead, he said, "What's so good about it?"

"We're both alive. You're not chained in the tower."

Ivan grunted.

"Well, what's so awful about it?" Helena asked. "The wound in your thigh was looking better yesterday. The others are healing nicely as well."

"I'm in Byzia instead of Rivak."

"That is a temporary condition."

Ivan grunted again and turned his face to the wall while she changed his bandages.

When she finished, she threw the old cloths into the fire, as she did every time she changed them, and added a log. "It's starting to get cold again," she said.

"I suppose that makes it certain that I'll be trapped here until springtime."

"Probably. Some travelers came through yesterday. They said winter has already come to the mountains." Helena sat on a bench near the fire. Ivan's happiness was not her responsibility, but his gloominess was starting to wear on her. "If you forgot for just a few moments that you hate us, you might find that it's not so bad here. Consider your stay an adventure."

"I'm not allowed to leave the room. That's hardly an adventure."

"You aren't well enough to leave."

"I wanted to. Yesterday. The guard wouldn't let me."

Helena glanced toward the front room, where Demetrios stood watch. "I'll talk to him."

She left Ivan and went to Demetrios. "Did he ask to leave yesterday?"

"Asked? Nay. He demanded."

"At this stage of his recovery, I think gentle exercise would do him good."

Demetrios glared at the door separating them from Ivan. "At this stage of his recovery, I think he should go to the tower. He's dangerous. I saw him in battle."

"Did he really capture Leo and wound your father?"

"I didn't see Leo's capture. But yes, he injured my father. And what's more, I saw him strike down Andronicus, Alexius, and Callinicus. Shall I have the chains brought in?"

Helena put a hand on the wall as shock made her knees tremble. Ivan had killed her betrothed? And captured her sister's husband? And mortally wounded Kyrios Basil's sons? Her first impression had been right. He was dangerous.

But dangerous was not the same as malicious, and Ivan didn't seem evil when she spoke with him. Moody and stubborn, yes, but not wicked. He had been under attack, and surely it was no sin to be a better swordsman in a battle he hadn't initiated. No, her latter impression of him was the correct one. His wounds embarrassed him, and he despised being a prisoner. He hadn't forgiven Kyrios Basil's men for what he saw as an unprovoked attack, but he wasn't evil. Chaining him would make it worse, not better. He threatened neither her nor the kastron.

"I think chains are unnecessary. He's a hostage, not a criminal."

Ivan overheard the conversation between Demetrios and Helena and knew the guard would have his way eventually. Ivan was their enemy, and he'd given them sufficient reason to lock him up. He would soon be shackled in chains or confined to a dungeon. He didn't want to spend the winter there. He wanted to spend the winter with his family.

After Helena's evening checkup, Ivan stared into the fire until it died. As the embers turned dull, he pulled on his boots and stood. He folded the blanket and threw it across his shoulder because he had no cloak, and he'd need warmth in the mountains. Then he grabbed an unlit candle and the slender knife Helena kept with her supply of herbs.

He eased the door open and peered into the outer chamber. The guard, the one called Niketas, slept on a three-legged stool with his back against the stone wall. His snores came rhythmically. Ivan considered clobbering the man and stealing his clothes and weapons, but the guards would change shifts during the night. If he knocked the guard unconscious, Ivan's absence would be discovered shortly. If he left the guard alone, perhaps no one would notice he was gone until morning.

Ivan took long strides and stepped softly, as if on a hunt and cautious of scaring the game away. Once past Niketas, he used the wall for support because his muscles were weak and his head still spun from time to time. The door on the far wall creaked when he opened it. The snore by the fire stopped, then restarted.

Stars lit the sky above him as Ivan stepped outside. He inhaled deeply—the first fresh air he'd breathed since the battle. All afternoon he'd had doubts about whether he should attempt escape, but the twinkling stars and clean night air convinced him. Freedom was worth the risk.

Moonlight and a few torches revealed a paved bailey. Ivan edged along the house until he reached the side and ducked into the space between the home and the chapel he'd seen from his sickbed. He waited there, resting and observing. Battlements about twenty cubits high surrounded the acropolis. The wall complicated his plans, but he wasn't ready to give up.

Across the bailey, a set of torches lined either side of a gate. The shadow of a watchman passed in front of one of the lights. The men who guarded the gates of Konstantin's grad wouldn't dare sleep while on duty, but the Greek soldier in the surgery had drifted off. Perhaps the one at the gate would be equally careless. If not, Ivan could claim he carried an urgent message to Thessaloniki.

Ivan doubted anyone would recognize him in the dark. To be sure, he shook out the blanket and wrapped it around him like a hooded cloak. He straightened his back, despite the pain in his abdomen, and stepped around the church. No one stirred. He took a few more steps, waiting for someone to shout.

Illness agitated his stomach, but he forced himself forward. He would have to get a horse because he wasn't strong enough to walk all the way to Serbia, and he might have pursuers to outpace.

Weakness and worry pulled at him as he slid past the buildings. A few times, he saw watchmen patrolling the top of the wall, but their attention was focused outward. A brisk wind led him past a kitchen, a keep, a cistern, and a bathhouse. He had to pause often as the dizziness returned, nearly blotting out his vision. If he could just make it outside the walls, he could find somewhere safe to sleep, and when he was rested, he could put more distance between him and this cursed fortress.

A torch burned in a bracket by the barracks. Ivan passed it quickly, then found the stables. He backtracked to the barracks' torch. He didn't dare take it—the watchmen up on the battlements and across the bailey at the gatehouse would notice if it moved. But he used it to light the candle, then shielded the small flame as best he could with the improvised cloak.

Inside the stables, Ivan paused to catch his breath and rub out the pain still eating at his side. Stalls of horses lined either side of a central aisle. He didn't need a warhorse because he didn't plan on battle. He wanted one with a gentle stride and a large store of endurance because the road to Rivak was long, and Ivan was weaker than he wanted to admit. A gray horse midway down the row suited his purpose. He clicked at the horse when it stepped toward him, and he ran his hand down its forehead and muzzle.

"I know it's early and dark," he whispered. "But I want to go home."

Ivan led the horse into the aisle. He needed a saddle and bridle, but there were none in the stables. He left the mare munching on loose hay and went to the wooden building next door. His side burned, and he had to stop and rest again. But he'd picked the correct building—and he would have known that even without the candle that he balanced amid a pile of loose horseshoes. The air smelled of leather and linseed oil. He selected an average saddle and hoisted it from its post, just as he'd done for years. But this time, as he lifted it, the ache in his side burst into a fiery explosion. Ivan dropped the saddle, and the pain brought him to the ground.

He breathed in through his nose and out through his mouth, controlling the rhythm of his lungs in an attempt to control the pulsing pain in his side. He pictured home: Konstantin, Danilo, Suzana, Marko, and Aunt Zorica. He wanted to see them again, badly, and he didn't want to wait until spring. He prayed, pleading for strength, and eventually, the pain ebbed. He stood, but standing upright made the pain worse again, so he hunched over. He left the saddle and grabbed the other items he needed, then returned to the gray mare. She was docile and patient as he slipped the bit into her mouth; he'd picked a well-trained horse. He led her into the other building so he wouldn't have to carry the saddle so far. The one he'd dropped still lay on the floor. He decided to use a different saddle, one still on its post so he wouldn't have to lift it from the ground.

"Over here, girl." The horse followed him.

They reached the post, but a wave of dizziness followed, and Ivan had to kneel until it passed. He was so weak that he couldn't keep his head from swaying into the wood. Eventually, the worst of it ended, and he struggled to his feet, then struggled even more as he raised a saddle onto the horse's back. His side burned, and his skin felt slick with sweat, but he got the saddle on the horse. As he clasped the buckles, he pictured his three-year-old nephew grinning with delight while he watched a falcon. As he filled the saddlebag with harnesses and other bits of tack, he recalled the sound of Danilo singing along with his gusle. Perhaps he could trade the extra harnesses for food the way he traded memories for strength.

Ivan had been able to mount a horse from the ground since he was small, but he wasn't going to try it now. He brought the horse to a table covered in pots of polish and bits of leather needing repair. The table creaked and wobbled when he climbed on—it wasn't built to hold his weight.

He caught his balance and tried to breathe through the new pain in his side. He had to keep going, had to get home. As he edged closer to the horse, the table tipped. His head banged into the wood as he crashed to the ground amid broken harnesses, cracked clay, and oily rags. He rested for a moment. The fall was a setback, but he could still make good his escape, as soon as he caught his breath and as soon as the throbbing eased just a little. He inhaled, then used his arms to push himself up, but nausea overwhelmed him, and he collapsed back onto the floor. He closed his eyes for just a moment, waiting for the dizziness in his head and the roiling in his stomach to pass.

Helena peeked into the great hall to see if her sister had felt up to breakfast. The table where Euphrosyne normally sat was empty, so it would be another quiet meal.

"Kyria Helena?"

Helena turned and recognized a young groom. "Yes?"

"I found a man in the storage room by the stables this morning. The soldiers took him to the surgeon's house and told me to find you."

She hoped Philippos didn't mean Ivan, but she had a feeling he did. Ivan could barely walk. What demon had goaded him into the rooms by the stables? She rushed from the keep and across the bailey to Petros's old chambers.

Demetrios met her in the front room. He wore leather lamellar on his torso and a frown on his face.

"You sent the groom to find me?" she asked.

"I did."

"Ivan was across the bailey this morning?"

"Yes. I told you he ought to be locked up." He sat on a stool and crossed his arms.

Helena stepped into the back room with a mix of emotions. There had never been a need to lock Ivan inside. Why chain a man when he could barely stand? Trying to escape in his condition was folly. But perhaps even more foolish was the way a small part of her hurt. She'd given up countless hours of sleep, crushed herbs until her hands were raw, and changed his bandages more times than she could count. And he had tried to leave without so much as a thank-you.

He sat in front of the fire with his back to her.

"Are all Serb warriors as reckless as you? To attempt escape is foolhardy in the best of times—and in your state, it is complete madness. Even a healthy man would freeze trying to cross the mountains this time of year."

He turned to glance at her but didn't reply. The skin around his eyes was swollen, and he held a rag to the right corner of his lips.

Helena put a hand on her hip. "Let me guess. You fell asleep, and the horse you planned to steal trampled you."

"No, my lady. The gray mare I planned to ride is far too intelligent to step on a man."

"A gray mare? You planned to take my horse?"

"I didn't know she was yours. But I compliment you on a fine taste in animals."

Helena's muscles were tight from her shoulders to her toes. She forced herself to relax. "If your bruises aren't from Cleopatra, where did they come from?"

"A parting gift from the guards who returned me to my prison."

Helena walked around to see his skin more clearly. She pulled the cloth away to reveal a cut, as if something had caught on his lips and torn the skin. It still oozed blood. She grasped his chin to turn the other side of his face into the light. He winced, and she let go in horror. She hadn't meant to hurt him. "Did you resist? Is that why they beat you?"

"I was asleep when they found me. Most of the guards offered their reasons while swinging their fists into me, but I believe it comes down to the fact that I am their enemy. When they attacked my brother's men, we fought more valiantly than they'd expected. We may have withdrawn, but we hurt them, and they won't forgive that any time soon."

Even though she stood before a fire, Helena felt cold. "Did Demetrios strike you?"

"Not that I remember, my lady. He and the stablemaster stood in the doorway while the others had their fun." Ivan kept his eyes on the fire as he spoke. No reaction made it onto his face or into his voice. She'd grown accustomed to him being stubborn and grumpy, and she wasn't fond of either mood, but the absence of emotion was worse.

She glanced toward the outer chamber but saw no one. The front door was open, so Demetrios must have stepped outside for a moment. Perhaps that was just as well, because disappointment in the soldiers welled up in her, clawing to be let out. Their ill behavior was almost as bad as Ivan's escape attempt.

No, it was worse. Ivan had planned to steal a horse—her horse, no less—but he hadn't hurt anyone for pleasure.

Helena rolled the sleeves of her tunic and tucked the pendant of St. Peter the Athonite into her dalmatica. "Let me wash the cuts." She gathered a rag, soap, and water, then added wine, needle, and thread to her supplies.

Ivan cooperated as she worked. Most of the cuts were small, but she put three stitches in the one on his lips. She made them small, and he held perfectly still while she sewed.

"Thank you," he told her as she finished.

Her hand paused over the bowl of water. He had never thanked her before, and the simple phrase warmed her heart. "You're welcome."

When he removed his tunic, Helena gasped. The damage was even worse there. She felt the newly formed scar in his side. "Does it hurt?"

He nodded.

Helena checked the older wounds on his thigh and shoulder and wiped away the blood that streaked across his skin. She was familiar enough with his body to know which cuts and bruises were new. "Did they use their fists or their boots?"

"Both."

She finished her work, anger burning just under the surface. She left and closed the door firmly behind her. Demetrios had returned.

"How dare you!" she said to him.

His face twisted in surprise. "What?"

"How dare you let your men beat him! Do you have any idea how hard I've worked to make him healthy again? You've set his recovery back days! And he is our best chance of getting Leo back. What if your men had killed him?"

"I would have stopped them long before they went that far—"

"You should have stopped them immediately!"

Demetrios took a deep breath and looked at the wall beyond her. "Kyria Helena, you are proving to be a gifted healer, but you know nothing of war."

"Was there a battle in the stables? If I remember right, the fight was fifteen days ago. And Ivan had no weapon this morning."

"He had one of your knives."

"Was he using it, or was he sleeping?"

Demetrios ignored her question. "How can you defend him? He captured your sister's husband, killed both your lord's sons, slew your betrothed, and wounded my father. And his friends did the same to a dozen others—my men remember that, and there is no one else to punish for it."

"What were the Serbs supposed to do when you attacked? Surrender? Did you even give them that chance?"

"They attacked our pronoia! We had to fight them!"

"No. Someone burned our fields, and you assumed it was the Serbs based on the words of one shepherd no one had ever seen before and no one has seen since."

Demetrios looked away.

Helena inhaled deeply, trying to calm herself. She had never yelled at a man before. But she had never seen such reckless cruelty before either. Every time she attended a birth, she was reminded of how miraculous each life was. To have the guards attack an unarmed, injured man was vile, even if he was their enemy. "No one enters this chamber without my permission." She pointed to the door that divided them from Ivan.

"Very well, kyria."

Helena went to get Ivan some porridge. Demetrios was gone when she returned, and Matthias stood guard instead. His son was the first baby she'd helped deliver when she'd moved to Byzia, but he didn't meet her eyes when she came inside, making her suspect he had taken part in the beating and now felt guilty about it.

Ivan seemed surprised to see her again when she opened the door to his chamber. He took the bowl when she handed it to him but didn't begin eating at once.

"Did they ruin your appetite?" Helena asked.

"No. But I'm confused. Who are you?"

Helena examined one of the bruises on his temple. The swelling was starting to purple. "Did they affect your memory when they hit you?"

"Kyria Helena, I've heard your name, and I recognize your title, so I know you are of noble birth. But in comparison to Kyrios Basil and his councillor, even in comparison to some of the guards, your clothes are plain. You serve me my breakfast and change my blood-soaked bandages, almost like a servant. Yet you can yell at the son of the tzaousios without retribution. I don't understand."

"You heard me speaking with Demetrios?"

He nodded as he stirred his porridge.

"I wasn't yelling."

"Of course not. Forgive me for suggesting it." A hint of a smile formed on his battered lips, followed by a wince. "Were you to chastise me with half as much indignation as you used on Demetrios, I would consider myself severely scolded, no matter the volume of your voice."

"You should eat." Maybe she had been too hard on Demetrios, but as she watched Ivan trying to spoon the porridge into the less-injured side of his mouth and grimacing as he swallowed, she didn't regret her words or her tone. "As for my clothing, I prefer simpler items for my work. I'd not wish to stain a carefully embroidered cuff when a child is born or be late when I'm called because I must change into something I can ride in. As for my place in society, it has altered so often that at times, I am no longer sure myself."

He met her eyes with that probing look that made her certain he understood far more than she spoke aloud. He didn't interrupt her, so she continued. "I come from old families. My great-grandfather was a Laskaris, but he lost his lands to a pack of Catalan mercenaries and, with his lands, his source of income. I was born in Constantinople, where he settled. But money and prestige do not last forever. From a young age, I knew I could bring little other than my name to a marriage, so it seemed wise to find a trade. My mother died shortly after childbirth. Some type of fever. The woman tending her was inexperienced, and I always wondered if my mother would have lived with better care. So I apprenticed myself to a midwife when I was twelve."

"A noble profession. Though that does not explain why I am your patient."

"The surgeon was killed in battle. That left me, if we wished you healed so we could trade you for Leo."

Ivan grunted.

"Leo is the reason I came to Byzia. He met my sister while in Constantinople for his family's wool business. It seemed a good match to marry the niece of a trading partner, and they liked each other from the moment they met. But Leo was only the nephew of the kephale, so though the marriage would save my sister from poverty, it seemed wise for me to continue my studies." Helena went to the herbs scattered across Petros's old table and started putting them away as she spoke. "My father was dead, and my uncle didn't wish to support me, so Leo arranged for me to finish my apprenticeship here. Now Leo is the heir, so my position is again changed."

Ivan had turned to watch her organize her herbs. "Leo is the heir?"

"Yes. And he will make a good kephale, when the time comes."

Ivan raised an eyebrow. "When I last saw Leo, he was trying to slay my brother. Forgive me if I do not share your high opinion of him."

Helena looked away. "Did you hurt him when you captured him?"

"I cut his forearm. I don't think it was deep, but it made him easy to disarm."

Helena had allowed herself to relax for a few moments, talking with Ivan as a friend instead of an enemy, but she couldn't ignore their differences completely. Ivan had fought against her people, and he wasn't sorry for it. And perhaps he had no reason for regret. He'd been defending his friends and his family.

"Will you continue as midwife when you are sister to a kephale's wife?"

Helena ran her fingers along Petros's copy of Trotula's medical compendium. "Yes. Bringing new life into the world is unlike anything else—I don't wish to give it up. But it seems I will remain only an apprentice. The woman I trained with died this past spring. The surgeon taught me some, but now he is also dead."

"We would be grateful for a midwife—even an apprentice—in my lands. The one who delivered me and my siblings died a few years ago—before my sister married—and then Lidija died in childbirth." As he spoke, the grief showed on his face, made starker by the damage the soldiers had done that morning. "She lived near to us, so her husband sent word. We expected she would be delivered when we arrived. But it took so long. And then the baby was too small, and my sister bled too much, and no one knew how to help her."

"Sometimes, there is nothing that can be done. I am sorry for your loss."

Ivan nodded. "The baby lived only minutes. I held her body, and she fit in one hand." Ivan held his arm out, as if he could still see his niece. "My aunt told me that women risk their lives to bring children into the world and men risk their lives to keep those children free. I suppose those are our roles, but sometimes, it seems too many die."

Helena glanced at Ivan. He was part prisoner, part patient, and he was turning her emotions upside down. She had visited graves from the battle the day before. Ivan was responsible for several of them. She should hate him. He'd killed her people and recklessly tried to escape instead of waiting until he could be exchanged for Leo. And yet, though she was angry with Demetrios and the other soldiers, she felt no anger toward Ivan. For him, she felt compassion. Was that treasonous?

No, kind feelings were never treasonous. But when she finished sorting the herbs, she left Petros's home and its prisoner. Conversation with Ivan shouldn't be so comfortable. Perhaps it was the location more than the person. In the same home, she'd told Petros about her dreams and vulnerabilities, but she'd opened up to few others. Why did she feel a connection with an enemy? His Greek was strangely accented, he'd been stubborn and uncooperative, and if his face had any appeal, it was hidden by bruises. She would have to guard her feelings with better diligence. She was supposed to heal Ivan, not befriend him.

CHAPTER EIGHT
LIKE A CAGED BIRD

IVAN DIDN'T PLAN TO STAY in the kastron all winter. His body needed rest, but he couldn't delay his escape long, or the mountains would be impassable. He shouldn't have tried so early. He'd been too weak, and now the guards were more cautious. Someone had nailed boards across the window, and they'd started locking the door at night.

"Good morning." Helena brought a smile and a bowl of millet gruel.

"Is it morning?" Ivan glared at the window. Only one small crack showed daylight. "It's hard to tell."

"Perhaps if you hadn't left without permission, you'd still be able to see the sky."

Her tone held rebuke, but what he hungered for was empathy. "Would you stay were you in my place?"

Helena didn't answer right away. "Probably. I'm not as brave as you. Or as foolhardy. And I'm used to others dictating what I must and mustn't do. Hold still so I can examine your new cut."

He obeyed, clenching his teeth as she examined the tender flesh.

"It looks worse today. All the bruises do."

Ivan put a hand to his cheek. "Then I must look like a demon. And you are not only kind but also brave to treat my wounds."

Helena's lips lifted in a brief smile. "It will heal, although it may scar." She touched the skin just to the side of his lips, the movement so light that he felt no pressure, only a pleasant warmth. "In any case, I learned yesterday that looks can be deceiving. I've seen the guards many times and never suspected they were capable of such cruelty. It's shameful. I spoke to Gregoras, and he reminded the garrison that you are meant to be kept whole so we can exchange you for Leo."

Ivan watched her check the wound on his shoulder. The guards had kicked him several times there, but her touch was gentle. "Your looks are not deceiving."

Helena met his eyes briefly. "Oh?"

"No. You are graceful and comely, in form and in soul."

Her fingers slowed on the bandage she'd been replacing.

Ivan thought he noticed a blush. What he really wanted was another smile. "Yours is the only smile I've seen since I arrived that was not mocking me or grinning at my pain. The servant who sometimes brings me food is not unkind, but I think she is scared of me. And the guards . . ." Ivan fingered one of the new bruises on his chest. "Well, you've seen how they treat me."

"They show it differently, but I think they are also scared of you."

Ivan stared at the fire. "I'm injured and unarmed. There is little for them to fear." He was as helpless as a lamb and as hated as a wolf.

Helena checked his abdomen next. The surrounding skin was more sore than usual as she felt it. He held his breath until she moved on to his thigh.

"Homer's Helen must have looked like you. But you are kinder than she."

Pink spots appeared on Helena's cheeks again. "You're familiar with Homer?"

"That's how we practiced our Greek."

Helena put some sort of ointment on his injured thigh. "Did you study *The Iliad* or *The Odyssey*?"

"Both. And I used to favor the stories of Achilles. But now I think I prefer *The Odyssey.*"

"Because it's about going home?"

He nodded. He felt a new kinship with Odysseus and his men—determined to go home but hampered and held up at every turn.

Helena finished bandaging his leg and put her hand on his. Her touch was so different from the guards'—calming, reassuring. "I have to go. There are several women under my care that I need to visit, but I'll come again tomorrow."

She came daily, and gradually Ivan could chew without pain and walk without dizziness. He enjoyed her visits, and sometimes he thought of her, even when she wasn't there. But far more often, his mind was in Rivak, and he began preparations for his next escape.

"What's this?" Helena asked one day. She held the scraps of bread Ivan had dried, wrapped in a cloth, and hidden in an empty clay pot. "You weren't thinking of . . ." She looked at the food again and pursed her lips. "You were planning to escape again?"

Ivan cursed himself for not finding a better hiding spot, but the room offered few choices. "It's my duty to escape."

Helena threw the dried bread into the fire. Ivan pushed himself to his feet, almost diving to save it. Instead, he watched it burn. What would he eat in the mountains if he had no bread?

"Who gave you this duty to escape?" Helena placed her hands on her hips.

"I did."

"Perhaps you ought to be more patient." Her words held a sharpness, but at least she hadn't called Niketas, who stood watch in the front chamber. His boot was responsible for the rip in Ivan's mouth.

Ivan sat on the bench with a sigh. "It's not just that. I miss my family. And I worry about them. My aunt's bones hurt in the winter. I used to rub her hands and feet each night. She won't ask for help, and I don't know if anyone else will remember to offer." If he came back before the worst of winter set in, maybe she'd forgive him for leaving without telling her and for taking Danilo with him.

Helena had seemed angry for a moment, but now she seemed sad. "You are close to your aunt?"

"She's been like my mother since I was young."

"Would she want you to risk a winter journey across the mountains or the anger of the guards?"

"No. My aunt is truly unselfish. Which is all the more reason for me to return to her, so that someone sees to her comfort." Ivan looked at the fire again. His aunt would manage without him. They all would. But they would miss him, and he missed them. "Camp fever swept through the grad when I was four. It took my mother and a sister, and it almost took me. My aunt saw me through the worst of it. I had fragile health most of my child-hood, but she never complained when she had to sit through the night with me or bathe me or spoon-feed me yet again. When I regained my health, I had to catch up on everything. Riding a horse, spearing something with a lance. Swordplay."

"By all accounts, you are a most accomplished swordsman."

"I had to prove myself." He remembered all the times he had shot his bow until his fingers had bled and shoulders burned, all the times he had sparred with someone taller and stronger than he until his hands blistered and his lower back ached. "If I am good at anything, it is because I worked twice as hard as anyone else to become that way."

"Including your stubbornness?" Helena seemed amused. He hoped that meant she'd forgiven him.

"The stubbornness I was born with."

Helena checked the herbs drying near the hearth. "Ivan, I know you long for your home, but you can't run away again." The sadness had returned to her voice. "Promise me you'll stay."

"That is like asking me not to breathe." Couldn't she understand how trapped he felt? How lonely and miserable he was? He had a duty to his family and to his people. If he was stuck in Byzia, he was failing them.

Helena faced him with slumped shoulders and downturned mouth. "If you escape, Kyrios Basil will send the entire garrison after you, and despite orders to preserve your health, I suspect they'll be just as vicious as they were the last time. Some of them want to lock you in the storeroom below the armory. It's cold, and it's dark, and the last man they put down there came out as a corpse. Please, please don't try again."

Her request was so earnest, and she'd done so much for him. He wanted to go home, but surely he could do something small for her. He reached for her hand, and she let him take it. "I give you my word of honor that I will not escape tonight."

"Would you like to walk outside with me?" Helena asked after she had replaced Ivan's bandages the next morning. Guilt still lapped at her for burning his bread and for not reporting her discovery to the guards. She should have told them, but she dreaded their reaction if they knew Ivan had planned another escape.

"Do you mean it?" His face had that wary look again, like a child promised a cake but convinced it would be snatched away from him.

"Yes." She scanned the boarded window. She would hate to be caged in a room with no sunlight. Maybe if he could leave from time to time, it would soften his determination to escape. "One of the guards must accompany us."

The enthusiasm on Ivan's face visibly dimmed, but he didn't ask to stay.

When Helena and Ivan walked into the front chamber, Demetrios stood ready. He offered Helena his arm. She took it so as not to be impolite, but she would have rather strolled with the prisoner. Demetrios was handsome and strong, but she'd seen the cruelty he allowed.

Ivan walked slowly and often needed to pause for rest, but the warm autumn sunshine seemed to do him good. The light caressed his face, throwing into stark clarity how pale and ill he still looked. She tried to imagine his face free of bruises and scabs, but she couldn't quite picture it. She would have to wait for him to heal before she decided whether he was handsome or homely.

Demetrios ensured that the outing was short. Given Ivan's health, Helena didn't object, though Ivan seemed reluctant to return to the room that formed his prison.

"Will you promise not to escape tonight?" she asked before leaving.

Sorrow crept into his eyes, and he looked at his hands before answering. Had he been planning escape again already?

"For you, my lady, I will stay until morning."

The next day, Helena waited until Demetrios was no longer on duty before she took Ivan outside. She told herself it was only because Demetrios hadn't enjoyed the walk the day before, that it had nothing to do with Ivan. But being with Ivan was far more fascinating than watching Euphrosyne's embroidery or enduring Kyria Domnica's gossip.

Matthias stayed where he could see the two of them but not always where he could hear them. Helena enjoyed the privacy as they strolled along the southern battlements. When they peered in, over the waist-high wall, they could see the buildings of the bailey laid out before them. When they gazed south, over a higher, second wall with toothlike crenellations, they could see the cottages and shops in the town below and the fields and woods beyond.

Ivan turned west, toward his homeland. "I wonder if they've had their first snow yet."

Helena knew nothing of the weather in Rivak. She wasn't sure if she should encourage Ivan to talk of home or if that would increase his longing, so she said nothing.

Ivan's voice grew wistful. "My nephew was enchanted with it last year. It wasn't his first snow, of course, but it was the first he remembered."

"How old is he?"

"Three. And forgetful. I spent most of the summer in Sivi Gora with my grandfather. Marko didn't remember me when I returned. I finally won his trust, and then I rode off to meet his father. He won't know me when I return. If I return." Ivan folded his arms across his chest.

"Spring will come. It does every year without fail, and then you'll be exchanged and return home."

"Not for long. I'm my grandfather's heir. He's let me spend most of my time at Rivak until now, but this was to be my last winter there, and I'm missing it because I'm stuck here." Ivan strode away.

Helena pulled her cloak more tightly around her shoulders. Was Leo taking his captivity as hard as Ivan was?

Ivan stopped and turned to her, his voice a plea. "You could give me a horse or a mule and let me go. I'll send the horse back—with Leo. You have my word."

"It's not my decision to make. And I'm not sure you're ready for a journey so long."

"I could manage it, if no one was around to pummel me with their fists."

Helena looked away. "I'll mention it to Kyrios Basil, but I don't think he is willing to risk so much on your word."

Ivan walked to the edge of the wall and put his hands against the crenellated stones. "It's your fault, you know."

"My fault?" She hadn't started the battle, and it wasn't her will that kept Ivan a prisoner.

"Not you. Your people. If your emperors hadn't been so absorbed in their civil wars, they could have held off the Turks. Instead, they invited them in, used them against one another, showed them the best roads and the most fertile lands, taught them how to defeat a Christian army, and now they're taking everything, bit by bit. Kostya wouldn't have been anywhere near Byzia if your rulers hadn't started the Turkish flood. Then there would have been no battle and no hostages."

"The Despot Manuel is fighting them." The Turks were Helena's enemy as much as they were Ivan's.

"The Despot Manuel is several generations too late. You should have given Constantinople to Kral Dušan. He would have kept the Turks back."

Matthias was closer now. He huffed. "Hand the empire over to a Serb warlord?"

Ivan met Matthias's scowl with a look of certainty. "Hand the empire over to a king who could have protected Christendom."

Helena agreed with Matthias. The Palaiologoi wouldn't have relin-quished the empire to an outsider. And though there had been whisperings that Stefan Dušan planned to march on Constantinople, he had died rela-tively young. Rumor held he'd been poisoned. Even if he'd lived, the land walls of Constantinople would have stopped his army, and the Serbs hadn't a navy to attack the sea walls. Dušan couldn't have conquered the city by force.

Yet Ivan was right about one thing: the imperial family hadn't kept the Turks out. It wasn't Helena's place to discuss defenses and threats, and it was practically blasphemous to speak ill of the emperor, but she knew Byzia's independence was precarious. Someone like Manuel might have done much good had he been born earlier. Now he had few options and an imperial father who had already surrendered part of his authority to the Ottoman sultan.

They didn't speak of politics as they continued their walk. When she no-ticed Ivan's footsteps slowing, she led him back to his quarters and checked his bandages. The bruises were no longer so dark, nor the sutured skin so puckered and red. The progress gave her twofold satisfaction: her efforts had worked, and Ivan's body was healing.

"Will you promise not to escape tonight?" she asked as she finished the last bandage.

Ivan's lips twisted as if he were in pain. "I'll not escape tonight."

She found that she wasn't in a hurry to bid him farewell. She checked some of the herbs hanging to dry, explaining their purpose when Ivan asked. After that, she fixed a few bandages that had been rolled in a hurry. The cloth was already functional, but she took her time, ensuring it would be neat as well, as if how tidy it appeared on a shelf might somehow affect how well it protected future wounds. Finally, when she could think of no other work to do in the surgery, she told him goodbye. His reply, given with a warmth that seemed like friendship, caused a smile she did her best to hide when she walked past the guard.

They soon fell into a pattern. Helena visited Ivan daily, and gradually their walks grew longer, and there was less of a need to change bandages and fret over possible infection. She grew familiar with his likes and dislikes, his moods and temperaments. They sometimes debated politics, but far more often, they spoke about their pasts. She admired Ivan's devotion to his fam-ily and was flattered when he showed interest in her healing techniques. She often felt stifled around other men—wary of saying the wrong thing and afraid of provoking disapproval. But Ivan seemed to accept her just as she was.

Every day before she left, she requested Ivan's promise not to escape. He was always reluctant, but he never refused her. Still, the pain she saw in his eyes each time he agreed somehow hurt her heart, and it was growing worse as autumn withered into winter.

Ivan wasn't accustomed to being inactive. He was used to riding horses and repairing chain mail, chopping wood for widowed merophs, and losing to Danilo in archery competitions. He yearned for freedom, for movement, and in the meantime, he yearned for his daily walks. Any chance to see more than a finger's width of open sky was better than the long stretches of time when he was locked in the surgery.

More than that, he liked Helena, and not just because she was the only person who spoke to him without fear or loathing. He would have liked her even if they'd met in different circumstances. She had the beauty of an icon, the mind of a scholar, and the kindness of a saint.

The morning air chilled them as they climbed the eastern tower. Helena wore a cloak of thick wool, and she'd found a similar one for Ivan to layer atop his undertunic, tunic, and hose. They'd been outside only a while when a burly man in a blacksmith's apron approached Helena.

"Kyria Helena?"

"Yes?"

"My wife is with child. And it's time."

Ivan admired Helena's passion for her work, so he tried to hide his disappointment that their time together and his time outside would end early. She glanced at Ivan, her lips pursed in silent apology.

"I'll go back with Niketas," he said. "And I will pray the delivery is successful."

"Thank you." She put a hand on his arm, bidding him farewell.

As he watched Helena leave with the blacksmith, he heard Niketas step closer. Ivan turned to face the guard.

"You will return to your quarters and give me no trouble." Niketas drew his sword. "Just because she's not here doesn't mean you don't have to behave."

Niketas was too stiff. Ivan could probably disarm him, steal his sword, and be off to the stables. But when he left, he wanted a head start. So, for now, he went meekly back to the surgery.

The servant girl brought his evening meal as light from the crack in the boarded-up window dimmed to darkness.

"Thank you," he said.

She nodded but wouldn't meet his eyes. She was probably still frightened of him.

"Any news of Kyria Helena or the baby she is delivering?"

The servant shook her head.

After he finished the bread and dried fish, the girl took the shallow ceramic bowl away, and the guard, Paulus, locked the door. Ivan walked to the fireplace, remembering another chimney, smaller than this one, that had once offered him escape. He grabbed a stick from the wood pile and used it to push the burning logs apart so the fire would die down sooner. On the boarded-up window, he heard the tap of raindrops, and it brought a smile to his lips. A dark night would suit his plans perfectly.

CHAPTER NINE
A DARK NIGHT

THE BLACKSMITH LIVED IN THE lower portion of the kastron, sharing a home with his younger siblings and widowed mother. His wife, Maria, had been in labor all day, and her pains came at regular intervals, but it was the woman's first child. Helena examined her again and predicted the baby would not come for a while longer. The blacksmith's mother seemed to know that. She sat on a bench in the corner, embroidering the cuff of a tunic. But the oldest of her daughters, a young woman of about thirteen, grew pale every time Maria travailed. Her needle had scarcely moved at all since Helena's arrival.

"Drink this." Helena handed Maria a goblet of wine heavily watered with a decoction of fenugreek and flax. "This will help with the pain and give you strength."

"I'm so tired. I can't do this much longer."

"You are stronger than you know." Helena wiped Maria's forehead with a damp cloth. "This may be the hardest day of your life, but it will also be one of the best days of your life." She held Maria's hand through another fit of pain.

"How much longer?" Maria sobbed.

Helena examined the birth canal and rubbed it with rose oil. "It's not yet time. But you're making progress." Helena felt the woman's hands and forehead next and went to add another log to the fire so Maria would stay warm. It was going to be a long night.

Since Helena hadn't asked him to stay, Ivan saw no reason to remain in the kastron. He stood before the table where she had crushed so many herbs and mixed so many salves. He was tempted to take the copy of *The Odyssey* that she'd loaned him, but he didn't want to rob her. His conscience already pestered him because he had no money, so he planned to steal food and a horse. He fingered a clean bandage, one Helena had cut, then scoffed at himself. He didn't need a token from a Greek woman. He was leaving, and soon his time as prisoner would be but a memory, a largely unpleasant one.

He pulled the woven sleeping mat to the corner behind the firelight, where it would be obscured if a guard looked in to check on him. Then he shoved a few bowls and logs under a blanket so it would resemble a body.

He'd spent the last hour cutting a blanket with the scissors Helena used for cutting bandages. He tied the last strips together, then looped the makeshift rope into a circle and slipped it over his right shoulder and across his chest. He pressed his ear against the locked doorway into the outer chamber and was met with silence.

The flames had died, but the logs in the surgery's hearth still glowed hot. Falling would be painful, but Ivan was willing to risk burns if it might mean freedom. He tied a wet bandage around his mouth and nose and dry ones around his hands. Then he stepped into the ash between the logs he'd separated. Even with the wet cloth, smoke stung his eyes and vexed his nose and throat. The warmth of the embers penetrated his boots and heated his feet.

The fireplace narrowed at about shoulder height. Ivan found a protruding ledge of stone and hoisted himself up. He couldn't have escaped this way the first time—he hadn't been strong enough. But he was mostly recovered now and soon stood on the small ledge. After that, it was a process of wedging himself up the flue, his back on one side and his legs on the other. Progress was slow at first, and the stones were uncomfortably warm, even through his clothes. In the dark tunnel, he worked by feel instead of by sight. His legs were stretched to nearly their full length, so he could move up the chimney only a bit at a time. But the chute narrowed as it went higher, and then progress was more rapid.

The slap of rain on stone grew louder, and the chute grew slicker. A few more squirms and a draft of fresh air brushed his cheeks. He was close. He'd studied the chimney on his walks with Helena. A louvered tile topped the flue, designed to release smoke and block out most rain. The southern end was broken, and he thought he could lift it. A burst of lightning brightened the sky for an instant, showing the tile only an arm's length above him. He pushed up with his feet and slipped. Panic snaked through him as he fell, but he quickly caught himself. In the darkness, he couldn't see how far he'd slid.

He was more cautious as he climbed again. His arms grew tired, and his legs shook with exhaustion, but he wouldn't give up. He could still turn back, and if he beat the soot from his clothes, the guards would never know he'd tried to leave. But he wanted to go home, wanted to be with his family. He might miss Helena, but he would miss nothing else about Byzia.

The cool breeze caressed his face once more, and at last, he could touch the louver. He slid it to the side and held it, scrambling up so he'd have more leverage. Rain splashed his skin, and the clear water brought with it relief from the smoke. He clamored through the narrow opening, then pulled the louver back into place. The slanted roof was slick and dark. Another burst of lightning flashed, revealing a watchman on the western battlements.

Ivan climbed from the roof and dropped into the bailey. Then he skirted around the chapel and kitchen and climbed the stairs of the eastern tower onto the wall walk. No one was within sight. He fastened the end of his rope to one of the merlons on the crenellated wall and lowered himself down. Both rope and wall were wet, but the wool of the blanket wasn't slippery, so he controlled the decent.

The rope was too short. He clung to the end of it, balanced against the wall, and waited for another flash of lightning and the clap of thunder that would follow. When the next streak flashed across the sky, he dropped into the cold, smelly moat, hitting the water at the same time the thunder met his ears. He swam across and crawled onto the bank, shivering with cold. The rain was a boon, masking his movements and washing away the moat's filth.

Ivan ran. People were still awake in the upper and lower portions of the kastron, and he wanted to put some distance between himself and the enormous crossbows in the towers and gatehouse. When he was past the town and some distance from the walls, he went back to the road. If he followed it, he'd come to a village before long, and by then, the village would be asleep.

He walked for a while, then ran again. The next village couldn't be too far away, because some of its inhabitants had watch duty on the kastron's walls. The rain tapered to a drizzle, and black silence surrounded him.

Eventually, a lightning burst revealed a small scattering of homes. As he drew closer, he saw two dozen of them, with low stone walls around their courtyards and gardens. He found the largest home and went to its stable. Ivan wasn't a thief, but these villagers' kephale had ambushed Kostya. They'd killed men and horses. War had been declared when Basil's men had attacked, and war seemed to change normal standards of right and wrong.

The stable had three horses. Ivan waited for a few lightning flashes to see them better. When the storm obliged, he picked what looked like the strongest of the three and led it into the open. He saddled it and was about to mount when a large bolt of lightning crashed nearby. The horse bucked, and though Ivan caught the reins, it took him several minutes to calm the dun stallion.

He mounted the horse and glanced over his shoulder at the rest of the village. The lightning had struck one of the small homes, and the thatched roof had caught fire. A fire was a divine gift. It would distract the villagers and explain why a horse had gone missing. He waited a moment, hoping the family inside would recognize their danger and leave, but nothing moved. Ivan needed to ride—he'd taken a good portion of the night coming to the village on foot, and he wanted to be far from the kastron when his absence was noticed.

He bit back a curse and urged the horse toward the home. Then he dismounted and ran along a partially built wall toward the chambers at the back of the courtyard. "Fire! Fire!"

Most of the rooms were only half finished. He went to the only one with four walls and yanked the door open. Light from the flames showed movement.

"Your house is on fire!"

Ivan saw a child asleep on a mat and scooped her and her doll into his arms. She was three or four and slept through the motion. He carried her outside, and only then did her eyes open. A woman followed Ivan, clutching an infant.

Someone other than the family must have heard Ivan's alarm because a bell began to ring. Ivan wanted to avoid a crowd. He set the little girl next to her mother and turned to leave before the village was fully roused. The woman and child were coughing, but they'd recover, and the other residents would help extinguish the fire. But then the woman said something that made him stop cold.

"Where's Theodora?" Her words were laced with fear.

"Who is Theodora?" Ivan asked.

"My other daughter—was she not in bed with Zöe?"

"No, there was only one child." Ivan glanced at the room. The roof was completely engulfed in flames. He swallowed his fear and ran back inside.

"Theodora!" Billowing smoke prevented him from seeing much of anything. He got on his knees and crawled along the floor, checking the children's mat again, looking in and under the larger bed. "Theodora!" The room wasn't large—probably meant to be a bedchamber when the rest of the rooms were completed. Where was she?

Each breath was choked with smoke, robbing his strength and leaving him dizzy. Ivan heard whimpering as he approached the table. Hiding underneath was a small girl dressed in a simple tunic.

"We have to leave!" Ivan shouted.

The little girl screamed. There wasn't time for gentle persuasion, so Ivan knocked the table over, grabbed the girl by the waist, and ran through the door. Theodora shrieked in terror. She clawed at his forearms and kicked her heels into his legs as he carried her. He set her down next to her mother and hunched over, trying to catch his breath. His throat had already been sore from his trip up the chimney. Running into a burning building had made it worse, and now he coughed and gasped for air.

Finally, he recovered enough to speak. "Are these all your children?"

"Yes." Tears streaked the woman's face. The baby wailed, Theodora whimpered, and Zöe bawled. "God bless you for your help!"

Ivan nodded and turned to go, but the way was blocked by villagers running to the fire. He tried to push his way through the crowd, but as the only stranger, he was conspicuous.

"Who are you?" a woman with bad teeth asked. Ivan stepped around her, but she grabbed his arm. "You don't live here."

"I was passing through and noticed the fire. Please release me." The woman didn't let go, so Ivan twisted from her grip.

She fisted her hands and placed them on her hips. "Passing through on foot? In the middle of the night? In a storm?"

Ivan looked around. Most of the villagers tried to smother the fire with dirt or water, but a significant portion of the crowd watched him. "Yes, and I must be on my way again." He gave up the idea of borrowing the stallion. He would make it past the crowd, walk from the village, and as soon as he was out of sight, he would run. There would be other villages and other horses.

"Your voice betrays you. You're foreign," she called after him.

"Why is my stallion out?" a large, middle-aged man with a rotund belly bellowed.

More of the villagers stared at Ivan, clear accusation in their eyes. He kept trying to move around them, but the group seemed to move with him.

The woman with bad teeth pointed a long finger at Ivan. "He's a horse thief!"

Ivan stepped back, still trying to get free of the villagers, but half a dozen of what had to be the village's largest men surrounded him. They closed in, blocking Ivan's escape and latching on to him.

"He should be whipped!" the owner of the horse shouted. The idea caught fire more quickly than the thatched roof of the village home had.

"Wait." Zöe and Theodora's mother pushed her way next to Ivan, still holding the crying baby close to her chest. "He saved my family. Does that not call for mercy? Let him leave in peace, on our mule if he desires."

"He must be punished!" another yelled.

Normal punishments included banishment, fines, or mutilation. Ivan wouldn't mind banishment, but he had no money, and he didn't want to lose a hand or an eye. He tried to jerk free of the men holding him, but after breathing in so much smoke, he wasn't strong enough.

"He's trying to escape. That proves his guilt." The owner of the horse crossed his arms and scowled. One of the men clubbed Ivan in the head, stunning him for a few moments before he could focus on the conversation again.

"Let him go." Zöe and Theodora's mother pleaded for him, but louder, angry voices drowned her out.

In the end, the villagers settled on a compromise, sentencing Ivan to a day in a pillory built by Latin crusaders. Eight men forced Ivan to the village square, shoved his head in the cut groove for the neck, held his hands in place, and slammed the top down, trapping Ivan's wrists and neck. The man who owned the horse Ivan had planned to steal fastened the device and strutted away.

It started to rain again.

The first while was not awful, other than the burning in his throat, the pain in his head, and the chill rain that ran in rivulets off his face. But by the time the sun rose, Ivan's body ached at being hunched in such an awkward position, and the damp had seeped deep into his bones, making him tremble with the cold.

Worse, another escape attempt had failed. Word would reach the acropolis, or a tracking party would make its way through the village. He didn't regret saving the little girl, but he did regret not running away the instant

Theodora was outside. Freedom had seemed so close, but once again, it had eluded him.

Maria and her husband sat together, gazing in awe at the healthy baby girl who'd been born at dawn. The blacksmith had seemed disappointed when Helena had announced a daughter rather than a son, but that emotion had disappeared the moment the baby was placed in his arms.

"You were right, my lady. This is the best day of my life," Maria whispered. Her eyelids drooped, and her voice was raspy, but her lips curved in contentment. "She's so beautiful."

Helena smiled. The infant's face was red and her skull misshapen from her journey through the birth canal, but those things would soon go away, and then the baby would be beautiful not just to the parents but to everyone.

Helena instructed Maria on how to nurse the baby, and soon the newborn turned from suckling to slumber. "You should sleep too."

"I'm so tired," Maria said. "But I cannot take my eyes off her."

"Let the baby's father or grandmother hold her until she wakes. You had a difficult night, and you need your rest." Helena held back a yawn. She hadn't given birth, but she was exhausted. "I'll return to check on you later." She turned to the blacksmith. "Send for me if she feels anything more than a dull cramp or if anything seems wrong with the baby."

The blacksmith took his daughter and told his wife to sleep. The tiny babe looked even smaller in his large arms. Helena felt a rush of joy. The mother and the child were both healthy, and there was love in this family.

The previous night's rain had slackened to a drizzle as Helena walked up the hill to the acropolis. The bailey was abnormally quiet, but she was too weary to wonder why. No one spoke to her until she reached the top floor of the keep and saw Euphrosyne in the hallway outside their bedchambers.

"Is the baby born?" Euphrosyne asked.

"Yes. A girl. And now I need a bit of sleep. Will you have someone wake me at noon so I can check on Maria again?"

Euphrosyne bit her lip and seemed to hesitate. "Yes, you should sleep. I'll wake you this afternoon."

"What's wrong?"

"Nothing that is likely to change over the course of your sleep. I'm glad the baby is come." Euphrosyne nibbled on her bottom lip again.

"Euphrosyne, what are you hiding?"

Her sister's mouth quivered for an instant before the words burst from her. "The prisoner escaped."

"What?" Helena had thought Ivan a man of his word, and he had promised not to leave. Then she remembered with a rush of dread. "It's my fault. I went to help with the baby. I didn't ask him to stay."

"Well, he left. How will we get Leo back?" Tears pooled in Euphrosyne's eyes.

"Has Kyrios Basil sent out a search party?"

"Several, but what if they don't find him?"

Helena took her sister's hand, feeling like a traitor. Part of her hoped Ivan would escape. She didn't want the guards to beat him again, as they no doubt would if they caught him. But she did want Leo back. And part of her wanted Ivan back. If he was truly gone, she would miss him.

Ivan spent the morning shivering. Every night since waking up in the acropolis, he had pleaded with God for the chance to escape, and last night, he had come so close. He stared at the ground, watching the rain beat a pattern into a nearby puddle. Despite the weather, the young boys of the village had woken early. Most of them threw handfuls of mud at him. A few threw stones or clots of manure.

By midday, the frequency of their hurled insults slowed. When a pair of small, bare feet stepped into his field of vision, he wondered if the village children had grown bold enough to hit him with sticks.

"Sir?"

The small voice surprised him. He looked up to see a face he recognized. "Hello, Theodora."

She held out a bowl containing some sort of gruel. "I've brought you some food."

Ivan remembered the kicks and the hysterical screams of the night before. "You're no longer frightened of me?"

Theodora blushed. "I was scared by the lightning, so I hid under the table when the storm began. I fell asleep there. When I woke, there was smoke and fire everywhere, like what I've heard of hell. So I thought you were a devil."

"Does your home still stand?"

"No. Papa was watching at the kastron last night. He came back this morning and says we can rebuild. His brothers will help. For now, we're living with my grandmother again." Theodora's face lit with a grin. "She says she will make me a new doll because mine was lost in the fire."

"I'm sorry for your lost doll. But I'm happy you're safe and that your grandmother will replace your toy." He hoped someone would replace her shoes as well, especially with winter coming.

"Mama says you saved us. But you're a stranger."

"I couldn't ignore a family in need."

Theodora's eyebrows scrunched together in concentration. "That is like a story Kyria Helena told me before my brother was born."

"Kyria Helena helped your mother?"

"Yes, and she told me about the Good Samaritan. He helped a stranger when he found him on the road. But what were you doing on the road in the middle of the night?"

"I was trying to go home." As he said the words, the pain of his failure hit him again, more intense than the discomfort of the pillory. He missed them all, and even if the exchange happened as planned, by spring, he would be needed in Sivi Gora. He would never again get to live with Konstantin, Danilo, Suzana, Marko, and Aunt Zorica.

"Where are you from?"

"Rivak."

Theodora took a few steps back, her mouth hanging open in surprise. "But that would mean you're a Serb. My father was fighting Serbs from Rivak the day my brother was born."

Ivan cursed himself for scaring away what was probably his best chance of a meal that day. Theodora seemed frozen in place. Watching her hurt his neck, so after a while, he looked away. But not long after, he saw the same pair of small, bare feet.

"Would you like your food now?"

"I would." Ivan glanced at his shackled hands and frowned. "If you're not frightened to feed a Serb."

Theodora fed him, one spoonful at a time. The meal was plain. The family's home had revealed they weren't rich, and now they had lost even that. But Ivan was hungry enough that he could have eaten four helpings of the gruel, and gratitude for the little girl was a bright spot in an otherwise bleak day.

"Thank you for rescuing me," Theodora said when the bowl was empty.

"You are welcome. Thank you for bringing me food. It was kind and brave of you to do so."

"How are you called?" she asked.

"Ivan, son of Miroslav."

"Ivan, son of Miroslav, would you like me to sing you a song? Kyria Helena taught it to me."

Ivan nodded as best he could while in the pillory, and Theodora began. "Off to wander, far away from Eden. Off to journey, through a land of woe. E'er a stranger, to the land of promise, till at last to heaven I shall go." Her voice had a sweet, childlike quality. But what struck him was the tune. He'd heard Helena hum it before, and he wondered if there was any chance that he would hear it again from her lips.

"My mother asks that you join us for supper when you're released at sundown. I'll return to show you the way. Will you come?"

"If I am able." He didn't want to disappoint the little girl, but he imagined most of the garrison was looking for him. "Thank you, Theodora."

"Good day to you, Ivan, son of Miroslav." Theodora stood on her tip-toes to kiss him on the cheek, then ran back to her grandmother's home.

When five soldiers rode into the village, Ivan recognized most of them. Demetrios had come, along with several who had pummeled him in the stable. His stomach tensed as they circled him in amusement.

"The great Serb warrior—a horse thief." Niketas laughed.

Demetrios paced in and out of Ivan's view. "The villagers were wise to treat you as a common malefactor. Perhaps we will follow their example." Demetrios went to speak with some of the paroikoi. While he was gone, the other four took turns tossing rocks into the air and watching them land on Ivan. They stung, but worse than the pain was the feeling of utter helplessness.

"He's sentenced until sunset," Demetrios said when he returned.

"Should we wait?" one of the guards asked.

"We've been out riding all day. The sooner we get back, the sooner we can eat," another said.

Demetrios thought for a moment. "We'll take him back now. But it seems obvious that he's getting too much to eat. Perhaps if we cut him to one meal a day, he won't have energy to waste on foolish escape attempts."

Ivan craned his neck to see their conversation. In the distance, Theodora watched, half-hidden behind a stone wall. Concern showed in her wide eyes and downturned lips. Then Niketas stepped in front of him, and she disappeared from view.

Ivan was unbelievably stiff when Demetrios unlocked him. All day, he'd anticipated instant relief when released, but the pain hardly subsided at all. Sharp aches needled down his back as he tried to straighten, and bitter disappointment choked his throat. He was parched, weary, and dizzy.

"Not much of a warrior now, are you? Caught by a few paroikoi." Niketas cuffed the back of his head. He hit the same spot the villager's club had. A bright flash crossed Ivan's eyes, and nausea churned his stomach.

Demetrios tied one end of a rope around Ivan's hands and the other end to his saddle horn. He mounted his horse and urged it forward. The rope jerked on Ivan's wrists, tugging him down into the mud. Demetrios halted long enough for Ivan to get back to his feet, then yanked the rope again. Ivan stumbled forward, but his limbs wouldn't work properly, and he ended up on the ground again. Rage boiled within him, but there was nothing he could do. He was helpless, weak, and at their mercy.

They had very little mercy.

The back of Ivan's head pounded, blood streamed from his nose, and the rope cut into his skin. The courser walked, but Ivan wouldn't be able to match its pace for long. He clung to a hope that the soldiers would tire of the slow pace and let him ride eventually. In the meantime, he ran.

As the sun passed the ninth hour, sweat ran down Ivan's face and stung his eyes. He couldn't wipe it away because his hands were tied. He had been a fool to try his first escape—he'd still been too weak, and he'd recognized that almost immediately—but as the wound in his abdomen twisted with pain and the gash in his leg sent throbbing daggers up and down his leg, he realized he was still insufficiently healed.

Ten more steps, he told himself. Then he pushed past it and set another goal. The horizon was fluid, and the men on horseback seemed as though they were swimming rather than riding. Ivan wandered to the left, but the rope jerked and pulled him back into a straight line behind Demetrios's mount. Five more steps. Four. Just a little bit longer.

The rope snapped, tugging Ivan to the ground. He crawled to keep up, desperate to avoid complete defeat, but soon he was being dragged. The rope bit into his wrists and dirt clung to his nostrils and dry mouth. Eventually, Demetrios stopped. Ivan pushed himself to his knees, breathing hard.

He would have traded a bag of Sivi Gora's silver for a mere sip of water, an entire year's take for his freedom. Hatred for his captors burned in his chest, mingling with despair.

"Get up," Demetrios ordered.

Ivan's legs trembled as he rose. Dust choked his throat, and blisters burned his feet. He picked out a beechwood in the distance. He would walk that far. He kept putting one foot in front of the other until they reached that tree, then until they reached another. Soon his head began to spin, and it was all he could do to keep stumbling forward. One of the soldiers yelled at him, but when Ivan looked toward the sound, everything was blurry. Demetrios seemed to be moving faster now. Ivan tried to run, but his legs wouldn't cooperate. He pitched forward into the dirt, and everything faded to black.

Ivan woke to something warm and wet on his face. He turned his head away from the stream and brushed against a thorn. Someone laughed in the distance. He tried to focus, and the smell suddenly overwhelmed him. It wasn't water. Ivan spat on the ground, though his mouth was so dry he could hardly make spittle. More laughter from the guards. Ivan tried to wipe the urine from his face, but there wasn't enough slack in the rope.

"Get up," Demetrios said.

Ivan struggled to obey. He fell four more times on the way back to the kastron, and each time, Demetrios dragged him a little farther than the last before stopping and allowing Ivan back to his feet. Ivan lost consciousness again just outside the kastron. One of the guards slapped him to revive him.

"Should we cut him loose?" one of the guards asked. "We need him alive if we want to exchange him for Leo."

Ivan hoped the others would listen, but Demetrios's voice didn't soften. "He has all winter to recover."

Exhaustion and humiliation clung to Ivan on the long walk up the hill through the town. Each step with his numb limbs was uncertain, but he wouldn't fall in front of the townspeople who lined the road to watch his progress. Demetrios rode through the acropolis gatehouse as the sun sank below the horizon, and Ivan collapsed on the paved bailey. His body hurt everywhere. No one had ever treated him with so much contempt, as if he were a pestilence or demon. He wanted to be home, where people loved and respected him instead of loathed and tormented him.

"Take him to the jail," Demetrios ordered Niketas.

Niketas kicked Ivan in the ribs. Ivan attempted to stand, but his arms shook and then collapsed when he tried to push himself up.

"Drag him if you have to."

Niketas and Paulus accepted the suggestion and lugged him across the bailey and into a small cell tucked between the barracks and the curtain wall. They left him with a few parting kicks and locked him inside.

Over the next week, Ivan grew familiar with every stone of his prison. No fire provided warmth. A narrow slit with bars where the wall met the ceiling was the only window, and it let in a disproportionately large amount of wind and a disproportionately small amount of light. The cell was barely long enough for him to lie down in, and the only bedding was a single, flea-infested blanket. The guards gave him food once a day, either water and gruel or water and dry biscuits. Every few days, he was ordered to switch out his bucket. There were no walks outside. And no Helena.

He prayed for relief, but none came. He missed his family with an intensity that left him aching. He could have escaped if he hadn't stopped at the village fire, he was sure of it. He'd tried to do the right thing, and his good deed had changed his circumstances from unpleasant to dire.

Sometimes as his stomach cramped with hunger and as he shivered in the threadbare blanket, he tried to remember the words of the song Theodora had sung.

Off to wander, far away from Eden. Far away from Eden, far away from Rivak.

He felt very much like a stranger in a land of woe. Even Helena had forgotten him. And so, it seemed, had God.

CHAPTER TEN
A SPY IN RIVAK

ISKANDAR STOOD IN THE BAILEY of Župan Konstantin's grody, plucking feathers from a beheaded pheasant. He'd come to Rivakgrad with a harrowing tale of flight from Turkish ghazis, and the župan's wife, showing mercy on a supposed refugee, had given him a job in the kitchen. Iskandar had never feared hard work, so he swept floors, cleaned pots, and did whatever else the cook instructed. Those he worked with were agreeable enough, despite their loyalty to a decrepit religion and their misguided admiration for their župan. When the time came to raid Rivak and its grad, he'd ask his father to spare them, especially the cook. Nevena had shown welcome to an outsider, and her talent was far too useful to waste on the end of a ghazi's sword.

The raid would come soon, he was sure of it. He'd long ago sent Ali with a message for his father, and since then, Iskandar had learned all he needed to plan a successful pillage. Now three of his father's ghazis waited for him in a nearby forest. Rivak was an inviting target, but Iskandar delayed because the Serbs were planning something big. A special guest, if rumors from the kitchen staff were to be believed. There hadn't been this much fuss since Danilo's betrothal ceremony, so Iskandar would stay to learn more.

"Danilo! Danilo!" The župan's son, Marko, ran toward the Turkish half-breed, his short legs churning up mud as he crossed the bailey ahead of his mother. Iskandar turned away, hiding his face. He hadn't realized Danilo was so near, and that could have been a fatal mistake. He'd spent weeks dodging the župan's cousin because Danilo might recognize him. Iskandar ducked into the shadow of the chicken coop.

Danilo picked the boy up when he came within reach and tossed him into the air before catching him.

"You throw him too high." Dama Suzana put a hand on her hip, but her voice held laughter, not anger. "What if you do not catch him?"

"I will always catch him." Danilo set the boy down. "Where is your husband? I'm to report to him."

"Kostya's at the grad's main gate, watching for Knez Lazar's envoy." Dama Suzana's face grew solemn, and her voice lowered to a whisper, something Iskandar could barely hear. "This is a larger step than any of the others we've taken. Even after all the planning and preparing, I'm afraid we aren't ready. I don't think we're strong enough if the sultan hears rumors of rebellion and turns on us."

"That is why we must keep it secret. And gather allies."

Dama Suzana forced a smile. "Yes, but sometimes I fear what freedom will cost us. Not in coin—we've saved, and with time, it can be replaced. But the cost in blood . . . That's what I worry about, especially since we lost Ivan."

"He'll come back."

Dama Suzana watched her son play with a pheasant feather. "That is what I pray daily."

Danilo clasped Dama Suzana's arm for a moment, then headed for the gate. Marko ran into the kitchen, no doubt to purloin a pastry. The boy was spoiled, but all the servants treated the child like royalty, so Iskandar did his best to mimic them. He would have preferred to smack the boy's little hands.

Iskandar had heard of Knez Lazar. His lands were to the north, some distance from Župan Konstantin's. An Ottoman army had slain the Serbian kral a dozen years ago at the battle of Maritsa, and the feeble-minded Serbian emperor had died soon after. Until Lazar, no Serb had been powerful enough to take a royal title, but the knez was now the most prominent man in Serbia. If Konstantin sought allies, he could do no better.

Iskandar had spent his time in Rivakgrad planning for a few ghazi raids. Instead, he'd uncovered evidence of treason. He needed to bring word to his father and to the sultan. But first, he would learn more of the župan's plans.

As the sky darkened, Iskandar helped serve supper. Usually, he avoided the keep because Danilo or the other men who'd seen him in Macedonia might recognize him. But the night's feast required more servants, and the need for information outweighed the need for caution.

The župan's family, advisers, servants, and guests all gathered in the keep's great hall. Tapestries graced the stone walls, and long tables spanned the rug-covered floor. The Greek captives were treated with courtesy and normally took their meals with the Serbs, but tonight, they'd been excluded. Instead, three extra lords were seated beside Župan Konstantin: Miloš Obilić, Knez Lazar's son by marriage; Župan Dragomir, whose lands bordered Konstantin's to the west; and Župan Nikola, whose lands bordered Konstantin's to the southeast.

In the background, a guslar maneuvered his bow across the string of his gusle and sang a song about Kral Stefan Dušan. Iskandar ignored the music and did his best to listen to the Serb lords. He stayed near at hand during courses of venison and pheasant, but the conversation revolved around agriculture and a building project at the Hilandar monastery at Mount Athos. It took effort not to yawn between refilling wine goblets.

When the meal ended, the women retired, and the servants and musician were dismissed. The hall grew quiet. Iskandar stayed, hidden in the shadow of the great hearth behind a pile of firewood. All that remained were Obilić, Dragomir, Nikola, Konstantin, Danilo, three of Konstantin's other men, and Dragomir's satnik.

Iskandar scowled. Why was Danilo included in the council? The half-breed was less than twenty and an outsider. Iskandar had never been invited to his father's private councils. They were both of mixed blood, but unlike Danilo, Iskandar at least looked like his people.

"Your messenger spoke of what could be termed treason," Konstantin said to Obilić. "And yet, I grow increasingly weary of fighting the sultan's battles for him. The tribute we pay could be better spent here on churches, roads, hospitals. And all my people live in fear of the child tax. So I am eager to hear more."

"The vassalage we have been under since Maritsa is mild compared to what will come," Dragomir said. "For now, Murad is content to gain strength through our military service and our tribute payments, but as he consolidates power, he will extend his control. I am not strong enough to stand up to the sultan. Nor is Župan Konstantin or Župan Nikola. But if we all unite, we stand a chance."

Konstantin leaned forward in his seat. "Father Vlatko has often quoted St. Sava: 'Only unity can save the Serbs.' Those are words of wisdom I am willing to test."

"Lazar will accept your allegiance, should you offer it. He has beat the Turks before," Obilić said. "There will be no child tax, no annual tribute. Just your loyalty in battle, to drive the Turks from all our lands."

Konstantin placed a hand on Danilo's arm and leaned over to whisper. Danilo nodded and stood, his eyes on the hearth.

As Danilo strode toward him, Iskandar slipped along the wall and through the door. He'd thought he was hidden. How had they seen him behind the firewood? And would Danilo follow? In Rivak, Iskandar was clean-shaven. During his time playing a Vlach shepherd, he'd worn a beard. That might not be enough of a change should he come face-to-face with the župan's cousin.

When he reached the bailey, he crouched behind a barrel. Danilo emerged from the keep a few moments later. He looked around and walked to the kitchen, where anyone would expect a serving man to go after cleaning the great hall.

Iskandar ran behind the kitchen to the stables. He was tempted to steal Župan Konstantin's new destrier or Obilić's fine stallion, but that would have been too conspicuous. He settled for a palfrey and rode to the gate leading to the causeway that connected the grody to the lower grad.

The guard there, Zoran, halted him. "Where are you going this time of night? On Miladin's horse?"

"Zoran! Stop him!" Danilo's voice shouted from across the bailey, but he was too late.

Iskandar kicked the horse, practically running over Zoran on his way to the lower grad. A bell rang wildly. Iskandar had expected to make it at least to the lower grad before the alarm sounded. How long would it take Danilo to saddle his warhorse and come in pursuit? Iskandar leaned low against the horse in case the Serbs sent arrows after him and rode the beast hard. Three gates led through the wooden palisade that surrounded the lower grad. He turned for the nearest one and raced across the moat before the guards could close the gate.

He fled along the road, gasping for breath as the chill night air swept past him. Eventually, the noise of the alarm faded. The hoofbeats of pursuing horses did not. He pushed the animal to keep galloping. If he reached his father's messengers, he'd be safe.

The rising moon highlighted thick trees in the distance, where his allies waited. It would be an ideal location to ambush the Serbs.

He slowed when he reached the tree line. "Hasan!"

"Iskandar?" The voice called from the distance.

Iskandar rode toward it. "I'm being followed."

"That's rather careless for someone who claims to be our father's best spy." The voice belonged to Iskandar's half brother, Nasuh.

"The information I discovered is worth a little skirmish. I think only two pursue me. We'll pick them off and then ride."

Ali, returned to Rivak with the other ghazis, threw a bow up to Iskandar. Next came a quiver. Then a scimitar.

"It would be better for you to hide," Hasan said. "These lands are under the sultan's protection."

"I've heard their plans. They have no loyalty to Sultan Murad. And we'll outnumber them."

"Complaints made in secret do not negate the orders of our sultan, young one."

Iskandar bristled at being called *young one*. But he wouldn't argue with Hasan, his father's most trusted warrior, a man who had made the hajj to Mecca and spoke more languages than Iskandar did. His father had honored Iskandar by sending a man of such stature to help him. Or had Hasan come because his father didn't trust Iskandar to make wise decisions without proper advice? "Very well." Iskandar dismounted. "But I plan to have an arrow aimed at the leader's back."

Iskandar tied the stolen horse to a tree a dozen paces from the road, then followed the others on foot as they rode to the tree line. Iskandar stayed far enough back to remain unseen, and the Serbs arrived at about the same time.

There were two, as he'd expected, but Danilo was not among them. That was unlike everything he'd seen thus far from the half-breed. But perhaps Iskandar had been too generous in his judgment. If the Christians weren't cowards, they wouldn't be losing their lands.

"We're looking for someone who may have traveled this road," Miladin said.

Hasan answered. "Oh? We have seen no one."

"Where do you travel?" Miladin asked.

"We are traders. We travel to Edirne. From Belgrade."

Iskandar bit his tongue to keep from correcting Hasan. The road from Buda through Belgrade and Edirne to Constantinople was some distance to the north. It didn't pass through Rivak.

"Have you had success trading with the villagers?"

Hasan feigned hurt pride. "We do not trade with mere villagers."

Miladin glanced around. He was no fool—Iskandar didn't doubt he knew something was amiss. But he let it go. "We wish you luck on your journey." He motioned to Zoran, and the two rode on, leaving Iskandar's group behind them.

"Shall I put arrows into their backs?" Iskandar had one nocked on his bowstring. At close range, it might pierce their armor.

Hasan held up a hand for caution. "Let them ride on."

"Can you read a map? Traders on their way from Belgrade don't take this route. They'll know you lied. And now they're ahead of us, and Konstantin's grad and all the rest of his men are behind us."

"Is your half-Vlach soul frightened?" Nasuh asked.

Iskandar wanted to send an arrow into his arrogant half brother's chest but shot back only words. "Don't underestimate them."

"Iskandar is right," Hasan said. "The sultan values the Serbs because they are good warriors. We should be wary. Iskandar, get your horse. We'll ride till the second watch, then rest. Ali, get him some different clothes so he looks like us instead of like a runaway kitchen hand."

Iskandar went back to the smooth-striding palfrey and patted its nose. The white splotches along the animal's neck shone gray in the moonlight. The horse was well cared for, with a healthy coat and strong muscles.

Something fell across Iskandar's right shoulder.

"Don't move."

Iskandar recognized that voice: Danilo. He glanced down and recognized the object too: the end of a spathion. Not far away, he saw Danilo's courser tied to a tree.

"Drop your bow and turn around."

Iskandar obeyed. The surprise on Danilo's face was almost worth facing a sword.

"The Vlach shepherd from Byzia. What are you doing here? And why were you spying on the župans and Obilić?"

Iskandar waited, certain Danilo's curiosity would keep him from slicing the blade into his neck.

"Who are you really? A Turk?"

"I am Iskandar bin Abdullah, and you made a grave mistake when you insulted me by leaving me tied and horseless." Then he yelled, "Hasan! We're under attack." Iskandar leaped back and pulled the horse between him and Danilo. A shrill whistled sounded, like the signal Danilo had used after the battle against Byzia. That meant there were more Serbs somewhere.

Someone shouted in the distance. One of Iskandar's friends? Or one of his foes?

Danilo lunged around the horse, and Iskandar barely had time to draw his scimitar to meet his enemy's blade.

It sounded as though a full-fledged battle were taking place nearer the road, but Iskandar had his hands full where he stood. Danilo swung his blade into Iskandar's with such force that Iskandar had to step back. He tried to get in a good strike, but Danilo met every move, almost as if he knew what Iskandar would do before he acted. The half-breed was a good swordsman. Unless Iskandar got lucky, Danilo would win.

A horse crashed through the trees, and an arrow pierced Danilo's arm. Danilo grunted in surprise and pulled back a pace, cradling his injured limb.

"Come, Iskandar," Hasan said. "Ali and Nasuh are dead. We must flee."

Iskandar couldn't find any sorrow over Nasuh's fate, but Ali's loss was a pity. He blocked another thrust when Danilo charged again. The blow had less force than the previous ones. Perhaps Iskandar would be able to finish him off after all now that Danilo was wounded.

"We must leave now!" Hasan loosed another arrow at Danilo, but the half-breed dove behind a tree, and the shaft missed.

Another Serb, Miladin, rode toward them, sword in hand. Iskandar mounted his stolen horse. Hasan had spoken wisdom. It was time to withdraw.

Hasan shot the horse out from under Miladin, then sent an arrow into Danilo's courser. The Serbs would be unlikely to catch them with wounded horses.

"Come!"

Iskandar took one last look at Danilo. He was on his feet again, running at Iskandar's horse. His injured arm hung unmoving at his side, but he hadn't given up. Iskandar longed for his bow so he could make sure Danilo would never trouble him again. But Miladin had gotten out from underneath his horse and was reaching for an arrow. Iskandar turned and galloped away with Hasan.

CHAPTER ELEVEN
DOOMED COURAGE

IVAN SPENT FIFTEEN DAYS CHIPPING out the mortar around the barred jail window. The cell was narrow enough that he could prop himself high up on the wall for hours at a time. With a bronze spoon as his only tool, progress was slow. But he had nothing else to do, and his desire to escape had grown stronger with his small taste of freedom and the squalor of his new quarters. For a time, he'd at least had Helena's company to look forward to, but now, nothing in Byzia held him, and longing for his family called him home.

When his task was complete, he waited until dark. He would let the guards grow drowsy, but he'd be gone before the second watch. He wanted as long of a head start as possible. The cell was in an out-of-the-way corner of the bailey, so he didn't think anyone would notice his absence until they brought his small once-a-day meal in the evening.

A watchman with a torch circled the bailey. Ivan had observed the routine time after time. Kyrios Basil's security had improved since Ivan's arrival, but the wandering watchman wouldn't pass Ivan's cell again until he had walked along the battlements, and he wouldn't look inside. Ivan pulled out the bars and the stone surrounding them, then crawled up and squeezed through. He probably wouldn't have fit through a hole that small prior to his capture, but extended illness and prison rations had left him scrawny. From the window, Ivan dropped onto the paving stones between the barracks and the stable. A partial moon showed an empty bailey, and torches highlighted the acropolis guards, so they would be easy to avoid.

He crept into the storage room beside the stables, borrowed a rope, and crouched below a row of saddles until the guard passed again. Ivan waited until the man was out of sight, then crept out. When the watchman reached the top of the battlement stairs, Ivan followed him, tiptoeing up the stone staircase, keeping a steady distance between him and the watchman. When he reached the wall, Ivan tied his rope to one of the merlons and tugged it snug. One of the guards would notice eventually, but perhaps not until daylight.

Ivan swung his feet over the wall, then grasped the rope and used his legs to keep himself several hand-widths away from the stones. He pushed and relaxed his grip, sliding closer to the ground, then tightened his hold on the rope as he came back toward the wall. He looked at the moat below and thought about tossing his boots across so they would stay dry, but he didn't have the rain to mask his sounds. He would have to swim quietly and endure wet clothing.

He had descended two-thirds of the way when he heard a whistle, and a sudden sharp pain slammed into his thigh. His left leg collapsed, and the rest of him crashed into the wall. The arrow that had pierced his leg burned with an agonizing pain all along the limb. He squeezed the rope as the clothing around his wound grew dark with spreading blood.

How was he supposed to make it home with an arrow wound in his leg? He took a deep breath, not ready to give up. Maybe Theodora's parents would help him if he could make it to their village. Shouts sounded above him. He had to hurry, and the need for silence had passed. He released the rope and fell into the moat with a splash.

The fall jerked the arrow, and the pain in his leg exploded. Frigid water engulfed him. He struggled to the surface, gasping for breath. The current manipulated the long shaft still stuck in his thigh, almost like a torture device, as he swam through the dirty stream. His movements were frustratingly slow, but he had time. The only exit he'd seen from the acropolis led into the town below. It would take a while for the watchmen to pass through both gates and circle back to Ivan.

Another hiss sounded, and a second arrow pierced Ivan's left arm, near the shoulder. His waterlogged clothing dragged him down, and he felt his feet touch the murky bottom. The muck would hold him if he didn't fight, so fight he did, back to the surface and all the way to the edge of the moat. He tried to pull himself out, but he was winded, and his left arm wouldn't work properly. He squeezed his eyes shut, trying to summon his strength. When he opened them, four guards stood before him. How had they reached him already?

Matthias pulled him from the water. The arrow in Ivan's thigh bumped against the ground, and Ivan almost blacked out at the wave of pain. Niketas called him a disparaging name and kicked him in the gut.

"Bring him," Demetrios said.

They plucked Ivan from the ground and dragged him along the moat to a small wooden bridge extending from the western tower. That was how they'd reached him so quickly. The tower contained a hidden postern. Ivan tried to squirm away from Niketas because his iron grip made Ivan's wounded arm howl with pain. Niketas only tightened his clutch. Their pace was too quick for Ivan to match, so every time they dragged him over an uneven bit of ground or a seam in the bridge's planks, agony shot up his leg.

They passed through the tower and into the bailey before they released him. Ivan managed to stay upright, barely. He put his right hand against a nearby wall for support as his head spun and his vision narrowed. He squeezed his eyes shut, shattered that this attempt, too, had failed.

"Put him on the ground."

Ivan opened his eyes long enough to recognize Gregoras. The nearest soldiers obeyed, forcing Ivan to the ground, facedown. Demetrios put a foot on Ivan's back, used a dagger to make a cut, and yanked the arrow from his arm. The arrow's exit was several degrees more painful than its entry had been. Ivan clenched his jaw to keep from crying out. Demetrios poured something on the wound—it smelled like wine—and another soldier bandaged it.

They shoved him onto his back. Their expressions showed mostly hatred, but Niketas's face showed satisfaction, and there was something different, almost sympathetic, from Matthias. Demetrios moved his foot to a spot just above Ivan's knee. This time, the jerk on the arrow pulled a cry from Ivan's mouth. His whole body shook in agony.

Ivan twisted his head to the side and vomited. He wasn't sure which was worse—his body pierced by arrows or his heart devastated by another failure. Was it so awful to want to go home? Why had God allowed him to chip away all the mortar only to fail now?

Two guards dragged him past the acropolis offices and into the southwest tower. They didn't follow the winding stone staircase up to the wall. They followed a narrow, slimy staircase down into the bowels of the earth. Not the slightest movement stirred the cold, fetid air. The torch Demetrios carried was the only light source.

The guards gave him a few parting blows with their fists and feet, shackled him in chains, and left him in the dungeon.

Helena heard the rumor over breakfast. Ivan had escaped again. And he'd been caught.

"The tzaousios was so angry, he asked Kyrios Basil to hang him." Euphrosyne leaned in so no one would overhear. "Some of the men are saying that a dead prisoner is better than an escaped prisoner. But if he escapes or dies, it will be hard for us to make Leo's ransom."

"They can't execute him for wanting to go home."

"The pass is snowed in. He can't go home until spring anyway. Sometimes I wonder if they'll really trade Leo for someone as dim-witted as our prisoner."

Helena jerked around, a protest on the tip of her tongue. Ivan was not dim-witted. But he was stubborn to a fault. "He can be reasoned with. And he keeps his promises. Every day that I asked him to stay, he did. If Kyrios Basil would just let me see him, I won't forget to ask again." She'd been requesting permission to see Ivan since the night of the rainstorm, but the answer was always no, and she daren't disobey.

Euphrosyne put her hand on Helena's. "He only stayed because he was not yet well enough to leave. Don't blame yourself for his stupidity."

Euphrosyne meant well, but she was wrong. Ivan wasn't stupid. Nor would he go back on his word. But if he made no promise, he had no reason to stay, and Helena doubted any cell would hold him permanently. The best way to keep Ivan in the pronoia was an appeal to his honor. Kyrios Basil stood, and Helena followed him into the corridor.

"My lord?"

The kephale turned. "Yes, Kyria Helena?" As he spoke, Gregoras came to stand at Kyrios Basil's side.

"I heard the prisoner escaped again," Helena said.

"He didn't get far." Gregoras folded his arms in satisfaction. "We caught him climbing down the wall."

"Is he hurt?" She tried to keep her face calm despite her concern over what the guards might have done to him.

"Yes."

"May I see him?" Helena clasped her hands in front of her skirt. "If he's not kept healthy, we'll have no hostage to exchange for Leo."

"Demetrios treated him." Gregoras shrugged off her concern.

"But Demetrios is neither surgeon nor physician." They should have called her.

"He helped you with our wounded after the battle."

"Yes, but he dealt with only the minor cases. He has not my experience."

Gregoras frowned. "Your experience? You are a midwife's *apprentice*. And a young one at that."

Rage boiled inside her like a pot steeping one of her herbs, but she forced the anger from her voice. "My care healed him before. He trusts me. And he is a man of his word. If we make him swear to stay, he will, and I believe I will be most effective in arranging said promise."

Gregoras huffed. "So, you would extract a promise from him and let him wander around at liberty? Perhaps ride out on a horse from time to time?"

"I would. After his first attempt, I had him promise me each night that he would stay until morning. And he kept his word every single time."

"Chains and arrow wounds will keep him here, lord." Gregoras waved Helena away. "We don't need promises that will soon be broken. I'm beginning to think we'd be better off finding another way to raise the ransom."

Alarm flared at the mention of arrow wounds. She had assumed there would be a few cuts and bruises from the angry feet and fists of the garrison. The truth was far worse. "Kyrios Basil, please. We need him for Leo."

"I will consider it," Kyrios Basil said. "But he's not our only option. For a time, trading him for Leo seemed the wisest course, but he's causing so much trouble that I'm no longer sure that's true."

The men turned and left Helena in the corridor, frustrated and worried. They didn't understand Ivan. She didn't either, not fully, but she was beginning to. If he did not die of his wounds, he would try to escape again and again and again. There would be no breaking this prisoner. Kyrios Basil could negotiate with Ivan, but he would never successfully command him.

A serving man turned a corner and rushed toward her. "Kyria?"

"Yes?"

"Someone has sent for you. A woman is struggling in childbirth."

Helena, Demetrios, and the paroikos who'd fetched Helena arrived in the village on the edge of the pronoia at midday. The paroikos was the younger brother of the soon-to-be-mother. Demetrios had insisted on accompanying them, but he hadn't told her a single thing about Ivan's capture despite her persistent questions during their journey. She had once considered Demetrios a friend, but now resentment simmered between them.

Helena heard the woman's cries across the little courtyard. She brought her birthing chair and bundles of herbs into the small chamber, where the travailing woman lay on a mat. An older woman knelt next to her.

"Is there water?" Helena asked.

"I'll fetch some," the older woman said.

Helena took the younger woman's hand. "I'm here to help."

The soon-to-be-mother sobbed with relief. Matted black hair stuck to her forehead, and paleness cloaked her skin. "It is taking so long. My mother said I should push, but the baby does not come."

Helena felt the woman's wrist while she waited for the water. Her pulse beat a quick rhythm against Helena's fingers. "This is your first child?"

The woman nodded, then her face twisted in pain.

"Breathe in through your nose and out through your mouth."

The woman tried to follow Helena's advice, but the second exhalation dissolved into a cry of agony.

When the birth pain passed, Helena spoke again. "What is your name?"

"Antonina."

"Antonina, today may be the hardest day of your life, but it will also be one of the best."

The woman's mother returned with water, and Helena scrubbed her hands and arms.

"I thought only Jews were so concerned with hand washing." The mother squinted at Helena's soapy hands, wary.

"I am Christian, but I find the washing beneficial." Anna, Helena's mentor, had learned everything she could, not only from her instructors at Salerno but also from a midwife in Thessaloniki's Jewish quarter. Christians they were not, but fewer Jewish infants died in the first fortnight. Jewish midwives might attribute it to God. Anna attributed it to better traditions. Helena simply wanted to save babies and their mothers and saw no harm in using a Jewish technique to help a Christian infant.

Helena tasked Antonina's mother, Constantina, with making Antonina more comfortable. As Constantina bathed Antonina's forehead with a damp cloth, Helena examined between the woman's legs. Her body was ready, and the waters had already dampened the mat she lay on. But the woman's hips were narrow. Though the swollen abdomen seemed normal for a woman about to be delivered, her thighs and breasts were too lean. Helena glanced at the mother. She, too, looked as though she did not have enough to eat.

"Have you been ill?" Helena asked Constantina.

"No, but this is a time of famine for us. May the pair of men who burned our fields be stricken with plague as punishment."

"We were told a passing Serb army burned your fields."

Constantina shook her head. "Just two men. Ghosts perhaps, but certainly not an army."

That meant Ivan's brother was innocent, yet Ivan was still a prisoner, wounded and locked away. Helena couldn't dwell on Ivan, not now. She and Constantina moved Antonina onto the birthing chair. Perhaps the different position would help the baby come. Antonina slumped forward in exhaustion, and Helena held her through another spout of pain.

"The next time the pain comes, push."

Antonina nodded.

Helena coached her through the next twenty spasms, helping her control her breathing, massaging her cervix between labors, and adding pressure to the abdomen when Antonina pushed. Still the baby did not come. Helena added mint and wormwood to water and gave it to Antonina to drink. She rubbed violet oil onto Antonina's skin. Still, no progress was made, and Helena began to fear for the baby. When she reached inside Antonina, she could feel the baby's head. The position was off, as if the baby were facing up instead of down, but Helena had assisted Anna with several babies birthed in that manner who were healthy afterward. Helena felt the womb, hoping for movement from the child, but she felt none. Perhaps the infant was as exhausted as the mother.

She gave Antonina another set of herbs to drink, and the young woman kept pushing, but her energy was nearly spent. Helena coated her hand with oil and tried to reposition the baby, but the head was firmly stuck in Antonina's narrow opening.

After another long series of struggles, Helena sat back. "I think you should rest through the next few to build up your strength."

They moved Antonina to the rush mat.

Constantina pulled Helena outside the room and whispered, "She is tiring."

"Yes. We can give her butter and honey for strength." Helena glanced at the sky. The sun had disappeared, and the world was growing dark. Once the birth canal was sufficiently open, the baby was normally born within an hour. Antonina had been pushing all afternoon and evening. Helena looked at Constantina and knew the mother suspected what Helena was sure of. "I fear the baby's head is too large for Antonina's hips." Helena paused, not wanting to continue. "Sometimes the baby has to be sacrificed, or both will die."

Constantina folded her arms as she thought. "The baby should have come by now. Let her push a few more times. If it still won't come, save Antonina."

Helena had watched Anna sacrifice the baby twice. Once, the mother had lived. The other time, both had died anyway. Helena didn't want to cut the baby apart, but if she did nothing, she was more and more certain that both would perish. "Does Antonina have anyone she needs to say goodbye to? The procedure carries risk."

"Her husband. He couldn't handle her cries, so I sent him away. He's finishing the cradle. And her brother."

Helena was about to have Constantina call for them when Antonina's cry tore through the air, loud and sharp. Helena pushed through the doorway and ran to the woman. Blood streamed from between her legs. Helena had seen it before, and in the back of her mind, she knew death would soon come, but she wouldn't give up without trying to stanch the flow. Antonina whimpered in pain, Constantina sobbed in sorrow, and Helena worked furiously to catch the blood, to reposition the baby, to somehow stop the inevitable. But all too soon, the blood stopped gushing, and Antonina grew still.

The mother was dead, but perhaps the child could be saved. Helena used her sharpest knife to cut into the dead woman's womb. The baby's head was stuck in the hips, but Helena grasped the shoulder and the base of the neck. On the third maneuver, the baby came free. Helena rubbed the infant's skin, cleared the infant's throat, and spanked the infant's backside. But nothing she did could change what had happened. Helena had hesitated too long, and she had saved neither mother nor child.

She laid the baby on a cloth. It would have been a son. Constantina's wails filled the room, blood soaked the mat and floor, and Antonina's lifeless eyes stared at the ceiling. Helena knew she should start washing the bodies, preparing them for burial. But all she could do was weep.

CHAPTER TWELVE
IN THE BASE OF THE TOWER

IVAN'S NEW CELL WAS BLACK, damp, and infested with rats. Chains gripped his ankles and wrists, and the wounds in his arm and leg burned and throbbed. From time to time, two guards unshackled him long enough to make use of the bucket in the corner of his cell. Occasionally, he was given stale bread or a thin porridge that made his intestines ache. When the guards left, they took the lights with them. Abandoned in the dark, Ivan finally acknowledged that escape was impossible.

That surrender seemed to cost him a piece of his soul.

Sometimes he prayed, but it was without hope. God didn't seem to be listening.

A visitor came eventually. Ivan wasn't sure how long he had been in the dungeon because he couldn't see the sky. He could remember three bits of food, so he supposed it had been three days, but the guards might have skipped feeding him a time or two. He squinted against the torchlight when Niketas and Paulus escorted one of Kyrios Basil's advisers into the pit.

"Do you know who I am?" The man spoke Slavonic.

"I don't know your name, but I recall your face." Ivan wasn't likely to forget the man who'd threatened to kill him because he wasn't Konstantin.

"I'm here because it was thought that you might listen to reason better if it were spoken in your own tongue."

"Who are you?"

"Kastrophylax Radomir."

"Radomir?" Hatred flared in Ivan's chest, and his hands strained against his chains. "I'd sooner run you through with a sword than take advice from you."

Radomir paced across the cell. "I thought that might be your initial reaction. You've heard lies about me all your life."

"They aren't lies." Konstantin, Miladin, and Župan Dragomir had told Ivan the truth. "You were supposed to set the watch at Maritsa, but you made an alliance with the Turks, and you left the army without sentries. You betrayed my father and my uncle. You betrayed your brother's trust. Serbia's kral and her best warriors died at Maritsa, and it was all your fault."

Radomir's lips hardened. "That is a twisted version of what really happened."

Ivan didn't believe him, and he hoped the dungeon's lighting wasn't dim enough to hide his contempt.

"You think well of my brother?"

"Yes." Ivan didn't hesitate. "Župan Dragomir is our closest ally, and he is an honorable man."

Radomir huffed. "That *honorable* man tried to cheat me of my inheritance. My situation was not unlike yours. My older brother was ward of my lands until I came of age. He kept all the best lands for himself and handed the bankrupt ones over to me."

Ivan put no faith in the man's words. Radomir couldn't know much about the inheritance arrangement planned for Konstantin and Ivan—he hadn't even known Ivan survived childhood. "So, you betrayed your people so you could avenge yourself on your brother?"

"That wasn't my intention. I sought help to claim my rightful inheritance."

"So you went to *the Turks* for aid?"

Radomir watched a rat venture from the corner of the dungeon. "Others have done the same, including several emperors in Constantinople."

"And look where it's taken us. They're encroaching on our lands, demanding tribute, forcing us to spill our blood in their wars, stealing our children for their army."

"I didn't come to argue politics with you, Ivan. I came to help you."

"I doubt that."

"Hear me out." Radomir paced to where the chain connected to the wall. From there, the chain ran through a loop in the ceiling, then along the wall until it split and connected to iron bands around Ivan's wrists. Radomir tugged on the chain, pulling Ivan's hands off his lap. Then he released it. "My grudge is not against you. If Dragomir is your brother's ally, so be it. Perhaps someday you'll accept the truth. In the meantime, I understand you are a man of your word. If you will swear not to escape, I have a thick wool cloak for you and permission to unlock your shackles. Think of it—even you cannot escape a cell such as this. I only ask that you accept what is possible and what is impossible. Make the promise. There is no need to worsen the winter with coldness and chains."

Ivan stared at the iron cuffs about his wrists. They were uncomfortable and heavy. The cold stone floor seeped the heat away from his body, leaving him shivering more often than not. Ivan couldn't escape the dungeon, not without help. Radomir was offering him warmth and the opportunity to walk. For a moment, Ivan considered it. "You are the devil himself, come to purchase my soul with a key and a cloak."

"Don't be unreasonable. We're not so different, you and I. You are a prisoner here—I felt a prisoner under my brother's wardship. I argued against Maritsa. My warning was ignored."

"The difference between us, Radomir, is that I rot in hell now. For your treason, you will rot in hell for all eternity."

Radomir grunted and paced. "I am a forgiving man. For Leo's sake, I will make my offer once again, despite your insults. Kyrios Basil could sell part of his lands to raise a ransom for his heir, but he would prefer an exchange of prisoners. You for Leo. That's better for him, and it's better for you. Shall I unlock your wrists?"

"Yes, so that I may speed you on your way to eternal damnation, but I'll make no vow with a traitor."

Radomir chuckled, a low, predatory sound. "You have no weapon. Do you intend to kill me with the insults that so imprudently roll off your tongue?"

"My hands would be sufficient. It may have been a Turkish weapon that struck down my father, but you are responsible."

Radomir's eyes flashed with anger in the torchlight. He grabbed the chain and yanked, forcing Ivan's hands above his head. Radomir looped the chain around a peg in the wall, making Ivan's position permanent. Then he walked over to Ivan and put his foot directly on Ivan's injured thigh, gradually increasing pressure. Ivan bit his lips to keep from crying out as the pain grew into fierce agony.

"We shall see what your hands are capable of after a few days like this. The time will come when you will regret rejecting my offer. And then you will beg me for mercy. I eagerly await your summons."

"That time will never come, you swine," Ivan said through teeth gritted in pain and anger.

Radomir cuffed him in the head and walked away. "In that case, give my regards to your parents when you see them. I expect your reunion will be soon. If you make it to heaven."

Radomir took the torch, leaving Ivan in darkness. His leg convulsed, and his hands felt bitterly cold. The rats seemed to know that Ivan could no longer shoo them away, and they grew bold, crawling in his hair and biting his neck. For a while, Ivan shivered uncontrollably in the cold cell. A thick cloak would have been welcome indeed. The only part of him that wasn't chilled was part of his left cheek where a lone tear had made a hot trail along his skin.

Time stretched into a seemingly endless period of pain and cold in the dark dungeon. Matthias lowered Ivan's chains and unlocked his wrists for the first meal after Radomir's visit. For a while, Ivan was afraid the damage had already been done, but eventually, the feeling worked its way back into his hands. The throbbing was unpleasant but also a relief. Radomir's malice wouldn't ruin his hands. Matthias replaced the chains when Ivan finished the dry bread, but he adjusted the links so Ivan's hands were no longer stretched above his head.

If he was fed once a day, then four days passed before anyone again spoke to him. Matthias looked as though he wanted to, a time or two, when the kitchen boy brought bread and Matthias brought the torch into the cell, but he always left before any words crossed his lips.

Ivan spent most of his time too tired and weak to be fully awake, too cold and uncomfortable to be fully asleep. Curiosity drew him from his stupor when the light of a torch pierced the cell and Matthias and a priest came inside. Matthias unlocked Ivan's wrists and glanced at the wound in his arm. "I'm sorry. It was my arrow that hit you. We could have surrounded you before you crossed the moat, but I was ordered to shoot."

"You're a soldier. You're trained to obey."

"I'm not obeying now. You are allowed no visitors. But someone should look at your wounds. Kyria Helena would be best, but she is forbidden from coming." Matthias put his hand on the priest's shoulder. "This is my kinsman. For his protection and mine, please keep his visit a secret."

"But when thou doest alms, let not thy left hand know what thy right hand doeth," the priest quoted softly.

Ivan tried to focus on the priest's face, but everything was blurry. "Your secret will be safe with me."

The priest removed the bandage on Ivan's arm and studied the damage in the torchlight. "If nothing changes, this will kill you." He felt Ivan's forehead. "You have a fever."

"Then why am I so cold?"

"I know little about the workings of disease. But if you remain here, there will be no prisoner exchange. Radomir has done your family wrong, but he has Kyrios Basil's ear. Send for him. Negotiate for medical care and a better cell, and do it soon, or you will be too ill to speak."

Speaking was already difficult. "Would you have told Daniel the same thing? To give in so that he might escape the lion's den?"

"We do not ask you to cease your prayers or forget your loyalty to God."

"You ask me to give my loyalty to a lord who isn't mine. I cannot do that."

The priest was silent while he checked the bandage on Ivan's leg. The wound's foul scent was strong enough to detect even over the already unpleasant smell of the dungeon. "Not your loyalty, just your obedience."

"Loyalty and obedience are tied. How am I to give one without the other?"

"Don't trouble yourself with rhetoric." The priest tossed the soiled bandages aside. "But please, think on Radomir's offer."

Ivan thought on the priest's advice as the man washed his wounds and gave him clean bandages, but Ivan couldn't make a promise with a demon like Radomir. God may have abandoned Ivan, but Ivan would make no pact with a devil.

CHAPTER THIRTEEN
A PROMISE TO HELENA

IN THE NINE DAYS SINCE Antonina's death, Kyrios Basil had eight times denied Helena's request to visit the prisoner. Helena was desperate to see Ivan. Euphrosyne was desperate to preserve her husband's best chance of ransom. So, the sisters went together and spoke to Kyrios Basil when there were no advisers nearby to counter their arguments.

"Please, lord." Euphrosyne sank to her knees. "If our prisoner is not kept healthy, how will we get Leo back?"

"The same way we plan to get the other men back: with money."

"But it would empty our coffers to pay all the ransoms, and already the paroikoi suffer with hunger. Would it not be better to preserve our resources for them?" Pleading filled Euphrosyne's voice. "We could move the prisoner to healthier chambers and put him under constant watch so he cannot escape again."

"We don't have the manpower to guard him nonstop. It should have been easier to hold a prisoner than raise the type of money we need, but this prisoner is proving an exception. We would have been better off letting him die for all the trouble he's caused us." Basil lifted his hand as if to dismiss them.

"He won't escape if he promises not to." Helena hurried to finish before he sent them away. "If he is stubborn in his efforts to escape, then he will also be firm in any promise he makes."

"Radomir offered him that option. He turned it down."

"Ivan believes Radomir responsible for his father's death." Helena swallowed. "Forgive me, lord, but you could not have picked a worse messenger."

Kyrios Basil frowned. "Radomir told me their common past would work in his favor."

"Radomir may have been unaware of Ivan's animosity. But the hurt, perceived or real, is deeply felt. Please offer him another way. We must not discard any options for Leo's return, and we may be running out of time."

Kyrios Basil sighed. "If he promises that there will be no more escapes, that he will stay until he is exchanged for Leo, then he can move elsewhere. The cell in the northwest tower. He will be chained at night and guarded, but you may attend him as often as his health requires."

"Thank you, lord." Helena almost sobbed with joy, but she knew convincing Ivan might be more challenging than convincing Kyrios Basil had been.

Euphrosyne wrote the stipulations on parchment, and Kyrios Basil signed and sealed it. Armed with the notice, Helena strode across the acropolis. Below the southwest tower lay the storeroom-turned-dungeon.

"The prisoner is allowed no visitors, kyria." She didn't know the guard who rushed over from the gatehouse, but he blocked the way with his bulk.

"I have permission from Kyrios Basil." She held out the letter and revealed the kephale's seal. "Do you read?"

"Of course." The guard slowly looked over the contents of the parchment.

"You understand the conditions?"

"Yes."

"I would like to see the prisoner now." Her hands trembled as she took the letter back.

The guard went to the gatehouse and returned with a torch and a set of heavy keys. When she followed him down the stairs, the first thing she noticed was the damp cold that penetrated her clothing and left her shivering. The second thing she noticed was the horrible stench. The smell almost made her vomit, and she was no stranger to unpleasant smells. She had never been to the dungeon before, and the chill that grew stronger as she descended the stairs was not entirely due to the temperature. But she was free to leave whenever she wanted, and that knowledge gave her the courage to proceed.

The sound of Ivan's coughs reached her while she was still on the stairs. What would she find when she saw him? Menacing manacles, empty for now, caught the light of the guard's torch. She took a deep breath to calm herself and nearly gagged. Ivan coughed again. It sounded as though the sickness went deep.

The guard unlocked the door and opened it for her. "We've found that he's not very responsive lately unless we give him a few good kicks. Shall I wake him for you?"

Helena hoped her glare was answer enough. She held her breath and strode inside. Ivan slept, huddled against the wall, half sitting, with the chains pulling his hands up to his shoulders. His bandages were soiled. Dark skin circled his eyes, the rest of his face was pale, and a rash was visible on his neck and hands. His breathing was labored and unnaturally quick. Each breath formed a small cloud of fog, but perspiration dotted his forehead.

Her eyes followed the chains to where they ended on the wall. The guard waited outside the cell. She handed him the letter so her hands were free to release the chains.

As his chains were lowered, Ivan's eyes opened. He squinted against the torchlight coming from the hallway. "Who is it?" His voice was raspy and weak.

Helena knelt by his side. "Do you recognize my voice?"

"Yes," Ivan gasped. "It is the voice of an angel. But I must be dreaming, for angels don't descend into hell." He coughed as he finished speaking, hard tremors that shook his whole body.

Helena felt his fingers. They were freezing. His forehead was the opposite. "I wanted to come earlier, but I didn't receive permission until now." Helena took one hand and studied the chafing that had left his wrists discolored.

"Thank you for coming."

"There are conditions, Ivan."

"What kind of conditions?"

"No more escapes. You have to stay until you are exchanged for Leo, on your word of honor."

Ivan looked away.

"Please, Ivan. What if Leo wants to come home just as badly as you wish to leave?"

"If he wanted to escape as badly as I do, he would have made it home by now."

"Not if he's in a dungeon."

"Rivakgrad has no dungeons this black or deep."

"Ivan, if you promise not to escape, you'll be moved to a room above ground. You'll be in my care again. You'll be chained at night, but during the day, we can take walks. As Kyrios Basil sees how well you keep your word, I'll convince him to give you more freedom. But you have to promise you won't escape anymore."

Ivan frowned. He opened his mouth as if to speak, but instead, he coughed.

Helena rushed to continue before he rejected her offer altogether. "I know you said that asking this promise was like asking you not to breathe, but is it not already difficult to breathe? If you aren't moved soon, you might not recover."

"It may be too late already."

"Won't you let me try?"

He glanced at her, then at the wall. He hadn't said the words, but she saw the refusal in his eyes.

Helena couldn't bear it if he died. She had to win this promise from him. She put her hand on his and tried a more personal plea. "If you won't make the promise because it is logical or because it is for your own good, will you make the promise as a favor to me?"

Ivan turned back to her, surprise on his feverish face.

"I've missed you. After you were shot, I lost a mother and an infant. Don't make me lose you too." Helena's voice cracked, and she was surprised to feel warm tears slipping down her cheeks. "Grief for them still grips me, and I'd only met Antonina that day, never did more than hold her dead son. But you . . . Ivan, you have become my dear friend. Grief over your death would haunt my every breath, and this may be our last chance to save you. If you refuse, I doubt Kyrios Basil will let me see you again. I don't want this to be our final goodbye."

The chains clinked as Ivan's hand turned and tightened around hers. "I'm sorry about the mother and child."

Helena sniffed, sorrow choking her once again.

Ivan coughed again, then spoke when he caught his breath. "I've prayed so hard that I could escape. I thought God would help me."

"Maybe you are meant to be here."

Ivan shook his head. "Why would He want me here instead of home with my family? Everyone in Byzia, save you, hates me."

Helena gripped his hand a little tighter. "God sees farther than we do. Perhaps, in time, you will see His purpose even in this. Please, Ivan, make this promise with me now, and maybe eventually, you will know why."

He closed his eyes and forced several slow breaths. Then he opened his eyes and met her gaze. For a moment, she feared he would turn her down.

But instead, he said, "I will stay until you give me permission to leave. I swear it."

Relief welled up inside her like a flood. "Thank you, Ivan. Thank you." She leaned forward and kissed his hot forehead, then whispered in his ear. "If the exchange fails, I will risk treason and help you escape myself."

His indecision had scared her, but now she focused on her work. "Your new chamber is in the northwest tower. There is a hearth outside it, so you will be warm, and it is above ground, so the air will not be so foul. I'll order a bath and have one of the guards escort you there."

"Which guard, my lady?"

Helena wondered why it mattered until she noticed the cluster of bruises along his jawline and remembered the guard's remarks on the need to kick Ivan to wake him. "Perhaps I'll send the guard to arrange the bath, and I will take you to your new room myself."

"I would prefer that, my lady."

Helena stood and strode to the guard. "I'll take the keys now." She held her hand out, and he relinquished them. "The prisoner is being moved to the northwest tower. Tell Pasara. She'll know what to prepare."

The guard left the torch in a bracket and disappeared up the stairs.

Helena unlocked the shackles around Ivan's wrists. "Do they hurt?"

"Yes, but I welcome the pain. It means I still have hands, and there were times I feared I would lose them."

Helena removed the chains from his ankles and let him stand on his own. He needed the wall for support, and when he reached his full height, he had to pause and cough deeply, uncontrollably. He rested his head against the cold dungeon wall as he caught his breath.

"Lean on me."

Ivan cooperated when she moved his arm around her neck. She noticed his limp as they stepped into the corridor outside the cell. The bandage tied around his thigh was filthy.

The first time she had wanted to examine his leg, he had protested. "Your leg wound. Will you let me look at it?"

"Anything you wish, my angel."

Helena felt her face go hot. "I'm not an angel."

"Who else delivers lost souls from hell?"

Helena felt Ivan's body shaking, either from cold or exhaustion, so she paused midway up the staircase for him to rest. "We're almost out."

When they finally made it to the bailey, Ivan blinked and squinted, then took in a lungful of fresh air. He looked as though he'd lost weight in the dungeon, but he was still heavy, and his unsteady limbs depended on her help. The walk across the acropolis to the northwest tower would be long, but she didn't regret her decision. The guard might have taken Ivan to his new chamber more quickly, but she didn't want to risk further mistreatment.

People from the town and villages crowded the acropolis. Helena ignored their stares. As she and Ivan passed the barracks, Demetrios stood in the doorway, his arms folded across his chest as he watched her. She gave him a pointed look, then turned away.

Helena's legs shook by the time they passed the bathhouse. Beyond that, they reached the northwest tower, and its stairway winded them both.

"Just one level up," she said when they came even with the wall. Helena was glad it wasn't more. She was tired, but more than that, she worried about Ivan's reduced stamina. They rested for a moment before climbing the last staircase, stumbling to the top room of the stone tower.

Half the space stored rock-slinging petroboloi and large crossbows. The other half was divided into two barred cells. A fire burned in the hearth, and steam rose in small swirls from a bathtub. Ivan took his arm from Helena's shoulders and slid to the floor.

Helena knelt beside him. "I shouldn't have let you walk."

"It is a comfort to know that I still *can* walk."

A servant laid out a mat in one of the cells. Someone had already brought chains, but she had Ivan's promise, so the chains were unnecessary.

"I'll give you some privacy." She glanced at his short tunic and the bandage over his hose. "Don't put those clothes back on. I'll bring clean ones when I come to care for your leg."

Ivan could barely walk, so she left one of the manservants there to ensure he didn't drown. By the time she returned with clean clothing and bedding, the servant was gone, and Ivan had fallen asleep on the woven mat in his cell. A linen cloth was wrapped around his waist. She added a log to the fire, wishing the hearth were inside his cell instead of across the room.

He slept through her examination of his arm and thigh. She tried to overlook the bruises that lined his abdomen. Gifts from the guards, she assumed. But she couldn't ignore the other changes she saw. When he'd first been wounded, his chest and stomach had been muscled and hard. Now his body was far too slender, and his flesh barely covered his ribs. She thought his arm would heal properly, but his thigh was infected, as were his wrists where the heavy shackles had chafed them. The wrists didn't worry her much; now that he was clean and out of the dungeon, she thought that they, too, would be fine. His leg was another matter. She would have to cut out the purulent parts. She put her head on his chest, listening to his labored breathing. That, too, gave her concern.

She covered him in a thick woolen blanket and went to the surgery to search through Petros's codices for remedies. She gathered items from the herb garden and the kitchen to make a potion that she hoped would fight the infection. She used up the last of the summer savory and had not quite enough spikenard, so she added more cowbane. She also took an old salve Petros had used on the blacksmith when the man had burned his wrist and the wound had festered. Perhaps it would help Ivan too.

On her way back, she saw Matthias walking from the keep, probably on his way home to his house in the town. "Matthias, will you help me with Ivan's care?"

"Yes, kyria, but I have no skill in healing."

"You have no malice toward the prisoner, and you have strong arms. Those are the only qualifications I seek today."

Ivan still slept when they reached his cell. She sat next to him on the rush mat and gently swept his brown hair back from his feverish forehead.

He opened his eyes and pushed himself into a seated position. He unfolded a knee-length tunic from the pile of clothes Helena had brought earlier. "May I put it on?"

"Yes, I examined your arm earlier. It is healing. Your leg is worse. I need to refresh the edges of the wound and sew it together. It will hurt."

"I can handle pain," he said with the smallest of smiles.

"I know, but I hate to be the cause of it. Lie down." Helena pushed the cloth out of the way when he complied. The edges of the wound were dried and discolored, and several pockets of pus would have to be cut out as well. She looked at both sides carefully, knowing the bleeding would make it difficult to see once she started.

She gave Ivan a piece of wood to bite. She would have given him wine as well, but Trotula said wine was harmful for feverish patients. She scrubbed his leg and located the best places for her incisions. "Matthias, you'll need to hold his leg still. Grip it above and below the wound."

Matthias rolled up his elaborately embroidered cuffs and took his position on the other side of Ivan. Then Helena began. Bit by bit, her sharp knife cut away the damaged flesh. She glanced at Ivan before she took up her needle. His jaw clenched the wood, and perspiration dotted his forehead. The arrow had entered the leg at an angle, making a wider cut than the one in the arm. Based on the shape of the wound, she suspected more flesh had been torn when the arrow had been removed than when it had entered. She gave it thirty stitches. Then she covered it with the balm from Petros's shelves and applied fresh bandages.

"There. Finished." When she spoke, Ivan squeezed his eyes shut, spat out the wood, and took several deep breaths.

She turned to her assistant, giving her patient a moment to collect himself. "Thank you, Matthias."

"You're welcome, kyria." Matthias took the rag she gave him and wiped a bit of blood from his hands. "Should I tell them to expect you in the great hall?"

"No. I think I'll eat with my patient this evening. Please take my greetings to your wife."

When Matthias left, Helena turned to Ivan. "Are you brave enough for me to salve your wrists? It may sting."

In answer, Ivan sat up and held out his left wrist. He kept it steady while she applied Petros's concoction and dressed it. They repeated the process with the right wrist.

"Thank you, Helena. I don't deserve a friend like you."

For some reason, the strength of his gratitude pricked her emotions. She was still determining the best way to respond when a servant interrupted them with food.

When the servant left, Helena looked at the bread and broad beans. It was a fast day, so there would be no meat, oil, or wine. "You're ill. You shouldn't have to fast, but perhaps the lighter fare is better for your condition."

Ivan obediently took the bread she handed him. "While I was in the dungeon, Radomir told me that if I promised not to escape, he'd unlock my chains and give me warm clothes. I said I would make no pacts with devils or traitors." He stared at the bread. "The promise I gave you is not so different, yet selling my soul to an angel does not seem like a sin."

"Your soul is still yours, Ivan. I have only your promise to stay until I release you."

They ate in companionable silence, though Ivan ate little and coughed much. When they finished, she felt his forehead again. The fever hadn't changed, but she found herself drawn to him, wanting to touch his skin to convince herself that he was really there, no longer chained, no longer in danger. His eyes followed her every movement, but his expression showed no wariness, no hostility, only faith in her abilities and in her character.

Since his promise, each glance, each gesture made it feel as though he'd entrusted her with not only his health but also his soul. She hadn't demanded anything so precious in the dungeon, but she intended to be worthy of the hallowed trust he'd given her.

The overwhelming relief Helena had felt when Ivan had moved to the tower disappeared as pneumonia ravaged his body. Constant coughing left Ivan weak, his fever grew worse, and by the end of the second day, he no longer recognized her when she tended him. The infection in his thigh didn't worsen—but nor did it improve. Helena found herself surviving on almost no sleep, and her prayers reached a new level of intensity.

"Any better?" Euphrosyne came into the tower as Helena applied a solution of cooling herbs to Ivan's face and chest.

"No." Helena said nothing else, afraid her voice would break.

Euphrosyne looked through the iron bars. "You're working so hard. I would tell you to rest, but so much depends on his recovery."

"How do you feel?" Helena turned to her sister. She doubted anyone else noticed, but Euphrosyne's thin frame was changing.

Euphrosyne bit her lip as she thought. "Hungry again. That is a relief. For a while, I had little desire for food. But I worry for Leo's sake. Can I do something to help?"

Helena shook her head. She had the herbs she needed. One of the kitchen boys brought pots of boiling water up regularly so Helena could make Ivan inhale the steam. There was little else anyone could do. In truth, Ivan would get better, or he wouldn't, and nothing Helena did was likely to change that outcome. According to Galen, nature was the best healer. Yet Helena was reluctant to leave. For the first time since Alexius died, Helena was afraid Ivan wouldn't survive. And if he were to die, she wanted to be nearby.

"If you think of something, you must promise to tell me. I will do anything to bring Leo back."

Helena nodded, but her motivations were far different from Euphrosyne's. Helena wanted Leo to come back. But tending to Ivan was no longer about having a healthy hostage. It was about helping a man she admired and cared for. He could be stubborn and unforgiving, but his heart held courage, kindness, and a loyalty she felt blessed to have earned.

When Euphrosyne left, Helena knelt next to her patient. "Ivan, son of Miroslav. You promised you would not leave until I gave you my permission. You do not have my permission to escape. And you do not have my permission to die. If you are a man of your word, you will get better."

CHAPTER FOURTEEN
ISKANDAR'S PLAN

Iskandar stood before his father to make his report. "Hasan slew one of them and injured their horses. But they killed Ali and Nasuh. Revenge will be sweet when we attack."

Abdullah bin Isa paced across the rugs of his tent, his arms behind his back and his head stooped in thought. "We won't attack."

"Why not? Rivak is rich, and now is the perfect time. The battle with Byzia's army left them weak. And they aren't loyal to the sultan. They're planning revolt—"

"Now is not the perfect time. You and Hasan made it through the mountain passes but only with difficulty. Our baggage wagons could not make the same journey."

"In the spring, then!"

His father shook his head. "You cannot attack Sultan Murad's vassals. He doesn't wish to lose their military service or their tribute money."

"But they're going to turn on him."

"Yes. I'll send word to the sultan. He'll be grateful for your discovery. But until he gives leave, you may not attack them."

Anger burned inside Iskandar's chest, so hot he didn't dare speak. His father was walking away from a golden opportunity—one Iskandar had been working to create since before harvest time. He fumed and sulked while his father called a messenger and charged him to take the news to Edirne.

Iskandar hadn't been in camp long, but he recognized the unease among his father's men. They were restless—it showed in the petty fights they picked with one another over foolish things such as which cut of meat they received. They were bored—it showed in the numerous cockfights. And they were impatient for action—it showed in the way they sharpened their scimitars and hoarded arrows.

Eventually, only Iskandar and his father remained in the tent. Had his father forgotten to dismiss him?

Abdullah bin Isa looked up from the embroidered cushion where he sat. "Iskandar, you have done well."

His father had never given him a compliment before, and the warmth of those words dissolved Iskandar's frustration. "Thank you."

"But you are not happy."

Iskandar took a moment to collect his thoughts, trying to speak with logic rather than emotion. "Your men are not happy. They need action, and Rivak is vulnerable. I worked hard to make it so. They would have made a rich target."

His father folded his hands together. "You must understand, Iskandar, that Sultan Murad is building a nation. That takes time and careful strategy. Our people have enemies in Rumelia and Anatolia. We're not invincible. Murad can't fight on all sides at once. Let him bring the Serbs into submission in his own way and in his own time. It's his decision, not ours." He stood and paced. "You are much like the sultan's son Bayezid. Capable and eager for attack. A raider rather than an empire builder. But what happens after the attack? That must also be on your mind."

"Yes, my father." Perhaps Rivak lay too far to the west, but Iskandar hated abandoning something he'd worked and schemed for over the course of several moons.

"What of the other men in the battle you arranged? The Greeks? Are they not also weak?"

"Weak, yes, but not so rich."

"Perhaps not. But something is better than nothing, is it not? The Despot Manuel has thrown off his allegiance to the sultan. We will be smiled upon for humbling his people."

Iskandar thought on it. No high mountains stood between Byzia and his father's camp. And though the Greeks weren't as wealthy as the Serbs, they weren't destitute. Leo's wife had worn fine jewelry. The kastron stored ample food and arms. And the villagers had tidy homes, orchards, and livestock. Allah willing, the pillage would be worth their time.

"Tell me, my son, how would you attack Byzia?"

Together they planned it.

CHAPTER FIFTEEN
A WINTER THAWING

IVAN WOKE TO HELENA'S HAND on his forehead, but her touch was the only thing pleasant about returning from delirium. His thigh ached, and his head burned, and he suspected that if he tried to sit, he'd be dizzy. His chest felt as if it were constricted by a heavy bowstring, and his limbs felt made of stone. The tower wasn't as damp as the dungeon, but the winter chill gripped him all the way to the bone. Beyond that, there was a weakness that grasped and held him.

Helena said he was improving, and he trusted her, but for several days, his body gave little evidence that she was right. Yet as the days passed, Ivan did grow stronger, a bit at a time. His coughing stopped, his fever disappeared, the wound in his leg closed, and the constant headache went from a roar to a murmur.

The weather had turned icy, but despite the cold, he hungered for fresh air and a larger expanse of sky than what he could see through the tower's narrow arrow loops. The first time he asked Helena if they could walk the castle walls, she put him off, insisting he rest. She said the same thing the next day and the day after, but the fourth time he asked, she finally relented. "Tomorrow."

On the day of the promised excursion, he stood and gripped the bars of his cell as soon as he heard footsteps on the tower stairs. The graceful folds of her veil and the long lines of her tunic and cloak were blue instead of white, but she looked like an angel. And the warmth of her smile seemed to make the chill of winter vanish.

He had to walk slowly, and frustration blanketed him like a cloak. He'd spent more time in bed than on his feet since the battle. It was like going back to his childhood, when camp fever had devastated his health. He'd trained and drilled and pushed himself to gain strength and skill. Now he was weak again. But the next day was better, as was the day after.

"What day is it?" he asked one cold winter morning while he walked with Helena on the battlements.

"Eager for spring?" The chill wind had turned Helena's cheeks and nose pink.

Ivan longed to pull her near and hold her until she was warm, but he wasn't sure how she'd react. "Yes. But also tired of not knowing. I lost track of the days long ago—but it must be after Christmas because the hours are getting longer."

"Tomorrow will be a fortnight past Epiphany, which makes today January nineteenth."

Ivan let out a small laugh to cover the sudden pang of homesickness. "January nineteenth."

"Earlier or later than you expected?"

Ivan shrugged.

"Then why is the date significant?"

Ivan shook his head, doubting a Greek woman would know much of Serb traditions. "It's not important."

"It must be important, or you'd not have reacted so. Tell me." Helena walked around to stand in front of him, her brown eyes staring up at him.

How was it that she read him so well? Ivan yielded. "Tomorrow is my family's Slava."

"What's a Slava?"

"A celebration of our family's patron saint, John the Baptist."

"How do you celebrate?"

It was the most important day of the year, with feasting, gathering of friends, and a blessing from the priest. But Ivan wouldn't be there to participate. "It doesn't matter."

The next morning, Helena didn't come. He was allowed outside his cell from sunrise to twilight, so he strolled the wall walk all morning, his thoughts across the mountains in his homeland. Images of Slavas past filled his mind: the joyous wishes from each guest who came to the grody's keep, the candle, the food, and the wine. The ache to be with his family grew and grew. It would have been his last Slava in Rivak, and he was missing it.

"Good day, Ivan."

He turned as soon as he heard her voice. "Good day to you, Kyria Helena." Her smile was brighter than normal, and held a hint of mischief, something he was not accustomed to seeing in her. A jeweled comb held her veil in place, and a golden belt cinched in the waist of a red dalmatica with richly embroidered cuffs. She held a basket in each hand; folded cloths hid the contents. "Shall I carry the baskets for you? They look heavy."

Helena handed them to him.

"You are dressed as if you plan to deliver no babies and change no bandages today. And the set of your mouth tells me you have a secret. What is it?"

Her smile deepened. "I have a surprise for you. For your family's Slava. I'm going to take you to my favorite place in the entire pronoia."

Ivan's curiosity burned as she led him down the stairs of the northeast tower and across the bailey. Outside the stables, Matthias held the reins to three saddled horses. One was Helena's, the gray mare named Cleopatra that Ivan had tried to steal during his first clumsy escape attempt. Matthias offered Ivan a glossy chestnut stallion.

"I'm allowed to ride a horse?"

Helena accepted her mare's reins. "If you stay with Matthias and me."

They rode through the gatehouse into the lower portion of the kastron. Ivan had been in the town only once, after he'd been recaptured at the village the night of the storm, the fire, and the pillory. It felt as if he were seeing the town for the first time. Tidy walls separated individual courtyards from the streets, and beyond the walls lay dormant fruit trees and homes with tile roofs. Helena grinned at him as he took it all in. They stopped at a home where Matthias collected a boy of about four and kissed a baby and a pretty woman in an elaborately embroidered dalmatica goodbye.

"His family?" Ivan asked.

"Yes. The older boy is the first child I helped Anna deliver."

They continued through the town and out its gate. About fifty paces later, Helena led them off the road into a meadow. On the far edge, she halted her horse. "I gather herbs here sometimes. It's not at its best this time of year, but it hasn't completely lost its beauty."

"This is the first time I've been outside the kastron walls without fear of capture. The newness is beauty enough for me, as is the company."

One side of Helena's mouth pulled with what Ivan suspected was pleasure. "Flattery won't make me release you from your promise."

Ivan dismounted and held out a hand to her. "It is not flattery. It is truth. The meadow is lovely. As are you."

She blushed as he took her waist and brought her to the ground. The added color in her cheeks made her seem more alive, and more vulnerable.

He didn't let go immediately. Matthias and his son were some distance away, and Helena's horse blocked their view.

Ivan had never been so taken with anyone. He'd seen beautiful women before. They'd stirred his curiosity and made his eyes linger. But Helena was different. He wanted to know everything about her and share everything about himself in exchange. When he looked at her, he saw beauty, but he also saw her compassion and her courage, her softness and her strength. She met his eyes for a long moment, then glanced at his lips, then away.

He released her waist, and after a moment or two, she moved to unload one of the baskets. It contained a meal and a blanket to spread on the ground. They ate and spoke and watched the birds hopping among the branches of a leafless mulberry tree for hours. Matthias and his boy tossed sticks and stones into the river, then rode around the clearing and through the woods. The sun sank lower, and shadows from the trees surrounding the meadow grew longer.

Helena shook with the cold.

"Take this." Ivan unfastened his cloak and held it out to her.

"Nay, then you will be cold."

As she spoke, he wrapped it around her shoulders. "Not as cold as I was in the dungeon. Thank you for saving me from that fate." He would have died if it hadn't been for her plea, he was sure of it.

"Thank you for letting me save you." Helena moved next to him—so close he felt each of her shivers. "I think this is large enough to share." She arranged the cloak across both their shoulders, and eventually, the trembling stopped.

Ivan turned to the woman beside him. "It's beautiful here, even in the winter. Is that what draws you?"

"Yes. And it is also a good place to find malache."

"And you use that to treat fevers?"

"Yes." Her eyebrows drew together in surprise. "You remember that?"

"I converse with few people in Byzia. I suppose that makes it easy to remember what you've told me." Her visits had always been the high point of the day, no matter how sick he'd been, no matter how much he missed Rivak. "Helena, when you promised to help me escape if the exchange fell through, did you mean it?"

"I wouldn't have said it if I hadn't meant it."

"Why?"

"Because you don't deserve to be a prisoner. You should be free." She met his gaze with earnest brown eyes. "And because a little girl named Theodora came from one of the villages to plead for mercy on your behalf. I promised her that you would return home someday."

"Theodora is too young to travel by herself."

"Her father accompanied her. That was a heroic thing you did, Ivan, to save her family from a fire and sacrifice your freedom by doing so."

"I didn't know I was sacrificing my freedom when I went back for her."

"Had you known what would happen, would you have acted differently?"

Ivan pondered her question, making sure he was telling her the truth about himself and not just the truth he wished about himself. "No. How could I act otherwise and live with myself?"

"You'll have your freedom again, Ivan. Someday. I promise." Helena put her hand on his. Her skin was cold from exposure, but her touch sent warmth coursing up his arm and into his chest.

"Thank you. I am blessed to have you as a friend."

Helena beamed, and it lit her entire face. "Happy Slava, Ivan." She leaned her head on his shoulder, and he caught the scent of rosewater in her hair.

He reached to brush a stray curl from her cheek. Then he touched her face again, trailing his fingers down the side of her jaw. She closed her eyes, and her lips curved up in contentment. Then Ivan remembered himself and withdrew his hand.

Their horses stamped in the background, Matthias and his son rode closer, and all too soon, it was time to leave. There had been no Slava cake, no priestly blessing, and no feast. At the end of the day, Ivan had to return to the acropolis that had become his prison. But despite that, he couldn't remember a more pleasant Slava.

Helena tried to contain the smile that threatened to burst from her as she entered the keep. She felt her cheek where Ivan's fingers had touched her skin and imagined his caress turning into a kiss. She hadn't enjoyed her first kisses, the ones Callinicus had forced on her, but Ivan's lips would be different.

The great hall filled as people gathered for the evening meal. "Kyria Helena, may I have a word with you?" Kastrophylax Radomir stood at her elbow and motioned her toward a quiet corner.

Helena followed him, her arms pricking with unease. She'd seen Ivan fingering the sores on his wrists one morning when Radomir had appeared across the bailey. When she'd pressed him, Ivan had told her of Radomir's abuse in the dungeon.

"I saw you ride out with the Serb prisoner today."

"He is back now. Matthias returned him to his chains." It wasn't fair that Ivan was condemned to spend all the dark hours locked in shackles. She had asked Kyrios Basil for mercy, but he'd refused to soften his decree.

"Why were *you* with him?"

"Today is his family's Slava."

Radomir grunted. "I fail to see how that involves you. Slavas are based on when a family embraced Christianity. I imagine your family threw off paganism several hundred years before his family did."

"Ivan is my friend." She hoped admitting as much wasn't treason. "I wished to help him celebrate."

"Let me give you some advice, kyria. Have a care, for your future and for your reputation. You were lucky with Callinicus. He was more interested in a pretty face than in a prudent match, and his uncle approved of you because you listened to him drone on about medical theory. But you are an orphan who has already lost several childbearing years. Marriages are meant to join families, and you have no family to speak of other than your sister. Now that Leo is heir, that might be enough to win you a worthy husband." Radomir gave a meaningful glance at Demetrios as he followed his father into the hall. "But if you continue strolling the battlements with an enemy, you'll throw that chance away."

"Ivan and I have done nothing improper."

"Improper behavior isn't necessary to ruin a lady's reputation. Being in a position where she *could* have done something improper is sufficient, especially when the lady in question has no parents to intercede for her and already pushes boundaries with her chosen trade. Take my advice and stay away from the prisoner. It's for your own good."

Her face felt hot as Radomir strutted away. What did he intend? He'd barely spoken to her before, so he couldn't be concerned for her welfare. Had he hinted that Demetrios would be a worthy husband out of friendship for Demetrios's father? Or was he merely trying to strike another blow at Ivan?

She didn't want the kastrophylax for an enemy, so she would be more discreet, but she didn't plan to take his advice. Ivan wouldn't abandon a friend because of threats against his reputation, and nor would she.

Ivan did his best to maintain the meager trust he'd earned from his captors. Helena had complete faith in him, and Matthias would talk with him, even spar with him using wooden swords, but everyone else eyed him with suspicion, from the blacksmith who shod horses while Ivan strode through the bailey to the servant who brought him porridge in the morning when Helena herself didn't come. He was allowed to attend worship services in the chapel and use the bathhouse during the day, but that didn't stop the glares or the bitter whispers.

The distrust and hatred that surrounded him made Ivan miss his family all the more. And yet, when he thought of leaving Helena, he knew he would miss her just as intensely come spring. He'd long ago predicted that his heart would be torn in two when he left Rivak for Sivi Gora. Now he suspected that another part of it would remain a captive of Byzia's midwife even after the exchange came.

Ivan strode past one glaring guard and crossed the bailey. Near the stables, he heard the sharp yells of the stablemaster.

"You lazy sod!" The fat stablemaster pushed a small groom from the stables with enough force to land him on the ground. Blood ran from the boy's ear and nose. The stablemaster gripped a thick wooden rod and held it with menace.

"What is the boy's crime, that you beat him so?" Ivan asked.

The stablemaster looked at Ivan and sneered. "It has nothing to do with you. Get on your way."

"First an answer, sir, for in my lands, a punishment like that is reserved for truly malignant acts." Beatings seemed common in Kyrios Basil's pronoia, but it was one thing to beat an enemy warrior. To pummel a child was vile. Ivan hadn't been able to defend himself while held hostage, but a burning frustration had simmered for months. Common or not, he was sick of standing by while the strong hurt the weak.

"He shirked his chores. It's none of your concern." The stablemaster turned his back to Ivan, dismissing him.

"But the tzaousios's men returned late—I haven't had time to care for all the horses yet." The boy's voice was choked with fear.

"I told you no excuses!" The stablemaster beat the boy across the back.

Ivan had seen enough. The groom had no control over when the guards brought their horses to the stable, and the stablemaster smelled of cheap wine. Ivan was unarmed, and he wasn't fully recovered from his illness, but the stablemaster seemed more bully than warrior. "I think you had better let him go."

"Or you'll do what?" The stablemaster turned around with a glare.

"Or I'll give you the same treatment you've been giving him."

The man huffed. "I'd like to see you try." He kicked at the boy a final time and then turned his anger toward Ivan, swinging the rod toward him.

Ivan ducked easily. As the man's momentum carried his arms to the left, Ivan threw his body into the man's chest and knocked him off-balance. He seized the wooden staff, yanked it away, and shoved the stablemaster into the side of the stable. Then he pinned the man to the wall with the rod across his neck.

Ivan glared up at him, applying steady pressure to his windpipe. "The next time you wish to take out your aggression on someone smaller than you, I suggest you go into the woods and find a wild boar to tangle with. If I ever see you lay so much as a finger on the boy again, I will do what I must to make sure you never touch him again."

Ivan saw resignation in the stablemaster's eyes; the man knew he'd been beaten. Ivan had hoped to see remorse, but that wasn't an emotion he could force. Somewhat reluctantly, Ivan released the lout. The man's hands went directly to his neck, rubbing what Ivan had bruised.

Ivan dropped the rod and turned to the boy. "What's your name, boy?"

"Philippos." He stared at the ground as he spoke.

"Have you worked in the stables long, Philippos?"

The boy nodded.

"The horses are well-groomed and well-cared-for. Be not ashamed to look any man in the face, because your diligence and hard work is noticed."

Philippos raised his head, his expression still wary. "I found you on the floor when you tried to escape." He pointed to the building that stored the saddles. Then his expression turned to alarm. "Look behind you!"

The stablemaster had grabbed the wooden rod and was swinging it toward Ivan's head. Ivan leaped out of the way. He kneed the man in the stomach and slammed his fists down hard on the back of his neck. The stablemaster fell to the ground, unconscious.

"What is going on?" Gregoras strode to the stables, Demetrios with him, spathion in hand. "I'll see you back in the dungeon for this!"

"It's all right, Gregoras." Helena's voice called from nearer the keep. When she drew closer, she spoke again. "I was watching from a distance and can explain what happened, but first, I would like to make sure the boy is unharmed. I'll meet you at the gatehouse when I've tended him."

Gregoras looked decidedly unhappy to follow Helena's suggestion, but he nodded his agreement.

Helena held out her hand to the boy. "Come with me, Philippos."

"Did you really see everything?" Ivan asked as he followed Helena to the surgeon's home. He watched for her whenever he wasn't chained in his cell, but he hadn't seen her. Of course, he hadn't seen the stablemaster either. He should have known better than to turn his back on someone like that. If not for Philippos's warning, the stablemaster could have broken Ivan's head.

Helena gave him a sly smile over the top of Philippos's head. "Perhaps you should tell me what happened so I know what to tell the tzaousios. I will trust your word, and Gregoras will trust mine."

Ivan held back a laugh, pleased that she would mislead the tzaousios to protect him. "Once again, my lady, I find myself in your debt."

The next day, the acropolis had a new stablemaster, and Ivan had a new friend. Philippos had already seemed in awe of Ivan after overhearing stories of the battle and Ivan's escapes from the guards. Like Ivan, he was an orphan, but unlike Ivan, Philippos hadn't been blessed with a doting aunt, protective brother, or loyal cousin. Ivan had seen boys like Philippos before—children who were treated poorly and came to believe what others thought of them.

For several days, Ivan had to remind the boy to look him in the eyes when he spoke rather than at the ground like a beaten dog. Then inspiration struck. If telling the boy he was a good groom wasn't working, Ivan would help Philippos gain the skills he so admired. After an all-too-brief visit with Helena, Ivan created a set of targets and fastened them to the inside of the curtain wall near the gatehouse. Then he went to speak with Matthias.

When Philippos completed his chores, Ivan held up the composite bow and quiver of arrows he'd talked Matthias into loaning him. "Would you like to learn how to use these?"

Philippos took the weapons with reverence. Ivan had him try the bow to make sure he was strong enough to draw it back. Ivan and Matthias had picked the smallest bow in the armory, then switched out the bowstring for one meant for a longer bow. The result wouldn't propel the arrow with as much force, but it still had a significant draw weight. Philippos strained, but he could stretch the string to his shoulder. Ivan helped the boy fasten his arm guard, and they went over nocking and correct posture. "Now pull it back to your right cheek and release."

Philippos's first shot hit the wall instead of the target. His face fell.

"Learning archery takes years. That wasn't bad for your first shot. Try it again, but keep your fingers relaxed."

They practiced until he could hit a target from a distance of five paces. The next day, he could do it from ten. The day after, from fifteen.

"If you keep improving like that, you'll be the finest archer in all of Byzia." Ivan put his hand on the child's shoulder, and Philippos seemed to stand a little taller.

Then Ivan's attention turned to the woman walking through the gate. Helena led her mare, and the horse carried the birthing chair and bundles of supplies. She wore red and blue with a golden belt. She was beautiful, and Ivan hadn't seen her in days.

She came to watch as Philippos hit his mark again and again. His fingers had yet to develop calluses, and his muscles had to be sore with learning the new movements, but determination carried him through.

After finishing his quiver and retrieving his arrows, Philippos's eyes drew upward. "How far do you think I could shoot an arrow from up there?"

"Let's have a look." Ivan surveyed the wall. Christophoros stood watch, and Ivan didn't think he'd begrudge their intrusion. He turned to Helena. "Would you care to walk with us?" She'd told him she couldn't see him so often now that he was healed, but deliveries were unpredictable. Since she'd just returned from a birth, everyone would assume she was still with the mother and infant.

Helena nodded. Ivan offered her his arm as they climbed the southwest tower. Her hand was warm on his arm, and she walked so near to him that her skirts brushed his legs.

"Ivan, do you think I could hit the church?" Philippos jumped up to see through an embrasure.

Ivan peered at the town. "Perhaps, but it's not a good target. If you miss, you might strike someone. And if your arrow hits home, you might commit blasphemy. See that tree there?" Ivan pointed to one outside the kastron.

Philippos followed Ivan's fingers. "Yes."

"That would be a good target, but not when the sun's so low. Some of the paroikoi might pass that way as they return home from their fields."

The battlements were designed to provide a clear view of any danger approaching the kastron and offer a safe haven for Byzia's bowmen. Whether by accident or design, they also yielded a breathtaking view of the sunset. Ivan stood as near to Helena as he dared while she watched the golden orb sink below the horizon. The end of the day was fair, but not as fair as the changing colors that played across her smooth complexion.

"The delivery went well?" he asked.

"Yes." Her visage, already showing contentment, now showed joy. "A daughter to go with two sons. She is small but healthy."

"I am glad. For their sake, and for yours." Several times during their walks around the bailey, bits of conversation had made him suspect she was still haunted by the mother and child she'd lost while he'd been in the dungeon. He had seen something similar from his brother and grandfather when they'd thought of men who'd died in battle under their command. Birth and battle were dangerous, death inevitable. So, he supposed, was the regret.

"Helena!" Euphrosyne's voice carried from the tower.

With a glance at Ivan and a flush of color, Helena spun around. "Yes?"

"It's a feast day. Come, you must change."

"I'll come in a moment."

"I think it best if you come now." Euphrosyne's eyes narrowed as she took in Ivan and his proximity to her sister.

Helena looked at the disappearing sunlight and at Ivan, then nodded in submission and followed her sister down the tower stairs. She collected her horse, and Ivan watched until she went inside the stables. The sun and Helena had both disappeared, and the coming night grew cold.

"Ivan. Ivan!"

Philippos had been calling his name for some time. "Yes?"

"What about that tree? Would it be a good target?"

CHAPTER SIXTEEN
STRANGERS ON THE WALL WALK

Iskandar bin Abdullah eyed the town at the foot of the acropolis, by far the largest in all of Byzia. A shoemaker, a smith, a potter, and a spinner lived nearby, among other craftsmen and traders. Its inhabitants tended their nearby fields and vineyards, their goats, pigs, and chickens. Some had mules or cattle. He doubted they had much coin, but they would have some with which to pay taxes. The entire kastron was protected by a stone wall, but the portion around the town was not as formidable as it appeared. Parts of the moat had grown shallow, and bits of the wall had lost their mortar and crumbled. Iskandar had easily snuck twenty of his men inside. Now they waited in a home his informant had said was abandoned.

"Ready?" Hasan asked.

Iskandar's charge was to draw the garrison into the lower kastron and engage with them long enough for his father's group to emerge from their hiding places and seize the acropolis gatehouse. They wouldn't hold it long—just long enough to throw open the postern gate at the western tower, let in the remnant of their forces, and gather Byzia's wealth. There would be jewelry, coin, food, stores of wool, and captives to be sold as slaves. Iskandar's diversion needed to last only until his father sent the signal. Then he would join him at the top of the hill.

Iskandar had never before been so trusted and valued; he'd been given a task of importance second only to his father's. "Yes, I'm ready." Iskandar and Hasan joined the others inside. "Give the order."

Hasan spoke to the assembled ghazis. "The time has come to win glory in Allah's name. Take what you will from the townspeople, but keep your wits about you. Once the alarm is raised, find a good position to attack from so you'll be ready when the garrison arrives."

The men disappeared into courtyards. Most of them would have a substantial collection of trinkets and livestock before an alarm was raised. And the town was but a prelude to the plunder they would find in the acropolis.

The church bell sounded. Iskandar hadn't expected it to ring so soon, but it seemed someone had already noticed their presence.

"Come, Hasan. We wait for the garrison."

When the bell rang, Ivan turned to Helena, who stood beside him on the wall walk. "Is that an alarm?"

A line of worry creased Helena's forehead as she stared at the church in the town below. "Yes. The last time I heard it toll like that, Kyrios Basil and his men rode away the next morning to attack your army."

"Kostya wouldn't invade in winter, even if he were seeking revenge." Ivan scanned the surrounding landscape. The town in the lower kastron and the meadows surrounding the walls seemed calm. But that sound—he needed a weapon. "Could it be a fire?"

"No, the sound for a fire is different." The ringing stopped abruptly. "I suppose it was a false alarm."

Ivan wasn't sure he agreed. Nor, it seemed, did Gregoras, who soon led a group of twenty men through the gate and into the town. Ivan walked along the wall with Helena to where they could better see the garrison's hunt. Perhaps it was only an accidental alarm, or perhaps the person ringing the bell had been forced to stop.

Four armed men emerged from the southwest tower. They wore turbans and layers of long robes. One pointed to Helena and Ivan, and all drew long curved scimitars and advanced. At their foreign calls, three additional men appeared from the western tower, cutting off all routes of escape.

"Try to stay behind me," Ivan whispered. The odds were against them, but he would defend her as long as he could.

"But, Ivan, you have no weapon."

"I know."

Before all seven men could surround them, Ivan moved toward the group of three, taking Helena's hand and bringing her with him. One of them strode toward Ivan in challenge. Ivan stepped away from Helena to meet him. The bandit sneered at his unarmed opponent and brought his scimitar down swiftly. Even more swiftly, Ivan ducked to the side, ignoring

Helena's scream and escaping the swing of the curved sword. With the bandit off-balance, Ivan grabbed his opponent's arm with both hands and shoved the man's forearm into the stone wall. The bandit's grip on his scimitar slackened, and a moment later, it was in Ivan's hands. With a grunt and a powerful slash, Ivan sliced the bandit's head from his shoulders.

Ivan chanced a quick glance behind him, making sure Helena was unharmed. Her scream must have been from fear—none of the bandits had accosted her. Yet. Ivan had little time to plan as the other six closed in. Now that he held a sword, they approached with caution. Ivan didn't wait for them. He ran at the closest one and sliced his scimitar across the man's abdomen. Then he crossed blades with two of the others. They kept him busy, both of them fighting him at once, but he warded off their blows and pushed them back.

"Ivan, behind you!" Helena cried.

Ivan knelt and rolled away from the man who'd approached him from the rear. In a moment, he was back on his feet, holding his sword in a high guard position and facing a group of three. He thrust his stolen scimitar down, literally disarming one bandit. He kicked a skinny bandit between the legs and knocked him into the third man. The two slipped in a puddle of blood. Had the inner wall not stopped them, they would have plummeted to the bailey below.

The skinny one caught his balance and yelled as he charged toward Ivan. Ivan blocked the man's blow, held despite the man's unexpected strength, then threw him back. He smashed his hilt into the other man's face before slicing his neck. When the skinny one came forward again, Ivan slashed across his shoulder, sending the man to the ground.

Five of seven were now defeated. Ivan turned around, panting for breath, but Helena was no longer there. Several valuable moments passed as he searched for her, finally spotting her between the remaining bandits as they dragged her toward the wall's western tower. One had his hand over her mouth.

Ivan grabbed a second blade from a fallen bandit, then sprinted after the last two. When he'd nearly caught them, he threw one of his scimitars into the back of the man on Helena's left. The man groaned and fell. The last one shoved Helena to the ground and turned to Ivan.

This one was the leader. His clothing was more ornate than any of the others, and the gray of his eyebrows and beard showed greater age. He drew his scimitar and attacked.

The other bandits had been poorly trained and predictable. This man, in contrast, handled his scimitar well and took advantage of Ivan's fatigue. Ivan met every blow, but each clash of steel sent a shock up Ivan's arms and forced him a step back.

Slash. Clang. Step. Ivan blocked the blows again and again. Gregoras had ridden out with the soldiers, but he'd left the watchmen. There were always several on the wall walk. Why weren't they coming to his aid?

The leader lunged and parried, slowly pushing Ivan against the inner wall. He drove his scimitar down hard against Ivan's blade, trapping it against the stone. With his free hand, the man grabbed Ivan's throat and twisted, forcing Ivan's body into an awkward angle. With his knee, the enemy placed strategic pressure under Ivan's thigh. Slowly but firmly, Ivan was being pushed up the wall.

Helena screamed again, but Ivan didn't understand her words. It was only a matter of time until Ivan's opponent tossed him over the wall to his death. Ivan's vision grew blurry, but he could still see Helena on the ground, where she'd been thrown. Ivan clawed and yanked and tried to break free, but instead, he felt himself sliding closer and closer to the top of the wall. The man was too big, too strong.

If he did nothing, Helena would be left defenseless. In a split second, Ivan made his decision. He'd been gripping his scimitar with one hand and trying to pry his attacker's hand from his neck with the other. He released his weapon and grabbed at his opponent with both hands. The enemy suddenly pushed Ivan so he was lying on top of the inner wall, balanced on a stone ledge only the width of a hand. Ivan gripped the wall with his legs and used his arms to shift his enemy's momentum in a new direction. Ivan hauled the man across his chest until the bulk of his attacker's weight tipped over the wall and the man fell into the bailey below. He heard the man's cry, heard a dull thud, and squeezed his eyes shut. He leaned in toward safety and dropped back to the wall walk.

His chest heaved, desperately seeking air, and he allowed himself several unimpeded breaths before getting to his feet. He looked about for danger, but the men on the wall walk lay still, and the enemy in the bailey hadn't moved. Just to be sure, Ivan plucked up a scimitar and sent it downward so it landed in the man's back.

Ivan stumbled toward Helena. Her hands were bound in front of her, her eyes wide and her face pale. She looked as defenseless as a butterfly in a hailstorm.

"Are you hurt?" He knelt and touched her shoulder.

She shook her head as he used a discarded blade to cut through the rope binding her hands. The bandits had drawn the cords tight enough to leave welts on her wrists. When she was free, he helped her to her feet. Ivan was covered in blood, but she crumpled into him anyway. He felt her sobs more than he heard them. They made her entire body quiver.

"All is well now. They cannot hurt you anymore." He gently kissed her forehead as her tears wetted his tunic. He closed his eyes and leaned his head on hers. His throat still burned, and his body ached from the fight, but she was unharmed, and that was all that seemed to matter right then.

Eventually, she caught her breath and stilled her tears. "I'm sorry, Ivan."

"Sorry? Why?"

"You had to fight seven men all alone—and I was too terrified to do anything but watch."

"I've trained to fight bandits, and your hands were bound. I am simply grateful I didn't fail you."

She was silent for a time. "I have witnessed death before, but never like this. Loss of life is something to be grieved, and yet . . ." She trailed off.

Ivan looked down at her. Helena's head was still buried in his shoulder, but what must she think of him? He wasn't sure all seven were dead, but the hurt he'd inflicted had been intended. "Shall I give you a few moments alone?"

In answer, she pulled herself closer to him, so he held her and rested his cheek on her head again. The sun had sunk, and darkness spread across the slain bandits on the battlements. A haze of light glowed from the lower kastron, and the smell of smoke was strong, but weariness outweighed Ivan's curiosity. Even if it didn't, he wasn't ready to release Helena. He might have held her for hours despite the cold and despite his exhaustion. When the bandits had attacked, he'd been worried for himself, but he'd been terrified for her. Feeling her next to him was proof that she was safe.

The calm didn't last.

"Release her, you villain." Ivan recognized that voice. Demetrios.

He didn't obey. "She's not my prisoner." Ivan scowled at the group of soldiers approaching by torchlight. "She is free to go if she wishes, but the decision belongs to her, not to you."

Demetrios drew his sword, and the other men followed.

"Please, Demetrios, Gregoras." Helena lifted her head from Ivan's shoulder. "Did you not see the bodies lying dead as you approached? The threat is past. Put your swords away, and make no more threats upon my defender."

"Kyria Helena," Demetrios began, "we have been attacked. Don't you realize where the bandits came from? They are clearly Turkoman. Should we not be concerned when we find you a captive of their vassal?"

"You fool." Ivan flung a hand at the dead bandits. "My people did not swear fealty to rabble such as that. Do not cross me—I would hesitate only a little to add you to the tally of men slain today."

Their faces were shadowed, so Ivan couldn't see the men's reaction to his words. He didn't care what they thought. Helena stirred, looked up at him, and smiled softly—letting him know she was on his side. She would no doubt do her best to smooth things over now.

"Helena—you are wounded!" Demetrios rushed toward her.

"Nonsense," Helena said. "When they pushed me down, I was stunned but not injured."

Even as she spoke, Ivan motioned for a torch and looked her over until he saw the red bloodstain Demetrios had noticed spread over a large portion of her cloak.

"Your cloak is stained. Do you feel no pain?" Ivan asked her.

"None." Helena unfastened her heavy wool cloak. She studied the blood spot carefully, then flipped the fabric over. The spot on the underside was significantly smaller. Helena grasped both of Ivan's hands in hers. Though spotted with blood, his appeared normal, until she turned them over.

"The blood is yours." She pushed his sleeves up to reveal a long, thin cut on his right forearm. "Did you not know?"

Ivan shook his head. He was sore in many places, but he had assumed the sting in his arm was merely a bruise or a scrape. He didn't know which enemy blade had sliced his skin.

"We'll go to the surgery. I will tend you there."

"We'll bring the other wounded to you as well," Demetrios said.

"There are others?"

"Half the town was burned to the ground. Several are wounded. More are dead, including the watchmen who were patrolling the wall." Demetrios studied the bodies, then turned to Ivan, no longer quite so hostile. "You slew five? With no weapon?"

"I took one of their weapons. And I cut down seven."

"I see only five bodies."

"One is at the bottom of the wall." Ivan glanced over the parapet. The leader's body was still in the bailey. Then he walked toward the others. One was alive, though Ivan doubted that would be true for long. Part of his bowels hung from his abdomen. The skinny man that Ivan had slashed in the shoulder was gone. "One is fled. He had an injured shoulder."

Gregoras sent Niketas and three of the others in pursuit.

"What of my sister?" Helena asked. "Is Euphrosyne safe?"

No one answered.

"Is she?"

"I don't know, kyria." Demetrios crossed his arms. "We fought a pitched battle in the town. We didn't realize a group had infiltrated the acropolis."

Ivan grabbed one of the scimitars from the ground. "Let's find her."

Helena led him away at once. Demetrios followed. She ran down the stairs, across the bailey, and into the keep. Nothing seemed amiss, though Ivan had little time to look for evidence that a group of bandits had infiltrated. He followed Helena through the great hall, up a flight of stairs, and onto the top floor of the keep. Helena turned west, then stopped and banged loudly on a door before throwing it open. "Euphrosyne!"

Helena's sister knelt in prayer in front of an icon. She turned in confusion. "What's wrong?"

Helena sighed in relief. "Nothing. I suppose nothing is wrong if you are well. I'm sorry to have alarmed you."

She turned to go, but Ivan stopped her. "There may have been more than one group. She should come with us so I can protect her."

Demetrios cleared his throat.

Ivan relented. "So you can protect her, if you prefer, but she should come. Are there other ladies in the keep?"

"Kyria Domnica," Helena said. "I'll ask her to join us after I speak with Euphrosyne."

Helena went to her sister. Ivan barely heard their words, but soon, Euphrosyne nodded and followed Helena. They stopped at another door, and a pale, somber-looking woman of about twenty joined them.

When they reached the bailey, Ivan ran to the stables, worried about what a desperate raider trying to steal a horse might do to a small stableboy. Philippos looked up from his work of brushing a stallion. The injured Turk must have left another way.

"What happened, Ivan? You're covered in blood."

Ivan gave Philippos a summary and promised a fuller account later. Then he joined the others in the busy surgery. Blood coated Matthias from his neck to his waist. He was still conscious, but lines of pain marred his face.

"Will you help remove his clothes?" Helena asked him.

Ivan took off Matthias's corselet and cut away the ruined tunic. Helena wiped the blood away and examined the wound. A deep cut bit into the man's side. The swing hadn't been enough to slice through the ribs, but the broken skin bled profusely.

"It will need stitches." She had Ivan hold a wine-soaked cloth over the wound while she went to the shelves of supplies and took a needle and silk thread. When Matthias was sewn up, she bandaged his wound and told him to rest.

A man from the town appeared next, his hand over his left ear, or that was what Ivan thought until Helena pulled his hand away. The ear was gone. Helena cleaned the injury with wine and then bandaged it.

Euphrosyne's face grew gray as she watched.

"Come sit by the fire." Ivan offered her his arm, and she meekly followed him to a bench near the hearth. The fire was full tonight—Ivan wouldn't have been able to climb through the flue had a blaze this large burned the night he'd escaped.

As Helena finished bandaging a soldier with a slashed arm, Gregoras entered the chamber.

"Are there more for me to tend?" she asked.

"No, kyria. The others died before we could bring them."

Helena's lips pinched in sorrow.

"We think it is safe now, should Kyria Euphrosyne and Kyria Domnica wish to return to their chambers." Gregoras kept his voice calm, but pain showed in his eyes.

Ivan glanced from Euphrosyne to Gregoras. "You will escort them and leave a guard nearby to be sure they are safe?"

Gregoras looked as if he were ready to reject Ivan's suggestion, but then his face softened. Perhaps he could see the wisdom, even when it came from an enemy. "I'll see them to safety and arrange watchmen for the keep."

Gregoras left with the two women. Matthias and the other injured men rested on rush mats. Demetrios watched from the door.

"Now it is your turn, and I'm sorry to have kept you waiting so long." Helena reached for Ivan's hand and led him to a bench.

"The other wounds were more pressing."

"Perhaps. But you are the one who saved me from being carried off to a fate I dare not imagine."

Ivan thought about saying he was in her debt for all the times she had nursed him back to health, but he was afraid that would make their mutual debts cancel each other out. He preferred them to be entangled.

She wiped at his arm with a wine-soaked rag. "It's been a while since I have had to patch you up."

Ivan exhaled slowly at the alcohol's bite. "And while I appreciate your care, I hope it will be a long while before I shall need it again."

"As do I." She finished bandaging his wound but continued to hold his arm. "Thank you for defending me so valiantly against such overwhelming odds. I was terrified for myself but even more so for you." She glanced behind her, to the doorway. Demetrios conversed with someone in the other chamber. Helena leaned in and kissed Ivan's mouth for one brief but unforgettable moment. "Thank you for saving me."

It took Ivan several heartbeats to recover from his surprise. Had she kissed him as a thank-you or as something more? "You are most welcome, my lady."

"Are you finished?" Demetrios studied them with hard eyes. Perhaps he had seen part of the kiss.

"Yes." Helena took her supplies back to the shelves.

"Then, I will escort you back to your chambers now."

"I wish to stay with my patients." Helena began rolling an unused bandage.

Demetrios clenched his jaw and turned to Ivan. "Very well. I will escort the prisoner back to his chains."

Helena whirled around. "What?"

Demetrios folded his arms across his chest. "His injury is not serious. You can check it tomorrow. In the meantime, we have limited men, and there is a risk that more raiders are nearby. We can't leave him loose tonight."

"He cut down seven of the bandits. If you are short of men, arm him, and be glad for the boon to your strength. You cannot lock him in chains when he proved his loyalty by saving me!"

"He's to be chained at night. That was the agreement when we released him from the dungeon."

Helena moved in front of Ivan, as if to somehow protect him from Demetrios. "He's a hero, not a prisoner."

"I'm afraid I must insist."

Helena looked ready to argue further.

Ivan stood. "I'll go. But I hope you will release me and arm me if more trouble comes. We are allies when it comes to defeating the type of vermin we saw tonight."

The muscles of Demetrios's jaw clenched, but he nodded.

"Good night, my lady." Ivan watched Helena's lips, wondering if she would grant him another kiss another night, when they had more privacy. He took her hand for a moment, then Demetrios seized him by the shoulder and turned him toward the door. Ivan allowed Demetrios to escort him across the bailey and up to his cell in the northwest tower.

"You're a fool," Demetrios said as he locked the chains around Ivan's ankle.

"Am I? Why?"

"Fall in love with Kyria Helena if you wish, but she'll never be yours."

"Oh?"

"Last spring, my father intended to ask Kyrios Basil for her as my bride, but Callinicus spoke first. Now Callinicus is dead, and as soon as it is proper, my father will speak to Kyrios Basil. Kyria Helena has always been fair, and now that Leo is heir, her worth has increased considerably. Kyrios Basil will use her marriage strategically to reward his loyal tzaousios and his tzaousios's worthy son."

"Will Kyria Helena have no say?"

Demetrios stood. The keys jingled together ominously. "Why should she? Kyrios Basil knows best. And he's certainly not going to give her to the miserable enemy prisoner who captured his nephew and killed both his sons." He slammed the cell door closed behind him, locked it, and strode away.

That night, Ivan had a difficult time falling asleep. Part of the problem was his arm. The swollen flesh throbbed with pain. Small cuts on his hands and bruises on his back added to his discomfort. Worry, too, remained that more of the Turks had infiltrated the kastron and might return with ill will.

But most of the problem was Helena. Ivan hadn't recognized his own intentions until Demetrios had laid them out. The thought of Helena married to Demetrios was bitter. Demetrios would be gentler with a bride than with a prisoner, but that was small comfort, because Ivan wanted Helena for himself.

One other detail interfered with Ivan's sleep. His lips tingled with a sensation he was utterly unfamiliar with. The memory of Helena's mouth on his was so powerful and so pleasant that he would gladly fight seven men again if his reward would be the same. And he would battle an entire army if he could win her for his bride.

CHAPTER SEVENTEEN
IVAN'S DREAM

SOMETHING ABOUT IVAN SEEMED DIFFERENT in the days following the attack. As Helena watched him teach Philippos how to arm a crossbow, she finally realized what it was. Ivan's raw stubbornness had softened into sober purpose. For a moment, she wondered if the attack had frightened him, but there was no fear in his eyes, nor, did she think, in his heart. As she approached, he smiled, and the motion contained a small hint of something. Admiration? Love? Or was Helena simply hoping that he felt the same emotions she did?

Philippos demonstrated his new skill for her. The poor boy scarcely weighed enough to arm the crossbow, but what he lacked in size, he made up for in determination as he lay on his back and used his feet to push against the bow arms while he pulled the string back.

From what Ivan had said about his own childhood, these two were not so very different. Ivan had lacked health, and yet he had become so skilled a swordsman that he could single-handedly defeat a band of Turkish raiders. She doubted there was anything he couldn't do if he resolved to do it.

Philippos shot his bolt, hitting the center of the target.

"Well done, Philippos," she said.

"Thank you, kyria." Philippos bowed respectfully. He'd changed since Ivan had befriended him. He had always been a polite boy, eager to please, but now he carried himself with confidence instead of trepidation. "With your permission, I will take my leave now. I am to prepare Kyrios Basil's horse."

Ivan took the crossbow. "I'll put this away."

Philippos ran off.

Helena studied her former patient. "They let you in the armory now?"

"Niketas and Demetrios don't. Matthias and Gregoras do."

"Will you walk with me after you've returned it?" Euphrosyne had warned her not to spend so much time with Ivan, and Radomir had made his threats, but Helena didn't care. She wanted to be with him.

"Gladly, my lady." He glanced toward the battlements. "Do you dare tread the walls again?"

"I do indeed dare, especially if you are with me."

She walked with him to the armory, waiting outside while one of the soldiers accompanied him in. The last time she had been inside the armory had been the day after her betrothal to Callinicus. He had offered to sharpen her knives for her, and she had met him there, not realizing there was no one else about until he'd held her against the wall and kissed her, fondled her, and demanded her cooperation as his bride-to-be. If Gregoras hadn't happened upon them, she would have had to scream—or submit. Even now, she was grateful she didn't have to go inside, where the memories themselves might be sharp enough to cut.

As Ivan came back outside, he thanked the guard and then focused completely on Helena, as if she were the only other soul in the entire fortress. He was so different from Callinicus, from everyone else she had ever met. They took the stairs to the battlements, quiet and comfortable together. The breeze was almost warm. The worst of winter had passed, and spring was coming. Normally, she longed for the warmer weather, the new growth of flowers and herbs, the longer days. But when spring came this time, Ivan would leave, and when he left, she was unlikely to see him again. That thought brought pain so intense, she could barely breathe.

"Are you well, my lady?" Ivan softly took her elbow.

"I am."

The concern in his eyes told her he was not convinced.

She tried to smile, but the effort was insufficient. "I'm only realizing it is nearly spring." She turned toward the mountains and leaned between two merlons. "Soon, the pass will be open."

"Yes." He balanced against the wall.

"What will you do when you go home?" She glanced back at him and watched his face grow thoughtful.

"First, I will see my kin. Then I will travel to Sivi Gora. And then, perhaps, I will build a wall, not unlike this one."

"A wall?"

"I'm to inherit my maternal grandfather's lands. They include a mine and a town. Right now, it's scarcely more than a village surrounded by wooden palisades, but I intend to see it grow into a city, one well-defended and prosperous."

"Prosperous for you?" She'd never heard him speak of money, and its mention surprised her, for their conversations had been frequent, and she was certain he wasn't greedy.

"Not just for me. I want the workers to eat well, and I want trade to flourish. Those who do not mine or farm can prepare furs or make belts to sell in Niš or Belgrade. We'll have bakers and butchers and craftsmen along with the merchants."

Helena pictured Ivan governing a small city of flourishing craftsmen. "I shall look for trade from your city and coinage with your face on it. Župan Ivan, ruler of the richest mine in Serbia."

"Don't laugh. I'm serious in my wish. Give me twenty years of peace, and I will make a great city."

"I wasn't laughing."

His hand brushed over hers, and a pleasant warmth followed his touch. "I think you were near to laughing."

After that, she couldn't help it. She did laugh, but not because of his plans. It was more a long-awaited release of the giddy feelings being next to him brought out. His lips turned up, and she knew she hadn't hurt his feelings. "What will you do with your wealth, Ivan?" she asked.

"Keep the city safe, with a stone wall and a well-trained garrison. And build churches, hospitals, monasteries, convents, that sort of thing."

"To secure your spot in heaven?"

He smiled softly. "I certainly hope so. But it's not just that. Where there is trade, there is opportunity. If the son of a miner doesn't wish to mine, he can apprentice himself to a tradesman. If a meroph has several sons and splitting his lands would leave them with insufficient inheritance, one can go into trade or work in the mines or join a monastery. But we're not anywhere near big enough yet."

He offered her his arm as they walked north. "Before the Great Mortality, my grandparents had seven living children. After the plague hit Sivi Gora, only my grandfather and my mother remained alive. The other families were hit nearly as hard. My grandfather canceled all rents because there were so few merophs left alive. He didn't want to see cultivated land turn wild again, so he encouraged them to farm as much as they could. They give us a portion of their crops in exchange for use of the land. Most of them have sufficient to feed their families and sell a surplus, but a prosperous city will need food. More than we have at present."

"So, you need more merophs?"

"Yes. And if the merophs thrive, everyone else will too. Monks can store grain against times of famine; nuns can nurse the sick. And I will build a beautiful church, but I don't want to build it alone. The butchers' guild can purchase a stained-glass window, and the weavers' guild can provide a tapestry, and so on with the masons and blacksmiths, the leatherworkers and the bankers. Then it becomes their church too. Their monument to God."

"Your dream is beautiful, Ivan." Helena smiled at the passion in his voice. "But you ask for twenty years of peace, and I do not think you'll have so long." There were too many enemies—the Turks, the Hungarians, rival lords, bandits, and pirates. "It's a pity. I've met few people who would use peace as well as you would."

"I shall do the best I can with the peace I am given, be it small or large."

"Then, you will do well, however long you have."

"You would fit well in my dream, Kyria Helena." His voice went soft, earnest.

"Would I?" She had trouble keeping an even pace as they walked, and she felt her face grow warm.

"Yes. A prosperous city needs at least one midwife. A growing population is vital to my plans."

"And where would I live in this city?"

"In a stone house that befits a Greek princess. Three levels high, with a center courtyard, decorated by flowers and fountains."

She glanced at the keep. The walls were strong, but the rooms were dark, and she would not be sad to leave it. "Where would I sleep in this house?"

"In a fine bed with a wooden frame and a mattress filled with soft wool. You would have fur coverings in the winter and linen ones in the summer and as many feather-stuffed pillows as you like to rest your head on at night. Or if you have been up all night seeing to a delivery, you could sleep during the day. We'll add curtains to shut out the sun."

Helena paused beside the northwest tower and looked toward the mountains. Ivan came up behind her and rested his hands on her shoulders. She turned to face him, catching her breath as she realized how close they were to each other. She didn't dare move. Their bodies had been near before, but this time, it felt different. He was so close that she could pick out the green, brown, and gray flecks of his eyes. Awareness of his height, his strength, of the pleasant form of his face struck her like a flaming torch.

"Where would you live, and where would you sleep?" Ivan's voice came in a whisper now. "You would live in my palace and sleep in my bed, as my wife."

"You would have me for your bride?" In that moment, there was nothing she wanted more than to spend the rest of her life with him.

"I would." He raised a hand to caress her face. She closed her eyes and leaned into his touch. Their lips were a mere palm apart, and that thought was both frightening and exhilarating.

"Ivan, I . . ." He touched her hair with his other hand, and she sighed contentedly. His warm breath crossed her cheek. She wanted to be his completely, wanted his lips on her mouth, her neck, his fingers on her skin, wanted to sleep next to him in a soft bed in his far-off city. She was certain he was going to kiss her, and she longed for it, but he pulled away.

Disappointment chilled her. Was it wrong to desire a kiss so fiercely? She opened her eyes and saw the reason for Ivan's delay. Philippos and Demetrios walked toward them from the direction of the keep.

"Kyria Helena!" Philippos called.

She straightened her veil and swallowed back her regret at being interrupted. "Yes, Philippos?"

"A woman in town needs your help."

"I'll go with you," Ivan said. "It's not safe for you to travel alone, even to the lower kastron."

"If you are going, I will follow." Demetrios put a hand on the hilt of his sword. "We can't have you escaping while Kyria Helena is occupied with other matters."

Ivan huffed. "I've kept my promise for months; why do you doubt me now?"

"I never stopped doubting you." Demetrios stepped closer, as if to make his advantage in height more obvious. And yet, despite Demetrios's size, if there were a clash between them, Helena expected Ivan to come out victor. Demetrios was broader, but Ivan was quicker, and there was a passion to him that made everything he did seem more meaningful, from a soft caress to a distant dream.

She didn't want the men to test her theory. "You may both come, but you mustn't bother the woman. And we mustn't keep her waiting. There is often little I can do in the early phase other than comfort, but sometimes that is greatly needed."

"It is not the early phase," Philippos said.

"All the more reason to hurry."

Ivan laid the sleeping three-year-old down on a rush mat and covered him with a wool blanket. The boy had been frightened for his mother, but sleep had finally taken him. He was about Marko's age. Ivan missed his nephew, missed the rest of his family. He hadn't fully thought of it when he'd asked Helena to be his bride, but he was asking a great deal of her. It was customary for a woman to leave her family and join her husband's, but the distance from Byzia to Sivi Gora was greater than what was usually asked.

Demetrios sat on a bench near the fire, arms folded and eyes narrowed. How much of the near kiss had he seen? Ivan had meant to ask Helena how she felt about Demetrios, but he didn't think she loved him. She valued military prowess, no doubt, but Ivan thought she valued kindness even more, and she would want to decide her own fate.

"I'm going to walk through the town to make sure nothing is amiss." Ivan pulled his cloak around him. The raid and the fire had left part of the wall collapsed and a wide swath of homes destroyed. The kastron was vulnerable, especially the lower portion.

"You'll do no such thing." Demetrios stood and took out his sword.

"Then, you will? Our goal is the same—that Kyria Helena come to no harm tonight. Surely you agree it is prudent to patrol the town at least once a watch?"

Demetrios slowly nodded. "Yes, but I'll not leave you alone so you can sneak off while I'm away. Come with me."

"Agreed. But I will no longer put up with the type of treatment I've received from your men in the past. If you threaten me, I will defend myself."

"I wouldn't waste the effort on someone like you."

Ivan went to the curtain separating them from the birth room and stood in front of it. The mother was in the middle of a labor pain, so he waited to speak until it ended. "Helena?"

Helena pulled the curtain aside enough to see his face. "Yes?"

"Demetrios and I are going to patrol the town. We'll repeat the process throughout the night, so if we're not here, we'll return soon. The boy is asleep. Do you need anything?"

"No. But Martina is progressing slowly. I expect we'll be here all night."

"I wish you both well." Ivan wanted to ask her if she would accept his offer of marriage, because not knowing how she would answer was almost unbearable. But now was not the time.

He followed Demetrios out the door, through the courtyard, and onto the road. Demetrios made no attempt at conversation. Nor did Ivan. He had enough to concentrate on, looking for Turkish scouts and keeping an eye on Demetrios. They circled around the town and came back along the main street that ran all the way to the acropolis.

They went out again during the second and third watches of the night. There were guards posted throughout the kastron, but Ivan had snuck past them before, so they were fallible. In between patrols, he tried to sleep, but sounds of the woman's travails kept him awake.

"You're quiet on your feet, I'll give you that," Demetrios said when they went out again during the fourth watch.

"It comes from playing hide-and-seek with my cousin. And hunting on foot."

"We normally hunt on horseback."

Ivan stared at a shadow. It moved, but it was only a cat. "Župan Dragomir once broke his leg while hunting on horseback. After that, he thought it best to spend part of the hunt on foot. It encouraged stealth and forethought, both of which are valuable in battle."

"You know Dragomir well?"

"His grandson married my sister, so he is my kinsman."

Demetrios led the way back to the main road. "Kastrophylax Radomir says Dragomir cheated him of his inheritance."

"I know not the details of the disagreement Radomir had with his brother, but I do know he betrayed his people at Maritsa. He is responsible for the deaths of my father and my uncle, and I'll not forgive him for that. Župan Dragomir has shown himself to be a wise leader and a generous host. Radomir has shown himself to be malicious and prideful."

"I would argue with you, for the sake of argument, but I can think of nothing good to say about Radomir."

Ivan looked at Demetrios. Neither said anything for a moment, and then both of them chuckled.

Demetrios lowered his torch slightly. "My father and Kyrios Basil respect him, so he can't be all bad. But after staying up all night, it is hard to remember what they see in him."

"You may sleep if you wish. I have promised to stay until Kyria Helena releases me, and I'm a man of my word."

"Sometimes I wonder . . ."

"What?" Ivan asked.

"Had you been born a Greek instead of a Serb and had you been a comrade rather than an enemy, we might have been friends. At least until we both sought the same woman for a wife."

The woman in question pulled the curtain aside when they returned to the home. "She's developed a fever, and I'm out of malache. Can you fetch me more?"

"From the surgeon's home?" Ivan asked.

"No. I used the last of that on Matthias, but there should be more in the meadow where I took you for your Slava."

"What does it look like?" Ivan had only seen it dried and crushed.

"It will be dead now, but the roots will help. It grows white flowers in the spring and blooms all summer. Some of the bushes reach near your height. It's also called malua or marsh mallowe."

"I know it. We have it in our land as well. And I will find some for you." Ivan turned to leave again.

"And I will assist him," Demetrios said.

The trek through the town and out to the meadow didn't take long, and Demetrios's presence was no longer oppressive. It was a pity their relationship hadn't thawed ages ago.

Once or twice, Ivan had seen the meadow dusted with snow, but there was none now. A line of trees followed the curve of the river, making it easy to spot, even in the predawn light.

"Speak of the devil," Demetrios said. "That's Radomir there. What is he doing out so early?"

Ivan followed Demetrios's gaze, and anger welled up inside him. Radomir had left Ivan and Konstantin orphans, robbed Danilo of his father, and thrown their people under a Turkish shadow. Yet the man was free, riding a fine stallion back to the kastron he had charge over as kastrophylax.

"He should be punished for Maritsa," Ivan said.

"And you would be the one to punish him?"

"I would. But justice has waited almost thirteen years. It can wait a little longer if my current efforts can instead help Helena's patient."

Ivan searched for the remnants of last summer's malache. All the toothed, lobbed leaves were shriveled, and the white flowers had long ago disappeared, but they finally found a clump a few paces from the river. Ivan pulled it up and paused. "Get down," he whispered.

Demetrios obeyed. "Why?"

"Look across the river." Ivan pointed out two men with turbans and scimitars. "Turks. Dressed much like the ones I met on the wall a few days ago."

Demetrios drew his sword. "What are they doing here?"

"I suspect they're scouts, planning another attack. I'll follow and see if the band they report to is large or small. You should take the roots to Helena and warn Kyrios Basil."

"I cannot give you leave to chase them. I'll go."

"I'm the wiser choice. You said yourself I'm light on my feet. And Basil and Gregoras will heed a warning from you more than they'll heed a warning from me, especially if Radomir's presence was no coincidence."

Demetrios's eyes widened. "You think he's involved?"

"He betrayed his own people to the Turks. Why would he not do the same to you, should the opportunity arise?"

"But you are their vassal."

Ivan bristled at the reminder. "We give them our tribute, not our love."

"All the same, I will go, and you'll not argue, for I am armed, and I won't lend you my sword."

Ivan nodded once in agreement. He was the better choice, but the longer they debated, the harder it would be to track the scouts. Demetrios ran to the trees and disappeared from sight.

Helena felt wet curls on the top of the baby's head. "Just a few more pushes and it will be over."

Martina's energy was nearly spent, but she nodded and waited for the next pain. A neighbor had joined them, and she helped support Martina on the birthing chair. With the next contraction, Martina bore down, and the infant's head emerged fully.

Three loops of umbilical cord had passed around the infant's neck, and the baby's face was blue.

"The cord is strangling it!" There was panic in the neighbor's voice.

The slippery cord had pulled tight, so snug that Helena couldn't get her fingers under it, at least not at first. She'd seen cords wrapped around infants before, but never this tightly. Helena cradled the baby's head, frantically trying to find some slack in the cord so she could loosen it and unwrap it before the infant perished. Finally, the shoulders appeared, then the rest of the baby gushed out with Martina's remaining waters. Helena pried a finger under one of the loops and loosened it. She turned the flailing baby around, gaining just enough length to fit the loop over the baby's head. The final two coils were easy to remove after that.

Helena smiled with relief as the infant's mewling filled the air. "You have a beautiful son."

Tears welled in Martina's eyes as Helena placed the plump infant in her arms. His soft wail soon grew to a healthy cry.

The neighbor put a hand on Helena's elbow. "You saved that baby's life."

"I only followed my training." Helena finished with the afterbirth when it came, then cut the cord. As she washed the baby in water with a bit of soda ash in it, she pondered the woman's words. Might things have been different if she hadn't acted quickly? Had she changed the course of delivery?

Helena had assisted with many childbirths, but of the mothers and infants who'd survived, all would have lived, even without her help. Helena may have sped the process or eased the discomfort, but she hadn't altered the outcome. This one—this one felt different. Ever since her mother's death, Helena had dreamed of saving lives. If the neighbor woman were to be believed, that goal was finally a reality.

Ivan returned not long after the baby settled into a quiet watchfulness, but Demetrios didn't accompany him.

Helena wiped her hands and went to talk with him. "Where is Demetrios?"

"We saw something. I need to tell Kyrios Basil, but I don't think he'll believe me. Perhaps if you came—or convinced your sister?" He handed Helena a clump of malache root.

He wouldn't ask for help if it weren't important. "I'll join you as soon as I start the roots."

As Martina and her neighbor admired the new baby, Helena washed and chopped the roots, then set them in boiling water. She pulled the neighbor aside. "Use this on her skin, and also have her drink it once it is cooled. Her fever isn't high, but it could worsen. I'll return this afternoon."

She sorted the supplies and left those she might need later. She handed the rest to Ivan to carry. As soon as they were outside, she spoke. "What did you see?"

"Turkish scouts. And Radomir. I didn't see them together, but I suspect they met. Demetrios followed the scouts. They could be planning another attack."

"A pity it had to happen today." She told him about the birth, about how the infant might have died.

"I'm sorry to pull you away from your triumph."

"When you put it like that, I feel guilty of excessive pride."

Ivan placed a hand on her shoulder. "You did well, and I'm happy for you. It is your dream to save babies and their mothers, and that dream came true today. Give the glory to God, but don't hesitate to enjoy the lives your hand has preserved."

The warmth of emotion pricked at her eyes. "How did you come to know my heart so well?"

"I would seek to know it better. I know I ask much, but I meant what I said on the wall. I would have you for my bride, if you are willing."

Helena smiled, glad he hadn't changed his mind, because there was nothing she wanted more. "My heart desires it. But the choice is my lord's, not mine."

Ivan's lips pulled down. "In that case, I regret trying to escape so often, for I fear Kyrios Basil will be firmly set against me."

When they arrived in the acropolis, Kyrios Basil stood in the bailey with Gregoras and Radomir. She hoped Ivan wouldn't ask for her hand immediately, because the kephale and tzaousios looked at Ivan with disdain. The kastrophylax had a similar expression but directed at her, probably because she hadn't followed his advice.

"Where is Demetrios?" Gregoras strode over to Ivan. "He went with you, did he not?"

"Yes. And I would speak to you and Kyrios Basil of what happened, but I prefer to tell only the two of you."

"Radomir will be privy to whatever you say, boy." Kyrios Basil folded his arms across his chest. "Where is Demetrios?"

Ivan launched a glare at Radomir and planted his feet, as if bracing for battle. "We went to the meadow to gather herbs and saw two Turkish scouts. Demetrios followed them. I believe he'll report back soon as to whether their group is small or large. What's more, we saw Radomir riding away from the meadow as we arrived. I believe he was meeting the scouts."

"Lies!" Radomir's voice was a snarl. "You murdered Demetrios and concocted this story to throw us off."

Ivan wouldn't murder anyone in cold blood—Helena knew that. But the other men would think only of what he'd done in battle, and an icy fear crept into her chest.

Ivan scowled. "Why would I kill my guard and then return to the kastron? If I wanted to escape, I would have fled. The Turks I fought on the battlements were real enough. So were the men I saw in the meadow."

Radomir huffed. "If they've returned, no doubt it's because you're in league with them. Demetrios saw your meeting, and you slew him to keep his silence."

Ivan opened his mouth to speak, but Basil spoke first. "Niketas! Paulus! Put him in the dungeon." As they ran over, their footsteps echoed like thunder claps. "If Demetrios returns, he can verify the story. If not, we can assume the prisoner is guilty. We've offered him far too much freedom, and he has taken advantage of us miserably."

"And what of Radomir?" Ivan asked as the two soldiers grabbed his arms, making him drop the birthing chair and the other supplies he'd been carrying. "He's a traitor!"

Kyrios Basil frowned. "He has served me well for many years. I'll not throw him in chains because someone like you accuses him."

Ivan yanked his arm free of Paulus's grip. "You need to warn the paroikoi and prepare the kastron for siege."

Niketas bashed the hilt of his sword into the back of Ivan's head.

"You mustn't hurt him!" Helena cried as Ivan slumped to the ground, unconscious. Helplessness welled up in her, just like the times she had watched women bleed to death and had been unable to stop it.

She tried to follow the guards as they dragged Ivan away, but Gregoras stepped in front of her. "Kyria Helena, if you leave this matter alone, we can perhaps overlook your latest indiscretion. But if you persist, we will have cause to doubt your loyalty."

Chapter Eighteen
Waiting for the Storm

Iskandar paced across the rugs of his father's tent, waiting for his scouts to return.

His father was dead—that much was clear. His band had never taken the gatehouse and had never sent the signal, so Iskandar had pulled his men from the kastron. But he hadn't given up hope of taking Byzia. If anything, he was more determined now. After years of craving respect and trust, he'd finally earned it only to lose it with his father's death. He wouldn't rest until he had his vengeance.

"Iskandar?" Hasan parted the opening.

"Have the scouts returned?"

"No. But a messenger has arrived from Edirne. Shall I send him in?"

Iskandar surveyed his tent, wondering what impression the unadorned panels and faded cushions would give. "He may enter."

The messenger removed his felt cap when he came inside, revealing a full head of coarse black hair. "Peace be unto you. I seek Abdullah bin Isa."

"Peace be unto you. Abdullah bin Isa is dead. I am his son."

The messenger took a moment to look Iskandar over from head to foot. "I bring word from your kinsman, Kasim bin Yazid."

Iskandar's half sister, Saruca, was Kasim's second wife. The first had been barren, and Iskandar's father had considered it no small triumph to marry his daughter to someone as close to the sultan as Kasim. "How is Saruca?" She was Iskandar's favorite sibling. She'd sometimes laughed when Nasuh had made fun of Iskandar's Vlach heritage, but she'd never initiated the torments, and she'd tended Iskandar's wounds after more than one scuffle.

"She has borne Kasim two sons."

His sister had reason to be happy, and he was glad for that. "Praise be to Allah. What is your name?"

"Cemal bin Salih."

"Welcome, Cemal. I look forward to Kasim's message."

"He says he is grateful for the news your father sent. He himself has been given the task of humbling the rebellious Serbs. He has had dealings with Rivak's župan in the past and looks forward to punishing him."

"With an army?" Iskandar was set on raiding Byzia, but Rivak was a richer target. If his sister's husband was sacking Rivak, he wanted to be part of it. He wouldn't abandon his quest for vengeance, but revenge on Byzia could wait.

"Kasim will use diplomatic means. He wishes you well and has asked me to serve you for the time being."

Iskandar eyed Cemal. Though not particularly tall, he was bulky with muscle. Was Iskandar to be honored that Kasim had sent help, or was Cemal a spy? "Are you a horseman or a foot soldier?"

"Either, depending on the need. But he did not send me to fight with saber or bow. My talent is bringing down walls, and he'll not need me in Rivak."

Iskandar hadn't planned a siege of Byzia's kastron. He preferred to lure the army out and destroy them in the open. Still, he wouldn't turn Cemal aside. He might prove useful.

"Also," Cemal continued, "some of Kasim's men seek an opportunity for plunder. They ride a day behind me, forty in number. If you will grant them an equal share in the pillage, they will serve you until Kasim again has need of them."

Forty men, plus a miner? That would bring Iskandar's group to one hundred. There was little they couldn't do with that many men. "Their share will be equal to my men's."

"That is what they ask."

Iskandar couldn't have been more pleased if he'd been granted a timar by Sultan Murad himself. He guided Cemal back outside and called for Hasan.

"Yes?"

"See that Cemal is fed and his horse cared for. Provide him a place to sleep. He is an honored guest, and will be with us for some time."

Hasan bowed slightly. "It shall be done. And the scouts have arrived."

"Good. Send them to my tent."

Iskandar didn't have long to wait. The two scouts entered, a prisoner held between them with his hands tied behind his back.

Ahmed shoved the man forward so he fell on his knees. "We caught him following us."

Iskandar studied the captive, a fair-haired Greek warrior. The man looked up and glared at Iskandar, and Iskandar recognized him. He switched from Turkish to Greek. "Why is the tzaousios's son following my men?"

"I will tell you nothing."

Iskandar laughed and spoke in Turkish. "He says he will tell us nothing. We shall see. What did you learn?"

Ahmed bowed. "It is as Davud said. Your father and everyone else in the party were killed by a Serb warrior."

"A Serb?"

"One they hold for ransom."

"And their strength?"

"About fifty, most of them foot soldiers with little training."

Iskandar would set a trap for them, luring them out by showing a small portion of his men so the Greeks would think they had the advantage. It had worked before. Allah willing, it would work again. He drew his scimitar and placed the blade against the prisoner's cheek. "Did anyone else see my scouts?"

The man didn't answer.

"If you don't cooperate, you're of no use to me, and I won't bother keeping you alive."

"As I said before, I will tell you nothing."

The defiance in the statement galled Iskandar. The soldier ought to be groveling, addressing Iskandar with respect rather than contempt. "So be it." He swung his scimitar and sliced the man's head from his shoulders.

Iskandar pulled back his robe so it wouldn't be stained with the blood gushing onto the carpet of his tent. He didn't regret striking down the tzaousios's son, but the damage to the rug was unfortunate. Next time, he would do his killing outside.

When the men wouldn't listen to her, Helena sought out her sister. Euphrosyne sat in her chamber, embroidering an infant-sized tunic.

"The Turks may be planning an attack right now. We have to prepare. And what's more, Ivan is the best swordsman we have. We ought to arm him, not throw him in the dungeon."

"Helena, listen to yourself," Euphrosyne's voice snapped. "You're repeating word for word what he's told you. His people are subject to the Turks. Why would he help us fight them?"

"He has before. I watched him strike down seven on the wall the night they attacked. He will be on the side of right, on the side of freedom."

Euphrosyne put the tunic aside and stood. "If I did not already hate him for capturing Leo, then I would hate him for what he has done to you. I warned you not to spend so much time with him. He's made you blind to reason, and now you believe everything he says."

Helena took a step back. She had never seen her sister so angry before. "Why should I not believe him? He's never spoken falsely before."

"Only to gain your confidence. If he's behaved well during the winter, it's because the weather has not been conducive to travel. I have no doubt that if we released him as a scout, he would flee home, and then Leo would remain their prisoner indefinitely."

"But what if he's right? Will you not help me? Help me release an innocent man from prison? Help me prepare the paroikoi for war?"

"War? Don't be ridiculous." Euphrosyne crossed her arms. "I will help you by seeing that Ivan stays in chains so he cannot further poison your mind."

"Euphrosyne, no!" If she continued shouting, it would only give her sister more evidence that she was too caught up in Ivan's fate, so Helena lowered her voice before continuing. "Do not punish him because you're disappointed in me."

Euphrosyne turned to the fire and didn't answer.

Helena left, swallowing back a mix of hurt and worry. Euphrosyne had turned on her, Ivan was in chains, and the entire pronoia seemed in danger of imminent attack. She didn't know how to mend the rift with her sister, free Ivan, or protect Byzia, but she did have responsibilities to Martina and her newborn son that couldn't wait until the other problems were solved, so Helena returned to her patient.

When she arrived, the new infant suckled at his mother's breast, and the mother's fever was gone. Helena said a silent prayer of gratitude. So many things had gone wrong that morning, but not for Martina and her baby.

Since her patient was well, Helena didn't stay long. She passed through the gatehouse and turned to the tower, walking down the cold, oppressive staircase. Luck was with her. Matthias stood watch.

"Matthias? Are you well enough for guard duty?" His fever had broken the day before, and she'd sent him home to his wife. She'd told him to rest, not to keep watch in a dank dungeon.

"This is light enough work. Though, to be honest, kyria, I was sitting until I heard your footsteps."

Helena glanced into the blackness of the cell. "May I see him?"

"Officially, he is allowed no visitors. But I'll let you in, for he told me what happened, and I believe him."

Once inside, it took time for her eyes to adjust to the darkness. "Ivan?" She heard him stirring before she picked out his form near the wall, struggling to his feet.

Helena went to him and felt the back of his head, fingering a large welt. "How hard did they hit you?"

"Which time?"

She was confused for a moment, then understood. The guards had beaten him again. "Did they break anything?"

"No. I don't suppose it's quite as satisfying to pummel a man who can't react, so I got off lightly."

She shivered through her thick cloak. "I'm so sorry, Ivan."

"You've nothing to apologize for."

"No, I do." She took his hands, feeling the iron cuffs around his wrists. "I should have let you go long ago, but I'll do it now. I release you from your promise. You are free to go whenever you can. I only wish I'd released you when you weren't locked in chains. Can you ever forgive me for making you stay so long?"

"You would have me return home now and leave you to face a Turkish attack alone?" She couldn't see the details of his expression but thought she heard a smile in his voice. "Nay, I will share your fate and defend you with my life, if I am able."

"I hate to see you here again, when you've tried to protect us." She stepped closer, and he lifted his shackled hands over her head, then lowered his arms so he was holding her. She leaned into his warmth and rested her head near his collarbone.

His lips brushed against her temple, and she no longer noticed the dungeon's damp chill. "This time is not so awful. My shoulder and leg are whole. And I've won your heart. That makes even a dungeon seem pleasant because it is near you. Now I intend to win your hand, and I shall put as much effort into that quest as I put into my escape attempts before you captured me with a promise."

"In that case, I am certain you'll succeed." The dungeon was black and cold, but he was warm and strong, and there was nowhere else she would rather be. She felt in the darkness, following the muscles of his arms up to his shoulders. Next, her fingers found his jaw and then his lips.

"Will you kiss me?" he whispered. "Just once."

His plea caught her by surprise, but she didn't hesitate, didn't give herself time to think it through. She placed a hand on one of his cheeks, guiding his face closer to hers. Then she met his lips with her own. He answered with a sweetness and a hunger that she felt all the way to her toes. Time seemed to halt, and all other senses faded except for Ivan's arms surrounding her and his lips exploring hers, imploring her for more. In the back of her mind, she knew no one outside the dungeon would approve, but she didn't care. Enemy or no, she loved him.

She ended the kiss to catch her breath but kept her face near his.

"I was mistaken, my lady." Ivan sounded as out of breath as she was. "One kiss such as that could never be enough, for it is a wonder that leaves me wanting ever more."

She kissed him again, running a hand through his hair to his neck, drinking him in. The darkness seemed to focus all her senses on him and on the way her lips tingled and her heart quickened. She sighed and almost pulled away, but he leaned in and continued the kiss until she felt dizzy in the most pleasant sort of way.

Matthias stomped in the hallway, and the door squeaked on its hinges as he pulled it outward. "Kyria, my watch will soon end. I think it best if you leave before Paulus comes."

Ivan lifted his chained hands again, releasing her. "The townspeople and the villagers should come to the acropolis for safety. And they must bring or destroy all their food. If there is to be a siege, they must leave nothing for the Turks."

"I'll warn them." She felt his lips with her fingers one final time, then turned to go.

"Father Symeon will help you," Matthias said as she walked past him.

"Thank you." As she climbed the stairs, she wondered how much Matthias had heard. But more than that, she wondered how long it would be until she could kiss Ivan again. She felt as light as a dove, buoyed up by a contentment that cradled her heart and brightened her hope.

The feeling dimmed when she approached the gatehouse and saw Gregoras and Radomir.

"Where are you going, Kyria Helena?" Gregoras asked. His voice and the set of his face seemed grim. Demetrios still hadn't returned; no doubt the tzaousios feared for his son.

"A woman gave birth this morning," Helena said. "I need to check on her and the baby."

Radomir frowned, but Gregoras waved her on.

She did visit Martina and the baby again, so as not to lie. They were both doing well. Then, following the advice she'd received in the dungeon, she went to Father Symeon, and he and two other messengers set out to warn the villages. Word passed around the town. The unrepaired wall and ruined homes made it easy to convince them that they were in danger, and the townsfolk began preparing for attack.

The fortress, in contrast, did nothing. For two days, Ivan stayed in the dungeon. Demetrios remained missing, cementing Kyrios Basil's conviction that Ivan was guilty of murder. Helena tried to visit Ivan again, but Euphrosyne and several of the guards seemed to hound her steps, and she daren't go while anyone other than Matthias stood watch. So she stole no kisses from Ivan, nor was she able to report on the kephale's stubborn refusal to prepare.

On the morning of the third day, Helena climbed to the wall walk and spotted a band of twelve paroikoi straggling into the kastron. As they came along the winding road through the town, she picked out one elderly man, three women, and eight children. The smallest child was carried on his mother's hip. The oldest child was perhaps thirteen. Among them was Constantina, the mother of the laboring woman Helena hadn't been able to save.

When they passed through the gatehouse, Niketas led them across the bailey into the keep. Helena walked parallel to them along the eastern wall. When she followed them into the keep's hall, a score of voices assaulted her senses.

Matthias stood near the door.

"What's happening?" she asked him.

"They were attacked. Their village is in ashes now."

"Ghazis?"

"Yes."

Kyrios Basil appeared from another doorway and walked to the front of the hall where Gregoras and Radomir waited. "Silence. I will listen to the reports one at a time."

Constantina stepped forward and bowed. "We discussed who should speak along the way, lord. I am prepared to tell you all."

Kyrios Basil motioned for her to proceed.

"They came yesterday, an hour before sunset. We posted lookouts after we received your warning, but even so, we had little time to prepare."

"What warning?" Gregoras asked.

"The message the priest brought, telling us to be wary of Turkish raiders and ordering us to gather in our foodstuffs. We've no spring plantings yet, and most of our harvest was burned, but we had our animals near."

"We sent no messenger." Gregoras scanned the hall, suspicion showing in his narrowed eyes and downturned lips. Helena fought the temptation to hide behind Matthias.

"Never mind that now," Kyrios Basil said. "Continue."

"They came with one of our soldiers." Constantina kept her eyes on the floor.

"What?"

"Part of him, anyway. His head was stuck on a pole, and they posted it in the crossroads as warning."

Gregoras gripped the back of a nearby chair. "Which of our soldiers?"

"One of the young leaders. With brown eyes and golden hair."

Helena slapped a hand over her mouth to hold back a cry. Demetrios. She had argued with him from time to time, but their quarrels hadn't erased her fondness for him. He didn't deserve a death so cruel.

Kyrios Basil laid a hand on Gregoras's shoulder and spoke gently to the woman. "Then what happened?"

"They said if we cooperated, they would do us no harm. They rounded us up at the crossroads. But some of the young women are fair, and when they wanted to have their way with them, we resisted. We had hidden our bows and our sickles." Tears rolled down Constantina's cheeks, though her voice was calm. "Their weapons were better than ours. They carried some of the young off. They slaughtered the rest, save us. We ran and hid."

Kyrios Basil seemed to falter as shock wrapped itself around him. "But there are twenty hearths in that village, perhaps a few more. Out of twenty families, you are all that remain?"

"Yes, lord. Other than those they took for slaves."

"How many in the Turkish party?"

"I saw twenty, lord."

The hall fell silent. Helena's heart sank. Demetrios killed. The villagers slaughtered. So many lost, even after a warning.

Kyrios Basil raised his voice so all would hear. "Gather our fighting men. At the sixth hour, we ride."

The next three hours were a hustle of activity. Helena bandaged a few small wounds on the refugees while the men prepared for war. She looked around the surgery—she still thought of it as belonging to Petros, but she supposed it was hers now. She feared to think of how full it might be when the army returned. Army. It was hardly an army. A dozen archers and two score men-at-arms was all they could muster.

They rode out, leaving Euphrosyne in charge of the kastron because she was Leo's wife, and Leo was the heir. The able-bodied men from the town went with them, leaving the upper and lower kastron largely defenseless. Matthias stayed because his wound was not yet healed. The only other men were under the age of fifteen, over the age of sixty, or clasped in chains in the dungeon.

"Euphrosyne?"

Helena's sister turned from the elderly steward she'd been speaking with. "I can guess what you want, and the answer is no. I will not release a prisoner while we are so inadequately guarded."

"But his warning proved true! The Turks did attack, just as he said they would. And if the battle goes ill, we may be next. You can double our strength by releasing him."

"But can we trust that strength?"

"Yes!" Helena gripped her sister's hands. "Yes, you can trust Ivan."

"He captured Leo."

"Because Leo was trying to kill his brother. Were I a warrior, I would do the same to defend you."

Euphrosyne glowered. "How do I know he won't slay our remaining guard and flee?"

"Because he promised to defend me."

"You personally?"

Helena glanced around, grateful the steward had gone. "Yes. He wishes to marry me."

"What?"

"And I wish to marry him."

"You are brainsick, Helena!"

"Not as brainsick as you if you do not release him when we are so desperate for his help. He is skilled and kind and honest. If for but a moment you could look past how he came to be here, you would recognize that he is a good man." Helena sank to her knees, still holding her sister's hands. "Please unlock his chains."

The clink of keys drew Ivan's attention and caused a swirl of nervous anticipation in his stomach. Were some of the garrison planning to pummel him for amusement? He squinted in the glare of torchlight as three shadows entered the dungeon. Helena, Matthias, and Euphrosyne. His worry turned to hope.

Helena took the keys from Matthias and bent to unlock the shackles fettered about his ankles. "You were right, Ivan. The Turks attacked."

"Where?"

"One of the far villages. Kyrios Basil led the men against the ghazis who did it. We hope our men will return in strength. But if they fail, we'll need your help."

"You shall have it, my lady."

Helena brushed her fingers against his cheek. He'd lost track of time in the dungeon, but however long had passed, memory of Helena and her kisses had sustained him. The path before him was as clear as calm water: he would defend Helena, and then he would marry her.

She unlocked the chains about his hands and examined his wrists. "They cut into your skin again, but not as badly."

Ivan stood, not feeling completely steady after sitting in chains for so long. "When did they set out?"

"They left midday," Euphrosyne said. "The eleventh hour now approaches."

"I imagine we have until dawn, at least. Probably longer, but we shouldn't waste any time." Ivan and the others climbed the stairs and emerged into the bailey. A few people were about, but no soldiers. "How many men are left?"

"You," Matthias said. "Me. A few gray-haired servants. And a handful of townsfolk."

They couldn't send help to the villages, and if the army failed, the villages would be vulnerable. "We ought to bring the other villagers to the kastron as soon as we can."

"I'll go warn them," Helena said.

Ivan caught her hand. He didn't think the attack would come tonight, but he didn't want to risk raiders catching her. "We'll find messengers among the servants. You and your sister ought to organize the people as they come. If we're besieged, we can't afford chaos within the walls. And you should prepare for wounded."

The elderly steward and the blacksmith's apprentice volunteered to warn the two villages that hadn't yet been attacked. As they rode off, Ivan, Matthias, and Philippos walked the acropolis wall. It had always been something that had held Ivan in. Now he looked at it with new eyes, trying to determine how well it would keep someone out. The walls of the lower kastron were still damaged. "I don't think we can defend the lower portion. We'll have to pull everyone into the acropolis."

Matthias nodded. "I agree."

"I'll warn them." Philippos looked to Ivan for permission, and when Ivan gave his nod, the boy went on foot to gather the town.

A river bordered the portion of the acropolis nearest the keep. A thick moat surrounded the rest of the kastron, and a thinner one divided the lower and upper portions. But the section separating the acropolis from the town had long been neglected. "Can we dig that stretch out?" Ivan pointed toward it.

"Yes. I'll see that it's done."

As the townsfolk came, Matthias took the able-bodied and put them to work digging out the moat by torchlight through the first two watches of the night. There were few men, for most had marched with Kyrios Basil, but the paroikoi women were accustomed to plowing fields and harvesting crops. They easily adjusted to moat sledging.

The bailey filled with animals as the people arrived with their flocks. Ivan put Philippos and some of the servants to work bringing weapons to the top of the walls, where they would be ready for use. He ordered others to pile firewood near vast pots that could be filled with liquid and boiled if a siege came. Ivan looked in on Helena once, but then a group from Theodora's village arrived, and Helena was too busy directing the newcomers to pause for conversation. The group included more men. He hoped they at least knew how to aim a crossbow.

During the third watch of the night, they finished their work on the moat. Then, while Matthias organized the lookouts, Ivan slept.

The next day dawned cloudless. Ivan relieved Matthias and gazed over the plains, meadows, and homes within sight. He had at his command a group of untested village lads and a handful of age-bent paroikoi. One of the graybeards confessed he could no longer see across the bailey, leaving three trained archers who could help Ivan and Matthias man the walls. Philippos, too, would be of use with a bow. The others might hurl stones or pour boiling water on the attackers if they came near the walls. But that was the extent of their strength. Would it be enough?

"I brought your breakfast."

Ivan turned at Helena's voice. "Surely you have more important things to do than bring me a bowl of porridge." He took it anyway when she held it out to him, because his stomach cramped with hunger.

"There are no wounded yet. I've assigned everyone a place to sleep, and the older children are feeding the animals, so my tasks are completed for now. All have had their breakfasts, except you and Matthias. I thought it best to let him sleep."

"Yes, let him sleep as long as he can. He's a good man."

"Can two good men defend an acropolis?" He heard the fear in her voice but also the trust. Whatever he said, she would believe.

Ivan had been pondering that question all morning. "Two good men, a handful of boys, and a few elderly farmers—I suppose it depends on what we're defending it from. I doubt twenty Turkish raiders can take the acropolis with its drawbridge up and its moat full. Kyrios Basil's attack ought to reduce their numbers. And the garrison knows the land. Even if the ghazis defeat them in battle, the local men will travel more swiftly than the Turks, so I expect we'll have reinforcements."

"You are kind to defend us when we've treated you so horribly."

Ivan set his bowl on the wall's ledge and ran his finger along the veil covering Helena's hair, following it to her chin. "You have ever been kind to me. And I would be a poor župan indeed if I stood by and let a band of Turkish raiders slaughter undefended paroikoi." He pulled his eyes away from Helena and back to keeping watch. "In my country, merophs work two days a week on their lord's lands. I think I shall change it. They shall work one day in my fields and spend the other day training for war. I don't wish my people to be defenseless should an enemy attack. I would have every man between the age of fifteen and fifty capable of defending my lands and my bride."

She put her hand on his. "I hope to be that bride."

"I will have no other."

"I fear Kyrios Basil will say no."

Ivan expected as much, but he wouldn't let Basil's rejection thwart his plans. "If the attack comes and I defend the kastron, I think I will have atoned, in his eyes, for my earlier escapes. If the attack does not come and Kyrios Basil returns to find the villagers' animals befouling his bailey, I may have to resort to abducting you, if I am ever released from the dungeon, where I am certain he will throw me." Helena's lips pulled up with mirth. "There's a long tradition of Serb grooms abducting their brides. It's mostly pageantry now, but it goes back to pagan times. Tell me, Helena, would you resist me as a captor?"

"I would welcome you as my liberator. But I prefer to gain permission, if it is possible."

Ivan wasn't sure which outcome he preferred. There was something innately appealing about sending Helena secret messages and stealing her away against Basil's will. But he understood her desire to seek her lord's approval.

Helena neared the wall to peer through an embrasure.

Ivan followed her gaze and picked out the cloud of dust still distant on the road. "I think we'll have word soon."

She held his arm as they watched what they assumed was a messenger draw closer. "Ivan, be careful. Either way, I'm concerned for your safety."

He kissed her forehead, inhaling her sweet scent. "Keeping you safe is my first goal. Staying alive to marry you is my second."

Eventually, the cloud separated into two riders. When they passed through the lower kastron, Ivan could tell they were Greek, not Turk. But why only two? They couldn't be riding for reinforcements because they'd left none behind. Perhaps they delivered news of victory, but to whom?

"I recognize them," Helena said. "Gregoras and Christophoros."

Ivan and Helena took the stairs to the bailey and pushed their way through the goats, sheep, pigs, and chickens. Ivan and one of the lads who had pelted him with rocks when he'd been in the pillory lowered the drawbridge and raised the portcullis.

Gregoras and Christophoros rode in. The tzaousios looked around, taking in the animals, the paroikoi children, and Ivan. "You are free and have not fled?"

"I am preparing for siege, though I hope my preparations won't be needed."

"Where is Kyria Euphrosyne?"

"In her chamber," Helena said. "I'll fetch her. And Matthias."

Gregoras and Christophoros dismounted, and Philippos came to take the horses. Blood stained Gregoras's uniform, and Christophoros sagged on his feet as he dismounted.

"Papa!"

Theodora ran past Ivan, her braided hair bouncing behind her as she fell into Christophoros's arms. Ivan was grateful for the glimpse—it reminded him that fighting the Turks would benefit more than just the aristocracy who lived in the acropolis. All were in danger. All would be required to sacrifice for victory. And all would enjoy the freedom if they prevailed.

When Euphrosyne, Helena, Matthias, and Ivan were gathered outside the gatehouse, Gregoras addressed them. "It may have been only twenty men who razed the village, but we ran into far more. They ambushed us with double our number. Kyrios Basil was slain."

Euphrosyne gasped.

Gregoras glanced at her. "Your husband is now the kephale, my lady. In his absence, you lead the pronoia."

"Are more men coming?" Euphrosyne asked.

"A few were taken prisoner. Most of the others fell. Christophoros and I were the only two who escaped."

"Do they pursue you?" Ivan asked.

"Yes. But some of them are on foot, and they have their baggage wagons, so they won't travel swiftly. But they are coming, and when they come, we must surrender. If we resist, they'll destroy us. If we arrange terms, we'll be spared."

"We ought to fight." Ivan laid a hand on the stone of the gatehouse. "The acropolis walls are strong. The Turks cannot long hold siege in winter. No crops are in the fields, and we've brought in all the livestock. What will they live on while they wait for us to eat through our stores? We can outlast them."

Euphrosyne hesitated, looking from Gregoras to Ivan and then back again. Helena, in contrast, seemed calm and stood with Ivan.

Gregoras straightened himself to his full height. "Kyria Euphrosyne, I strongly recommend we come to terms. Ivan did not see them in action, and he has little reason to care if we're massacred when our resistance fails."

"If you come to terms with them, they will take your prettiest girls for the sultan's harem and your healthiest boys for his janissaries." Ivan had heard of the child tax, and he loathed the forced conversion that followed, from Christian to Muslim, from family to military foe. "The remainder will be left with extravagant taxes to pay the bill of tribute, and your paroikoi will either starve to make payment, or you'll renege on your agreement when they cannot pay, and then the Turks will come back in greater numbers. Stand up to them now, or you and your people are as good as slaves."

Gregoras glared at Ivan. "You say that only because you're not one of us."

"No. I say it because it's true and because I would not have the few people in Byzia who have befriended me suffer the way my people have under Ottoman vassalage. I know what it's like to bear that yoke. And I know what it's like to have others dictate whether you will eat and if you will see the sky. Why surrender your freedom when you are surrounded by a strong wall and your stores are filled with food?"

Gregoras cleared his throat and turned to Euphrosyne. "I will repeat what I said earlier, kyria: I recommend we come to terms."

"They'll only keep the terms while it is convenient for them to do so," Ivan said.

Gregoras ignored him. "You stand for Kyrios Basil now, Kyria Euphrosyne."

"No," Euphrosyne whispered. "I stand not for Kyrios Basil but for Leo. What would Leo wish?" She glanced around at the walls, at the goats and the pigs in the bailey, at the paroikoi hauling water from the cistern. "How many days can we last?"

Helena answered. "I don't have an exact count, and we still wait for the last village, but the cistern is full. If we're cautious, it should last us until Lent, even with no rain. The paroikoi brought grain. Combined with our own stores, I think we can last one hundred days, and that does not include the animals."

"But what will the animals eat and drink?" Gregoras gestured to the full bailey. "There is enough fodder for the horses, but this many animals will devour it within a fortnight."

"Eat them first," Ivan said. "It will save the grain and be good for morale."

Euphrosyne shook her head. "If we eat all the animals, how will we replace them, even if we do withstand the siege?"

"Animals can be replaced with coin. Freedom, once lost, can only be won with blood." Ivan kept an eye on the road. It was still clear.

"How large is the Turkish party?" Euphrosyne asked.

"Close to a hundred," Gregoras said. "Very few were slain."

"A hundred?" Euphrosyne's mouth hung open for a moment. "Against how many?"

"Three men-at-arms." Ivan counted himself, Matthias, and Gregoras. "Five archers." Ivan counted Christophoros, Philippos, and the three older paroikoi who had served Basil before. "Plus a dozen or so lads who can be trained within a week to be of some use."

"A hundred against eight?" Euphrosyne looked as if she would side with Gregoras.

Ivan had to change her mind before she made a mistake. "It is not that simple. Look at the wall." Ivan stretched his hand out, gesturing at the stones. "It is surrounded by water so they cannot approach it. If they wish to harm us, they'll have to come within range of our bows. If they attack, we are sheltered. If they camp and try to wait us out, they will run out of food. We have the advantage, regardless of their numbers."

The veil over Euphrosyne's head flapped in the wind as she thought. She looked at Gregoras, at the animals, and at her sister. "Ivan, would you risk my sister's safety for your pride?"

"No, kyria. Nor would I risk her freedom because of a fear that we can conquer."

Euphrosyne reached for Helena's hand and gripped it with her own. "Then, I believe Leo would want us to fight."

CHAPTER NINETEEN
SIEGE

THE LAST GROUP OF VILLAGERS came with their flocks and the remnants of their harvest at the eleventh hour. The Turks came at nightfall.

Ivan and Gregoras watched from the wall. After agreeing to resist the Turks, Euphrosyne had given Gregoras command of the defenses. Resignation still outweighed enthusiasm, but the tzaousios took to the task with competence and organized the men much as Ivan would have. He also prepared Greek fire, mixing as much as he could, given their limited supply of bitumen and sulfur. Ivan had thought the weapon that burned even on water was only legend, but Gregoras assured him it was real. He primed the copper and bronze syphons to propel the fire at the enemy and gathered the wine vinegar to douse it should the Turks have a similar incendiary weapon to use against the defenders.

They had a supply of crossbows, large and small, and a pair of petroboloi, but no teams to work them. They had all the bows, lances, and lamellar corselets they could want in the armory. And they had the food and water that would make time their ally. A calm resignation settled over the acropolis.

Campfires began to glitter in the field to the west of the kastron, but the fires were too distant to hit with arrows. A pair of Turks rode into the lower kastron, visible in the moonlight. "Scouts." Ivan raised his bow.

"No, not yet." Gregoras lifted his hand.

"Those two are either the leaders or their most experienced scouts. Striking them down will weaken our enemy."

"If you provoke them, we'll have to fight tonight."

"Then let us fight tonight. They're weary from their march."

Gregoras shook his head. "My eyes no longer see so well in the dark. I'll be of more use in daylight. Matthias is not fully healed, and Christophoros is weary from our ride. A night's rest will do them good. And neither of us has had a chance to find out what sort of villagers came across the draw-bridge before we shut it. Let us set a watch and rest. The attack will come soon enough."

Ivan tried to hide a yawn.

Gregoras's jaw hardened into something almost like a smile. "When did you last sleep?"

"Last night's fourth watch."

"Sleep the first three watches tonight. You can organize the men before dawn. Go get some rest."

"But who will stand guard?"

The tzaousios had just admitted to poor vision. Ivan didn't trust him to maintain an all-night vigil.

"Send up a dozen lads. Then sleep."

Ivan relented. Helena and Euphrosyne had assigned the paroikoi places in the keep and barracks. Ivan slept with the other soldiers in Radomir's old home. He found the home's former owner distasteful, but the arrangements were an improvement over sleeping in chains.

Philippos shook him awake before dawn. Ivan climbed to the top of the wall and found a well-rested Matthias and eight village women maintaining watch.

"Women?" Ivan asked.

"Just during the night. Had we been attacked, I would have sent them away, but now the men will be more rested."

The moon had set, and the sun had not yet risen. Ivan peered at the Turkish camp and counted a score of glowing campfires. "Any movement throughout the night?"

"No. They have pickets, I suppose. But they would have had a long march yesterday. I imagine they needed the rest. As did we."

Animals filled the bailey, so Ivan took the wall to the keep. He didn't take time to count them, but he supposed close to a hundred paroikoi slept in the hall. He didn't wish to wake the women and children, but he wanted to speak with the men and older boys. He woke a handful of them.

"We have to organize. Have all the men and boys over twelve assemble in the bailey." Ivan went to the barracks next and did the same thing.

Thirty came. Less than half were between the ages of twenty and forty, but Ivan himself was a few years short of twenty, and he didn't think youth an impediment. Fifteen claimed to have skill with the bow or crossbow. Ivan tested them as the early morning light roused the animals and illuminated the targets he had placed on the wall for Philippos.

Seven were excellent. Another three were competent. The other five could work the crossbow but couldn't hit the target.

Ivan chose two older men from the skilled group and assigned them the task of training the others. "You five will help man the wall." Ivan pointed to the others with good aim. "The rest of you will practice. If called, you will help cast stones at the enemy or assist in loading crossbows for those more likely to hit their targets."

Ivan returned to the wall walk in time to see the new day stretch itself over the enemy camp like a golden piece of silk.

Matthias came to stand beside him. "They've had breakfast and groomed their horses. I suppose they'll attack eventually, but it seems they do not wish to attack on empty bellies."

Not until the sixth hour of the day, when the sun was high and shadows were short, did five riders approach under a flag of truce.

Ivan watched from the wall. Philippos was with him. "Go get Gregoras," Ivan told him.

Philippos ran off, and by the time the Turks had reached the moat in front of the western tower, Gregoras was climbing the last stair onto the wall.

"I am Iskandar bin Abdullah, ghazi of Sultan Murad, leader of the Divinely Protected Well-Flourishing Absolute Domain of the House of Osman. You will surrender to me, or we will enslave and destroy you." The man who spoke was about thirty years of age, with leather armor over blue robes. But Ivan spent more time studying the man to his left, Radomir.

Ivan looked to Gregoras to answer and was surprised to see rage in his eyes.

"Iskandar bin Abdullah, you have plagued us long enough. I remember your face—you led us into needless battle at harvest time, with false tales of Serb atrocities. You are the one who burned our fields! You will pay for it! And you will pay for the ambush you drew us into two days ago. On my word, either you or I will die before this is finished!" Gregoras turned to his former comrade. "And you, Radomir! Twice traitor! You will burn in hell for what you have done! No penance can wipe out your sin!"

Radomir's charger stamped its feet, but Radomir held it steady. "Don't be a fool, Gregoras. We offer you terms. Surrender, and pledge your loyalty to the sultan. What is a thousand hyperpyra a year if it buys your protection from the Ottomans? Be wise, my old friend. There cannot be more than five of you left to defend the acropolis. Leo is lord now. Give him something to come home to. He was never quick to fight and would not be so now."

"Shall I shoot them?" Ivan slipped an arrow from the quiver at his waist and nocked it onto the bowstring.

"No." Gregoras spoke softly. For a moment, Ivan thought Gregoras might give in to the Turks, but he continued, speaking only to Ivan. "We will honor the flag of truce. And he's right. Leo wasn't eager to attack your brother's men because he wasn't convinced they burned the fields. But now we know who was responsible, so not even Leo would hesitate." Gregoras stood taller. "The talks are over. Leave before I let my archers have you."

Radomir laughed. "You have no archers. Unless you are referring to that Serbian filth who stands beside you. Surrender. Or prepare for death."

Radomir, Iskandar, and the other horsemen turned and rode back to their camp.

Gregoras watched them go with a grimace on his face. "We will be avenged, you and I." He clasped Ivan on the shoulder. "Me, for my son and my lord. You, for the battle that left you prisoner here for a long, needless winter."

Ivan had never doubted the need to resist, but Radomir's visit renewed his determination. The same seemed true for Gregoras, who threw passion and energy into their preparations.

"You watch here for now. The moat is most narrow between the upper and lower kastron. Be prepared to move if necessary." Gregoras assigned one of the better village archers to a spot on the wall walk between the gatehouse and the southeast tower. "Christophoros, take the southwest corner. They might not know it, but the moat is partially filled there."

"We dug it out," Ivan said.

Gregoras grunted. "In that case, I hope Radomir remembers it was once shallow. If they attack there, they'll have a harder task than they realized."

The sun shifted, and as the ninth hour approached, the ranks of Turkish raiders came forward for battle. Their archers, perhaps two score in number, formed a line twenty paces from the wall. Horsemen waited behind, just out of bow range. On order from Iskandar, the Turkish archers released their projectiles at the acropolis. Their swift arrows rained over the walls, tapping onto the battlements and into the courtyard below. Ivan had cleared everyone from the bailey when the enemy had marched forth, so the only thing the Turks hit were the livestock. But that didn't make the shower of arrows any less intimidating.

Ivan had a composite bow and three crossbows among his siege weapons. He could launch arrows more quickly with a bow, but a crossbow sent its bolts with greater force. While the Turkish archers, standing in an orderly line, awaited the command for their next volley, Ivan shot two of them with crossbows. He shot a third as Iskandar gave his next order, then ducked behind the wall when the next deluge of Turkish arrows fell. Philippos took the emptied crossbows and gave them new bolts, lying on his back and using hands and feet to pull the string back.

"Can I try?" Philippos asked as he finished reloading.

Ivan looked at the eagerness in Philippos's eyes and at the sharp points of the fallen Turkish arrows and suddenly understood why Konstantin had insisted that Ivan stay with him in the cart even when Ivan would have been more useful as part of the rear guard. Sometimes, the needs of the heart clashed with the needs of the battle. Ivan didn't want Philippos to get hurt, but he understood the boy's desire, and he couldn't deny him the chance to fight for his freedom. "Wait until I say."

Ivan peered through the embrasure and shot another archer. Turkish arrows had a better range and were more accurate than the Greek counterparts, but they were also lighter and hit with less force. He wasn't sure Philippos's too-large hauberk would stop a well-aimed arrow, but between the chain mail and the wall, perhaps Ivan could keep the boy safe. "They're getting ready for the next volley. After it hits, you may aim."

The Turks released another hail of arrows. Then Philippos, Ivan, and several other archers shot back. Philippos made his first kill.

Ivan kept close watch on Philippos as the afternoon wore on. The Turks gradually lost their synchronization, which made it harder to return shots. Gregoras had issued orders to change position after every five shots, so the small number of defenders, mostly hidden and constantly moving, made difficult targets for their enemy.

The Turks pulled back as the sun sank below the horizon. Ivan watched them withdraw to their tents, wondering when they would come again and what they would try. He paced the walls, making sure none of the men were wounded. An arrow had glanced along Christophoros's arm, but the armor he wore had protected the skin. The others, too, were unharmed.

As darkness settled, the cooks prepared a solemn feast. The horses and few cows had all been safe in the stables, as had as many of the flocks as could fit there or in the unused buildings of the acropolis. But plenty of pigs, sheep, goats, and fowls had met their end and would now be used to feed the defenders and the defended.

Ivan had never eaten in the acropolis great hall before. He sat across from Gregoras on a bench before a long rectangular table, sharing a rack of lamb seasoned with marjoram and coriander. Matthias was on duty outside, with lookouts taken from the villagers.

No one ate so much meat under normal circumstances, and that made the mood almost festive. Ivan was sure the cooks and butchers would preserve much of it, but for now, everyone was allowed to eat their fill. He was glad it wasn't a fast day.

"We held well today. We hurt them more than they hurt us," Gregoras said between bites. "But it will take more than that to make them leave. Tonight, I want to organize the watch differently. We must take care not to overtire our men, but if there's an attack, we must have instant reinforcements." Gregoras looked beyond Ivan and motioned for someone to join them.

To Ivan's delight, Helena approached and sat beside him. Women often dined at separate tables, but tonight was different.

"How went the day for you?" Gregoras asked.

"The children were restless, but we managed. I organized a group of women to shift supplies around. They cleared one of the vaults at ground level so we can put animals there, though I know not how well they'll like it."

"They'll like it better than being skewered by arrows." Gregoras took another bite of his meat.

"We've also cleaned out the saddle room so more animals can be sheltered there. The villagers do not wish to eat all their flocks, if it can be avoided."

Helena's hand lay in her lap. Ivan took it in his own beneath the table. "Put the sheep and goats away first. Pigs have larger litters. They'll be easier to replace."

Helena nodded her agreement.

A bell sounded. Ivan jumped to his feet and grabbed his sword, arrows, and still-strung bow and ran from the hall, Gregoras not far behind him.

"Fire!" someone shouted.

The buildings along the eastern wall were made of stone. They wouldn't burn. But the stable, storage room, and barracks on the western side were made of wood, and the stable's roof was only thatch. Ivan recognized the source of the fire as dozens of flame-lit arrows clattered onto the bailey and burrowed into the more susceptible roofs. The majority of the arrows fell on the more vulnerable side. As former kastrophylax, Radomir knew all the weak points of the kastron's defenses, and he would have told the Turks where to aim.

"Get the horses!" Ivan called to the men running around the bailey, tripping over panicked sheep and frightened chickens.

Ivan went to help, but Gregoras held his shoulder. "I'll organize them here. See to the men on the walls. The fire could be cover for an attack."

Ivan took the steps to the top of the wall two at a time and found Matthias directing the counterfire along the west wall. He had only a handful of archers, and the enemy had cover of darkness, so he was having little success.

"I sent the women to the armory, where they would be safe, but that means no one is watching the eastern wall."

"I'll look." Ivan rushed to ensure they weren't under attack from more than one side.

The southern wall where the acropolis and town met appeared as it had the last time he'd looked, but from the eastern wall, above the surgeon's stone home, Ivan spied shadows moving near the moat below. He waited for the moon to come from behind a cloud and cast its light, and when it shone, it revealed a dozen enemies who carried logs and ladders toward the acropolis. While the defenders fought the fire, the Turks intended to sneak over the wall.

Ivan aimed his bow and hit one, then another. The cries of his victims sounded over the crack of the flames and the shouts of those who fought the fire. The Turks shot back, but Ivan had the wall for protection. He shot a third enemy before the rest scattered into the black night, leaving behind their partial bridge. Ivan would deal with it later. First, he had to ensure there weren't any other attacks.

When he reached the top of the keep, the full extent of the fires was visible. The river protected the keep walls, and the river was thicker than the moat, so he moved quickly along the wall there, trusting the water to protect that part of the acropolis. He slowed as he rounded the corner and headed past the bathhouse, back to Matthias and the others.

Ivan shot five arrows into the Turkish archers still casting their fiery shafts over the wall. They were more distant than the other group had been, so he couldn't see if any fell, but the Turkish archers soon withdrew.

Ivan looked into the bailey. It seemed Gregoras had saved the barracks. The stables still smoldered, but as Ivan watched, a line of villagers relayed earthenware jars of water and shovel-loads of manure onto the flames.

When he was certain the Turks were gone, Ivan circled the walls once more, finding them calm. When he returned to the bailey, the flames had died out. Torches set in brackets outside the church and the barracks cast a dim light on what was left of the stables.

Gregoras nudged aside a goat and walked to meet Ivan. "We saved the horses. So they can be shot tomorrow by Turkish arrows." He jerked his head in frustration, then gestured to the saddle room and the barracks. "The damage to those is minor, so that's something."

"They tried to come over the wall, there." Ivan pointed to the surgeon's house. "Can you spare a few men to help me retrieve the equipment they left?"

Gregoras nodded. "Yes. Radomir undoubtedly told them about the postern there."

Ivan knew there was a postern gate in the western tower—he'd been hauled through it once before. He hadn't known there were more. "How many gates are there?"

"Three. One in the western tower. One in the eastern. And the gatehouse."

Ivan took in the exhausted faces of the paroikoi who'd fought the fire and then the dead animals littering the bailey. "Did we suffer any casualties?"

"Three were injured. I sent them to the surgeon's house and fetched Kyria Helena to care for them."

"How serious?"

"One is severe. The others less so. Wait here." Gregoras disappeared up the western tower and returned with Matthias. Ivan followed them to the eastern tower.

"They caught us by surprise tonight." Gregoras grunted as he unfastened and pulled open a doorway scarcely big enough for a man. "But we can outlast them. We'll water the barracks roof tomorrow night, same with the saddle room. There is little they can burn after that."

Matthias motioned for Ivan to grab a set of nearby planks, which they used to create a footbridge across the moat. Gregoras covered them from the doorway while three village women and two archers watched from above to warn of any approaching enemy. Once across the moat, Ivan checked the bodies of the men he'd shot. They were all dead. He helped Matthias bring the ladders across the moat so the enemy couldn't retrieve them. When they and the footbridge were back inside, Gregoras closed and secured the postern again.

Other than the bleating of goats and lowing of cows, all was quiet. But they knew the Turks would attack again.

Helena cut an arrow from a village woman's upper arm and searched the wound, finding fragments of wool cloak and cotton tunic. She picked them out and washed the wound with wine, then stitched it together. The woman was silent while Helena worked. Helena had helped her deliver twins two years before, and she had been brave then as well.

Helena bandaged the arm and hoped it would heal well. "Rest it as much as you can until the wound closes."

The next patient was a boy, perhaps thirteen years old. An arrow had grazed his thigh but hadn't stuck there. Helena pulled up the boy's tunic and motioned for him to take off his hose.

His young face set in a grimace. "Can't you heal me while I'm dressed?"

"I must see the wound to clean and treat it."

He frowned.

"Come, you are acting like Ivan. Normally, it is wise to stay clothed, but now is an exception."

"Like Ivan? The man who leads the siege?"

Gregoras was the nominal leader, but Helena wasn't surprised that the boy looked to Ivan instead. "Yes. Ivan came to me with an injured leg. Except his wound was on the left thigh, and yours is on the right. And he had other wounds as well. Are you hurt elsewhere?"

The boy shook his head. And then he took off his hose so Helena could better see the injury. His tunic came to his knees, so he was able to maintain most of his modesty. She cleaned the wound with wine, which caused the poor youth to yelp, but the salve she used seemed to soothe him. She covered the injury with a clean bandage.

"The cut will continue to hurt for a few days, but it's not deep, so you will recover. For now, you must rest."

He nodded.

The third patient lay under a thin linen cloth. She was a village woman, and the Turkish arrow had struck her too near the heart. She had died soon after being brought inside.

Helena heard the door open and went to the front chamber. Ivan stood in the doorway, a torch in hand. The armor he wore made him seem invincible, but she looked him over, fearing he was injured.

He put his torch in a nearby bracket. "I heard some are wounded."

"Yes."

"Three?"

Helena nodded.

"How are they?"

"Two are bandaged. If they escape infection, they ought to heal. The third is dead."

Ivan frowned. Then he opened his arms, and she stepped into his embrace. His armor made him feel different, and he smelled of smoke and river, but she drew comfort from his strength and sympathy.

"I'm sorry, Helena," he whispered. "I didn't mean for any of the villagers to be harmed."

War was ugly and unpredictable, and they were only at the beginning. "Promise me it will be worth it in the end."

"It will. We'll withstand them, and your lands shall remain free."

Helena gripped him tighter. She could ignore her fear when she stayed busy, but deep down, she felt trapped. They had walls to protect them, but compared to the walls of Constantinople, they were like twigs to a log. There were few defenders, they couldn't send for aid, and not everyone was as strong as Ivan. "One of the men from town said God has forsaken us, and that is why we're under siege. Perhaps he's right. I've seen so many times when good has not won." She thought of all the babies she had lost and of the mothers.

"Sometimes, it is not the absence of God's blessing but instead a lack of effort that keeps us from our desires."

"You think you can change God's will?"

"No. But I do not believe the God who created us intended us to be miserable. He won't save us from the Turks if we do not try. But if we do our best, He'll guide our efforts."

She raised her face to look at him, and his hazel eyes seemed to capture her own. She'd always believed she had little control over her life, but Ivan was starting to change that perception. If anyone could change their future and reorder their fate, he could.

"I will do everything in my power to defend you, my lady."

Her heart filled with peace. "Then, I have nothing to fear."

CHAPTER TWENTY
SILENCE AND SHADOW

ON THE SECOND DAY OF the siege, the Turks used manjaniqs to hurl stones at the curtain wall. The paroikoi lowered rugs and bales of wool to lessen the shock to the stone. The walls held, but several goats were smashed by the projectiles. Gregoras tried to train a group of youthful paroikoi to operate a petrobola, but catapulting with accuracy took practice, and the enemy was too dispersed for the inexperienced team to hit.

During the third day of the siege, the Turks attempted another attack, similar to the first day's but from behind wagons and shields. It kept Ivan and the other defenders from resting, but neither side drew blood.

On the fourth night, the Turks infiltrated the lower kastron, pulled down a long section of wall, and launched a night raid on the acropolis. One man made it to the top of the fortress walls before Matthias beheaded him and cast the ladder off.

When the sun set on the fifth day, Iskandar's men brought in a battering ram, shielded by a roof laden with wet animal hides. The main gate held but only because Gregoras blasted the attackers with Greek fire, scorching the ram and its operators.

By the sixth day, the Turkish manjaniq teams were so accurate that one boulder hurled from a far-off siege engine came within a cubit of Ivan's position on the tower.

And so it went.

Ivan gradually moved archers from training to duty. Their store of arrows and bolts was adequate, but Ivan didn't want to waste any, so he made the paroikoi practice until they could hit the center of their target nine out of ten shots and then repeat their skill the day after.

A fortnight into the siege, fewer animals filled the upper kastron because they'd made room for goats, sheep, and cows in the acropolis offices. Pigs, chickens, and geese still roamed the bailey. The besieged had food, water, and more archers.

But on the fifteenth day of the siege, exhaustion made Ivan stumble down the tower stairs on his way to bed. The next day, he nearly fell asleep on watch. He noticed frequent yawns from Matthias and Gregoras, and he found Philippos snoring softly when he was supposed to be standing vigil.

Something had to change. The handful of men inside the acropolis grew wearier with each passing day. A paroikoi named Bardas had recognized the sound of miners at work. The Turks were attempting to excavate beneath the walls, and the besieged didn't have the manpower to try a countermine. The enemy had begun their work sheltered in the homes of the lower acropolis, so none of the defenders knew when the mine had started or how close it was to their walls.

Matthias joined Ivan on the battlements. "If they make it under the tower and start a fire, they'll bring the wall down. And if our walls are breached, we're finished."

"We need more men."

Matthias half chuckled. "Yes. But I don't know how we're supposed to get them. We could send a messenger out, but even if he made it to Thessaloniki, it would take time for them to send reinforcements. And they've got their hands full there. Çandarlı Halil Pasha threatens siege. Manuel won't want to provoke Murad's vizier any more than he already has."

"Iskandar is a ghazi. He does his own will, not the will of the sultan or the sultan's vizier."

"For now. Ghazis have been given official positions before, when they're successful."

"We will make sure Iskandar is not successful." Ivan pointed to the Turkish camp. "There are men in that camp who can help us outlast the siege."

"Why would the Turks fight for us instead of Iskandar? They aren't yet starving."

"Not the Turks. Their prisoners."

Matthias put his hands between the crenelated top of the wall and looked out. "How would we get them?"

"With silence and shadow."

Ivan waited until the third watch of the night to set his plan in motion.

"I still don't approve," Gregoras said. "If something goes wrong, we're finished."

"But if something goes right, we're victorious." Ivan removed his cloak and adjusted his leather chest strap as Matthias came into the armory, still rubbing sleep from his eyes. Three others, men from the villages, were already prepared. "We've known about the mine for two days, but they may have started it the night they arrived. We must end things before they undermine our walls. I dare not wait any longer."

"And if you fail tonight, are we to surrender?" a feminine voice asked.

Ivan turned to see Euphrosyne standing with hands on her hips. Helena stood behind her, bleary-eyed and quiet.

"I won't fail."

Euphrosyne turned to her sister. "Talk some sense into him. He'll listen to you."

"Does everyone in the acropolis know our plans?" Ivan asked Gregoras.

"No." Gregoras looked over the row of swords and picked out a sharp spathion. "But Leo's wife deserves to know of your gamble."

Ivan turned to the ladies in time to see Euphrosyne nudge her sister with her elbow.

"What do you plan?" Helena's eyes had an apologetic cast, as if she wanted to trust Ivan but wasn't quite willing to reject her sister's request.

"A raid on the Turkish camp. We'll free the prisoners and set fire to their supplies. If we succeed, we'll have more men, and they'll have to raise the siege earlier because their stores will be gone."

"And if not?" Euphrosyne asked.

"If not, we will be even more short of men." Gregoras folded his arms across his chest. "And when the Turks bring down our walls, they will take the acropolis."

"If they destroy the wall, we're already too weak to stop them." Ivan helped Matthias dress in a hip-length sheet of lamellar. "And if we try to starve them out, who do you think will starve first? The Turks or their prisoners?"

Helena glanced at her sister. "It may be a gamble, but I trust Ivan's judgment. We should let them go."

"I think it prudent to exercise caution," Euphrosyne said.

"If we stay behind the walls, the Turks will finish their tunnel and take the acropolis. If we go out and are slain, the Turks will finish their tunnel and take the acropolis." Ivan handed an iron helmet to Matthias. "This is our only chance to change that fate."

A vein on Euphrosyne's neck twitched, either in fear or anger. "Why did you not mention this when we decided to resist?"

"I'm sorry, kyria. I did not expect a group of ghazis to have the skill to mine. But we did resist. It's too late to change that decision. But I can change the direction the siege is headed tonight."

Euphrosyne sighed and nodded a lukewarm approval. "If your skill is half as great as your arrogance, we have nothing to worry about."

"Euphrosyne!" Helena's eyes widened. "He is risking his life for our benefit. How can you insult him?"

Euphrosyne turned to leave. "Easily. I have only to remember Leo."

Helena watched her sister go, then turned to Ivan. "I apologize for her behavior."

Ivan didn't mind the insults if they were followed by Helena's defense. He took her hand for a moment. "You're not responsible for her words. No doubt she misses her husband and grows weary of sharing her home with the occupants of three villages and one town."

A smile crept across Helena's face, warming her countenance. It disappeared when Philippos came into the armory and selected a lamellar cuirass and a pair of knee-high greaves. "Surely you're not taking Philippos? He is too young!"

"Not so young that he can expect mercy should the acropolis fall. He moves with stealth, and his aim is true, even in the dark. But no, I'll not take him to the camp. He'll stay near the wall to guard the bridge to the postern."

Gregoras gave the boy the sword he'd picked out earlier. Ivan ran his hand along the long, triangular cavalry shields before grabbing a smaller round one made of wood, animal hides, and iron. He slung it over his shoulder and motioned Helena toward the bailey.

"You should be sleeping," he said to her.

"I cannot sleep while you are outside the walls."

He took her hand again. "In that case, perhaps you should prepare the surgery. I hope there will be no need for your healing skills, but I imagine some of the prisoners will need your assistance, even if our raid goes exactly as planned."

"Does anything ever go exactly as planned?" Helena turned toward him, her lips drawn with worry.

"No." Ivan hesitated, then ran his fingers along her cheek. "Sometimes, they are better."

She relaxed with his touch. "Be careful. I couldn't bear it if you did not return."

Ivan touched her soft lips with his thumb. He wanted to kiss her mouth, but they weren't alone. "I shall do all I can to return to you, my revered lady."

Gregoras and Philippos left the armory. Ivan kissed Helena's hand before following the tzaousios and stableboy to the western tower.

"I regret my earlier remarks," Gregoras said. "You're right. We have two unpleasant options. Of the two, this is the better choice. God go with you. We'll monitor as best we can from the walls." Gregoras handed Ivan a small trumpet with a leather strap. "Three bursts and we'll open the main gate and send out what strength we have. Use it only as a last resort, for if we open the gates, there is no guarantee we can keep the enemy out."

Ivan tied the horn to his belt, positioning it where it wouldn't hit his sword or dagger. Matthias, Bardas, Isaakios, and Himerius waited at the western postern.

"Have you noticed any watchmen?" Ivan asked Isaakios, who had come from the wall walk.

"Not this night, nor any other. They must keep their sentries close to camp."

"Then, I will have to silence them." Ivan drew his dagger from its sheath and tested the blade for sharpness. Sneaking up on a Turkish sentry and slitting his throat was a different type of war, but if he didn't kill them during the night, within a few days, they would breach the walls and slaughter all who sheltered inside the acropolis. Father Symeon had absolved the garrison of their sins at sunset, so Ivan's soul was clean.

They laid the footbridge over the moat, and Ivan was the first across. Matthias came next, then Philippos, then Bardas. The man's bow case banged against his spathion. Ivan glanced around. Would the sound carry to the Turkish camp? As the last two men crossed, Ivan helped Bardas rearrange his weapons so he'd be silent. Ivan forced himself to relax, but he couldn't ease the tight sensation in the pit of his stomach. So much rode on the success of their mission—his life, Helena's life, and the future of every man, woman, and child inside the acropolis.

Radomir yawned. "I'm not sure this is wise. Would it not be better to wait until the tunnel is finished and the wall brought down?"

Annoyance flashed in Iskandar's chest, but it quickly subsided. "You told me yourself they can't have more than three or four decently trained men inside the acropolis. If we disrupt their sleep tonight and tomorrow, it will be easier to defeat them when the wall is breached."

"Won't your soldiers be just as weary if they have to stage raids around the clock to keep the defenders occupied?"

"I am more concerned with bad morale than with weary bodies. Allah favors the bold. And so do my men." Iskandar didn't add that their supplies were dwindling. If he failed to fill his men's bellies, they'd desert him. "We've given the defenders too many quiet nights. I don't want them to have so much as an hour of peace from this night forth. Come. We leave at once."

"As you wish." Radomir gestured his submission with a lowered head and followed Iskandar outside.

The wind bit into Iskandar's nose as he gathered the men he would need. He'd selected Radomir so he could point out which areas of the acropolis were most vulnerable to flame. He took with him five others. He would use this raid to train them so they could, in turn, lead raids to keep the Christians on edge. If there were really as few warriors as Radomir said, it would be easy to wear them down and, Allah willing, take control of the acropolis.

Iskandar studied the sky. No moonlight would reveal their approach. Clouds obscured the stars. Other than the twinkle of campfires, all was black. The Christians would have no warning.

Ivan held up a hand, signaling his men to slow. The embers of dying campfires glowed throughout the Turkish camp. They were close enough that the scent of smoke tickled his nose and the occasional sound of horses greeted his ears. If the Turks had sentries, they would be nearby. Ivan motioned the other four men to a copse of trees. He went forward, stepping cautiously. A shadow passed in front of a fire, blocking the flames for a moment before the fire reappeared. The sentry paced back and forth somewhere between Ivan and the fire. Ivan waited, his eyes searching for other shadows that might be other sentries, but any other watchmen must have been on another side of camp.

Ivan's throat felt dry as he crept closer. Could he sneak up on the sentry without being heard? And could he silence the man before he sounded the alarm? Ivan slid his dagger into his hand and hunched over to make his shape smaller as he stepped through the dry mix of tall grasses and weeds. Gradually, the guard became visible, even when he wasn't crossing the fire's light. Ten paces away, Ivan went to his knees and crawled forward, gently pressing into the ground so none of the vegetation would snap and alert the guard.

Ivan waited in a depression while the guard walked within a body's length of him. The sentry stamped his feet and stared up at the sky, then turned back, his head in constant movement as he scanned toward the acropolis and then toward camp. But he didn't look down. As he strode past, Ivan leaped to his feet and plunged the dagger through the man's leather armor, thrusting it between his ribs. Ivan slapped his other hand over the guard's mouth and held him until he stopped struggling.

Ivan returned to his men more quickly than he'd left them. "Come. One of the guards is down. We'll sneak in that way."

They approached the camp, slowing as they reached the first tents. The wind sent ripples across banners on poles near the tents. Prisoners wouldn't be held inside tents marked with horsetail banners, so he led the group on along the edge of the encampment. Most of the enemy was quiet, and light from the campfires showed men as mere shadows. If spotted, Ivan hoped his group would be taken for friendly sentries.

They passed four more tents before they reached the supply wagons. Ivan whispered to Bardas. "Stay here. If you hear a commotion in the camp, we've been discovered, and I want you to burn everything. Otherwise we'll put these to the torch on our way back."

Bardas nodded and hid beneath a nearby wagon. A campfire burned not far away, so he'd have an easy source of flame when the time came.

After passing two more tents, Ivan caught sight of the prisoners. Twelve of them lay on the ground, tied together, while a Turkish guard stood over them. They weren't in the center of camp, but they weren't on the edge either. The dark and the distance made it impossible to judge if any of the prisoners were wounded. Ivan wanted to avoid open battle when his numbers were so small. Would they need to eliminate the men inside the nearest tents, or could the prisoners sneak past them without waking anyone?

"Matthias. Check if a second man guards them."

Matthias nodded and moved off.

While he waited for the report, Ivan borrowed Himerius's bow and nocked an arrow against the bowstring. He knew exactly where to aim to make sure the guard died before he raised a warning.

"Himerius." Ivan tipped his head toward a nearby tent. "Slay anyone who tries to leave."

As Himerius drew his spathion and moved into position, Ivan assigned Isaakios to another tent near the prisoners, with the same instructions. When Matthias came back, Ivan was ready.

"I saw no one other than a sentry pacing the outside of camp."

Ivan nodded. "When this one falls, release the prisoners. I suspect some of them wouldn't trust me even were I to unlock their shackles."

"They will trust you after this."

Ivan doubted that, but he wasn't sure who slept in the nearest tent, so he didn't snort his disbelief. Nor did he have time for a discussion on whether the same soldiers who had beaten him and piddled on him would suddenly respect him.

A nearby campfire illuminated Ivan's target. The man rubbed the back of his neck and folded his arms across his chest. Ivan drew his bow and released the arrow. It slammed into the man's throat. If he cried out, the sound was weak, softer than the gentle thud of his body hitting the ground.

Matthias hurried forward. Ivan drew another arrow and looked about for any alerted enemy. Time stretched out painfully while Matthias found the keys on the dead guard and unlocked the shackles, then cut free those prisoners who were tied with ropes. How many would need help walking? Two rose, then three. Ivan joined Isaakios at the front of the closest tent.

"Share out your spare weapons and lead them back to the postern."

Isaakios led the first six away: three men and three women. Matthias took a scimitar from the slain guard and handed it to one of the freed soldiers. Then he helped one of the wounded to his feet and offered his shoulder for support. As they came closer, Ivan recognized the wounded man: Niketas. He supposed they were on the same side now, but he was glad their roles were partially reversed and he was no longer a vulnerable prisoner. A freed paroikos supported a second wounded prisoner, another of Gregoras's men.

"Take them back," Ivan told Matthias. "Himerius and I will bring up the rear and help Bardas destroy the supplies." Ivan handed the bow and quiver to one of the healthy prisoners. To another, he handed his dagger. Ivan was left with only his sword and shield, but now more of his party could fight.

As Matthias's group disappeared behind a tent, Ivan glanced at Himerius. He watched his comrades, not the tent. The flap few open, and a bare-headed Turkish warrior sliced his scimitar into Himerius's back. Himerius cried out and crumpled to the ground. Their secrecy vanished as the Turk called out an alarm.

Ivan rushed toward the man who'd struck Himerius. He dodged a swing and replied with a slicing stroke across the man's unarmored chest. The Turk stumbled backward into the fabric of his tent, bringing the tent down on top of him.

Two men emerged from another tent and ran toward Ivan with raised scimitars. One blow hit Ivan's wrist guard and glanced away, biting into Ivan's skin but not disabling him. Ivan parried a barrage of blows from the two Turks. Cries from deeper in the camp diverted one man's attention for an instant. Ivan twisted away from the second man into the distracted one, chopping at his neck. As that man fell, the other man charged, but Ivan met his swing and shoved him back. He struck blows as quickly as he could until the Turk couldn't match his speed and Ivan's strike dug into the soft flesh of his side. The man pulled his arm in to protect his wound and retreated. Ivan let him go.

Five Turks ran toward him. Ivan bent briefly to confirm Himerius was dead, then dashed after Matthias. Ivan had defeated more than five before, but he didn't want to try his luck against odds like that tonight.

As he ran around a tent, a group of four men emerged, blocking his path. He could have barreled past them and tried for the acropolis, but that would draw nine men after the wounded. Ivan turned from the camp, running into the darkness, parallel to the acropolis rather than toward it. He prayed the nine would pursue him instead of the others and hoped Bardas could destroy the supplies by himself.

The noise from camp grew louder and fiercer. Ivan glanced over his shoulder for a moment. When he looked forward again, a Turkish figure stepped from the shadows directly in front of him. Another sentry. He raised his scimitar, and Ivan raised his sword. The Turk was larger, and his stance was firm, but Ivan had momentum on his side. He swung hard enough to drive the man's scimitar to the ground, then elbowed the man's nose. He pulled his sword from where it held the other weapon and sliced into the man's neck.

Ivan felt the sticky warmth of blood but didn't dwell on it. A quick peek behind him showed that most of his pursuers still chased him. It showed something else too. The camp glowed as if a bonfire lay at its center. Bardas had succeeded.

The farther Ivan ran from the camp, the harder it would be for the Turks to see him, so he continued forward, through grass and into trees. He'd thought his lance wound healed, but the flesh beneath his scarred abdomen burned. His sliced forearm stung, but the gash wasn't deep. Finally, he slowed, listening for pursuers. With the camp in commotion, he couldn't hear them. Either he'd lost them, or they'd gone back to battle the fire consuming their supplies.

Ivan cut back toward the kastron. If the Turks tracked down Matthias or Isaakios, then his friends might need reinforcements. Ivan almost scoffed. He was one man—hardly worthy of being called *reinforcements*. They had freed the prisoners and destroyed some of the Turkish supplies, but if they didn't make it back inside the acropolis, their foray would be for naught.

A group came into view as Ivan neared the walls. Seven men. He guessed it was Isaakios's group. Matthias's would have eight, if Bardas joined them, and none of the shadowy figures appeared injured. He almost called to them, but Župan Dragomir's hunts had taught him the value of silence. The fire may have distracted the camp, but that didn't mean a shout wouldn't stir up trouble. He'd had enough of that for the night. An ache in his head had been present most of the siege at various levels of intensity, but the pain had jumped after his sprint away from camp. He slowed, catching his breath from the run. How far away was Matthias's group? He checked behind him but saw no one in the darkness.

When he turned back, he stopped walking. It wasn't Isaakios's group. Nor was it Matthias's. Rather than iron helmets, turbans took shape in the darkness. Ivan had nearly run into a Turkish raiding party.

One of them shouted, and all of them turned. Ivan stepped back, tempted to run again, but he didn't want to turn his back on the enemy. The outlines of their curved bows were visible in the darkness, and at this range, he doubted his armor would prevent an arrow from piercing his skin.

"Greek scout, you have two choices. You can surrender, or you can die."

Ivan recognized that voice. Radomir. He didn't answer, didn't bother to correct them that he was Serb, not Greek. Ivan's shield hung from his shoulder. He brought it round to protect his chest as he lifted his sword. A pity he'd given away all his other weapons.

An order sounded in Turkish, and two men moved forward. The first ran at Ivan, bellowing something violent. Ivan blocked the downward strike of the scimitar with his shield and thrust his sword into the man's abdomen. The man dropped to the ground. His partner called out, and two more Turks joined him.

They approached as a team, steady and disciplined. He would have to fight them all at once, and they looked formidable. A gust of wind stirred the hair on the back of Ivan's neck. He stepped away and to the right, trying to string out the men so they couldn't all strike in unison. But the three attackers were quickly upon him.

They all brought their scimitars around at once. Ivan twisted away from one of them and used his sword and shield to block strikes from the other two. The next strikes from the Turks were less coordinated, and Ivan met them one by one, always moving to keep from engaging with them all at once. But he couldn't win against them. It was all he could do to block their thrusts. Every time he saw an opening, he had to block a blow instead of slashing at whoever was vulnerable.

A shout sounded behind him, and the four men from Isaakios' group ran past Ivan to engage the three Turks. With a handful of swift strokes, they slew all three.

Ivan breathed deeply, trying to force more air through his body. Where were the final three members of the Turkish party? "Did you see where the others went?" he asked.

"No."

"What of Matthias's group?"

"I've not seen them."

Radomir was out there somewhere. He knew the Greeks, and he knew their kastron. Did he suspect how they'd left the acropolis?

Ivan untied the trumpet from his waist and handed it to Isaakios. "Take them through the wall in the lower kastron to the main gate." Ivan had a suspicion Radomir would lead the Turks to the postern, and he didn't want the women or the wounded involved in a skirmish. "Three bursts and Gregoras will open the gate and come to help. Don't blow it until Matthias's group comes, and only if you can make it inside without the Turks following you. At least three are still out here, plus those at camp and the mining crew."

Isaakios nodded and rounded up his group. "What will you do?"

"Philippos is supposed to retreat across the bridge and close the postern if anyone other than a friend comes, but I want to make sure."

"Take someone with you."

Ivan put his hand on one of the newly released prisoner's shoulders. He had thick muscles beneath his rough wool tunic. "You. Come with me."

The man followed as Ivan ran off, slowing only when they neared the moat outside the western wall. Lookouts patrolled the wall walk, but Ivan couldn't make them out. Would they recognize him? He didn't dare shout a greeting. Somewhere, the remnants of the Turkish raiding party waited.

Philippos stepped into view, and Ivan felt a tug of relief. The boy was safe.

Something whistled past Ivan's shoulder and tore into the paroikos's chest. He dropped. Ivan followed him to the ground. "Get down, Philippos!" Ivan checked the paroikos. He squirmed in pain as blood gushed from his wound. But the arrow had hit something vital, probably his lungs, and his struggle against death was brief.

Where had the shot come from? There was little light, so the archer had to be close. Ivan crawled forward until he lay next to Philippos. "Stay down."

Philippos tucked himself into a dip in the ground. "Where are they?"

"I don't know, but I'll find them."

Ivan crept away from the moat. Were he lying in wait, he would pick a sheltered spot, such as the group of trees thirty paces away. He crawled forward, keeping his movements slow. He made a wide path before approaching the copse from the back. His side ached, and so did the cut on his arm, but he forced himself forward.

He was almost on top of them when he saw them: a Turk with a scimitar standing behind a tree, someone kneeling with a bow, and a third man in slightly different dress: Radomir.

Ivan reached for his dagger before remembering he'd given it to someone else. He wasn't afraid to fight them, but he preferred not to engage them all at once. Even the wind seemed to pause while he planned. Then, as the breeze picked up, Ivan ran for the Turk standing behind the tree.

At the last moment, the archer turned. As the bowman scrambled to his feet, Ivan smashed his shield into one of the men's faces while he lifted his sword and thrust it into the archer's thinly armored abdomen.

Radomir, the only member of the trio still standing, stepped back and drew his sword. "Who are you?"

"I am Ivan, second son of Župan Miroslav. And you, Radomir, will now pay for betraying my father to his death."

Radomir huffed. "You would be wiser to surrender or run home to your brother, but I've had enough dealings with you to know you would choose foolishness. Come, Ivan Miroslavević, and meet your death."

Ivan let the desire for revenge consume him. He ran at Radomir and hammered his sword into the traitor's. Radomir shoved back, haughty enough to laugh as he blocked Ivan's second thrust.

"You would be better off joining the Turks, Ivan Miroslavević. In time, they will control your lands, your people, your destiny. If you resist, you'll be punished. If you cooperate, you'll be rewarded."

Ivan swung his sword into Radomir's hard enough to drive the vile man backward. "Perhaps I care more about what is right than about what is wise."

"Then you are as big a fool as your father was." Radomir swung from below and knocked Ivan's shield askew.

Ivan recovered and thrust at Radomir. The Serb traitor met each blow, but Ivan kept it up, harder, faster, and forced Radomir closer to the moat. The older man was growing weary. Ivan was, too, but this was the man responsible for his father's and his uncle's death. Ivan wasn't about to let a scratched arm and a fortnight of heavy guard duty end his chance for vengeance.

With a desperate blow, Ivan knocked Radomir's sword into the ground. He kicked it from Radomir's hands and knew he'd won the duel. He raised his sword for the death strike, but he heard something behind him. He turned just in time to block the scimitar of the Turkish man he'd thought he'd knocked unconscious.

"What a pity," Iskandar said. "Just when you were about to take revenge on him for your father's death. But I'm afraid now you must answer for the death of my father." Iskandar pointed to the acropolis. "You killed him on that wall along with five of his men. I am most pleased to finally meet you face-to-face. I was afraid you would never leave the protection of your wall." Iskandar kicked Ivan in the thigh.

Ivan stumbled backward, but he stayed on his feet and regained his balance in time to meet the next blow from Iskandar. "Your father attempted to abduct a lady. I defended her then, and I will defend her until I draw my last breath."

Iskandar sneered. "In that case, you will defend her only a few moments more." Iskandar charged forward. He was a good swordsman, almost as good as his father, and Ivan was drained, but he met each of Iskandar's strikes. Blades clashed, and both men grunted with the effort. Then Ivan gouged the man's shoulder, and Iskandar drew back in pain. Ivan was about to pursue when he heard a muffled cry.

"Drop your sword, Ivan, or the stableboy dies."

Radomir held Philippos in front of him, a sword pressed into the boy's neck.

"If I drop my sword, will you release him?"

Radomir huffed. "No. He's worth something in the slave markets. But you would rather that, wouldn't you, than see him gutted before your eyes?"

Ivan dropped both his shield and his sword.

Three blasts came from the other end of the acropolis. Isaakios was calling the remaining guard out.

Radomir turned toward the noise. Philippos stomped on Radomir's insole, and the traitor grunted in pain. Philippos kicked, ducked, and ran free.

Ivan plucked up his sword and ran at Radomir. He swung it into Radomir's blade and knocked it from his hands. Slowly, Radomir raised his arms.

"Across the moat and inside with you, Philippos. As quickly as you can. Fetch some of the other lads." Ivan looked around, wondering where the wounded Iskandar had gone. He didn't see him anywhere.

Ivan pushed Radomir to the ground and tied the traitor's hands with his belt. He took Radomir's dagger and slid it into the top of his own boot. "Across the footbridge."

"I can't balance with bound hands."

Ivan glanced about, making sure the way was still clear. "You will balance, or you will drown. It makes little difference to me." Ivan poked his sword into the man's back to prod him forward. "I am tempted to run you through now, but the paroikoi have been deprived of far too much since harvest. I won't deprive them of their chance to see justice."

"Ivan, the men are all gone, but I've brought some of the women." Philippos's voice called out.

Ivan ran Radomir across the bridge and pushed him toward five sturdy women. The paroikoi had lost family, homes, livestock, and crops, and anger at the traitor showed on their faces. Ivan wasn't sure Radomir would still be alive when the women were through with him, and he didn't really care.

Ivan pulled in the footbridge and secured the postern door. He took an offered lance from one of the women, then he raced across the bailey. Even the animals seemed to sense his urgency and dispersed before him. He passed under the open portcullis and across the open drawbridge. As he reached the lower kastron, he ran into a full-fledged skirmish. The numbers looked roughly even. The Turkish sapping party must have attacked.

"Fall back!" Gregoras shouted.

Ivan stabbed a roaming Turkish soldier with his lance, then cut into another with his sword, freeing the Greek fighting him. Bardas. Together they beat off a rushing pair of Turks, then joined Matthias and two other armed paroikoi.

The Greeks withdrew toward the gate, keeping the Turks from the drawbridge. Matthias and Bardas were capable of holding their section, so Ivan went to help Gregoras, who marked what passed for the far end of the Greek line. Ivan was nearly there when an arrow dug into the tzaousios's side. Gregoras grunted and began slipping to the ground. Ivan caught him and pulled the man's arm around his shoulder. "Hold on. I'll get you inside."

Ivan fought off two more Turks with his free hand, then passed Gregoras to one of the paroikoi. Ivan remained as part of the rear guard with Matthias and Bardas.

"All together," Ivan said. "Back one step at a time." He used a backhand swing to deflect a Turkish blade and stabbed with his lance.

When they passed inside the portcullis, the women manning it let it slam down. Two Turks had slipped in, but Ivan and Matthias slew them. Ivan turned about, looking for more Turks, but it seemed the acropolis was once again safe.

Confusion reigned in the bailey for a few more moments as villagers ran to see if family members were among the freed prisoners.

They'd done it. They'd released the prisoners, put a torch to the Turkish supplies, and returned. Or at least, most of them had. They had gained twelve and lost three.

Ivan took an offered cloth and wiped the grime from his forehead, still trying to catch his breath. He searched for Gregoras and eventually found him under Helena's care in the surgeon's home.

"How bad is it?" Ivan asked.

Helena shook her head and blinked away a tear.

"I will soon join my son." Gregoras's face was pale and his breathing raspy. He reached out a hand, and Ivan took it in his own. Not long ago, the gesture would have been impossible, the hatred between them too strong. Now sorrow tightened Ivan's throat. "I am glad you came," Gregoras said. "I was wrong about you. In the end, you saved us."

CHAPTER TWENTY-ONE
WHEN THE SWALLOWS RETURN

THE NEXT DAY, THE GHAZIS packed their camp and raised the siege. Niketas, acting kastrophylax, had condemned Radomir, the former kastrophylax, to death by hanging. Ivan watched the traitor dangle from the end of a rope. The hangman had miscalculated the length, so Radomir had been doomed to a slow death by strangulation rather than a quick death from a broken neck. The crowd jeered, and some of them clapped when the body finally stopped twitching. Ivan had never liked executions, but he felt satisfaction that Radomir's threat was gone.

After the hanging, Ivan went with Matthias and Bardas to examine the mine. The dark opening reminded him of the dungeon, so Ivan was relieved to stand watch while the others went inside. He didn't expect to see the enemy in the lower kastron, but there were plenty of hiding places should a Turkish rear guard wish to stir up trouble.

When Matthias came out, his face was pale. "They can't have been more than a day's digging away from the walls."

"I'm glad we risked a sally," Ivan said. "We couldn't have saved the acropolis if we'd lost our wall."

Matthias rolled up the rope he'd used for measuring. "It wasn't just about the acropolis. It was about the people inside, and that included my wife and my sons. I'm in your debt, Ivan. Sivi Gora will be blessed to have you as their župan."

Iskandar shivered. His eyes gradually opened and adjusted to the dim lighting as snatches of the last few days flooded his memory. He remembered returning to his smoldering camp and collapsing at one of the few unburned tents. Hasan had worked on his shoulder, sending bolts of pain through his arm and chest. He had next woken in the back of a wagon, but the ground was still now. He lay in a tent.

"Effendi, are you awake?"

"Hasan?"

"Yes."

"Where are we?"

"Three days from Edirne."

Iskandar tried to push himself into a sitting position, but the agony that ran through his shoulder when he moved was so intense that he could barely breathe. "Why do we travel for Edirne?"

Hasan lifted a dim oil lamp and lit a second, bathing the tent in warm light. "We couldn't continue the siege. Our supplies were burned, and we lost twenty men that night. We almost lost you."

"I didn't give permission to raise the siege."

"No, effendi. You were nearly dead. And Kasim's men insisted. We had no choice."

Hasan shouldn't have given up the siege without orders. Iskandar had killed men for smaller offenses. He spotted his trunk in the corner of the tent. He could order Hasan to fetch his scimitar, and when he complied, Iskandar could strike off his head. Or had he lost his blade? He couldn't remember if he'd brought it back or if he'd dropped it when Ivan had gotten in a lucky strike.

It hadn't been entirely luck. The Serb had skill with the sword. But the boy was destined for death, and Allah willing, Iskandar would be the one to provide it. The day of reckoning had been postponed, but it would come.

"How many of my men are left?"

"Twenty-three."

"And our supplies? The loot we've gathered?"

"Most was burned. We've conserved the remnant as much as we can." Hasan frowned, the lamplight making the creases around his lips more pronounced. "We took a wagon from some peasants and scrounged sufficient food. I think we'll have enough to pay the men off, but there will be nothing left."

Nothing left? How could Iskandar recruit more ghazis when his most recent campaign had met with failure? He could offer neither plunder nor glory. "So you took me back to Edirne?"

"Yes. Perhaps with Kasim's influence, the sultan might find a place for you."

Iskandar glanced at his trunk again, glad he hadn't smitten off Hasan's head, for the man had thought clearly; he had come to the same conclusion as Iskandar but come to it earlier.

The ghazi life had served his father well, but perhaps it was time for Iskandar to move beyond pillage to something more. He remembered his father's words about not just raiding or conquering but also building a nation. If the sultan would give Iskandar a chance to prove himself, he would work to strengthen his people. And if he put his skills in the service of the sultan, he had a feeling he would eventually have his revenge on both Greek and Serb.

"You're somber today. Is something wrong?" Ivan asked Helena as they meandered along the northern wall together.

She forced a smile. She was being selfish, finding sorrow in something that would mean so much to him. "The swallows have returned. That means spring is here."

Ivan glanced at the mountains in the distance. His face betrayed neither relief nor sorrow. "The exchange will come soon."

"Yes." Her throat tightened.

"Will you come with me?"

She ran a finger over the embroidered pattern of her tunic. She didn't want to part with him, but she couldn't leave her sister now, not when Euphrosyne had begged her to stay. "My sister is with child, and there are no other midwives in Byzia. I would like to stay until she is delivered. Can you wait?"

The edges of his lips drooped, a contrast to the contented look he'd had just a few moments earlier. "I am eager to return home, and how will Leo be present for the birth of his child if I'm not exchanged for him? When will the baby come?"

"Early summer."

"Then, we'll arrange the betrothal during the exchange, and I'll come back for you at the solstice." He slowed, taking her hand in his. "Would that be acceptable?"

"Yes." It would be perfect. She could see Euphrosyne through childbirth and the early weeks when infection was most common. And then she would have Ivan.

"Good. Because I am looking forward to our wedding, and I wouldn't want to delay it for anything of less importance than the birth of a niece or nephew."

She studied his face, healthy and turned toward her. Strange that half a year ago she had not known him at all, and now he seemed almost a part of her. "Will your brother agree to our marriage? And your grandfather?"

"My brother will find it a relief that he doesn't have to find me a bride himself, and my grandfather will be pleased that the blood of imperial families runs in your veins. I think the bigger question is whether Leo will give permission. And how much you will miss Byzia when I've taken you to Sivi Gora."

Helena wasn't overly worried about Leo. If he said no, she would wait for Ivan's message, visit a patient, and not return. She would miss her sister and the friends she'd made, but she would not mourn her move. "Byzia has been my home less than five years. I will be content adopting another as long as you are my husband. Though you will have to be patient with me as I learn your language and customs."

"I can begin preparing you now. What words shall I teach you?" Ivan clasped his hands behind his back as they walked around a tower and into view of a watchman.

"Since I am a midwife, I suppose I should learn things like, 'The child is a boy,' or, 'The child is a girl.'"

Ivan said the words in Slavonic, and Helena did her best to repeat them. The amused smile on his face made her think she did a poor job of it, but she would improve with time and practice.

"What about 'Rest,' 'Push,' and 'The pain will only last a while longer'?"

Ivan taught her those phrases, then had her try several more.

"What were the last ones?" Helena asked.

"You are strong."

She repeated it again in Slavonic. "And the others?"

"You are beautiful. I want to be with you forever."

Helena met his eyes. She'd suspected the last few phrases weren't meant for the birthing room, and the last one confirmed it, as did his face. Helena had never been adored before, not that she could remember. Ivan's admiration for her was written on his face more clearly than lampblack on parchment.

"I have another for you." He paused, then spoke a set of words so tenderly that she wondered if it was something religious.

She did her best to repeat it and was rewarded with a wide smile. "What does it mean?"

"It means, 'I love you, and I want you to kiss me.' You won't need it for your work, of course. And you can use Greek, if you prefer, but that's a phrase I suspect you'll want to use most nights."

Helena's cheeks felt warm. "Will I?" She glanced at his lips and remembered them pressed against hers in the dungeon. He was right. His lips were like an angel's. She wanted that feeling, that closeness, over and over again.

"Is that not why Jesus performed His first miracle at a wedding feast, because marriage is blessed of God? It is His intention—a man and woman, joined together as husband and wife."

She didn't reply as they approached the southeast tower and went inside. Narrow arrow loops lit the spiral stone staircase.

"I'll go first, to frighten off the rats."

Helena stepped aside to let Ivan pass. The theories of Trotula encouraged marriage, too, as a way for the hot and dry nature of a man to balance with the cold and wet nature of a woman. But she didn't need a priest or a physician to tell her marriage was good. She felt it in her heart whenever she imagined Ivan as her husband.

She followed him, and midway down, where the brick of the upper level changed to larger foundation stones, he slowed and turned. She stopped on the step above him. Their lips were level.

"Helena?" his whisper was gentle and smooth, like new silk.

"Yes, Ivan?"

"I love you, and I want you to kiss me."

The air around them seemed to change, and breathing suddenly took effort. The way was wide enough that she could walk past him if she wished. Or she could turn around and go back to the battlements. He had given his plea, but the choice was hers. He didn't lean toward her or press her. He simply waited. She touched his face, and he closed his eyes as her fingers moved along his cheek and jaw. She ran her hand down his neck to his chest. Underneath his tunic, his heart beat just as hard as hers. In the still air of the tower, she felt the warmth of his breath as she closed the distance and met his mouth.

His lips responded immediately, clinging to hers with tenderness and persistence. One of his hands circled around her waist and drew her closer. In that moment, everything was perfect. Ivan adored her, and she worshipped him. Soon they would be joined as husband and wife, and perfect moments would follow as frequently as blossoms in the spring—abundant and beautiful. His mouth moved over hers again, and her thoughts vanished, swallowed up in breathless wonder.

CHAPTER TWENTY-TWO
THE EXCHANGE

As Ivan crossed the bailey that afternoon, Matthias called down to him from the wall. "Someone's coming. A messenger, I think."

"Just one?"

"Yes."

Ivan used the tower stairs to climb to the wall walk. He paused midway, on the step where he'd kissed Helena a few hours before. Helena, his future bride. It wasn't official, but it was certain. A marriage alliance would cement the peace between Konstantin and Leo. Everything Ivan had heard about the new kephale suggested Leo was quick to show gratitude, and Ivan had helped keep Leo's lands free. Beyond that, Ivan had the ear of his brother. As part of the bride-gift, he would ask Konstantin to release the other Greek prisoners without ransom, and surely that would convince Leo. But even if Leo refused, Helena had promised to run away with him. She would be his one way or another.

Matthias kept his hand on his crossbow and his eyes on the rider who trotted along the road running through the town. "I don't recognize him."

Ivan peered into the distance, and hope stirred. Black hair. Skilled horsemanship. The end of a bow visible at the man's side. Joy surged as the man drew closer and Ivan scanned the face, one he knew better than his own, one he had missed every single day since the skirmish with the Greeks. Danilo. "You can put your crossbow away. He's my kinsman."

"If he's anything like you, I should gather more weapons, not fewer."

Ivan smiled. "He's riding along the main road—by himself. War is not his intention today."

Danilo slowed his horse as he came nearer the acropolis. The drawbridge was down, and the portcullis was up, but Danilo was alone and wary.

Ivan watched his cousin gaze along the top of the wall and raised a hand in greeting. "Danilo!"

He could pick out the exact moment his cousin recognized him. The tense set of his limbs relaxed, and his face broke into a grin.

Ivan waited until his cousin had ridden across the drawbridge before he barreled down the tower stairs and ran into the bailey. Danilo waited, with several guards milling about him. He dismounted as Ivan reached him.

"Seeing you alive is an answer to many, many prayers." Danilo opened his arms, and they embraced. Ivan had been waiting for months, pleading with God for a reunion with his family. Relief that his captivity was almost over made something in his throat catch. Danilo held him for a long moment. "I wasn't sure what I'd find when I arrived."

His cousin's Slavonic words were like a balm to Ivan's ears. "It's good to see you, Danilo. I've missed you."

"And we have all missed you. But what are you wearing? Greek armor?" Danilo brushed a hand along Ivan's shoulder guards. "And do the Greeks know nothing of scissors? Why is your hair so long?"

Ivan laughed. His hair normally fell level with his ears. Now it touched his shoulders. "I've been busy."

"You look well. When I last saw you, I feared it would be the final time in this life."

Ivan had scores of questions for his cousin but asked only the most important one. "Is Kostya coming?"

"He's camped a few hours away with most of the garrison. I'm here to arrange an exchange. They are open to the idea?"

"Yes. They want Leo back."

"And the others?"

"They would like them back too. They have little to bargain with, but I have a few ideas." Ivan studied his cousin's face as they walked toward the keep. Danilo's neatly trimmed beard was thicker, but he seemed otherwise the same. "What of that girl Kostya found for you?"

Danilo's lips made a crooked line. "She is pleasant to look upon and pleasant to talk with. But she is young. In their eagerness to join our families, her brothers forgot she is but fourteen. We are betrothed, but it will be a lengthy betrothal."

"Do you like her?"

"Yes."

It was strange to Ivan, Danilo's acceptance of a bride that he found agreeable rather than one he was in love with. And yet, that was what Ivan had always expected for himself: an arrangement made by others. Pleasant but not passionate. Meeting Helena had changed all that.

They passed the stables, and Ivan motioned Philippos over. "Will you care for my cousin's horse?"

The boy took the reins. "Certainly, Ivan." He looked at Danilo with open curiosity.

Ivan turned to a passing guard. "Bardas, will you find Kyria Euphrosyne and ask when she can meet about her husband's release? I imagine Niketas should be told. Kyria Helena and Father Symeon as well."

"Yes, Ivan." Bardas rushed ahead of them toward the keep.

Danilo lifted an eyebrow. "I am pleased you're not locked up. But I did not expect to find you ordering around the Greek watchmen."

Ivan glanced at the northwest tower. He no longer slept there, and he was no longer chained at night. "I spent time in a dungeon and in a tower. But things have changed since then. A Turkish ghazi laid siege to the kastron, and I helped defend it."

"I hope that's all you did against the Turks."

Ivan stopped walking. "You hate the Turks as much as I do. Why shouldn't I help the Greeks fight them?"

"What did you do, Ivan?"

"It's a long story."

"I need to hear it."

Ivan gazed around cautiously, though he wasn't sure why. Everyone inside the acropolis knew Ivan's role in the siege. "I suggested they resist when the ghazis arrived. The tzaousios was in charge, but he heeded my counsel. And I led a raid that drove the Turks away."

Danilo looked over Ivan's armor with a frown. "Well, dressed as you are now, I suppose they thought you were just one of the Greeks."

Ivan didn't know what was going on, but he'd always been honest with his cousin and saw no reason to hide the truth from him now. "Radomir was working for them. He betrayed Basil's army and went over to the Turks. He knew who I was, as did the Turkish leader."

"Ivan, we are sworn vassals of the Ottomans. You can't go to war against them!"

"But their leader was only a ghazi. He wasn't acting on the sultan's orders. Iskandar was simply pillaging a weak pronoia."

"Iskandar bin Abdullah?" Danilo's face went hard.

"Yes."

"We've had dealings with him since you were captured. Please tell me he is dead."

"No. I wounded him, but he was well enough to escape while I captured Radomir."

"And what happened to Radomir?"

"They hanged him." Ivan motioned to the spot where he'd been executed, though the gallows had long ago been cleared away.

Danilo straightened. "Well, I suppose finding you alive and Radomir dead tips the balance in favor of celebration."

"What happened with Iskandar?"

Niketas and Bardas strode toward them. Danilo shook his head. "I'll tell you later."

Danilo didn't have time to explain anything else to Ivan that day. After agreeing on a location for the exchange, Danilo retrieved his horse so he could reach the Serb camp before nightfall.

"You'll have a long ride," Ivan said.

"I've had long rides before." Danilo seemed to hesitate. "I wish I didn't have to say goodbye again so soon, but I'll see you tomorrow. After that, we can put this whole mess behind us and get you home again." Danilo clasped his shoulder. "Until then."

Ivan watched him ride away. Helena stood beside him at the gatehouse, but she didn't speak until Danilo had disappeared into the town. "You wish you could go with him now."

"Yes."

"I'm sorry my sister is so stubborn."

"Your sister is prudent. It would be foolish to release your hostage to his friends without receiving your own man first."

"Under normal circumstances, but you have proven your honor again and again."

Ivan took her hand for a moment, grateful for her trust and dreading their upcoming parting. "You'll come tomorrow?"

"Yes. I'll accompany my sister and try to convince her to be on our side should Leo hesitate. Matthias will speak for you as well. Even Niketas."

Ivan pursed his lips. "Had you told me that three moons ago, I would have called you mad."

"Niketas took his time coming around, didn't he?"

Ivan crossed his arms and nodded.

"You're worried. Why?"

Ivan relaxed his arms, surprised she could read him so easily. "Something happened while I was gone. It involved Iskandar, but Danilo didn't have time to explain."

Helena laid a hand on his elbow. "He frightens me."

"He also frightens Danilo. And that is no easy task."

"Does he frighten you?"

Ivan didn't answer right away. Before today, Iskandar had been but a Turkish ghazi. Skilled but not invincible. But to have left such an impression on his cousin . . . "Yes."

Ivan rode behind the carriage where Helena and Euphrosyne sat. Father Symeon and Matthias rode next to him. Niketas and five other guards, most of them more paroikoi than soldier, rode ahead. Helena had suggested her sister stay at the kastron, given her condition, but Euphrosyne was eager to see her husband. The carriage bounced and jerked about on the rough road. Ivan didn't envy the women inside.

Ivan wanted to see his brother again, he wanted to be free, and he wanted his betrothal to Helena made official, but the horses plodded along at an irritatingly slow speed. Finally, the party came around a bend, and the foliage bordering the road opened to reveal the Serb camp. Two score armed men stood ready, half lining the approach to camp, half standing guard near a canopy.

When he was almost to the first Serb guard, Niketas reined in his horse and held up his hand to signal a halt. Ivan tossed his reins to Matthias and dismounted. He opened the carriage door and offered his hand first to Kyria Euphrosyne as she climbed out, then to Helena. Both wore their best clothing: silk stolas, embroidered tunics, decorative collars, and delicate hats with golden thread and dangling medallions.

Niketas's eyes pinched in irritation. "I thought we agreed to wait for my signal before you dismounted."

"I've been waiting all winter," Ivan said. Helena nudged him slightly with her elbow, reminding him that they might need a good word from Niketas. "I apologize, Niketas. Are you ready to lead the party forward?"

Niketas looked over the camp. "I don't like it. We're outnumbered."

"My brother is a man of honor. He'll not attack you without provocation."

Niketas turned to the group of Greek soldiers. "Stay with the horses and carriage for now. Matthias, you may join us. Ivan, you will stay at my side until I give you permission to leave. Is that clear? And you will give me your sword."

Ivan could see Konstantin, Danilo, and Father Vlatko waiting in the shade. He handed over his sword—it had come from the Greek armory, after all. He kept the short dagger in his boot. It, too, was Greek, but Niketas hadn't asked for it.

Niketas and Ivan led. Father Symeon escorted Euphrosyne behind them, and Matthias walked with Helena behind her sister. Niketas's frown grew deeper, and the knuckles gripping his sword hilt grew white as they strode through the Serb guards. Ivan recognized all of them. Bojan grinned at him. Miladin nodded in respect. Kuzman and several others murmured, "Welcome back, Ivan."

Niketas stopped at the edge of the canopy.

"May I leave now?" Ivan asked.

"Not until they release Leo."

Konstantin walked forward. Ivan was sure he'd heard and understood Niketas, but Konstantin's steps were firm and confident. He ignored Niketas and placed a hand on each of Ivan's shoulders, then pulled him into an embrace. "Long have we prayed for your safe return." Konstantin released Ivan and turned to Danilo. "Bring Leo." Then he faced Niketas. "Am I to negotiate with you?"

Niketas hesitated. "With Kyria Euphrosyne."

Konstantin nodded and extended his arm to the cushions and rugs spread under the canopy. "Make yourselves comfortable, please."

Ivan helped Helena to a seat and then offered his assistance to Euphrosyne, but she looked past him, gasped, and ran into Leo's arms.

After a long embrace and a few whispers, Leo helped his wife to a cushion. He turned to the Greek delegation. "Niketas. I am pleased to see you. Though I expected Kyrios Basil would come himself, or send Gregoras."

Niketas bowed his head. "Kyrios Basil is dead. As are both your cousins and your tzaousios."

"W-what?" Leo stuttered in surprise. "How?"

"Andronicus and Alexius were wounded in battle against them." Niketas nodded toward Danilo and Konstantin. "They died soon after. Kyrios Basil fell when the Turks ambushed us, and Gregoras when we drove the Turks away."

"Does any of the pronoia remain?"

"Yes, lord. But it has been a hard winter."

Leo sat next to his wife, his face somber and pale.

"Leo, I am sorry for your unpleasant news." Konstantin sat across from him. "It seems you are to negotiate your own release. May I suggest we trade your freedom for my brother's?"

Leo nodded. "Yes."

Konstantin looked at his brother. "Ivan, you are now free."

It was only a simple sentence, but it cast off the weight of captivity he'd been carrying since the battle. Helena met his eyes and smiled.

"How do you propose to ransom your four other men?" Konstantin asked Leo.

Leo shook his head as if to clear it. "It seems my pronoia is weaker and poorer than I left it. Would you give me a moment to discuss matters with Niketas and Father Symeon?"

"Of course. That is available for your use." Konstantin pointed to a nearby tent.

Ivan stood. "Kostya, might I speak with you?"

"Yes. Come." Konstantin led the way to his tent. Inside, Ivan recognized the blanket on the bedroll, the chest beside it, and the stool in the corner. The interior was a little piece of home. "Do you have any idea how worried we've been all winter? I was terrified Danilo would come back with news that you'd died months ago." There was a hint of scolding in Konstantin's voice, like the time Ivan hadn't properly cared for his horse after being caught in a rainstorm, or the time Ivan had fallen back asleep after Konstantin had awakened him for guard duty.

"Well, I'm here now."

Konstantin sighed as he sat on the stool. "Yes, you're here now. What suggestions do you have?"

"Turkish raiders attacked Leo's pronoia."

"So Danilo said. Iskandar?"

"Yes. They destroyed one village, burned half the town, and looted everything else. The Greeks managed to save most of their crops, but they lost a good portion of their animals. They have little in their treasury, and their lands are unlikely to recover this year or the next."

"So you think I should accept a small ransom?"

"Actually, I have a different idea. Kyria Helena. She is Kyria Euphrosyne's sister. I wish to marry her."

Konstantin stared at him. "You wish to marry?"

"Yes."

"Careful, Ivan. Marriage could be the most painful thing you ever do."

"What?" Why would Konstantin say something like that? He adored his wife. "Did something happen to Suzana?" Panic welled in Ivan's chest. He had assumed everything would be just as he'd left it when he returned to Rivak, but what if he, like Leo, had ill news to hear?

"Suzana is in good health."

"Did you quarrel?"

"No."

"Then, what happened? I thought you loved your wife."

"I do." Konstantin folded his arms. "And I love my son. But I'm going to lose him, Ivan, and it hurts. Worse than any injury on the battlefield, worse than when our parents died." Konstantin broke off, the muscles of his jaw tight.

"Is he ill?"

"No. Marko is healthy."

"A raid? Did the Turks attack? The Hungarians?"

"There was no raid. Only an Ottoman spy who overheard us meeting with Knez Lazar's envoy. You know how long we've been working toward revoking our vassalage. We've made progress, and I thought we were close. Another year perhaps, and then we'd be ready. But after Iskandar sent his report to the sultan's court, Sultan Murad requested an extra tribute payment. The man he sent to deliver the message is someone I have known and loathed since my first campaign for the sultan. Kasim bin Yazid. To have that man in my grody, to be forced to honor and obey him—" Konstantin's jaw clenched, and he shook his head. "But that's not the worst part. Murad doesn't just want an extra tribute payment. He also wants a hostage. Marko."

"No! He's too young."

"Murad doesn't care. I would fight him, but we aren't strong enough yet. And after the last payment, we'll need two years to prepare, not one. But even then, how can I revoke our vassalage, knowing my son will be executed if I do?"

"Marko can't go." Ivan's throat felt dry, and desperation made his hands clench. "He's only four. He would forget his family. He would forget his faith, his very identity."

Konstantin frowned. "We live in dark times. I've always known that someday an enemy might take my son's life on the battlefield. The Turks are worse. They will steal his soul."

"We have to fight."

"We're not ready. We would lose, and then we'd be back in the same position only weaker, with no hope of recovery."

"Would they accept someone in his place?"

Konstantin hesitated. "Danilo offered to go. Kasim is here, in the camp, probably making sure we don't form an alliance with the Greeks. He wouldn't take Danilo. It must be a member of my household."

Ivan pictured his nephew. How would he cope in the Turkish court? He was scarcely more than a baby. He needed his parents, needed tutoring from Father Vlatko. What would the Turks teach him? Marko was far too young, far too impressionable to stand up to a power like the sultan. Ivan didn't like the alternative, didn't like what it would cost him, but he could see no other way.

"I am of your household. I will go in his place."

Konstantin looked up with tears in his eyes. "I would never have asked it of you."

"I know."

"You can maintain your identity, at least, but I can no more rebel, knowing it would mean your death, than I could provoke them, knowing it would mean Marko's death. We'll have to remain faithful to the foe who slew our father."

"No." Ivan straightened. "If you need two years, then I will be a hostage for two years. Then I will escape."

"They won't let you walk from Adrianople whenever you please."

"I can do it, Kostya. I almost escaped from the kastron. I would have eventually, but I promised Helena I wouldn't." As he said her name, the full weight of what he'd agreed to do slammed into him. Helena. Would she wait two years for him?

Helena watched Serb servants offering pastries stuffed with honey or plum jam to their guests. She tried to understand the Slavonic words as they spoke among themselves, but she had little success. She had learned to read Latin in order to study the works of Trotula, so she was sure she would eventually learn the language of Ivan's people. For now, she could gather meaning from gestures and expressions.

Leo, Niketas, and Father Symeon returned. Leo's overwrought expression softened when he saw Euphrosyne again. Had he noticed the change in his wife's body? Had she whispered it to him when they'd been reunited, or was that happy news to come later?

Niketas sat next to Matthias as Leo joined his wife. "Where did they go?"

Matthias motioned to the tent where Ivan and his brother had disappeared. "They went to discuss . . . something." Matthias's gaze fell on Helena for a moment, and he stifled a smile. It seemed he suspected the subject of the brothers' discussion and approved.

Niketas folded his arms across his chest. "Ivan knows we have little to trade with. But he also knows how badly we need four good men."

"He'll be fair with us," Matthias said.

"We cannot afford fair."

Ivan and his brother emerged from the tent. Konstantin motioned for Danilo, and the three of them spoke in whispers, their expressions grim. Ivan had been certain his brother would agree to the marriage, but what if he'd been mistaken?

Instead of returning to the canopy, they disappeared behind a jumble of tents. Something was wrong. Ivan's face had showed grief, not joy. Helena put a half-eaten pastry aside, her appetite gone. She would bring no wealth to a marriage and little prestige. She was an orphan and old for a bride. If Konstantin insisted his brother find a better match, would Ivan side with his brother or with his heart?

Eventually, Konstantin and Danilo came back into view. A few moments later, Ivan and another man appeared. He wasn't a Serb. A neatly trimmed beard covered his chin, and a white turban was wrapped about a red cap on his head. The man was Ottoman. Helena had known Ivan's people were bound to Sultan Murad by vassalage, but she hadn't expected an Ottoman dignitary to travel with them. Did Ivan need Ottoman permission to marry?

When they arrived, Konstantin held a gracious hand out to the Turk. "May I present Kasim bin Yazid. He is visiting us from the court of Sultan Murad."

Konstantin's face remained polite, devoid of emotion, but Helena saw disdain in the eyes of the nearby Serb guards. Kasim was not a welcomed guest.

"My lady?" Ivan bowed to her. "May I have a word with you, in private?"

Helena nodded, but Euphrosyne cleared her throat. "I am not sure that is proper."

Ivan kept his eyes on the ground and his voice meek. "If Matthias stood as chaperone and if we stayed in the open where you could see us, would that be acceptable, Kyria Euphrosyne?"

Helena caught Euphrosyne's eye and was certain her sister would protest because she still held a grudge against Ivan, but it was Leo who spoke. "Yes, that will be acceptable."

Ivan assisted Helena to her feet and offered her his arm. She took it, frightened of whatever had changed their plans. Ivan looked unsettled. Matthias followed them but stayed several paces back to give them privacy.

Ivan spoke in a whisper. "Do you love me enough to wait two years for me?"

A chill ran through her as sudden and cold as if she'd fallen into the moat during winter. "I would wait a lifetime for you, but I thought we'd marry this summer."

"Before Iskandar laid siege to your kastron, he followed my brother back to Rivak. We've long chafed at our vassalage, and Kostya made plans to revoke it. Iskandar learned of those plans and reported to the sultan. To weaken us, Murad demanded a double tribute. And to ensure our good behavior, he demanded a hostage. My nephew."

"But your nephew is still so young."

"Marko cannot go. It would ruin him. But we aren't ready for open war against Murad. So another hostage must go. And it must be a member of Konstantin's family." Ivan paused, waiting for her to come to the obvious conclusion.

Helena could barely breathe. "You?"

Ivan nodded.

"But you only just regained your freedom!"

"What would you sacrifice for your family, for your people?"

Helena thought of her sister. If it were her niece or nephew, would she not make the same choice, no matter how painful? "I understand why you must go, but I mourn your captivity, and I grieve the change to our plans."

"I will regain my freedom, but I have to be patient. And I'm asking you to be patient with me. I have no right to ask it, but will you wait? When this is over, will you still be my bride?"

"Yes." Helena wished they weren't exposed to so many eyes. She longed to be in Ivan's arms again. She needed that comfort, that strength, because it felt as though the thing she wanted most in life had just been yanked from her grasp.

"If anyone asks, I took you aside to learn your feelings. We've told Kasim I will be hostage until Marko is ten."

"But that would be six or seven years. You said two."

Ivan glanced back at the canopy. "You mustn't tell a single soul what I'm about to say, not even your sister."

"I will keep your secrets, Ivan."

"I won't be in Adrianople for six years. And Marko will never go, not at age four nor at age ten. The tribute set my brother's preparations back a year. He will pay the tribute next year, but the year after, I will escape. We'll be ready to defend ourselves then, and we will succeed. And then I will come for you. We will have two winters apart, but we will be together by the third. I promise."

Two winters apart. She had a feeling both would seem colder and longer than normal. "If anyone can escape Adrianople, you can. But I ache for what you will have to suffer. I think you'll be even more alone there than you were in the kastron."

"I won't be completely friendless. Danilo has offered to come with me."

Helena tried to be brave despite the raw hurt in her chest. "Then, you shall have your cousin, and I shall have a niece or nephew until we can be together."

"When we are finally married, I will make it up to you, I swear it." He took one of her hands in both of his. "I love you."

"And I you." She gripped his hands. Those hands were capable of defending a kastron and slaying any foe, but they were always gentle with her. She released them reluctantly and unhooked her necklace. "Take this." She placed the pendant of a bearded saint in his palm. "St. Peter the Athonite was also a soldier, and he was also a prisoner of the Saracens for a time. But he escaped and fulfilled his vow, as I know you will."

They returned to the company under the shade of the canopy. Ivan gave a nod to his brother, and then Konstantin and Leo discussed a six-year betrothal and the release of the other men who'd been taken during the battle last autumn. Ivan didn't participate. He held her necklace in his hand and gazed into the distance, toward the home he had longed to see all winter, the home he would now be exiled from for two more years.

For a few moments, Ivan had been free. She had seen the relief in his eyes, noticed the change in his bearing. Now he would have a longer trial, a longer time as hostage, and her heart broke for what he would have to endure before they could begin their lives together.

Helena felt a pair of eyes on her and glanced up to see the Ottoman diplomat. How much did he understand? And how much did he suspect? Kasim looked to be nearly fifty. Gray streaked his beard, but old age had not yet hit his body. He was a warrior still, with keen, piercing eyes.

She did not like the way he looked at her.

CHAPTER TWENTY-THREE
AN HONORED HOSTAGE

IVAN LEANED ON THE WOODEN fence, watching an Ottoman horse trainer tire out a beautiful gray stallion. Ivan's armed guard stood a few paces behind him. His second winter in Adrianople was ending, and it would be his last among the Turks. Konstantin's next tribute was expected midsummer. The week before it was due, Danilo and Ivan would make their escape.

Often, Ivan thought of where he might be instead. In Rivak, with his brother and nephews. Konstantin had two boys now, though Ivan had yet to meet the youngest, born a year and a half ago. Or Ivan could have been in Sivi Gora with his grandfather, building a prosperous town. Or he might have been with Helena. Anywhere with Helena would seem like heaven.

But his time among the Ottomans was a postponement, not a final sentence. And life as an honored hostage was not completely unpleasant. They had lessons most mornings, learning Turkish and Arabic, studying the Koran and philosophy. They trained with Turkish sipahis in the afternoons, practicing sword work, archery, and unarmed combat. In the evenings, when they were locked in their chambers and free of their guards, Danilo played his gusle, creating familiar melodies. Sometimes he sang as well. Other nights, they reminisced of their childhood in Rivak or spoke of their plans for a future in Sivi Gora.

The Ottoman trainer tried to saddle the spirited stallion. He succeeded, but the horse reared up and looked as though it would need settling before it let anyone mount.

"You enjoy watching the breaking of horses?"

Ivan turned. He'd heard someone approach, but was taken aback to see Bayezid, one of the sultan's sons. "Yes. You have many fine animals here." After nearly two years in Adrianople—Edirne, as the House of Osman called it—Ivan understood Turkish, but the foreign words still felt awkward on his tongue.

Bayezid lifted his chin slightly in what passed for a nod. "We do. Though it is the process that interests me more than the horses themselves."

"Oh?"

"Breaking horses is not so very different from breaking men. Breaking nations. Submitting them to our will. I watch them"—Bayezid motioned to the trainer and horse—"so that I might better break my Christian vassals when I am sultan."

Bayezid was not Murad's only son, so it wasn't certain that he would follow his father as sultan, but Ivan didn't think it prudent to point out that fact. Nor did he know how to respond to the prince's statement. Did Bayezid suspect that Konstantin would soon revoke his vassalage? Were his words a veiled threat?

"I don't hate Christians," Bayezid continued. "My mother was born Christian. And one of my wives is Christian. But they must know their place and who is master. Just like the horse."

Ivan clenched his jaw shut to keep from saying something he'd regret.

Bayezid scowled as another group of Ottomans approached the training grounds. Even before the men were close enough for Ivan to pick out their faces, he guessed one of them included Bayezid's half brother Yakub. Despite his family's constant bereavements, Ivan had grown up surrounded by love. But things were different among the sultan's sons, perhaps because they had different mothers or maybe because their inheritance would be either a sultanate or nothing. Serb and Greek tradition divided a family's assets among any surviving sons, thus Konstantin was to inherit the geographically larger lands from their father's family, and Ivan was to inherit the smaller but richer mining town from their mother's family. But the sultan's lands would not be divided. Whoever was not heir would depend on Murad's successor to decide what, if any, inheritance he would have.

The brothers greeted each other with cool politeness when Yakub and his entourage arrived. Bayezid and Yakub were as different as two brothers could be. Where Bayezid was bold, Yakub was thoughtful. Where Bayezid was brave, Yakub was cunning. And where Bayezid was direct, Yakub was beguiling. Both were vipers. Their youngest brother, Savcı, had been executed over a decade ago after rebelling against their father. Taking the possible heirs from three to two had only made the fraternal hatred stronger.

Yakub's followers included Kasim bin Yazid, who greeted Ivan with a bow. "Ivan Miroslavević. Any word from your lands as of late?"

Ivan swallowed back his distaste—something he had become proficient at since arriving in Adrianople. "All is well as of the last letter."

"Your new nephew? He is strong?"

Ivan hated that Kasim knew so much of his family. "Yes. Pavle is healthy."

"Good. Another future warrior. The Serbs make fine soldiers, do they not, Yakub?"

Yakub turned from Bayezid and examined Ivan as if he were examining a horse. "Yes. I have served with them before." He glanced at Kasim. "Will you take any when you leave?"

Kasim shook his head.

"Are you preparing a campaign?" Ivan asked.

"Yes."

"May I ask where?"

"To a city in need of humbling."

Ivan galloped along the enclosure, threw his hat in front of him, and shot it with his arrow. He slowed his mount at the far end of the training field and waited for Danilo to make his pass and join him. They and the sipahis they trained with had repeated the drill two dozen times thus far that afternoon. The Turks wanted their vassals to be skilled when called to battle on their behalf.

Danilo's shot was perfect, as always. He guided his horse to Ivan's side and glanced around to make sure no one could overhear them. "I ran into Iskandar today."

"Oh?"

"He told me that he will someday strike your head from your neck and place it on a pole in revenge for his father's death. And he will do the same to me. He only delays because we are currently esteemed hostages and he would not wish to impinge the honor of the great sultan, leader of the Divinely Protected Well-Flourishing Absolute Domain of the House of Osman."

"Pompous fool." Ivan hoped the insult would lessen the fear. It didn't. "Were he not so dangerous, I would laugh."

"He's preparing a campaign."

"He told you?" Iskandar liked to brag, but surely he knew the value of discretion for military matters.

Danilo shook his head. "He didn't know I was still there."

"Did he say where?"

"No."

Several of the sipahis drew near, so Ivan and Danilo paused their conversation. They didn't think the others understood Slavonic, but they didn't want to chance it. They repeated the riding drill, then stood before targets and bent their bows the required one hundred times for the session.

After the archery, Danilo picked up a scimitar and motioned for Ivan to spar with him some distance from the other pairs.

"Kasim is also going on campaign," Ivan said as they crossed blades. "Do you suppose they go together?"

"Perhaps. It's early for campaign season." Danilo twisted to block one of Ivan's swings. "I wonder where they're going. I saw twenty baggage carts."

"Kasim said there was a city in need of humbling."

Danilo huffed. "Edirne? I hear it needs humbling."

"I prefer to call it Adrianople." Both their fathers had died on a campaign meant to restore the city to Christian hands, so Ivan would use the city's Christian name. "I wouldn't put palace intrigue past Iskandar, but they wouldn't need many baggage carts for that, would they?"

Danilo lunged at him, and Ivan drew him back, farther from the others. He leaped onto a water trough and parried a few of Danilo's strikes. Then he flipped over a large pithos of clay and struck the scimitar from Danilo's hands.

Danilo frowned and retrieved the lost weapon. "More?"

Ivan nodded.

"They changed the guards at the southern entrance today. Four now instead of two."

"Do you think it's permanent?" Ivan asked as he blocked one of Danilo's thrusts.

"I'll keep checking. If it is, I think that will change plan four."

Ivan thought as his scimitar and Danilo's rang against each other. "Make it less desirable than plan eight, but more desirable than plan nine?"

"Unless it's raining."

Ivan signaled a break, and they both lowered their blades. "That message from Kostya can't come soon enough."

"I don't expect it until midsummer."

"I know. I'm just sick of this city, sick of the Ottoman court. Bayezid deigned to speak with me today. Told me how his Christian subjects must be subjugated much like his horses. I wonder if he knows how much we hate them."

"We'll be free again. Soon."

Ivan hoped Danilo was right. They spent their days studying the Turks, learning their tactics and analyzing their skills. When the time came, they would have firsthand knowledge of how their enemy waged war. But they also knew how vast Sultan Murad's resources were. They could beat an army of Turks on the battlefield, but if that happened, Murad could summon his other vassals and recruit new warriors from his far-flung sultanate. Serb manpower could not be replenished so easily. That meant they would not only have to win but also win decisively.

Iskandar rode up to Kasim. "The scouts have returned. The way ahead is clear, effendi."

"Good. Ride with me a while."

Iskandar obeyed. He had followed every command from Kasim since the failure at Byzia. But that failure would soon be avenged.

"Tell me more about the kastron. Where does the noble family live?"

"In the keep, on the north side of the acropolis. The gatehouse is on the south, and the offices and armory. Most of the buildings vulnerable to fire are on the west. The rest are stone."

"Yes, that is what Cemal has told me."

"His tunnel would have worked had we been given more time."

Kasim smiled. "This time, we will not be hurried away from the walls. But I don't think we'll need a tunnel. We come not as raiders but as an army of the sultan."

"You honor me in asking me to ride with you, effendi. I am eager to complete what I was unable to do two years ago." Iskandar wasn't sure why Kasim had followed his suggestion to attack Byzia. It held little wealth, nor did it threaten the ongoing Ottoman siege of Thessaloniki. Yet seeing it finally captured would bring Iskandar much contentment.

"I have my reasons for wanting Byzia."

Curiosity burned in Iskandar's mind, but he held his tongue. Iskandar's defeat had left him without followers or resources. He owed everything to Kasim. He would not voice impertinent questions. But he did turn to look, asking with his eyes.

"The sister of the kephale's wife."

Iskandar remembered her vaguely. "What of her?"

"I will have her for my own."

"But Saruca has given you three sons, and you took a third wife only last summer." Iskandar had complicated feelings about Kasim's latest marriage. He was jealous, for his sister's sake, and envious. The Bulgarian bride was beautiful.

"One can never have too many sons. And I am allowed four wives, so four wives I shall have. My fourth will be a sweet addition. The moment I saw her, I knew I had to have her."

CHAPTER TWENTY-FOUR
THE FALL OF BYZIA

HELENA LAUGHED AS HER NIECE uttered a long sentence of earnest gibberish. "She's speaking so well now."

Euphrosyne had a dalmatica of samite on her lap, but she watched her daughter, not the thick silk she embroidered. "I understood none of the words."

"Yes, but the *rrr* sound is new. So is the *na*. Soon, she will be able to say Aunt Helena. Or Jelena, if she wishes to use the Slavonic pronunciation."

Euphrosyne turned back to her embroidery. "Your engagement is scheduled to last another four years. By then, she'll no doubt be able to say either. And by then, I doubt you'll want to go."

Helena bit her tongue rather than correcting her sister. Ivan would come for her this summer or fall, and she still yearned to marry him with a desperation not unlike a drowning woman seeking air. She plucked her niece from the ground. "Ah, young Kyria Irene, I caught that yawn. Off to bed with you." Helena sighed as Irene laid her head topped with curly brown hair on her shoulder. "I'll take her."

"Thank you."

As soon as Helena approached Irene's bed, the child arched her back and nearly escaped her aunt's arms.

"Oh, no, my little one. You shall have a nap." Helena held back a giggle as she rocked her niece and sang her a lullaby. She was glad to have watched her grow this much, but she often thought of how life might have been had the Turks not stolen Ivan away from her. Perhaps she would have had a child of her own by now. Irene relaxed as Helena laid her in her bed and covered her with her favorite blanket. She would miss Irene almost as much as she missed Ivan. He would come soon, she was sure of it. The second winter had passed, the swallows had returned, and the paroikoi were in the middle of spring planting.

Euphrosyne no longer sat in her chambers when Helena left Irene, so Helena went to the great hall. Commotion filled the air. Leo and Niketas spoke with Matthias while Euphrosyne stood to the side and wept.

"What is it?"

Euphrosyne didn't answer. Tzaousios Matthias caught Helena's pleading look and walked over to explain. "Paroikoi report an army of Turks approaching. Several hundred strong."

Dread crept through her veins. "Not again." Leo had done his best to rebuild the pronoia since returning two years ago, but Matthias's men numbered only forty. Even if they recruited paroikoi, they would be hard-pressed against an army so large.

"It's Iskandar again, but this time, he comes not as a raider but as a servant of the sultan. He's not in charge. A man named Kasim bin Yazid is, but Iskandar knows our tactics. And it seems he wants revenge."

"When will they arrive?"

"Three days, most likely." Matthias crossed his arms. His mouth was a grim line.

"We must do what we did before, and do it quickly," Helena said. "Send word to the villagers and gather in the animals and the crops. We'll have more men to guard the walls this time—"

"Don't be foolish," Niketas broke in. "There are no crops ready to harvest. And we can't call in the paroikoi during planting, or we'll all starve, even if we do manage to defeat the Turks. We can't survive a siege. Nor can we meet them in open battle. We'd be far too outnumbered."

Helena wanted to argue. Surely there was some way to resist. And yet she remembered all too well the last siege. The timing had been in their favor two years ago, after the harvest but before the spring planting. Now time was against them.

"What will we do, then?" she asked.

Helena watched the preparations, wishing they could do more. Matthias drilled his men, the soldiers polished their armor and sharpened their weapons, and thirty paroikoi joined the garrison. But they went about their tasks with fear in their eyes and trembling in their souls. None had the determined confidence of Ivan.

When the Turks arrived, trailing smoke plumes in their wake, Helena watched from the wall. Matthias stood nearby.

Helena shivered. "There were not so many last time."

"No, kyria." Matthias straightened his shoulders. "But we are more now than we were then. And I believe we are wiser."

"There is not so much grain this time."

"And there are fewer animals to eat it."

Helena nodded, trying to follow Matthias's example of courage. But she couldn't help thinking one persistent thought. "I wish Ivan were here."

"As do I."

The Turkish army didn't attack at once. They set up camp in the meadow, and then a group of seven rode to the gate of the kastron under a white flag of truce. Helena wasn't invited to the negotiations. Only later, when the Turkish delegation returned to their camp, was she called to the great hall.

Leo sat at the head of the room, Euphrosyne by his side. Niketas and Matthias flanked them.

"Helena . . ." Leo paused and looked away.

Helena tried to glean some clue from his form, but she saw only defeat and sorrow. Niketas's lips, partially open and curving down, suggested surprise and distaste. Matthias would not meet her gaze, nor would her sister. Matthias seemed angry. Euphrosyne's pale skin showed shock.

"Helena," Leo began again. "We have come to an arrangement that will avoid battle."

She thought of the men on the walls and of how many of them might fall and of the village children who might starve. Peace was preferable, but at what price?

Matthias cleared his throat, and Leo began again. "As part of the terms, you are to marry one of their leaders, Kasim bin Yazid."

"What?" Surely she'd misheard him. She was to marry Ivan, not an enemy Turk.

"We have nothing to bargain with save your hand in marriage. We cannot resist, or they'll kill half of us and enslave the rest. Iskandar threatened to raze the pronoia if we reject their demands. They've requested gold, and we have little, but we will give what we can and pawn Euphrosyne's jewels for the rest. They require my supplication as their vassal, and I have no choice but to comply. And they've demanded a Greek bride of noble birth." Leo lifted a hand toward her. "You are the only option."

Helena flinched. "I am promised to Ivan Miroslavević, future župan of Sivi Gora."

"There was no betrothal ceremony."

"But I pledged my word. You pledged your word and received your men back in exchange! Ivan promised he would come for me, and I am patient enough to wait." Panic touched her words with shrillness.

Leo's jaw was tense and his words terse. "Circumstances have changed. Either you marry Kasim, or our villages will be burned and our paroikoi enslaved and slaughtered."

Helena's throat tightened. How could she marry someone who threatened to destroy her people? But how could she refuse when the lives of so many hung in the balance? "Surely there is another option."

"None that we have found." Leo stood and paced the floor. "I am not pleased, but I have no choice."

Helena stood silent for a long time before she answered. She wanted to marry Ivan. But that possibility had been trampled into the dust by the arrival of a powerful Ottoman army. If Byzia resisted the Turks, they were almost certain to lose, and defeat would result in her death or her capture. How could she refuse Leo's command when they had almost no hope of victory and fighting would mean the death of so many? Was her ever-narrowing chance at escape worth the price in blood?

"Then, I have no choice." The words came from her throat as a whisper, and they took all hope from her soul.

"Father Symeon attended the deliberations." Leo paused his pacing. "He insisted you be allowed to stay Christian. They won't force you to convert. It's an offer more generous than you would have received from a Latin bridegroom."

The enormity of it all hit her like a rock flung from a petrobola. She was to marry a man she didn't know, an enemy. She'd seen him once—when his demands for a hostage had forced Ivan to postpone their marriage. Now he would destroy their plans permanently. She was to be cut off from her people and her faith. She wouldn't see her niece grow, wouldn't be present to help Euphrosyne with the next child. She would learn not Slavonic but Turkish. Ivan would be but a memory, forever haunting her as to what might have been.

Leo, his wife, and their advisers watched her. The weight of their eyes was as oppressive as a wool blanket on a blazing summer afternoon. She blinked back tears and asked to be dismissed.

Leo nodded, and she went to her chamber.

"Helena?" Euphrosyne stood with a pale face and red-rimmed eyes in the doorway of Helena's bedchamber. "May I come in?"

Helena nodded, not trusting her voice. Hours had passed since Helena had been told her fate. She had spent most of the time since then crying.

"I'm sorry, Helena." Euphrosyne sat on the bed next to Helena and took her hand. "I tried to think of anything I could to keep this from happening. Matthias said we should fight, but there are too many this time. They'd outlast us or call for reinforcements." She wiped a tear from her cheek. "In the end, I'm selfish. I don't want my sister married to an infidel. But more than that, I don't want my husband executed and my daughter enslaved and the villagers killed."

"No one wanted this. But we have no choice." Too many would die if they resisted. And if they failed, as they eventually would, Helena's fate would be the same. Better to make her sacrifice now, when it could save the rest of the pronoia.

"I wish you could have married your Serb. I didn't like him, but he would have made you happy. And he would have been a better husband than a Turkish ghazi."

"Is Kasim a ghazi? I thought he led sipahis."

Euphrosyne squeezed Helena's hand. "Whoever he is, I wish he were not your husband-to-be. I would rather see you married to a Hungarian or a Venetian and forced to join the Latin heresy than married to a Saracen. But he is older than you. Perhaps you will be a widow soon, and then perhaps they will let you return."

"Who would have thought that a prospective bride would be so eager for widowhood?"

Euphrosyne made a sound that was half laugh, half cry. "I brought you something. I wanted to send you with my favorite icon, but your new husband might see it as an idol, so I decided on this instead." She handed Helena a leather-bound codex.

Helena opened the book. The pages were paper rather than parchment. Each letter was carefully formed, and illustrations decorated every other page. "It's beautiful." She looked at the title. The gospels of Matthew, Mark, Luke, and John. The cover and the illuminations made the book worth as much as a horse. "Don't you need this? To sell for tribute money?"

Euphrosyne shrugged. "We might find a buyer eventually. Maybe a trader from Genoa would want it. But I would rather it go with you. Your copy of Galen cannot be your only companion in exile."

Exile. That was what it felt like. The familiar lines of a song came into Helena's head: *Off to wander, far away from Eden. Off to journey, through a land of woe. E'er a stranger to the land of promise, till at last to heaven I shall go.* The words had never before felt so true.

CHAPTER TWENTY-FIVE
A QUIET, BITTER GARDEN

Ivan and his guard navigated through a crowded bazaar, the largest in Adrianople. People could buy almost anything here: perfume from Constantinople, fur from Serbia, balsam from the Holy Land, or cardamom from beyond the Mongol Khanates. Ivan passed a rug merchant's booth, then a vendor selling fragrant bread. He'd lost guards to the distractions of the market before, but today, he wasn't trying to escape, and his guard stayed near. This one had been assigned to Ivan just a few days before. They never stayed long. Ivan suspected it was because a guard who had spent little time with his charge wouldn't hesitate to turn executioner should the order be given.

Ivan was growing restless in the Ottoman capital. He was fed up with the guards who hounded his every step, weary of showing respect to men he despised, tired of feigning loyalty while planning revolt. Before Ivan had begun his exile, Konstantin had told him not to stay beyond St. Vitus Day of the second year. Ivan had spent two winters in Adrianople, and spring was coming. They were only a third of the way through Lent, still four moons away from St. Vitus Day, but after nearly two years, the end finally seemed in sight.

He avoided a group of ghazis in tall red hats of felt and left the market and its crowds. When he sought solitude, there was a place in the city where few of his guards would follow him: a Christian church.

Ivan walked reverently into the basilica when he arrived. As he passed from the narthex to the nave, he looked over his shoulder, making sure his guard hadn't followed. The distance from his captor made it easier to breathe. In the past, it had also made it easier to arrange help for their planned escape, but he and Danilo had everything set now. Today's visit was just for peace. Ivan inhaled the incense-sweetened air and studied the clerestory, where light from the windows cast a golden glow over the images of saints.

He was too late for the matins service, so he made the sign of the cross, touching his forehead, chest, right shoulder, and left. Then he prostrated himself, kneeling before the icon of John the Baptist and touching his forehead to the ground.

As he finished his prayer, he heard footsteps behind him. Tension and wariness hardened his muscles just long enough for him to turn. When he saw who it was, he relaxed and stood. "Matthias? Father Symeon?"

"Ivan, it is good to see you." Matthias's face did not match his words. He seemed grieved, as though he had just come from burying someone. "You have changed."

"I am two years older." Ivan wore a beard, and he was no longer the thin stripling he'd been when he'd been captive in Byzia. "A sadness seems to haunt you, my friend. What is wrong? And why are you here among the Turks?"

Matthias motioned to the narthex, and they walked there. "Iskandar came against us again, this time with a man named Kasim bin Yazid, and they would have taken the kastron. Leo pledged his loyalty to the sultan to avoid a battle."

Ivan had suspected Kasim and Iskandar were campaigning together, but to hear that they had gone to Byzia . . . that they had taken the lands Ivan and the rest of the pronoia had fought so hard to defend . . . The bitterness was like a mouthful of pepper when expecting honey cakes. "Kyria Helena—was she harmed?" His hand went to his chest, where he wore her pendant of St. Peter the Athonite under his tunic.

"Kyria Helena is in good health. But . . ."

Ivan glanced outside, making sure his guard wasn't watching. "But what?"

"I'm the bearer of bad tidings. As part of the negotiations, Kasim demanded Helena for his wife."

"What?" Ivan felt as though he'd been pierced by a lance again. Disbelief, anger, and horror all clawed at his soul. "But she's promised to me." He and Helena loved each other. They'd planned a life together. For her to instead be given to a man as vile as Kasim was unthinkable.

"None of us wished it. But there were too many of them. She bought our lives with her marriage."

Ivan could barely breathe. Byzia fallen. Helena given to another, to a hated enemy. "Has the wedding taken place?"

"It's to take place tomorrow."

Ivan gripped Matthias's arm. "Where is she now?"

Helena took off the heavy golden bracelets she'd been given as part of her marriage gift and placed them on top of a trunk, next to the bright-red veil she was to wear for her wedding the next day. She fingered the dangling gold earrings that an old woman had pierced her ear lobes with a few hours ago. She was unused to their weight, but she didn't dare remove them. She might not be able to get them back in, and she didn't want to give the woman who'd placed them in her ears another reason to yell and slap. She didn't understand Turkish, so she wasn't sure who the women were who had spent the evening preparing her for the wedding. Relatives of Kasim, she supposed.

The night before her sister's wedding had been so different. Euphrosyne had been ecstatic. But Euphrosyne's bridegroom had been a young, handsome man of her own people, and Leo's wealth had meant continued comfort. Kasim was wealthy, too, of course—he had to be to support three other wives in addition to Helena. Euphrosyne had spent the eve of her marriage laughing and celebrating with their relatives. Gentle remarks and blushes had revealed her eagerness for the wedding. Helena had been jostled about by four women who had treated her like a doll to be ornamented, with no consideration for modesty or decorum. Her skin felt slippery after they'd threaded away all unwanted body hair, and she barely recognized her hands underneath the elaborate henna drawings. She dreaded the upcoming ceremony. Even more, she dreaded what would follow.

Her chamber felt stuffy. A cushion was set out for her to lie on, but she didn't feel like sleeping. She felt like weeping. She went outside to the courtyard garden, pulling a shawl around her shoulders to ward off the cool night air. She gazed into the heavens, where the stars shimmered in a cloudless sky like pearls on an embroidered dalmatica. It would have been a perfect spring night were it not for what was to happen the next day.

Two fortnights had passed since Leo's capitulation. She couldn't blame him—he'd had no choice. The mighty could dictate to the weak. Such had held true since the beginning of time, and it would not change until Christ

Himself returned and ruled the earth. At least she had been spared marriage before the journey. Kasim had wished it, but Helena had begged for a reprieve. She couldn't have endured the long travels while adjusting to life as a consort.

Matthias had given her sympathy on the journey, and Father Symeon had given her comfort. This life was not the end. There was hope that the next would be better. Saying goodbye to them without crying had been a task she had barely been equal to. Now, alone in the garden, the tears came. She had already accepted her lot, her duty to her people. But on this, the night before her sacrifice, she couldn't hold back the waves of grief as she knelt on the ground next to a fountain.

She wept, and then she sobbed, and then she sniffled. In time, she was calm. Life was capricious. Why should she be spared hardship? At least her suffering would have purpose. She inhaled slowly, deeply, and sent up a silent prayer for courage.

A small piece of pottery hit the ground an arm's length in front of her. She bent to pick it up. It hadn't been there before, she was sure of it. Then another hit to her left. She walked toward it, then toward a third piece and a fourth.

"Helena?" The whisper came from the wall.

She stepped closer. She should have been afraid, but so few people in Edirne knew her name that it had to be a friend. And that voice still made her heart beat a little quicker. "Ivan?"

An elm grew just beyond the high garden wall, and Ivan waited among the branches. He lowered himself from the tree and stood before her. He was fully man now, taller and broader through the shoulders than she remembered. His beard had come in, but he wore it short, so it clung to his jaw without obscuring the shape of his face. She reached for his hands and clasped them in her own, touching him to make sure he was real.

She had wondered if she would see him in Edirne, had wanted a chance to say goodbye.

Yet now that he was here, she wasn't so sure. Saying goodbye would only bring more pain. He was still everything she wanted in a husband, and knowing that their marriage would never take place tore her to pieces.

Ivan's words came in a rush. "I saw Matthias and Father Symeon. They told me what happened in Byzia. And they told me of Kasim's demands. You cannot marry him."

She should have known he would object. She would object, too, if the consequence of rejection were not so heavy. "I have no other choice."

"You have this choice: Escape with me. Tonight. Before you're married."

That was what she wanted more than anything—to escape Kasim and wed Ivan. But so many would die if she gave in to her own desires. "I have to stay. If I leave, Kasim will take his army and destroy Byzia."

"We'll fight them off together—your people and mine." Ivan ran his hands up to her shoulders.

His touch still made her skin tingle with warmth, and she had difficulty forming her next words. "Kasim's sipahis are too swift. Leo's paroikoi would be slaughtered before messengers could even reach your lands, let alone before your army could march to their aid." She'd already thought of uniting against Murad, had spent hours with Matthias, discussing the chances of success should they resist. But they had both been practical enough to see they were doomed. Kasim's army was too strong, and his was but a small part of Sultan Murad's power.

"Why would they slaughter paroikoi? The land has little value if there is no one to farm it."

"They could bring new settlers, make an example of my people. Would you have them kill Theodora and her family and a hundred other families just like them?"

Lines of pain crossed his face. "Of course I want them safe. But what of your happiness? Does it count for nothing?"

Somewhere along the road to Edirne, Helena had come to accept that the rest of her life would bring her little joy. "You must be happy enough for both of us."

Ivan shook his head in disbelief. "I cannot be happy with you married to Kasim. My brother has campaigned with him before, and he is evil. I've met him and others like him, and I know how they treat women. Helena, you would be worth less than an old warhorse to him."

"The same might be said of many Christian husbands."

His hands moved to hers again, cradling them in a plea. "But you are not choosing between Kasim and some other stranger. You are choosing between him and me. And I would be devoted to your happiness. I would love you and cherish you and honor you and put your well-being above my own. I cannot let you marry him, not while I have breath left."

She believed every word he said—had they wed, he would have treasured her, but that was never to be. She hated the Turks for breaking not only her heart but his as well. "You must allow it, Ivan. There's no other way." If there had been any other option, she would have found it and clung to it.

"But what of your promise to me? I love you, Helena. I want you for my wife. Every day I've been trapped here, I've told myself it was worth enduring because in the end, I could have you. How can I walk away and let you marry another—someone you have no love for? You think I'll leave you to misery for the rest of your life? Nay, we must escape tonight. We'll fetch your things, and I'll help you over the wall." He led her a few steps toward her chamber.

Helena pulled her hand away and squeezed her eyes shut, trying not to cry again. A profession of love like that should have lifted her to the clouds. Instead, it made the agony worse. But her misery would not be eternal. "I cannot leave. But Kasim has seen many winters. Fifty, I think. I'll serve my time as his wife, and when I am widowed, I will go to a convent and spend the rest of my days there. But perhaps it will not come to that. I've seen many women die in childbirth who wanted to live. Death for me would be an early respite."

He touched her again, on the elbow, imploring her. "I'll abduct you. We'll leave signs of a struggle, and you'll simply disappear. If you're taken against your will, the punishment cannot fall on your people."

"And you and Danilo would disappear at the same time? They would know, Ivan."

"Danilo and I could come back, if needed, to throw off suspicion."

Helena considered it. Her hopes rose for an instant before crashing down again. "Kasim knows we were promised to each other. If I disappear, he'll suspect you, and then both our people will be punished for our choice. We can't ask others to give their blood for our happiness."

"You would have me mourn out my days with a heart crushed to dust instead? Will you try nothing?" The desperation in his voice pierced her.

"You mustn't mourn for me."

"Then, I will wait for you. Thirty years, if needed."

His offer was tempting, but it wasn't fair to him. She might die before Kasim or be past childbearing age when she was finally free, if that day ever came. Ivan deserved a family, and the Turks had already forced him to wait too long. "You cannot wait for me. If you were to die in battle, would you expect me to spend the rest of my days in mourning?"

"That would be different."

"I'm not a warrior. I cannot sacrifice my life on a battlefield. But there is more than one way to give your life for your people. You mustn't deter me from my sacrifice any more than I would deter you from risking your life by going to war. Go live your dream, Ivan, as if I were dead."

"But you are not dead." He brushed a finger along her face. Despite the anguish in his voice, his touch was still tender, and her resolve almost melted. His words held truth—she was not dead, and being near him still stirred something deep within her, something that made her feel even more alive. But that only made the pain sharper.

Ivan continued his pleading. "How can I live my dream while you are enslaved in an infidel's house? Please, Helena, let me rescue you!"

"I'm sorry, Ivan, more than you know. I would rather have been your wife, lived in your city, borne your children." Her voice cracked, and she lost her battle with the tears. She folded her arms, trying to contain the agony bursting from her heart. "But that is not to be. Go, and know I wish you well."

"You wish me well? And yet you tell me I must live without you. I would rather be drawn and quartered than see you as Kasim's wife. It would be easier to live without my legs than to live without you, Helena. We should fight." He spoke too loudly for the garden, and she feared someone would hear.

Helena replied in a whisper. "You cannot stop the Turks, Ivan. They are too strong and their numbers too great. You can't defeat them any more than I can save every infant and every mother who delivers by my hand."

"Why have you lost hope?" He took her hands again. "We've beaten them before. We can do it again, without carving out my heart and laying you at the foot of a Turk. We don't have to accept this!"

"I already have accepted it because there is no other way." Helena drew in a shuddering breath. "You must leave. And you must promise me that you'll be happy again."

His face twisted with emotion. "A promise like that would be a lie, no matter how long I live."

"You once thought you couldn't stay in the kastron until spring. But you did."

His hands fell away from hers. "I should have left. If I had, I wouldn't have given you my heart only to have it thrown back at me, trampled into pieces. Would that I had killed Leo in battle, before he sold you to the Turks to cover his cowardice. He should have fought."

"Had you not spared him, Kyrios Basil would have let you die."

"Better to have died than to have fallen in love with you and see you marry Kasim. I offer to rescue you, and instead, you choose misery? You marry him and wound me more deeply than any of your soldiers ever did." He stepped away from her, every bit of him brimming with bitter rage.

How could she help him understand? She still loved Ivan, but refusing Kasim would bring consequences she couldn't live with. "Would you stand at the foot of the cross and tell the Christ to come down and walk away, to reject His purpose because it is not pleasant?"

"That was different."

"Yes. It was different. He had the entire world to save. I have the lives of a handful of paroikoi. But how could I face Him if I did not make this sacrifice? I am only one person. Is my happiness of more value than their lives and their freedom? Would you have me abandon them to Turkish pillage?"

"They are not free if they are under the Turks." His voice was dull now, as if some part of him had died. "No matter what you sacrifice, they will not be free."

"But they will be alive."

"Is life as a slave worth living?"

"That is not a choice for me to make. Nor you." Her words came out more sharply than she intended.

Ivan turned away as if he'd been slapped. Neither of them spoke for several long moments. The only sounds were the weeping of the fountain and the lamentations of a nightingale.

"I would not have us part in anger," he whispered. "I have another phrase for you to learn."

The words that followed were not the Slavonic sounds she expected, but Turkish ones. "What does it mean?"

"It means 'Allah has commanded husbands to be gentle with their wives.'"

She couldn't meet his gaze. Had he known that was one of her fears? If he was trying to protect her after her marriage, then perhaps he had finally accepted what must come. "Is it from the Koran?"

"No. But it sounds like it could be, and perhaps Kasim will think it is."

"Thank you," she whispered. "I'm sorry, Ivan, that I cannot keep my promise to you and that I'm causing you such pain. I have felt the same pain, only I've had two fortnights to live with it. Familiarity does not make it less severe, but I have learned to accept it."

"And I am sorry that I do not have a thousand ships to launch for your rescue. If I did, I would save you and your people." He reached for his neck and then took her hand, returning the pendant she'd given him when they last parted. "I think you will need this more than I will."

She looked down at the image of St. Peter the Athonite. She almost told Ivan to keep it, but he was right. She did need it, as a reminder of her faith. If only it could conjure up the help of St. Nicholas and St. Simeon. They'd helped St. Peter escape his prison, but there would be no miraculous release for her. "Build your city, Ivan. I will think of it, from time to time, and imagine its grandeur, and that image will buoy me up. I want to believe that somewhere in this world a people are led by a župan who is brave and good, even if it is not my fate to be part of it."

"I will build my city because it is my duty. But the most important part of my dream will be gone."

She reached for him, and he took her in his arms a final time. His fingers ran through her hair, and she felt his strength, his warmth, and his pain. "Goodbye, my dear, dear friend."

"I will wait all night, in case you change your mind."

"I cannot change my mind, or the lives of Byzia's paroikoi are forfeit." She stepped away reluctantly. Her burden was so great that she felt she would be crushed. And added to it was the weight of Ivan's sorrow. He deserved so much more than their broken dreams.

As she walked back to her chamber, she heard him singing new lyrics to a familiar tune.

"I have loved you since I first did see you. With this people, we do not belong. I will leave here, never to return near. All that's left of us shall be this song."

If misery had a voice, it would have sounded exactly like Ivan's in that quiet, bitter garden.

CHAPTER TWENTY-SIX
HEART OF DUST

"You can't stop eating."

Ivan glanced across the chamber at Danilo. The two were alone, for the moment. They'd skipped the day's lessons and training because Ivan hadn't been in the mood for them, hadn't been in the mood yesterday or the day before or the day before that. He wasn't fully in control of his emotions, and he didn't want his anger slipping out while he was armed. That was the overwhelming feeling—that he wasn't in control. The Ottomans were. They were in control of everyone and everything.

"How many members of the Ottoman court do you suppose we could kill before we were stopped?"

Danilo raised an eyebrow and paced in front of Ivan. "Well, if we wanted to take out a few and then escape—"

"I don't care about escaping."

"Well, in that case, two each, at the very least. Far more if we planned it right." Danilo turned when he reached the edge of Ivan's vision. "But unless we planned it very carefully, they would punish our family."

Ivan sighed. He couldn't avenge himself by attacking Murad and his court or Kasim and his household, but that didn't stop him from wishing he could. "I've never hated anyone this much. I've fought, and I've killed before, but this is something deeper." The loathing was so thick, he nearly choked on it. "I feel as though God Himself has betrayed me."

Danilo made a few thoughtful paces across the chamber. "Perhaps God sees farther than you."

He'd expected words like that from Danilo. But Danilo hadn't seen his Greek angel sacrificed to a vile Turkish warlord. Losing Helena was worse than losing his freedom, worse than losing his health, worse than losing his life.

"I'm going to give you some advice, Ivan, because you're my cousin, and more than that, because you're my friend. And then I'm going to leave the room because I don't think you're going to like it, and I don't want to argue with you."

Ivan grunted.

"I like Tatjana, but I've only talked to her twice, so I can't say I've ever been in love before. Which means I don't know exactly what it's like to have the woman you've cherished for years added to your enemy's private harem."

"Are you trying to pour salt on my wounds?"

"Sorry. I should have phrased that differently. Ivan, I don't know what you're going through. But I do know a few things. Moping about won't help her. Refusing to eat and spending half the night punching your pillow won't help her. Nor will losing your strength and giving up on your brother's plans do anything to help Kyria Helena or your family or your people. You are duty-bound to serve them. Do not let this setback—no matter how devastating—become your Achilles' heel. You're stronger than that. Let this be one more reason to drive the Turks from your land, one more reason to strengthen Sivi Gora so it will hold them back for a hundred years. Be the leader I have always known you could become, the leader I would postpone my own wedding for so I could follow you into two years of exile in Edirne."

"Adrianople. Call the city its Christian name."

Danilo smiled briefly. "Adrianople." He looked around to make sure they were still alone. "Supper will be served in an hour. I expect you to be there because four days of no food is too long for even a mighty župan. And when Kostya revokes our vassalage, our people will need a mighty župan. Rise to the occasion, Ivan. We need you."

Danilo left. Ivan listened until the sound of his footsteps faded into silence. Danilo was right. Ivan knew it, but he wasn't ready to accept it. He'd worked hard to earn Helena's heart and the right to her hand, and he'd waited two years to have her. And then she'd been stolen from him.

He stood. One of the pillows came off the cushion he'd been sitting on, and he kicked it across the marble floor. Ever since Helena had refused his rescue, he'd bottled up his frustrations as much as he could, afraid that anything more than violence to a pillow would escalate into something he couldn't control. But something had to change. He plucked a vase from its spot on top of a carved pillar and hurled it across the chamber.

It crashed into the wall and broke into a hundred pieces. Just like his heart.

He hadn't done anything so childish since he'd been four and his father had told him he couldn't see his mother because she was dead. Ivan's memory was faint that far back, but according to Konstantin and Aunt Zorica, Ivan had swiped his arm across the table and swept a dozen dishes to the ground in his frustration. Destroying the dishes hadn't brought his mother back. Nor would the ruined vase free Helena.

And yet, Ivan felt better. The smashed vase had vented his emotions just enough to allow him to think clearly.

Helena had sacrificed for her people. The requirement was cruel: submission to Kasim bin Yazid.

Ivan would also sacrifice for his people. His requirement was much different from hers. His duty was to carry on despite the wounds to his soul, despite the shattered state of his heart.

Helena was lost to him. Sivi Gora remained. He would pour all his energy into building a prosperous, able people, and pour all his blood, if needed, into ensuring their freedom. He would have his revenge on the Ottomans. But he would wait until the proper time.

Ivan trimmed his beard, changed into a fresh robe, and went to supper.

A fortnight had passed since Helena's wedding. She woke early, when Kasim's first wife, Bahar, sent her to draw water. Kasim was wealthy enough to have servants, but the real master of the house was Bahar, so Helena accepted her assignment and did so without words, for she still spoke almost no Turkish. Bahar was Kasim's age, though her hair was grayer than his. She had no children. Desislava, Kasim's third wife, said Bahar was barren and ordered the other women around as punishment for being young and fertile.

Helena balanced the heavy amphora on her hip as she brought it back through the courtyard garden. Water sloshed out the top and soaked her tunic. It probably weighed as much as Theodora, but it wasn't as heavy as the guilt would have been had Helena refused her fate and allowed Theodora and all the others to be enslaved or killed.

She took a moment to rein in her emotions before taking the water inside. Since entering Edirne, she'd felt constantly on the verge of tears. Her new husband was rough instead of gentle, demanding instead of giving.

He didn't hurt her for pleasure, and he didn't yell, but their time together left her feeling used instead of loved. Maybe it would have been different if she hadn't known how it felt to be adored, if she hadn't spent two years planning to share a bed with a man she desperately longed for. Knowing she had sacrificed passion and friendship for subjugation and indifference made everything about life in Kasim's home bitter.

Helena and the other women took their breakfast of gruel sweetened with honey in the women's harem. Arabic scripts and painted vines decorated the walls, and soft cushions lined the chamber. When the meal was finished and she'd completed the tidying-up tasks given her by Bahar, Helena sat on a low cushion and took out the book Euphrosyne had given her.

Saruca, Kasim's second wife, said something to her, but she didn't understand.

Desislava spoke Greek, albeit with an accent. "She says, 'If you were more playful, perhaps Kasim would call you more often, and then you could sleep longer in the mornings and would not be Bahar's slave.'"

Saruca smiled at Helena as Desislava translated. Then she followed her youngest as he toddled into the courtyard. She had three children, all sons, and that gave her a standing that not even Bahar could challenge.

"I prefer drawing the water."

"So do I." Desislava ran a hand over her swollen abdomen. "But it is not for me to choose. It all depends on Kasim's wishes." Desislava glanced at the book Helena held. "Do you read?"

"Yes."

"What is your book?"

"The gospels." Helena handed it to Desislava, who leafed through the pages with reverence.

"In a church in Târnovo, there is a window like this." Desislava pointed to one of the illuminations.

"Is that where you're from?" Helena knew Desislava was Bulgarian and that her marriage to Kasim was much like Helena's. Forced.

"Yes. And you?"

"Constantinople, when I was young. Then my sister married, and we moved to a pronoia, where her husband's uncle was kephale. I planned to move to Serbia next, but I was brought here instead."

"Serbia? Why?"

"I was betrothed to someone. I shouldn't speak of it. That possibility is now dead." But memory of its loss still brought tears to her eyes every night.

Desislava looked over more of the pictures. "Did you love him? The other man?"

Helena knew she shouldn't answer, but the word still escaped her lips. "Yes."

"And did he love you?"

Helena nodded.

"You are blessed to know that someone once loved you. My mother loved me. My father used me to buy peace. And Kasim uses me in the hope of having more sons. It would have been comforting to have someone besides my mother love me as a person rather than a tool."

"It doesn't feel like a blessing. Right now, it's more like an unhealed wound. A festering one that will need amputation because it will never heal on its own."

"I suppose it is also a hardship, to know you might have been happy instead." Desislava handed the book back to Helena. "Will you read it to me? I've been here almost a year, and that's what I miss most."

"How old are you, Desislava?"

"Fifteen."

That meant the poor girl had been married to Kasim at age fourteen. Helena's own twenty years prior to arriving in Edirne seemed generous in comparison. She had lost much, but so had Desislava. Their lives seemed doomed to misery the way an herb along a footpath was doomed to being trampled. But they still had one source of hope, and Helena began to read from it. "'Whosoever shall lose his life for my sake and the gospel's, the same shall find it.'"

Helena was not a martyr or a saint, but she felt as though she'd lost her life. Yet the words of the scriptures calmed her. Her sacrifice for her people had cost her dearly, but maybe, just maybe, she would not feel lost forever.

Time passed, and Helena's life developed a pattern. She grew used to putting away the bedding every morning and learned to carry water vessels on her head instead of her hips. When she and Desislava had free time, they read from the scriptures together, drawing comfort from the life of the Savior and from their friendship. Life was not happy, but nor was it miserable.

After years as a midwife, she found the scope of her new station confining. With no women or infants to tend to, the days stretched out and often felt without purpose. She had less to do, but even so, she felt less vigorous. From time to time, she made brief escapes from Kasim's home when she went to the bathhouse or the bazaar with the other wives. She didn't like the elaborate headpiece and veil she was required to wear when in public, but she looked forward to the excursions, even if they were brief. The city was more familiar to her now, with its new Islamic buildings and its older Christian ones. Both types of architecture were lovely, in their way. The food was pleasant, though it was different from what she was accustomed to, and it sometimes left her stomach unsettled. The servings were plentiful, and perhaps that was why her tunic now fit more snugly across her chest.

She paused one morning on her way to the garden fountain and recoiled at a newfound realization. It wasn't the Turkish food that drew her tunic tight and made her nauseated and less vigorous. She'd been married to Kasim for two moons. And during that time, her menses had not come even once. She was carrying his child.

She should be happy. A baby was a blessing. She didn't love her husband, had no desire to give him anything, but a baby would be innocent, in need of her love and care. Even if she never grew to love Kasim, surely she could love an infant, regardless of who the father was. A child would give her days purpose and ease her loneliness.

Would it be a boy or a girl? She tried to picture it, but the wisp of hope dissipated. A son would grow up to be just like Kasim—bloodthirsty, arrogant. The Muslims showed great respect to their mothers, but as a Christian, Helena would always be an inferior. And if the child were a daughter, what life could she look forward to? A life like that of Bahar or Saruca? A daughter was destined to a life almost as wretched as her mother's.

Helena kept it secret for a week before confiding in Desislava.

"Our children can grow up together." Desislava took Helena's hands in hers and smiled. "And you will have something over Bahar—perhaps she will stop treating you like a slave."

Helena wasn't ready to tell Bahar, though she didn't care if Saruca knew. The lithe second wife was aloof but not unkind. She supposed she should tell Kasim, but she put it off.

Another week passed. Bahar sent her to fetch water early one morning, as usual. Helena went down the stairs into the courtyard, then crossed through the garden. She was still fiddling with her veil when she heard a voice.

"Dama Helena?"

Helena stopped midstride. Barely visible in the shadow of a peach tree was a man. At first glimpse, she thought him Turkish, but he wore no turban on his head, he'd used a Serbian title, and he'd spoken Greek, though with an accent. Ivan's kinsman crouched between the trees and the periwinkle-covered wall. She let the veil fall from her face. "Danilo?"

"Yes. Ivan asked that I come and offer you another chance to escape. If you're not happy, let us take you elsewhere. Ivan knows he cannot have you while you're married to another, but he would see you safely away from Edirne. You can enter a convent or travel to Constantinople or Mystras. Surely you would be happier elsewhere?"

Helena frowned. Would a convent take a woman expecting a baby? She could find satisfaction as a midwife in a Christian city, but what would become of her people? "The circumstances that compelled me to marry Kasim haven't changed."

"Ivan predicted you would say something like that, but he wanted to offer you a final escape. He would have come himself, but he feared he'd sin by coveting another man's wife."

"And if I agreed to go? Would he not covet me then?"

"If you agreed to come, he would generously endow a convent or a monastery as penance. Or risk hellfire if he sinned in the process of taking you somewhere safe, where you could be happy."

Helena glanced around the garden, making sure no one watched their conversation. How like Ivan, to sacrifice and risk for her, even when they couldn't be together. "How is he?" His mournful song from their last goodbye whispered through her mind, breaking her heart all over again.

Danilo didn't answer immediately. "His sense of duty is strong, so he will continue his work. But he is pained with worry for you. I've never seen him so melancholy." Danilo shifted in the shadows. "He asked me to see how you are. You look unhappy."

"I am unhappy. Would that console him, do you think?" She suspected his pain was similar to hers, and she longed to soften it. If only she could mix herbs into a salve that would ease both their grief.

"I think he would rather you be content. But if that contentment came from another man, it might make his own pain worse."

A cook entered the other side of the garden. Helena fastened her veil to her headpiece, leaving only her eyes visible. She couldn't stay much longer. "You must tell Ivan what you think is best. I want him to be happy. More than anything, I want him to have joy. Tell him I am miserable, or tell him I am blissful. Whatever it takes to help him move on."

"You evaded your guard?" Ivan asked as soon as Danilo returned.

Danilo nodded and held up a waterskin. It had been full of plum wine when he'd left. Now it looked empty. Some of their guards avoided alcohol, in compliance with Mohammad's teachings. But many of them didn't.

"Did you find her?"

"Yes."

"Will she leave?"

"No."

Ivan looked away. He hadn't thought she would. Yet a sliver of hope had burrowed into his heart that perhaps her time with Kasim had changed her mind or somehow had changed the conditions that held her in Edirne. "Was she happy?"

Danilo didn't answer.

"Well?"

"She told me I should tell you whatever would best enable you to move on."

Ivan studied his cousin's expression. It revealed nothing. "I'm interested in the truth. Did she have bruises? Is he beating her?"

"I saw only her face and her hands. There were no bruises there. Nor was there anything obviously wrong with her movements."

Ivan folded his arms across his chest. Just because Kasim hadn't bruised her face or broken her legs didn't mean he wasn't hurting her. Ivan had heard Konstantin's stories from campaigns in Anatolia. Kasim had battered women before. He might do it again. "What did she say?"

"She said she wants you to be happy." Danilo sat next to Ivan on the cushion. "She's sacrificed a great deal for her people. Perhaps it would be best if you didn't add to her burden by permanently mourning her."

"She won't know whether I'm happy or sad, so I don't see how I'm adding to her burden."

"Do you plan on pining over her for the rest of your days?"

Ivan scowled. "Right now, I am planning to leave Adrianople. And I never intend to return, unless I'm at the head of a vast army planning its conquest."

Danilo raised one eyebrow, as if considering whether to change the subject back to Ivan's lost love or move it forward to their escape. "I suggest a variation of plan five. The oil-wrestling at Kırkpınar is in two days' time. It should serve our purposes."

Ivan nodded. They had received Konstantin's warning the day before. He would have sent it far enough in advance that they could wait two days for an opportune chance to escape. "You'll alert the man about the horses?" The guards didn't follow Danilo as closely as they followed Ivan. Even if they did, the Greek Christian they planned to purchase horses from was a leatherworker. Danilo could buy a belt, and no one would suspect the visit was anything more.

"Yes."

"Palfreys, not destriers."

Danilo's lips turned down in a familiar expression, one he'd been making for years. Normally, he reserved it for Nevena, Konstantin's cook, when she tried to turn the boys out of the kitchen so they'd stop snitching her freshly baked pastries.

Ivan uncrossed his arms and met his cousin's gaze. "We'll have a long ride."

"What if we're pursued?"

"If the two of us are attacked, it would take more than a warhorse to even the odds."

"But a proper warhorse would help."

Ivan almost smiled at his cousin's pouting lower lip. "Palfreys."

CHAPTER TWENTY-SEVEN
KIRKPINAR

Soldiers, wealthy timar-holders, craftsmen, and peasants crowded the grassy fields of Kırkpınar. Not a woman was in sight. The scent of sweat and olive oil from the wrestling matches blended with roasted lamb and sliced melons from vendors selling food to spectators. Ivan watched one of the pehlivans lift his opponent over his head, winning his match amid the dozens of other contests. Ivan's newest guard stood behind him.

Danilo was late. Ivan wasn't ready to panic yet, but he felt eager to leave. He'd been eager to leave since the day he'd arrived as hostage.

A deep chuckle bellowed down the field from where a pair of boys attempted to pull each other to the ground. Ivan turned and recognized the laughter's source. Hatred welled inside him, stronger than he'd expected.

Ivan had defended Byzia. Kasim had defeated it.

Ivan had fallen in love with Helena. Kasim had married her.

Did the large soldier laughing at the young wrestlers know how completely he'd bested Ivan, how thoroughly he'd devastated and demoralized him? Kasim looked up and met Ivan's eyes. His laughter turned to a sneer. Yes, he knew.

Ivan stalked away. Provoking Kasim wouldn't free Helena or her people. It would probably backfire and make things worse for Ivan's lands because the Ottomans had their eyes on expansion. The moment he and Danilo left, the Ottomans would be free to attack. Ivan prayed Konstantin was ready.

Danilo slid next to him and lowered his voice to a whisper so the guards wouldn't hear. "The horses are waiting. About a half mile to the north, by a hill and a copse of trees. But Iskandar is following me. I think he suspects something."

Ivan had seen the scar on Danilo's arm, and he remembered the friends he'd lost during Iskandar's siege. "He's dangerous."

Danilo nodded once. "He's closer now. I think seeing the two of us together makes him nervous."

"We'll split up. Slip away to the horses when you can. Be there by the tenth hour, even if you can't lose him."

Danilo nodded again and walked away. A few strides later, Ivan checked over his shoulder to see how closely his guard tailed him. The hairs on the back of his neck prickled when he saw Iskandar conversing with Kasim.

Having multiple enemies was dangerous. Having enemies who cooperated with each other was even worse.

The crowd cheered as a muscled pehlivan raised his opponent over his shoulders, thus gaining a victory. Ivan wasn't surprised. Though their height was roughly equal, the winner was significantly larger. He bowed his bulky body and kissed his defeated rival's hand to show respect for the man's age, then lifted his oiled arms above his head in a gesture of triumph.

"He's about your height. I wonder how a match between the two of you would shape out."

Ivan recognized that voice. Kasim stood a few paces away, surrounded by members of his entourage, looking to Ivan for a response. Ivan glanced at the champion pehlivan. "I'm not a wrestler."

Kasim scoffed. "Neither is he. Cemal bin Salih is one of my soldiers, a specialist in sapping walls. This is his first tournament."

"His success reflects well on his leader. You must be pleased. No doubt your training is key to his current triumph."

"You would better appreciate his training after a round against him, I think."

Ivan had watched the matches the year before, and he and Danilo had practiced what they'd seen—without the olive oil. Ivan had no desire to wrestle a champion like Cemal. "Wrestling is not a tradition among my people."

"I insist."

"I'm a hostage, not a slave. I respectfully decline." Ivan turned to walk away.

"It is your right to decline, of course." Kasim matched Ivan's pace. "But I am in the mood for a struggle. A violent one. If you won't provide one against Cemal, I shall have to have one with my newest wife."

Ivan paused midstep and squeezed his eyes shut. He had neither the desire nor the time to wrestle Cemal, but he couldn't leave Helena to suffer the consequences of his refusal. "And if I agree?"

"If you agree, then the next time I wish to enjoy one of my wives, it will be as a contented man who has no reason to be rough."

Ivan's fingers itched to grab his dagger from his boot and plunge it into Kasim's chest, but if he struck Kasim, the surrounding guards would finish him. Ivan could do his brother and his people no good if he were dead, so he nodded his agreement. Across the field, Iskandar seemed thoroughly absorbed in one of the matches. With Iskandar distracted, Danilo was probably losing his guard and heading off to the horses. Ivan ought to be joining him, not playing Kasim's games, but he didn't have much of a choice.

"My servant will see that you're given the proper clothing." Kasim motioned one of his men forward. "Make sure it is a good match, or my Greek beauty will writhe in pain." He turned abruptly and sauntered away, his neck erect and his stride confident.

"This way." Kasim's bulky servant nudged Ivan toward a tent some distance from the field. Ivan's guard followed them.

What would Kasim consider a good match? Would an hour be sufficient, or was Kasim seeking something more like the original Kırkpınar match, which had lasted an entire day? The opponents, two Ottoman soldiers, had both died from the struggle, then their army had gone on to conquer Adrianople. Ivan peered at the searing summer sun. The hours were longer this time of year. Even if they'd been in the middle of winter, lasting an hour against Cemal, or anyone else, sounded as though it would tax every bit of his limited wrestling abilities. Danilo and Ivan had spent more time at swordplay than at wrestling, but they'd done enough to know that wrestling demanded copious amounts of strength, endurance, and clearheadedness.

Danilo appeared in the edge of Ivan's vision, his eyebrows scrunched together in inquiry. Ivan motioned him over.

"What's going on?" Danilo asked.

"I am to become a pehlivan."

The bewildered look on Danilo's face would have brought laughter under different circumstances. "Why?"

"Kasim insists. That is why."

Danilo walked beside him in silence. Ivan would give him a better explanation when they were alone. He didn't think Kasim's servant understood Slavonic, but he didn't want to risk it.

The servant called to another man in rapid Turkish. He brought a piece of clothing and gave it to Ivan. "You may change in there." He pointed to a tent. "Leave your clothes inside."

Ivan went in, taking Danilo with him.

"Why does Kasim want you to wrestle?" Danilo whispered.

"Because taking the kastron I defended and marrying the woman I loved wasn't enough of a humiliation."

Danilo flipped the flap of the tent open a crack. "We don't have time for this."

"I know."

"My guard hasn't found us yet, so there's only the two nearby. You deal with your shadow, and I'll knock out Kasim's man. Then we'll make for the horses. Our absence will be noticed sooner, but that can't be helped. We'll still have a chance."

Ivan shook his head. "I have to give Kasim a good match."

"No, you don't. But you do have to get away before the messengers arrive to tell Murad that your brother refused to pay the tribute this year."

"It's not that simple."

"Why? You want to show him up to satisfy your pride? What about prudence? Your duty to lead your people?"

Ivan removed his boots and hose and put on the kispet he was to wrestle in. It covered the skin from his hips to just below the knees. "This is not about pride. This is about what I owe Helena. Kasim said that if I don't wrestle, he'll hurt her."

Danilo frowned as he checked outside the tent again. "From what I've heard of Helena, she knows all about duty. Her duty to her people required her to marry someone like Kasim. Your duty to your people requires you to get home as quickly as possible. We'll be needed when Murad sends his army for revenge."

"I can't sneak off and let Helena suffer because of it. You've heard the stories from the campaigns in Anatolia. You know what Kasim is capable of." Ivan stripped off his knee-length tunic so he was naked from the waist up. He handed Danilo his coin pouch and his dagger. He planned to come back for his clothes, but if something changed their plans, they needed the coins for their journey, and the extra weapon might prove useful.

Danilo put Ivan's pouch into his own and tied both to his belt. He slipped the dagger into his boot. "Ivan . . . you can wrestle every man on this field, and it won't do anything to change the fact that her husband is vile and her life with him will always be unpleasant."

"There is a difference between an unpleasant life and a tortured one."

"Yes. And I suppose you know all about it because of your tortured heart."

"She healed me after this, Danilo." Ivan pointed to the scar along his abdomen. "Regardless of anything else, she saved my life—more than once. I owe her this."

The tension in Danilo's jaw softened, and he crossed his arms in resignation. "Maybe you do. But try not to get hurt, because when this is over, we need to ride."

Slick olive oil poured down Ivan's neck and across his chest. He did his best to coat his skin. As one official poured oil over the pehlivans, another man spoke in rapid Turkish, explaining the rules. Ivan knew how it worked. Cemal would win if he exposed Ivan's umbilicus to the sky, if he lifted him over his shoulders, or if he picked him up and carried him five paces.

Danilo helped spread the oil across Ivan's back. "Hold out long enough to satisfy Kasim, then let's get out of here," Danilo whispered. "Cemal's had at least one match. Maybe he's tired. But for you, time is more important than winning."

Ivan nodded. He didn't have to win, needn't feel shame or pride about his performance. He just had to put up a decent fight and come out able to ride home.

Kasim and Iskandar spoke to each other twenty paces away. Ivan glanced at them, then at his and Danilo's guards. "What I haven't figured out yet is why. Is this just another humiliation from Kasim? Or am I missing something?"

Danilo poured more oil on him. "I haven't figured it out either. Be careful."

The official motioned Danilo away, and Ivan stood facing Cemal. They were the same height, but the similarities ended there. Closely cropped bristles surrounded Cemal's round head. Hair covered his massive chest, and the oil seemed to make the muscles of his torso bulge.

The two bowed to each other and gripped hands.

"Begin."

Cemal surged forward, forcing Ivan back. Cemal was every bit as strong as he looked. Ivan regained his footing and stopped the charge, for the moment.

They pushed against each other, changing positions slightly. Ivan tried to grab Cemal's arm, but his hand slipped on the oiled skin. Cemal slid behind Ivan and gripped him around the waist with one arm. Ivan drove into the forearm, barely twisting free.

The two faced each other again, a few handspans apart. Cemal slipped an arm around Ivan's wrist and pulled it up, pinning it into Cemal's armpit. With his other hand, he gripped the waistband of Ivan's trousers. His movements were so quick that Ivan could barely follow them. Their heads were close. Ivan felt the prick of Cemal's mustache and the sweat running down the man's cheek. He pushed Cemal's shoulder back, but not enough to free his hand.

Cemal tugged on Ivan's trousers, nearly yanking him off-balance. It took all Ivan's strength to keep from being pulled over. Then Cemal released the kispet and swung his arm around to whack the back of Ivan's head. The pain jarred him for a moment. In the distance, he recognized Danilo's voice raised in protest amid a multitude of jeers and shouts. But Ivan had seen others do the same thing. Cemal's move was legal.

Ivan pushed forward, and Cemal shifted just enough for Ivan to pull his hand free. They separated for a moment. Ivan took a cautious step sideways. Cemal matched him, and they circled the grass for a pace before trying to grab each other's shoulders again. Cemal slid a hand between Ivan's arm and abdomen and pulled him off-balance as he slipped behind him. He yanked Ivan's back to his chest and wrapped his arms around, pinning Ivan's arms to his sides. Even with the oil, Ivan couldn't slip from the hold.

Cemal's hand shot down Ivan's trousers, following the line of his scar. Ivan had seen enough matches to know it was common to reach inside the waistband. But it surprised him how much leverage Cemal suddenly had as he twisted Ivan off his feet. Ivan grabbed one of Cemal's legs to keep from being hoisted over the man's shoulders. He doubted he'd satisfied Kasim's thirst for a struggle yet. Cemal heaved on the trousers, and Ivan wondered which would break first—his skin or the leather kispet.

Cemal yanked again, but Ivan's grip on the man's leg was firm enough to keep Cemal from an immediate victory. Ivan hung upside down through a few more tugs. Then he grabbed behind Cemal's other knee and ripped his foot off the ground. They both tumbled into the thick grass. Cemal grunted in pain and ripped his hand from Ivan's kispet.

Ivan tried to scramble to his feet, but Cemal grabbed his knees and kept him in the grass. Cemal got to his feet, still holding Ivan's knees, and plowed Ivan's chest and face into the ground. Ivan balanced on his outstretched arms and his face. Dirt invaded his nostrils. He couldn't see and could barely breathe. He'd watched more than one pehlivan defeat his opponent by pushing his face into the ground and nearly suffocating him. Cemal bent lower, his head near Ivan's kidneys. He applied steady pressure, then bursts of added force. Ivan couldn't balance like this forever. He could roll. Then he'd be able to breathe, but from that position, it would be a simple matter for Cemal to pin him. Ivan coughed into the grass. It felt as though the bones of his back were being crushed together.

He couldn't see, but his hearing was still sharp. "Like the barrows, Ivan!" Danilo called out.

Ivan felt befuddled, as if he'd had too much wine. The pressure on his torso was almost unbearable. What did Danilo mean? As boys, they'd played on the barrows, but what did that have to do with wrestling? Danilo and Ivan had practiced archery there, hunted there, and sparred with swords there, but they'd never tried to bury each other headfirst in the earth.

Then it hit him. They'd often gone to the barrows, wrapped themselves in old cloaks, and rolled down the hills. They'd be dizzy, rest, and do it again. Danilo was telling him to roll.

Ivan wasn't sure it would work, but he was desperate. He twisted, rolling onto his back. Cemal was probably hoping for just such an opportunity to pin his opponent to the ground. But as Ivan twisted, he ripped his legs free and swiped them under Cemal's, knocking him to the ground. The two grappled in the long grass for a few moments, but neither could get a decent grip on the other.

Cemal backed away for a moment, giving both of them a chance to regain their footing. Cemal went for Ivan's shoulders. Ivan shrugged underneath him and brought his hands around, trapping Cemal in a hold so his hands extended behind Ivan's head, where he couldn't do more than feebly swat at Ivan's skull. Ivan held his head back so Cemal's headbutts were less effective.

Cemal twisted and yanked, but Ivan held on. He couldn't win the match by holding Cemal there, but he thought Cemal's efforts to escape wearied him more than Ivan's efforts to hold him did. For the moment, that was enough. It was a break of sorts. Cemal grunted and pulled. It wasn't a restful break.

The sun's rays warmed them, and the smell of olive oil and sweaty men replaced the scent of grass and soil. Cemal used his head to knock at Ivan's collarbone, but Ivan didn't dare let go. A bruised collarbone was a small price for the momentary reprieve. Cemal could do far more damage if he were free.

Kasim strode to the official and whispered in his ear. Perhaps the match had grown too dull for Kasim's taste. Maybe he'd find it more satisfying if Ivan tugged Cemal around a little more. Ivan took a tentative step to the right, pulling Cemal with him. Moving seemed risky—Cemal might figure out a way to escape. But it might lead to opportunity.

Could Ivan pin the man he now held in an arm lock? Or lift him over his head? Cemal jerked his arms apart and almost broke Ivan's hold. He did it again a few times, but Ivan was prepared for it, so he held.

"We will pause the match," a Turkish voice said.

Ivan looked at the official to confirm. Cemal's arms went slack, and Ivan released him. The two bowed slightly to each other and separated, Cemal to Kasim and Ivan to Danilo.

"Now they give you a break, when you're finally winning."

Ivan took the cloth Danilo offered and wiped the oil from around his eyes and the dirt from the rest of his face. "I'm not winning."

"You could have fooled me."

"I'm just not losing for the moment. There's a difference."

"You broke his hold. He couldn't break yours."

Ivan shook out the cloth and wiped at the back of his neck. "His hold. You could have been a little clearer with your clue."

Danilo pursed his lips. "If I had been any clearer, Cemal would have known what to expect."

Ivan lifted his face skyward. His neck was sore, and so was the rest of his body. "I'm not made for wrestling."

Danilo handed him a clay cup of water. "You're doing better than they thought you would. Keep it up. I know I said you only needed to hold even with him long enough to impress Kasim, but there's more to it now. The better you do, the more they'll think twice before attacking us."

"So, now you're saying I need to win?"

"If you can."

Ivan finished the water and applied more olive oil. Cemal spoke with Kasim. Ivan wasn't convinced that he could beat him, but surely their skirmish had been enough of a struggle to appease Helena's husband. "I could let him win, and then we could leave."

Danilo shook his head. "Show weakness and you put our people at risk."

"Any ideas on how to beat him?"

"His arms are stronger than yours, but your legs seem about equal. If you can neutralize his upper body, you'll have a chance. Otherwise, keep moving. You're quicker than him."

Kasim sent Cemal off, and immediately, the official motioned Ivan back to the field. Ivan and Cemal bowed to each other, and then the official ordered them to begin.

Cemal didn't lunge toward Ivan immediately. Ivan held back, wondering what type of trick his opponent was planning.

"You are skilled," Cemal said.

"Not as skilled as you."

"I am more practiced, but that is not the same thing."

They both circled the spot of grass.

"I have learned wrestling for years," Cemal continued. "It is a tradition among my people. Think what you could be if it were your tradition as well."

"Our tradition is with the sword. I would readily agree to a contest of blades over another round of wrestling."

Cemal shook his head. "You have been among my people two years, yes?"

"Yes." Two years and sixty-five days, each one of them time stolen from his family and his people.

"And have you thought of joining us? Say the Shahada now, and I will be witness to your conversion. We will go to an imam, and he will also witness it. You will be greatly honored."

"I was born a Christian, and I will die a Christian."

Cemal glanced to the side of the field. "And your mixed-blood companion? Does he feel the same?"

Ivan's anger flared. "Mixed blood? If my kinsman's blood is mixed, it is a combination of courage and loyalty. And yes, he feels the same." They'd talked about it before. Both would die before they renounced their faith.

"It's a pity you will not see the true faith. I will give you a final chance, for I noted your courage during the siege of Byzia when I nearly mined your walls, and I would welcome you as an ally. Conversion to Islam might save your life."

"I will again decline."

"You are a good soldier, are you not?"

Ivan nodded, wary.

"Then you understand that I, too, am a good soldier. And I must be obedient." Cemal lunged at Ivan.

Ivan hadn't meant to let his guard down, but he wasn't quite quick enough to escape. Cemal grabbed one arm and reached for Ivan's shoulder. Ivan blocked the shoulder, grasping at Cemal's wrist. With his other hand, Cemal dug into the flesh of Ivan's arm and clawed at him. It was no more painful than the other moves had been, but it surprised him. When Ivan pulled away, four lines of blood marred his bicep.

Cemal's lips turned down, almost as if in apology. "I'm afraid the rules will be a bit different this round."

"I thought the rules were established years ago."

"Only if they are enforced." Cemal ran at Ivan's torso and nearly toppled him.

Ivan grabbed one of Cemal's arms and held it. But the rest of Cemal's body was too far away for the hold to be useful. Ivan tried to yank him closer, but Cemal's freshly oiled skin slid from his grasp. Cemal reached for Ivan's waistband, and Ivan ducked away. He lunged for the bottom of Cemal's kispet and grabbed at the leather. Cemal tottered but stayed on his feet.

Remembering Danilo's advice, Ivan rushed at his opponent before Cemal could fully regain his balance. He slipped behind him, thrust his hand into the kispet, and lifted Cemal off his feet. Ivan panted as he took a step forward, carrying Cemal, but before he made even half of the five paces required to win, Cemal's foot pounded into the side of Ivan's head. His vision turned black for an instant, and he lost his grip on Cemal.

The kick hadn't been an accidental flailing. It had been forceful, intentional, and well-aimed. The move was illegal, but the official said nothing. The crowd of onlookers roared—but Ivan couldn't tell if the noise held approval or protest. He backed away to let his head clear as Cemal scrambled to his feet.

Cemal recovered more quickly than Ivan. He reached for Ivan's waist-band, and Ivan leaned in so it would be harder for Cemal to maneuver. He blocked Cemal's hand and tried to get behind him, but Cemal was too swift. The wrestler attacked again, taking Ivan's shoulder and gripping the kispet, but Ivan twisted away and managed to give Cemal a solid knock on the back of the head with his fist. He would have rather kicked him in the ear to make things even, but he had the feeling that he wouldn't get away with flouting the rules.

As they turned, Ivan glimpsed Danilo arguing with an official, but he didn't have time to watch. Of course Danilo would be upset that Cemal was winning with unfair moves. In all the matches Ivan had watched, he'd never seen any of the other pehlivans break the rules. They might push the boundaries, but it was a matter of honor to follow the guidelines, and few Turks would risk their honor. Had Cemal's conversation been an explanation? He was following orders. And surely for him, obedience to Kasim was more important than respect for the rules.

Ivan had to end it, quickly. His head pounded—he couldn't take too many more maulings from Cemal and still make his escape. He feigned a grab at his opponent's kispet, and when Cemal moved to deflect it, Ivan grabbed the man's arm and pulled it in with his elbow, holding it next to his ribs. He used his free hand to block Cemal's other hand. Then he put pressure on Cemal's forearm, bending it until Cemal cried out in pain.

Cemal tore his hand away and yanked at Ivan's kispet. Ivan slid on the oil-covered grass. He would have kept his balance under normal circumstances, but Cemal saw what was happening and dove into Ivan's legs. They hit the earth in a jumble of oiled skin and slick breeches. Somehow, in the process, Cemal kneed Ivan between the legs. Ivan fell inward. He told himself to keep fighting, but the pain was paralyzing. It wasn't a legal move, but the official either hadn't seen it or didn't care.

Ivan grunted. Inhaled. Tried to rise.

Before he could, Cemal was behind him, slipping an arm around Ivan's neck and pulling, blocking Ivan's breath.

"I told you the rules would be different this round. And I offered you a chance. You could have chosen conversion. Instead, you chose death." Cemal's words came in gasps, as if he were just as exhausted as Ivan was. "Why are the Serbs so stubborn?"

Was that the purpose of the match? An elaborate assassination, one that could be called an accident? Would a messenger tell Konstantin that Ivan's pride had led him to reckless sporting? And would Konstantin believe it?

It wouldn't matter. Either way, Ivan would be dead.

Cemal's grip grew tighter. Ivan tried to pull Cemal's arm away. He clawed at it, bashed his free elbow into Cemal's ribs. But he couldn't get any air. He heard Danilo's voice, but couldn't understand the words. His vision blurred. He planted his feet on the ground and pushed with all his might. Cemal's grip loosened enough for Ivan to inhale, but then Cemal's arm clamped back around Ivan's throat.

If Ivan broke the rules, he would lose. If he kept them, he would die. He stomped on the inside of Cemal's foot. Cemal's arm moved ever so slightly, and Ivan bit it as hard as he could. Cemal cried out, and the pressure on Ivan's neck eased enough for him to slip from Cemal's grasp. Ivan spun around and punched Cemal first in the nose, then in the left eye. Blood spewed from Cemal's nose, and rage filled his face as he stumbled back. He growled and looked like he was about to charge. But Ivan felt something sharp cut into his back.

"Stop! At once!" Three Ottoman soldiers in brightly colored robes surrounded Ivan, the tips of their spears pressing into his unprotected skin. He glanced around and found Danilo on his knees, with soldiers on either side of him, holding his shoulders down and pulling his arms back. The guards soon pushed Ivan into the same position.

"What is the meaning of this?" Bayezid, the sultan's son, stepped forward, with Kasim at his side. Ivan hadn't noticed Bayezid before. He must have arrived after the match had begun.

"Perhaps that is a question best answered by Kasim," Ivan said. "He forced me into the match and ordered Cemal to kill me."

The sultan's son glared. "You were not following the rules."

"Cemal broke them first."

Bayezid shook his head. "Not the wrestling rules. You came here as hostage to ensure your brother's cooperation." Bayezid held up a folded piece of parchment. "Your brother refused to send tribute. He broke the rules." Bayezid eyed Ivan, then Danilo. "You are no longer honored guests. You are prisoners. And you will be executed for your deceit."

CHAPTER TWENTY-EIGHT
THE SOUND OF TURKISH DRUMS

How had Bayezid received Konstantin's rejection so quickly? The message telling Ivan and Danilo to leave had arrived but a few days ago. Ivan gazed up at the sultan's son, loathing him and all he stood for. "Are you the sultan, that you can order his hostages killed?"

Danilo nudged Ivan with his knee. "Don't anger him," he whispered.

Ivan usually listened to Danilo, but he didn't have anything to lose. If Bayezid ordered their execution and walked off, Kasim and Iskandar would carry it out. Better to test Bayezid's resolve and question his authority than to do nothing.

Bayezid stared down at Ivan for a long moment, then turned to Kasim. "I return to Anatolia tomorrow. I wish to see their impaled bodies along the road when I ride out."

Ivan cursed. Of course. They did have something to lose. The manner of execution. Iskandar stood at the edge of Bayezid's entourage, grinning in satisfaction. As Bayezid strutted away, Iskandar and Kasim strode forward.

Kasim spoke first. "You're very predictable, Ivan Miroslavević. I knew you would try to run. And I knew exactly how to keep you here. Fool. I don't beat my wives. I have much better uses for them." Kasim sneered at the two Serbs kneeling in the grass, then followed Bayezid.

Iskandar made no move to follow. Perhaps it was his task to oversee the executions. "You almost made it, didn't you?"

Ivan watched Bayezid hand the parchment to one of his attendants, then mount a magnificent horse and ride away. "You received news of Konstantin's rejection quicker than I expected."

Iskandar smirked. "We requested the tribute early this year. The group you watched ride out was our second delegation, a decoy. It included our swiftest riders so that when they met the first group, they could bring us word at once. We could never figure out what the signal from Rivak would be, but we knew it would come. So we held all messages from your brother for at least a fortnight before giving them to you." He motioned to the guards. "Take them off the field. We mustn't spoil any more of the matches."

Eight guards and Iskandar escorted them away from the pehlivans. All the wrestling matches had stopped. Cemal stood in the distance, one eye swollen shut. He watched the prisoners being led off the field until he met Ivan's gaze and turned away. Other observers didn't hide their interest as they followed the two disgraced hostages. The executions wouldn't take place on the Kırkpınar field, but they would be public. Fear, dread, and regret swirled round Ivan. If they'd left only a day earlier, they might have escaped. Instead, their enemy had outsmarted them, and a cruel, agonizing death would be the consequence.

Iskandar halted just beyond the tent where Ivan had changed his clothes before the match. "Here." Several of the guards held the onlookers back as more pressed in from behind. Other guards, three on each prisoner, forced Ivan and Danilo to their knees again.

Iskandar picked up a long wooden pole. One end had been sharpened into a point and lubricated with oil. "This one will suit you nicely. If we follow your spine, perhaps you will still be alive to watch Bayezid ride out tomorrow." He waved the sharp end in Ivan's face. "It is hard to put into words how eagerly I've awaited this day. A chance to avenge my father's death. When you were a hostage, I couldn't touch you, no matter how well my spies followed your movements, no matter how vulnerable you were. But you're no longer under the sultan's protection. Farewell, Ivan Miroslavević, one-time defender of Byzia and disloyal vassal of Sultan Murad."

Iskandar nodded to the guards, and they pushed Ivan to the ground on his stomach and held him so he couldn't move. One straddled his back and one held each of his arms. None of them was quite as muscled as Cemal, but there were three of them, and they weren't worn out from a wrestling match. Ivan's head still spun from Cemal's kick and near strangulation. He hadn't a hope of escaping.

The beating of his heart seemed loud, like a semantron calling the faithful to worship. Did it know it would soon beat its last? Sometimes it took a week for the impaled to die, but maybe Ivan would be lucky and be dead before he had to witness his best friend's impalement. Danilo had voluntarily followed him into two years of exile. Ivan was sickened to think that this was what he had led him to.

If this was to be his end, Ivan wanted to die bravely, so he clenched his jaw so it wouldn't tremble and told himself not to grovel.

Danilo had other plans. Ivan heard him roar as he barged his way to his feet and threw one of his guards into the tip of the pole. Danilo ripped a spear from the other guard's hands and struck down the man kneeling on Ivan's back, then jabbed his elbow into another guard's face.

Ivan rolled and twisted from the grasp of the two guards who'd been holding his oil-slicked arms. He grabbed a fallen guard's spear and gutted the nearest man, then stole that one's weapon.

"Come on, Ivan!"

Ivan followed Danilo into the crowd of onlookers, but not before catching sight of Iskandar. His eyes were narrowed into livid slits, and his mouth was open in rage, calling out orders.

The crowd parted for the two armed refugees. When the spectators weren't quick enough, Danilo shoved them out of the way. Ivan kept glancing back, but at least a few members of the crowd stayed between them and Iskandar's retinue.

They pushed through the last of the bystanders to where the crowd thinned. Men still rushed toward the group, drawn to commotion like vultures to carrion. Ivan and Danilo kept their spears in hand and fled for their lives across the fields of Kırkpınar.

Ivan wore no shoes, and bits of rock struck his feet. Better for his foot to be impaled with gravel than for his intestines to be skewered on a pike. Bloody feet and sore lungs were nothing compared to what he ran from. He wasn't fully recovered from the match against Cemal, but training with sipahis had left him tough.

Ivan checked behind and saw Iskandar directing a pair of bowmen. "Danilo! Archers! Curve to the left!"

Danilo obeyed without looking back or breaking step. They ran back to the center, then to the right. Arrows whistled past them, but they dodged each missile. They were almost into the trees, where they would have cover.

Then three Ottomans armed with scimitars blocked their path.

What I wouldn't give for a sword. Ivan would have said it aloud, but he was panting too hard.

"Barrel through," Ivan told Danilo. They didn't have time to slow down and carefully prepare their assault. They were outnumbered, and the enemy had the better weapons, so he and Danilo had to use their speed to the utmost advantage.

The Ottoman swordsmen spread out to make certain Danilo and Ivan couldn't bypass them. They raised their scimitars in disciplined unity, ready to strike. As they converged, Ivan skewered one and pushed him into another. Danilo used his spear shaft to block his opponent's blade, then thrust the tip into the man's neck.

Ivan yanked at his spear, but it wouldn't pull free of its victim. He grabbed the scimitar from the dying man's hands. He blocked a strike from the other guard, shoved him back, and ran on.

"This way!" Danilo called. They were ahead of their pursuers, even with the delay the swordsmen had caused, but the Kırkpınar fields were a flurry of movement. Some soldiers continued to give chase, and others fetched horses. Time was not on Ivan and Danilo's side.

They ran past a camp of traders, over a small stream, and around a hill. Ivan skirted boulders, hopped over logs, and stubbed his toes so often he lost count. But around the hill, in a grove of trees, waited four horses. Two were saddled. Ivan could guess which horse Danilo had intended for himself, because a strung bow and full quiver hung from the saddle. A boy leaped to his feet as Ivan and Danilo ran into the shade. Ivan freed the reins from where they were tied to a branch.

Danilo handed the boy some coins. "If you know what's good for you, you'll run away and pretend you never saw us."

The boy nodded and disappeared into the trees.

Ivan grabbed the lead rope for the spare palfrey and mounted his horse. By then, Iskandar had arrived.

Ivan had to admire his courage. The ghazi had outridden his men, and now he was vulnerable. Iskandar charged toward them, forcing his horse over fallen logs and across the uneven ground. Danilo drew out his bow and launched an arrow at their enemy. At the same time, Iskandar's horse reared up. Iskandar tumbled to the ground, and the arrow flew into the stallion's underbelly. Danilo drew another arrow, but horse and rider were on the ground, hidden among the undergrowth.

Iskandar's men were not far behind, a score strong, mounted on swift horses.

Danilo launched arrows into the grass where Iskandar had fallen, but between the horse and the brush, Ivan couldn't tell where the arrows hit, and he doubted Danilo could either. Iskandar's men drew within bow range, and arrows struck the ground all around Ivan and Danilo. One pierced the hindquarters of Ivan's spare horse. Ivan cut the lead rope to leave the horse behind. It would only slow them down now. Ivan wanted Iskandar dead, but they couldn't wait. "We have to ride."

The two kicked their horses into a gallop as another shower of arrows flew toward them. Their mounts were steady and fast and had little to carry other than the riders. That would be to their advantage, for their pursuers wore heavier armor. But they had such a small lead. Could they keep it and extend it enough to escape the torture that awaited them if they failed?

War drums sounded, spurring the Turks forward, and spurring Ivan and Danilo to swifter flight. The guards from Kırkpınar followed hard. Ivan leaned forward and kicked his horse into a faster pace. He and Danilo had planned dozens of escapes, but none of them involved trying to outpace a pack of Turkish pursuers like this. The wind rushing past him chilled his bare skin, just as knowledge of what awaited him upon capture chilled his heart.

Gradually, the arrows fell farther behind them, and they rode out of bow range. Bit by bit, Ivan and Danilo stretched their lead. They urged their horses to keep a hard pace, and the Turkish riders shrank to shadows and then to blurs. The sun sat low on the horizon. Soon, it would disappear, and then the darkness would be their ally.

They pushed their horses hard into the twilight, even when they tired and wanted to ease the pace. Their pursuers faded until, eventually, Ivan and Danilo felt confident they had outrun them.

When they could no longer see anyone behind them, Danilo turned south. "We should stay off the road. They might have some way of signaling other garrisons."

Ivan turned his mount off the smooth, dry road and into the fields kept lush and fertile by a nearby stream. "You picked good horses." On lesser animals, they wouldn't have made it, but now they needed a slower pace. Even their one remaining spare was flagging.

Danilo scanned the area, looking for pursuers. "You picked dangerous enemies."

"I didn't pick them. They picked me. Well done back there. I fully expected to be displayed on a stake for Bayezid's departure tomorrow."

"I couldn't let us die like that. It's not a dignified death. And what would become of our souls? You haven't confessed, have you, to being in love with another man's wife?"

Ivan grunted. There were Christian priests in Adrianople, but they were Greek instead of Serb. He would have been more comfortable with the priest he'd grown up with in Rivakgrad or the one he knew from Sivi Gora.

It wasn't his fault Helena had been forced to marry someone else. Their love had been pure when it had blossomed. Now he wondered if those feelings, no longer so innocent, would ever fade. "Your soul would be fine. You haven't done anything you need to confess, have you? Other than killing all those Turkish guards this afternoon?"

Danilo's mouth pulled into a small circle. "Was that a sin? Killing them?"

"I don't know. I'm not a priest." Ivan chuckled. After the tension of the afternoon, he welcomed the lighter mood.

Danilo's shoulders visibly relaxed. "I'm sure Father Vlatko will travel with Kostya's army. If it was a sin, he'll prescribe the proper penance."

"If we're going into battle, he'll probably grant absolution. And then I'll have to put Helena from my mind completely, or I'll be in perpetual penance." He'd left her behind, physically. Banishing her from his heart would be more difficult. Maybe impossible.

Danilo pointed to a knoll ahead of them. "We should pause there and see which horse is most in need of rest. Then we can switch off again at nightfall."

Ivan checked behind them. He saw no one, only long shadows following them like signal flags. Iskandar would have access to trackers. They'd abused their horses today and couldn't expect their mounts to perform so magnificently again and again, but they had to maintain a good pace, or they'd be overtaken and impaled.

Ivan shuddered to think how close they'd come to death. "Danilo?"

"You don't have to thank me. You would have done the same thing had our positions been reversed."

Ivan fought a smile. How had Danilo known Ivan was about to thank him for saving his life yet again? "Actually, I was going to ask if I might have some of your clothes when we check the horses. I'm cold." Ivan still wore only the kispet.

"Of course." Danilo sounded flustered. "We'll have to stop in a village to buy shoes and such, but you can have my cloak or my tunic, whichever you prefer. I think the cloak is warmer."

"Danilo?"

"Yes?"

"Thank you for saving my life."

CHAPTER TWENTY-NINE
ACQUAINTED WITH MISERY

HELENA WOKE SLOWLY. THAT WAS how mornings arrived now, no longer suddenly but a bit at a time. She was more weary than normal as she sat up, but at least her nausea was finally under control.

Kasim had returned home later than expected the night before, missing the evening meal. Helena hadn't heard why. She wasn't sure she cared. If she stayed ignorant of palace intrigue, perhaps she wouldn't be punished if someone other than Bayezid succeeded Sultan Murad as sultan. Kasim, a longtime friend of Yakub, had switched his support to Bayezid. That was all she needed to know. Bahar and Saruca could gossip about why and what it meant all they liked.

Saruca worried that Kasim would be punished with lower prestige, a smaller home, or even exile should Yakub take the throne instead of Bayezid. Saruca had more to lose than Helena did. Helena had already lost everything important to her. Could any of Yakub's punishments for the wives of Bayezid's supporters be worse than her current fate—marriage to Kasim?

She sighed and got out of bed. Wallowing in self-pity would do her no good. There were worse men than Kasim. And though she was unhappy in Edirne, she might be even more unhappy if sold into slavery or left without food and shelter.

Helena washed her face and dressed. Bahar ordered her to get the water. As she went outside, she felt a slight pain, the normal discomfort that came with the growth of a baby. She moved her hand to her abdomen, slightly rounded under her long tunic. Perhaps that was why Saruca fretted so over Kasim's alliances. She had children. And her children would suffer if their father did.

Bahar called her back.

Helena paused on the stairs. "Yes?" Helena turned and was startled to find Bahar right behind her. Her face displayed a scowl, which was nothing new. She yanked the earthenware pithos away and looked inside. Helena wondered what she'd done wrong this time. Then Bahar shoved the vessel back into Helena's arms as if the pithos were a weapon. Helena stepped back to keep her balance, but she misjudged the distance to the next stair. She fought to stay upright for several long moments, then she tumbled.

She tried to catch herself with one hand, but it slipped. She lost her grip on the container, and it hit the stair above her as she bumped first her shoulder, then her hip on the steps. She couldn't stop and let out a scream as she banged against every single one of the ten stairs leading to the courtyard below.

Her momentum finally wore out on the tiled landing. Pain erupted from her hips, legs, and head. She groaned and tried to sit. She glanced up at Bahar, who looked away. Why had she used so much force when she had thrust the pithos at her? Had it been intentional? Desislava ran out the door and raised a hand to her mouth when she saw Helena crumpled at the bottom of the stairs. She flew down them with surprising grace for someone so far along with child.

"Helena, are you all right?" She knelt next to her and gently brushed a finger along what felt like a bruise.

Helena winced. "I fell." A sudden rush of nausea started in her throat, went down into her stomach, and then came back up. Helena turned and vomited on the ground. The motion hurt her abdomen, hurt her hips, hurt her head.

"You need to rest." Desislava helped her to her feet. "Put your arm around my neck; I'll help you balance." They slowly made their way back up the stairs and into the house. Bahar was no longer there. Saruca gave Helena a sympathetic twist of her lips as she came out with another earthenware pithos.

Helena sat on a cushion, still dizzy with pain and uneasy with worry. The fall hadn't broken bones, but the way she'd hit the stairs made her anxious.

The cramping began within minutes.

The bleeding lasted hours.

Desislava stayed with her, fetching more rags to catch the blood, bringing Helena water and suggesting she try a little bread.

"Sometimes women bleed." Desislava's voice shook. "It doesn't always mean the baby is gone."

Helena took Desislava's hand, grateful to have a friend. "Sometimes women bleed and keep the baby, but they do not bleed this much." Helena held back a sob. She had experience enough to judge. "I'm going to lose it."

"I hate Bahar." Desislava's words were quiet but intense. "She pushed you, didn't she?"

"Did you see?"

"No. But I saw the resentment in her eyes when she learned you were with child. And I saw the look she gave you when you walked out the door."

When it was over, Helena no longer carried an infant. Her womb was empty, and so was her soul. She hadn't realized how much she had wanted a baby until it was gone.

Helena tried to console herself. Kasim might be disappointed, but she owed him nothing. Her husband still frightened her. He wasn't cruel but nor was he kind. He took his pleasure and gave her none in return. He had little patience for her rudimentary Turkish, so they didn't converse. How could affection of any kind grow when there was no communication, no tenderness, just greed and subservience?

Yet Helena mourned the loss of an innocent life. Any baby, even one born of a slave, was a miracle. And for a few years, at least, Helena would have had someone to love and would have been loved in return. She had given up so many of her dreams. Would she have to give up hope of motherhood as well?

Desislava returned after taking away some of the blood-soaked cloths. She would have her baby soon, and Helena felt a pang of jealousy. She imagined Bahar feeling the same emotion, only much stronger because she did love Kasim, and far more often as Saruca had given birth to three sons and then Desislava and finally Helena had been found with child. She could understand the bitterness. But she didn't understand how it could grow into a temptation to throw another woman down the stairs, if that was what had happened. A painful welt had formed behind Helena's left ear, and memory of her fall seemed foggy.

Desislava handed her another cup of water. "Have you heard the news?"

"What news?"

"Everyone is talking about it. Two hostages escaped from Kırkpınar yesterday. It's why Kasim was late. He was hunting them."

Helena felt a strange tightness in her chest. "Did he find them?"

"No. They disappeared."

"Do you know their names?"

"No. But they were Serbs."

Ivan and Danilo were gone, Helena was sure of it. She thought of Ivan's city, his dream. He would make something beautiful and prosperous, a place where no one starved and everyone had opportunity. He would build a grand church, the streets would be paved, the walls would be strong, and church bells would sound the hours. Supported by a successful mine, the city would grow and thrive.

Perhaps Ivan's heart had already moved on. He'd been shocked when they'd last met, too upset to see past the pain to his duty. But he would not shirk the task ahead of him. His broken heart would heal, and he would find someone else to share his life with, someone else to bear his children. And maybe, when Helena was old and Kasim was dead, maybe then Helena could visit the city and see the splendor Ivan had created.

"There is talk of war," Desislava continued. "They've revoked their vassalage. If they're left unpunished, others may follow."

Helena's vision of a flourishing city vanished, replaced with an image of Ivan standing alone against an army like the one that had threatened the kastron. In truth, others would be with him. He might even have a fortification to protect him and his men. But how could they withstand the full fury of the Ottoman army? It seemed far more likely that Ivan, like her baby, would soon be gone.

Days passed. Helena had seen countless miscarriages, so why was it so hard to shake her own? She didn't even like the father. Perhaps that was part of the problem: she couldn't rely on Kasim to help her through the grief. A baby would have been something good coming from her otherwise desolate station.

New life was coming to the home regardless. Desislava's time was near, and Saruca was with child again. Saruca was horribly sick, so Helena spent much of her time watching her youngest, Evhad. He was a sweet boy, enamored with birds and insects, and Helena enjoyed following him around the garden. She tried not to think of what he might grow up to become.

"Helena?" Something in Desislava's voice made Helena tense with worry.

"What is it?"

Desislava stood in the doorway, slightly hunched over, her face twisted in pain. She panted and grasped at her abdomen. "I didn't think it would hurt this much."

"When did the pains start?"

Desislava took a deep breath. "Just now. But it's gone."

"It will return, many times. You can rest, or you can walk around the garden with Evhad and me. Sometimes walking makes the pains come more quickly."

"Why would I want the pains to come more quickly?"

"Because then the baby may come sooner. It's hard to say how long it will last. If you walk, perhaps you will have the baby tonight. If you rest, perhaps tomorrow."

"But it's still morning, not even the third hour of the day. Will it take so long?"

Helena took the girl's hand, remembering Desislava had never witnessed a birth before. "First babies often take their time. I can't tell you how long or how short it will be."

Desislava frowned, then gasped as the pains hit her again. "Will it hurt any less if I rest?"

"No."

"Will you help me walk, for now? I would rather have the baby sooner."

Helena helped Desislava stroll around the garden until noon. After that, Desislava wanted to rest. Two Muslim midwives came, and Helena was demoted from midwife to merely fourth wife.

The next day at sunset, Desislava was still not delivered.

"Why won't the baby come?" Desislava whispered. Tears streaked her face, and her breath came in painful gasps. Her hair hung limply around her face, and she barely had the strength to stay on the birthing chair.

Helena had examined Desislava from time to time over the past two days. Her body had progressed normally. Helena had watched the other midwives' techniques—most of them similar to her own. They hadn't done anything wrong, but Helena, and probably both other midwives, knew why the delivery had stalled: Desislava's petite pelvis was too narrow.

Helena took a cloth and wiped the perspiration from Desislava's forehead. "You've been pushing a few hours now. Why don't you rest for a few pains, then we'll try again?"

Desislava gripped Helena's hand. "I'm going to die, aren't I?"

Helena tried to speak, but her voice caught in her throat. She swallowed. She had to be brave for her friend. "It is far too soon for you to give up. I've helped women who took much longer than you have." But none of them had been in the final phase for so long.

"And their babies? Were their babies well?"

"Many were healthy."

One of the Muslim midwives wrote something on a scrap of parchment, then washed the ink off and gave the water to Desislava in a cup. Helena didn't think the ink water would help any more than the talismans they'd put under Desislava's cushion, but she didn't think they would hurt either. The other midwife continued her incantations.

Bahar and Saruca had come and gone throughout Desislava's travails. They stood off to the side now, and their conversation suddenly became angry. Bahar's voice grew in volume. Saruca whispered back, spitting her words at Bahar. For just a moment, fear seemed to consume Bahar. She glanced around the chamber. Helena and the two midwives watched, all attention for the moment on Bahar rather than on Desislava. Then Bahar said something low to Saruca and left the chamber. Saruca followed not long after.

One of the midwives went back to massaging the birth canal. The other prepared herbs. Helena washed again and checked the baby's position, but neither alignment nor presentation was the problem. The infant's head was simply too large to fit through Desislava's pelvis.

Helena cried as she cleaned. Her back was to Desislava so her friend couldn't see. Part of her tears were selfish—she'd grown to love Desislava. If she died, who would she speak to? No one else knew her language. And even when Helena's Turkish improved, no one else understood her culture, her beliefs. She would be truly friendless.

Beyond her own hurt was the enormous injustice. Desislava hadn't wanted to come to Edirne, hadn't asked to be Kasim's wife, hadn't longed to bare his child. And though Kasim would value a son, he showed little tenderness for his fragile young wife. Would he even mourn her death? There was an underlying belief that the woman was merely a vessel caring for her husband's seed. If the vessel broke, what was the loss? He could always remarry.

Saruca returned in her most commanding posture and ordered the two midwives away.

Helena was shocked. Had Saruca given up? The situation was dire, but sending the midwives away while Desislava still lived seemed harshly premature. Was Desislava's life not worth fighting for? Was it because she was only the third wife? Only a Christian?

"Where are they going?" Desislava mumbled.

Helena combed back some of Desislava's damp hair with her fingers. "I don't know. But I will help until your baby comes. And I have brought many children into this world." If Helena was to be in charge of the delivery, she would make something stronger for Desislava's pain. She doubted her friend would survive the delivery, but she could at least ease her final agony. She didn't have her own herbs, but perhaps a servant could track down some mandragora, if Helena could figure out the correct word in Turkish.

Helena squeezed Desislava's hand. "I'll be back. I'm going to see what herbs they have in the kitchen." Helena stood, but before she took two steps, Bahar returned. She checked the chamber, then brought in an elderly woman. Bahar didn't stay.

Helena watched the woman wash and examine Desislava. The woman's clothes weren't the Muslim style. She was a Jew. She softly hummed a tune Helena didn't recognize as she felt the baby, touched Desislava's head, and stoked the fire.

She unpacked her bundle. When Helena saw the knives, she had a good idea of what would happen. Either the new midwife would slice open Desislava's abdomen, killing the mother and saving the baby, or she would sacrifice the baby to save Desislava.

The new midwife began cleaning Desislava's abdomen with wine, and Helena could guess what that meant.

"It's too soon." Helena put her hand on Desislava's stomach, stopping the woman's work. She couldn't let her give up on Desislava, not yet. "You must give her more time."

The woman raised an eyebrow at Helena. She probably didn't understand, so Helena tried her best Turkish. "Not time."

"She is past time," the Jewess replied in Greek.

"You can't kill her."

"I do not intend to kill her."

Helena looked back at her friend. Desislava was too caught up in pain and exhaustion to follow the Greek conversation. "Do you plan to sacrifice the baby?"

"No."

"Then, why are you here? The baby's head is too large for her pelvis. Eventually, the afterbirth will detach, and she'll bleed to death."

"That is why I must act quickly. If you wish to help, I expect you to wash."

Helena did as ordered. The Jewess gave Desislava something to drink, and soon, Desislava drifted off to sleep. The woman cleaned a knife with wine and heated an iron until its end reddened with heat. She handed it to Helena. "Be ready to press the iron on anything that bleeds too much." Then the woman cut into Desislava's side.

Helena held Desislava's daughter as the Jewish midwife cleaned her knives and gathered the blood-soaked rags. Desislava slept, pale, but alive. At Saruca's insistence, the baby wore a little skull cap with a pearl and blue beads on a tassel to ward off the evil eye. Helena didn't believe in the evil eye. But until an hour before, she also hadn't believed a mother and child could survive a birth such as the one she'd just witnessed.

Rebekah, the midwife, had cut Desislava open, taken the baby and the afterbirth out, and then dressed the wound. It was unheard of. It was impossible. Yet it had happened.

Saruca came into the chamber and spoke with Rebekah. She smiled, then left again.

Rebekah chuckled softly.

"You have performed a miracle. Why do you laugh?" Helena touched the baby's perfect little nose.

"Because she is pleased the child is a girl. Her status as the only wife to bear Kasim a son is secure."

"Have you helped her? Is that how she knew to send for you?"

Rebekah tested the end of the iron to make sure it was no longer hot before putting it next to her knives. "No. Saruca's sons have all been born without complication."

"Where did you learn that technique?"

The woman doused a rag in wine and ran it along Desislava's pinned-up abdomen. "It is a secret my people have guarded for many generations."

Helena thought of all the women who might have been saved if such a procedure were more common. "Why haven't you shared your knowledge?"

"Because most people do not look kindly on things they do not understand. Some Muslims believe a child born in this manner is a devil. Neither they nor the Christians wish to associate with us. Not under normal circumstances."

"Would you teach me?"

Rebekah didn't answer.

Saruca returned with a tray holding copper bowls of minced mutton and rice. Saruca sometimes served Kasim, but not his other wives. Why hadn't she sent a servant?

Saruca spoke to Rebekah.

"She wishes me to translate for her," the midwife said. "You are sworn to secrecy. If anyone learns how the child was born, she'll be considered cursed, and she'll be rejected. Not even Kasim is to know."

"I understand." The incision would leave a scar, but she and Desislava would come up with something to explain it away. "What of Bahar?"

Rebekah and Saruca spoke back and forth, and the Jewish woman nodded. "Bahar thinks the infant is a child of the devil. But she will say nothing because Saruca threatened to tell Kasim that Bahar caused your lost child if she even whispers of a Jew entering the home."

"But how did she convince Bahar to let you come?" Jewish and Christian midwives weren't allowed to attend Muslim women. Desislava was Christian, but the house was Muslim, and the child would be Muslim. Kasim wouldn't approve.

"Saruca reminded her that if this woman died"—Rebekah pointed to Desislava—"Kasim would likely take a new wife. And the new wife might be just like Saruca."

Saruca smiled, and Helena understood. Desislava and Helena were young and pretty, but they didn't have Kasim's ear. Helena could barely speak a full sentence in his language. But if Kasim married a younger version of Saruca, Bahar would lose even more influence with her husband.

Helena had caught Bahar studying her reflection, fingering her wrinkles. Her age showed, and she was without children in a culture that valued offspring above any other contribution a woman could make. Another wife like Saruca would surely be unbearable.

"I must leave soon, but first, I will explain what to do as she recovers." Rebekah showed Helena how to tend Desislava's sliced abdomen. It was not so different from the time Helena had mended Ivan's wounds. Then the Jewish midwife left, leaving Helena to care for Desislava and the baby.

The baby was perfect—plump and healthy, with a lusty wail whenever Helena tried to put her down. A child of the devil? No. A child of miracle. Desislava stirred, and tears came to Helena's eyes. She had been mourning Desislava's certain death only a few hours ago. Then Rebekah had shown Helena that what had always seemed impossible was instead a reality. If that was true with the birth of a child, might it also be true for the other things Helena had always assumed were out of reach?

CHAPTER THIRTY
DISLOYAL VASSALS

IVAN AND DANILO RODE SIDE by side, keeping their horses at an easy pace. They'd been on the road almost a fortnight and hadn't seen their pursuers since the day they'd left Kırkpınar. They were almost home, and the threat of impalement now seemed behind them.

"You're quiet today," Danilo said.

Though Ivan longed to reach Rivak, concern tempered his excitement. "Do you suppose he'll recognize me?"

"Kostya?"

Ivan nodded.

"You're two years older, you have a beard, and you're dressed in rags, but you haven't changed *that* much. If you wish to exchange clothing with me so you're more presentable, I will gladly do so."

Danilo had offered a dozen times before, but Ivan's answer had always been the same. "I don't need your clothes." The mix of a fine horse and a tunic scarcely fit for a peasant had earned Ivan curious looks when they'd passed through villages. But that wasn't what bothered him.

"Ivan, I've known you since you were born, and you were my only friend these last two years. I know your moods. Something worries you."

Trying to hide his feelings from Danilo was like trying to hide a watchtower built on a wide steppe, so he confessed. "What if I'm not ready?"

"Ready for what? To see our family again?"

"No." Ivan hungered for time with his family, to be somewhere familiar, with people who shared his beliefs. "I have a feeling we'll be at war soon, and I think my grandfather will expect me to lead some of his men. What if I'm not ready for that?"

"Of course you're ready. I saw you when the Greeks attacked, what, three years ago? You proved yourself then, and your skill has only grown since. You saved the Greek kastron, and in Adrianople, you were more than a match for every Turkish swordsman who wanted to test himself against you."

"But I wasn't leading anyone when Kostya's army was ambushed, other than maybe you." Ivan was destined for leadership, but throughout his childhood, he'd trailed behind Konstantin and Danilo, following them, learning from them, striving to be like them. Danilo deferred to him now, had done so for years, but Ivan hadn't done anything to earn that respect other than be born a župan's son rather than a župan's nephew. "And a siege is different from leading men in battle."

Danilo raised an eyebrow and gave Ivan half a smile. "You led the raid to free the prisoners."

"That was only a raid. It wasn't meant to turn into a skirmish."

"But it did. And you won."

He had won, he supposed. Iskandar had left. But he had lost Gregoras and several others. And in the end, it hadn't mattered. "I won the day, but Iskandar returned with Kasim, and the kastron surrendered."

"Only because you weren't there."

"I'm not so sure. Kasim brought a large army." Ivan and Danilo had trained with sipahis. They knew firsthand what an Ottoman army could accomplish.

"He will bring a large army again. We will lead a large army to oppose him. And I will be at your side when the battle begins."

Ivan didn't doubt Danilo's loyalty. But could they win? His cousin never lost confidence in him, even when Ivan doubted himself, but Danilo's confidence wouldn't win a battle. Ivan had saved Konstantin when Leo had tried to kill him. He'd held the kastron in Byzia with a mere handful of men. But for all that, he hadn't been able to save the woman he loved. What else would he fail at despite his best efforts? It would take a miracle to defeat the Turks. If God hadn't let him save Helena, when she meant everything to him, how could he expect divine help with anything else?

They reached the borders of Rivak as the afternoon heat grew to its full summer warmth, and they rode to Konstantin's grad that evening, just as the sun disappeared over the horizon. The guard at the gate blocked their entry. "Danilo? Weren't you in Adrianople?"

"I am back."

"I am glad for that, Danilo." The guard glanced at Ivan. "But I'm not allowed to let anyone pass whom I don't recognize. I'm sorry. Your companion will have to wait for approval from Konstantin or Miladin."

Ivan chuckled at Danilo. "And you said I hadn't changed much." Ivan remembered the guard's face, or at least a slimmer version of it, but he couldn't remember the man's name, so he supposed that made them even.

Danilo frowned at the guard. "Don't you recognize Ivan Miroslavević, brother of the župan?"

The guard's mouth opened in confusion as he stared at Ivan.

"Ivan does not need your permission to ride into his own city."

Ivan held up a hand to stop his cousin from giving the guard further reprimand. "It's all right, Danilo. I have changed. And it's not my city." Coming back to Rivakgrad was like coming home, but it wouldn't last. His destiny had always lain to the north, in the lands he was destined to lead as heir of his maternal grandfather. For years, he'd imagined bringing Helena along as his bride. That dream was gone, but his duty to Sivi Gora remained.

Another member of the garrison came to see the reason for the delay. This one Ivan knew without question: Bojan.

"Ivan? Danilo? We expected you ages ago."

Ivan dismounted and embraced the man who had taught him how to ride a horse. "It is good to see you again, Bojan. Although I remember you being taller."

"I haven't shrunk. But you've grown. Your brother will want to see you. He'll want to see you both." He looked up at Danilo. "Come."

They followed the main road past neat wooden homes and then led their horses on the causeway to the upper grad, set on a hill above the rest of the town. The first person they saw in the bailey was Marko. Ivan called out to him and waved. The boy waved back but without any zeal. He was exactly as Ivan remembered him. But that couldn't be right—Marko was six now. And hadn't Marko stopped sucking his thumb? Only when an older boy came around a corner and ran into Danilo's arms did Ivan realize his mistake. The little boy sucking his thumb and waving at them halfheartedly was Ivan's new nephew, Pavle.

Danilo spun the real Marko around and set him on the ground. "We need to see your father. And your mother and great-aunt."

"Come on." Marko ran off, expecting them to follow at the same pace. They were weary after a full day in the saddle, so they didn't bother keeping up with him. He was older now, but he was still the carefree boy Ivan remembered rather than a hostage in Adrianople, and that was something to rejoice over.

Konstantin met them before they made it to the stairs of the keep. He embraced Ivan first, then Danilo. "I am overjoyed to see you both, for many reasons." He put his hand on Ivan's shoulder. "But what are you wearing?"

"Getting away from Adrianople was more difficult than expected."

Konstantin lifted one side of his lips in a cross between a smile and a grimace. "I was afraid of that. First, you can change, then we'll feast. After that, we can discuss your journey and the plans we've made."

"I think they'll come after us. With an army."

"We're expecting them."

Danilo disappeared—probably to see his mother. Ivan trimmed his beard, washed, and put on fresh clothing. Everything was comfortable, familiar. He was no longer prisoner, hostage, or refugee, and being a free man was liberating, even if that freedom would soon be threatened.

Ivan went to the great hall and was hugged and grasped and looked at until he was exhausted. Suzana commented on his increased height and officially introduced him to his thumb-sucking nephew. Miladin asked him what he had learned of Ottoman tactics. Aunt Zorica suggested he would make a handsome husband for some lucky woman, and Danilo quickly did his best to steer his mother's conversation a different direction.

"Were you on foot for the journey? Is that why it took so long?" Konstantin asked as they were served a rich stew of roasted lamb and vegetables.

"No. We had horses, three for most of the journey. We sold one outside of Prilep. But they were delaying your messages. We didn't receive your warning until a few days before they knew you'd refused tribute."

Konstantin set his spoon down. "I should have sent multiple messengers."

"We're here now, mostly unscathed."

"I'm glad you are both safe. It's been a long time, and I imagine the time has seemed even longer for you. Grandfather wasn't pleased to lose you for two years, but he said you did the right thing, going in Marko's place. I owe you everything, Ivan. Thank you for saving my son. I'm sorry for what your time as hostage has cost you."

Ivan nodded. Konstantin didn't know the half of what his time as hostage had cost him. But it wasn't Konstantin's fault. Nor was it Helena's. The blame lay with the Turks. Ivan stored up his anger because a confrontation with them would come soon enough.

"There's more, Ivan. Grandfather's messenger arrived today. He's ready for you. He's camped about a day's ride to the north with his army. It's a magnificent host—horse archers and heavy cavalry, well-equipped footmen. But he doesn't plan to lead it himself. He intends for you to lead it."

Ivan put aside the bread he'd been about to bite into. "He's entrusting me with all his men? I had thought I might serve under him, or under you. Command a section, not an army."

Konstantin fingered his goblet but didn't drink from it. "I would have liked that, in some ways. I've only just gotten you back, and we never had the time I wanted. First the Greeks, then the Turks kept you from me. And now I'm losing you to your destiny." He met Ivan's eyes. "It is time for you to become the župan of Sivi Gora."

Ivan had always known he would one day inherit his grandfather's lands. And he had always been intimidated by the tall, stern man who dug precious metals from the ground with the skill of his miners and held the Hungarians at bay with the might of his army. Now he and his grandfather were the same height, and Ivan was no longer a beardless youth, but his grandfather still wielded an unmistakable presence.

"They will follow your orders because they are well-trained. And they will respect you because you are my heir," his grandfather explained as they rode through the camp to view the men. There were fifty heavy cavalrymen, forty mounted bowmen, and eighty foot soldiers. "If you wish to earn their love, see that their needs are met. If you wish to earn their loyalty, lead them to victory."

Ivan gazed on the faces of those he would take into battle. He'd spent most summers in his grandfather's lands, but he hadn't visited Sivi Gora since before his capture in Byzia. If the men remembered him, it was as a boy.

"Knez Lazar has a good mind for strategy. And he's faced the Ottomans before. He defeated them at Dubravnica, so listen to him. But don't hesitate to offer your advice. You've seen the Greeks in battle and fought with them. You've trained with the Ottomans. You know the enemy more than most of us. Use that to your advantage."

Ivan nodded.

"My most experienced men are as old as I, plagued by gout or old wounds. Goran's father served me well from the time your mother married your father until his death four years past, and since then, Goran has continued in his father's place. He will serve you well. His skill is not strategy, so don't ask for his advice on when to charge and when to retreat. But he'll arrange for your men to be fed, find fodder for the horses, and see that the camp is organized. He's not bad with the sword, but I've learned to value his ability to organize over his ability to fight."

"Goran. I remember him." He'd defeated Ivan in a sparring match when Ivan had been thirteen and Goran seventeen. The next year, Ivan had won.

"My men are valiant in battle. But you don't know them, and they haven't seen you for three years. Will you bring any from Rivak?"

"One. The son of my father's sister."

"Danilo?"

"Yes." Ivan would never be able to repay his debt to his cousin. Danilo had given up two years to join Ivan as a hostage, and now he would forsake Rivak and follow him to Sivi Gora. That dependable friendship was Ivan's anchor in a sea of change and disappointment.

"So, Konstantin will be deprived of brother and cousin." His grandfather grunted. "I gave my only surviving child to Rivak. It is fitting that I'll take back two young warriors now. You'll need to march in a week. Stay near Konstantin, Dragomir, and Nikola in case you run into trouble. But you'll be better off camping separately; otherwise, you'll have trouble finding sufficient water and grazing for the animals."

"So much to know."

The stern lines of his grandfather's face softened. "Goran will remind you of water and forage. Set Danilo in charge of scouting. Find someone to organize a guard for the camp. Someone else to see that the men don't get into quarrels with each other."

"Will they?"

"Difficult to say. Kral Dušan felt quarrels were inevitable and sought only to ban others from joining in. It's been my experience that fights are unlikely if the men stay busy and if loot is divided fairly."

Ivan looked at the fighting men, then studied the camp. The men-at-arms were assembled, but many of the heavy cavalrymen had brought their own servants, and they still milled about camp. They, too, would need to be fed. Remembering his time in Byzia, he thought that they, too, could be trained to fight. He would have them learn to use crossbows, at least, should they need to defend the camp. But who would he put in charge of keeping the camp secure from outside intrusion and free of internal strife? "Do you have any recommendations for which of your men I should trust with camp security?"

"They are your men now. Get to know them. See what you think."

Ivan's grandfather had never been one to smooth the path ahead. If it was something Ivan could do himself, his grandfather always let him struggle until he figured it out on his own. But this time was different—Ivan was leading men into battle. The consequences had moved beyond the bruised muscles and soaked clothing that most of his prior learning experiences had involved.

After reviewing the troops, Ivan went back to his tent. He would stay with the men from now on, preparing with them, training with them, eating with them. His grandfather planned to take a new name and retire to a monastery near Sivi Gora. Ivan would be able to visit from time to time—but only if he won against the Turks.

"Župan Ivan?" a voice called.

Ivan parted his tent flap and found an errand boy standing outside. "Yes?"

"There is a group to see you."

"Show them in."

Ivan expected soldiers from his grandfather's army—his army now—most likely those who thought they deserved a place as trusted advisers. Ivan wouldn't make any decisions based on one discussion, but it would be worthwhile to meet them, to see which were respectful, which had fragile egos, and which seemed resentful of their new župan.

But only one man entered, and he was no stranger.

"Matthias?"

Matthias smiled and walked toward him. Ivan went to embrace him, but before he closed the gap, Matthias lowed himself to one knee. "Great župan, it gives me much pleasure to see you again, and to see you free of Edirne."

Ivan felt a stab of pain at Matthias's mention of the Ottoman capital. He was free, but Helena was not, and that made his liberty incomplete. "Rise, my friend. I am glad to see you, though yours is not a face I expected to see. We're nowhere near your land's normal trade routes."

"We're not here on trade."

"What do you seek? Surely my company alone is not worth a journey of such distance."

"You underestimate your worth, lord. But, no, I did not come to be social."

Ivan motioned for Matthias to sit.

Matthias stayed on his feet. "I'm afraid I again bring troubling news. Kyrios Leo is dead."

Leo. Ivan had several strong memories of him. He was the warrior who'd tried to kill Konstantin. He was the uncertain ruler who'd agreed to let his wife's sister marry a formal rival. And he was the coward who'd broken that promise and used Helena to buy peace. "How?"

"Poison, though we cannot prove it, of course. Even if we could, we suspect it was the Ottoman overseer who is now bey of Leo's holdings."

"What of Kyria Euphrosyne and her child?"

"She moved to Constantinople. She has an uncle there, in the wool trade. She and her daughter will be cared for."

"But they will have no inheritance."

"Not in Macedonia."

"And Kyria Helena's sacrifice?"

Matthias didn't answer.

"She married Kasim to save her people, and all they got from it was one short spring of peace. And she is stuck a slave until either she or her husband meet their deaths."

Matthias bit his lip. "I argued for battle when they first appeared. So did she."

Ivan sat on a wooden chest and leaned forward, his elbows on his knees. "I saw her before she married him. I begged her to run away with me. But she wouldn't risk her people's safety." The pain of that night washed over Ivan anew. *I shall leave here, never to return near. All that's left of us shall be this song.*

"Lord, there are some who remember your defense of our acropolis. We would not serve the Turks, but we would serve you."

Ivan nodded. "You are welcome here. I would be glad of a familiar face."

"There are more. Many of the paroikoi see little difference in paying rents to an Ottoman lord instead of a Greek lord. But some would prefer to live under your rule, if you will have them. They number twenty paroikoi and four men-at-arms, plus me and my family."

"Of course. The boy mentioned a group. But I'm surprised there are so many."

"We know no one in Mystras or Constantinople. And Murad has his eye on Thessaloniki. We've lived through sieges before, and they have shown us the value of leadership."

"I have lands that need cultivation, a wall to build, and a growing population to defend. All refugees from Byzia will be welcomed." Ivan stood. "Perhaps God Himself has sent you to me because you are needed." Matthias might not know the language, but he knew how to organize a watch. What's more, he'd long ago earned Ivan's trust.

Matthias clasped his hands behind his back. "I will be glad to serve you however I can. It took me some time to recognize your worth, but I have seen it clearly for several years now. Some who came with me recognized it immediately. You will be glad to see them, I think."

"Where are the others?"

"A few wait outside your camp. Niketas and most of the paroikoi are with the wagons, perhaps an hour's ride away."

"Niketas?" The two had settled into an uneasy truce after the siege, but Ivan wouldn't have called their relationship friendly.

"He hopes you will forgive him for his poor treatment of you. Seeing the second siege and Leo's death changed his mind about many things."

The two left the tent and found part of Matthias's group waiting ten paces away. Theodora stood next to her father, Christophoros. The girl ran to Ivan, then stopped a few paces away and bowed. Her face had grown narrower, her hair thicker, and her limbs lankier.

"Theodora, I am pleased to see you."

She grinned and turned to her father. "I told you he would recognize me!"

"Where is the rest of your family?"

"With the carts, lord," Christophoros said.

Next, Ivan's eyes fell across Isaakios and Bardas, men who had helped him and Matthias free the captured prisoners. He grasped their arms and welcomed them. They were dressed as Matthias was, in lamellar mail, with swords hanging from their belts. He'd known them as villagers with a bit of skill with the sword. He would test them later, but it looked as though they were now warriors instead of a leatherworker and a butcher.

The person he was most desperate to see held the reins of two horses. Ivan walked toward him and clasped the boy in an embrace. "Philippos, you are at least a head taller than I remember you."

Philippos laughed, his voice deeper than it was in Ivan's memory. "I have practiced what you taught me every day since you left. I won't disappoint you, Župan Ivan."

Ivan watched those who had come—most alive only because of Helena's sacrifice, her final gift to him.

His eyes stung just a bit to think of their faith in his leadership, their willingness to follow him to a foreign land. He didn't think Philippos, Matthias, or any of the others would disappoint him. He prayed that he could live up to their trust.

CHAPTER THIRTY-ONE
A THIRST FOR VENGEANCE

HELENA WASHED THE JEWISH MIDWIFE's knife and needle in water and then in wine. Rebekah had reluctantly agreed to let Helena learn from her, and she had just witnessed another miraculous birth.

"It is good to see you smile," Rebekah said.

Helena glanced at the new mother holding a newborn son. "There are many things here to be happy about."

Rebekah gathered the bloody cloths. "Sometimes, you have to search diligently to find joy. Other times, it is as plain as the coo of a new baby."

Was that Helena's problem? Was she unhappy only because she wasn't looking hard enough for the good?

"You are often sad." Rebekah spoke it as a statement, not a question.

"It is difficult to be married to a man not of my faith. I did not seek to be his wife."

"Esther did not seek her marriage either, but God used her to save her people. Perhaps in time, you, too, can be an influence for good on behalf of your people."

Helena pondered Rebekah's words as she sneaked back to Kasim's home. She wasn't allowed in public without an escort and certainly wasn't allowed to associate with a Jew, but ever since Desislava's baby, the balance of power had shifted among Kasim's wives. Saruca was dominant now, and she wanted Helena to learn all she could, in case Saruca needed help when her next child was born.

She found Saruca and Desislava together in the women's quarters, practicing a dance. The two had grown closer of late. Saruca was a patient tutor, helping Desislava learn how to care for her infant. Saruca might not have been so gracious had the baby been a son instead of a daughter, but

Desislava was so young herself, with no mother nearby to help her learn. She needed Saruca.

Their friendship left Helena even more isolated. Had Esther felt like that? Friendless? Trapped in a marriage she didn't want? Would Helena ever have enough sway with Kasim to soften his heart toward the Christians the way Esther had softened the heart of the Persian emperor toward the Jews? Or would she have to bear children first and hope that they would be merciful to their mother's people? The Muslims gave great honor to their mothers. She admired that in them even more than she appreciated their fine soap or the melodious call to prayer that sounded five times a day.

Helena smiled at Saruca and Desislava's dance. The movements were supposed to benefit a women's abdomen so she was better able to bear children, but there was also something seductive about the dance. Desislava, still recovering from her unconventional delivery, made her dance steps conservative, but Saruca swayed her hips and rolled her stomach with a dramatic flair. Her condition showed now, and she was hoping for another son.

Helena had felt relief when her menses had come six days ago. But as she thought of Rebekah's words, she realized she ought to adjust her hopes. Kasim was her husband, and Edirne was her home. Helena's duty was to do the most good she could in whatever sphere she'd been placed. Feeling sorry for herself benefited no one.

Saruca's youngest, Evhad, ran through the swirling fabrics to Helena and lifted his arms. She picked him up, wondering how long he would love her. Perhaps, for now, she could make a difference in the life of this one little boy. And that was something good, no matter what he grew up to become. Life was better with service; she had witnessed that when she'd watched Ivan take Philippos under his wing. Life in a harem in Edirne was not what she'd pictured when she'd planned her life, but perhaps it was time for her to trust God again and actively seek for what good she could offer others. She had sacrificed for her people, and it had been the right thing to do. But surely that was not the end of her life's purpose.

Bahar stormed into the chamber and broke up the dance. She uttered a long string of rapid Turkish. Helena caught only a few words: now, war, horses.

"What did she say?" Helena asked Desislava.

Desislava swallowed and made jerky movements with her hands. "Kasim is campaigning with Lala Şahin Pasha. And you are to go with him."

"What?"

"He usually takes Saruca."

Of course. He would take one wife when he went to war, not his entire household, and Saruca couldn't go because she was with child. Desislava couldn't go because she had a newborn. And Bahar was bitter. She wouldn't make a journey more pleasurable. That left Helena.

Desislava gripped Helena's hand. Her brow crinkled in worry. "She also said something about leverage."

"Leverage?" What on earth could that mean? "Where are they going?"

"They ride against the Serbs."

Ivan dipped his boukellaton in his vinegar, softening it so he could eat a piece without breaking a tooth. After twenty days on the campaign trail, the fresh food was gone. But there was still salted fish and plenty of hard, twice-baked biscuits of millet or barley. Goran had proved as good as the old župan had promised when it came to planning for food, water, and campsites, and that had made their journey uncomplicated.

The old župan—that was what the men called Ivan's grandfather. They called Ivan the young župan. And at times, Ivan felt his youth and inexperience, but he rode often to meet with Konstantin, Župan Dragomir, and Župan Nikola. Ivan had the larger army, but they had more experience, and he was grateful to learn from them.

Morale among his men remained high. Ivan now recognized all their faces and knew most of their names. With Matthias and the other Greeks, his camp numbered one hundred seventy-seven fighting men and sixty-nine grooms, pages, and other servants. Ivan had assigned a man from Sivi Gora named Cyril to keep the peace in camp. Cyril had once been Ivan's bodyguard, when enemies had threatened the family and Konstantin had been forced away for service to the sultan. So far, Cyril had needed to take no action save breaking up one drunken fight. And so far, Ivan had heard not a single complaint about the hard biscuits that made up the majority of their diet.

Horse hooves sounded, and Ivan stood as Danilo rode in with someone Ivan didn't recognize. Ivan's cousin had stayed busy throughout their journey, organizing scouts and training the camp followers. Ivan didn't expect to use them in battle, but they'd made enough progress that they'd be able to defend themselves should they run into the Turks.

Danilo and his guest dismounted, and Philippos ran to take their reins.

"Ivan!" Danilo waved him over. "This is one of Knez Lazar's sons by marriage, Miloš Obilić. He brings news."

The fine lines crossing Obilić's face suggested this was not his first campaign, but his movements had been spry when he'd dismounted. He was a warrior in his prime, with quality armor that looked as if it had seen its share of action. He scanned the camp, his bright eyes seeming to observe everything, and then he nodded his approval at the neat rows of tents and the ditches and embankments around the edge of camp. "Your security is good."

"Thank you," Ivan said. "I once raided a ghazi camp with the man I've put in charge of security. We know how easy it is to overcome a few watchmen." Ivan gestured to his tent. "Come, I will have someone bring food." He hoped Goran had something better than hardtack and dried fish to serve the knez's son by marriage.

When the three had settled inside, Obilić spoke. "Knez Lazar's scouts have located the Ottoman camp. Sultan Murad himself has not come. Lala Şahin Pasha leads them. They are numerous but mostly akincis."

"Like ghazis?"

"Yes, but cooperating with the army."

They would be less disciplined, less fierce than sipahis. But Lala Şahin Pasha had won many battles, including the one that had killed Ivan's father and uncle. "How far is their camp?"

"About a day by foot."

Ivan offered Obilić a goblet of malmsey wine. "When does Knez Lazar plan to attack?" Serb, Bosnian, and Bulgarian armies had all gathered under Lazar's leadership. They were ready.

A corner of Obilić's mouth lifted. The lopsided smile suggested he was privy to insider information. "Not yet."

Ivan felt himself frowning. "Do they know where we are?"

"No."

"Then, what are we waiting for?"

Obilić took a sip of his drink. "How are ghazis paid?"

"Plunder."

"Yes. If they can't find us, their ranks will grow restless, and they'll break up for raids or pillage. When that happens, we'll attack."

Ivan glanced at Danilo. He seemed to like the plan. Ivan's instincts urged instant attack, but his grandfather had spoken highly of Lazar, so Ivan would trust the knez. "And until they split?"

"We stay alert. And out of sight."

Iskandar rode into camp after another unsuccessful day of scouting. He dismissed his men, handed his horse to a groom, and went to Lala Şahin Pasha's tent to report. A horsehair standard marked their leader's tent, staked in the center of camp. When he entered, Kasim and the pasha regarded him from the plush cushions on which they sat.

"Did you find them?" Kasim asked.

"No."

"Perhaps they are too frightened to come against us in battle." Kasim looked to their leader.

The pasha leaned into a pillow that matched the red and gold embroidery of the tent panels. "We'll send out the teams again tomorrow. If they find nothing, we'll consider our options."

Iskandar hesitated for a moment, then spoke. "Effendi, the men are restless. They need action."

The pasha lifted an eyebrow. "Are you dictating tactics to me?"

"No, effendi." Iskandar bowed deeply. "I am only offering you what information I have."

"I want information about Lazar's army, not about my own."

"As you wish, effendi." Iskandar bowed again and turned to leave. If he left now, perhaps he wouldn't say anything else to upset the pasha. He wanted to win the general's approval, not create an enemy. Serving Kasim had brought Iskandar far, but Iskandar was not content to serve someone of Kasim's status forever.

For a time, he had thought to gain Bayezid as an ally. He'd come to the prince's notice by keeping the two Serb hostages at Kırkpınar until news of Rivak's treachery was confirmed, but any good his work had done had been wiped out when Ivan and Danilo had escaped. Iskandar rubbed his arm where one of Danilo's arrows had sliced his skin. He couldn't afford another failure.

"Wait a moment, Iskandar." Kasim stood and strode about the tent with his hands clasped behind his back. "Effendi, Iskandar has led ghazis before. He knows their strengths and their limits. Releasing the men for plunder could prove wise. We are on Lazar's lands. If we burn fields and sack villages, Lazar must react—or test the loyalty of his subjects. If he can't defend them, why should they give him their taxes? Even if you don't provoke him into action, at least the men will be satisfied. They'll serve you well if their time here rewards them with riches."

The pasha was silent for a few moments. "Tomorrow, we will send out the normal scouting parties. The day after, if we see no sign of the enemy, I will take your advice into consideration. You may go now, both of you."

Iskandar nodded, then waited for Kasim outside the tent.

"You would do well to learn how to speak to your superiors." Kasim glanced around them. The camp buzzed with soldiers and horses going to and fro, but no one was close enough to hear his words.

"Lala Şahin Pasha would do well to listen to those with more experience than he."

Kasim frowned. "Perhaps he would listen more if your tone were less insolent. Give him the information, but let him make the conclusions. He is our appointed leader, and he won't appreciate anything that smells of usurpation. He may not know the Serbs from Rivak, but he's waged far more campaigns than you have."

Iskandar bit the inside of his lips and did his best to accept the reprimand with humility.

"Come." Kasim pointed to his tent, one almost as large as the pasha's. Its proximity to the camp center was a sign of Kasim's importance.

Iskandar followed him inside. Kasim's Greek wife was preparing food. Kasim clapped his hands twice. She bowed and slipped behind a curtain into another part of the tent.

"You brought her? Are you sure that was wise?"

Kasim bristled again. "That's your problem, Iskandar. You must stop questioning the decisions of your leaders."

"But she could escape from here far more easily than from Edirne."

Kasim huffed. "She won't escape. A camp full of soldiers is a hazardous place for a beautiful woman. And she might not be loyal to me, but she is obedient. I have my reasons for bringing her."

"Namely?"

"I first saw her not long after your failed siege in Byzia, when I was gathering a hostage and ensuring Župan Konstantin made no military alliance with the Greeks. And I saw the way she looked at the župan's brother when they thought they'd be betrothed." He folded his arms across his chest. "She has never looked at me that way. Instead, I find her pillow wet with tears, and if she trembles in my arms, it is with fear, not pleasure. But perhaps if I strike down Župan Ivan in battle and show her his severed head, his memory will finally disappear. Only then will I own her completely."

CHAPTER THIRTY-TWO
THE EVE OF WAR

A TWIG DUG INTO IVAN'S thigh as he slithered through the underbrush away from the Ottoman camp. He'd watched for hours, but as the sun sank lower on the horizon, his view grew less and less useful. With the sun behind them, men and tents were mere outlines now, and Ivan could see no details.

When he'd distanced himself from the camp, he gave it a wide berth, then made another slow crawl through long grasses and shrubs to the thick copse of trees where Danilo kept watch from the north side of the camp. The nearest tent lay only sixty paces away, so Ivan rose cautiously. Sudden movements might be seen.

"Their routine is changed today," Danilo whispered from a tree branch.

Ivan peered into the camp, wishing he could see inside the tents. "Do you think they march tomorrow?"

Danilo pointed to the right side of camp, along its fringes. "Those men are preparing their evening meals as normal. But over there, it is different." Danilo pointed to the left. "They're saddling horses."

"Raiders?"

"I think so."

"Good. How many of them?"

"A third of the camp, I would say."

"Do they take their baggage with them?" For a quick raid, they would leave their tents and most of their supplies behind and return in time for breakfast. For a longer raid, they would set up camp closer to their target. And that would leave the remaining portion of the Ottoman army vulnerable.

"I can't tell yet."

Ivan thought of joining his cousin in the tree, but he trusted Danilo. Better to stay hidden and wait until the Turks made their move.

Eventually, a group rode westward with one packhorse for every rider. It seemed their return would not be immediate.

Ivan and Danilo waited until dusk before returning to the forested vale where Matthias waited with the horses.

"Did you see anything?" Ivan asked.

Matthias shook his head. "It's been quiet here."

The three of them rode for their camp, strung bows in hand since they were still near the enemy. They had traveled less than a Roman mile when an arrow struck Danilo's horse. It tumbled, throwing Danilo into the ground, where he lay completely still.

Ivan pivoted toward the arrow's origin and saw two Ottoman warriors. Ivan launched an arrow into one, and the second ducked behind a cluster of stones.

"Do you see any others?" he shouted at Matthias.

"No." Daylight was fading. They'd been lucky to see the first two.

"Keep an eye out." Ivan kicked his horse toward the attackers, keeping his shield up to block any additional shots. If the man who'd shot Danilo's horse told the pasha of the Serb scouts, there would be no surprise attack. The pasha would recall his raiders, and the chance to defeat the Ottoman army while it was divided would be lost.

Ivan rode past the rocks. The Ottoman scout ran toward a pair of horses in a depression. Ivan drew his sword as he reached the fleeing Turk and leaped from his mount. He caught himself on the man and brought him to the ground. Ivan sprang back to his feet and held his sword next to the man's neck as he turned around.

Ivan recognized the face. "Cemal?"

Cemal glanced along the sword to Ivan.

"Are there others, or just the two of you?"

Cemal didn't answer. Nor did his gaze waver.

Ivan scanned the nearby shadows, watching for trouble. "On your feet. And don't try anything. You'll find my skill with the sword better than my skill on the wrestling field."

Cemal stood slowly, keeping his hands where Ivan could see them.

Matthias rode up, and Ivan relaxed enough to look to his cousin. Relief washed over him when he saw Danilo standing in the distance. His fall must have knocked him unconscious for only a while.

"Are you scouting?" Ivan asked Cemal. "Answer truthfully because I don't have fond memories of our meeting in Kırkpınar. Cooperate and you will live. Refuse and you will die."

Cemal peered at his fallen companion. "We were released to plunder. My friend said a smaller group would be better because we wouldn't have to split our takings so many ways. But when we saw you, we knew Kasim's reward for your capture would be better than anything we could take from a petty village."

Ivan used Cemal's belt to tie his hands together. "How many in the camp are off pillaging?"

"A quarter, perhaps, when I left. More were to leave after us, more in the morning."

"When are they to return?"

Cemal shrugged.

Ivan let the tip of his sword sink into Cemal's skin. "I want answers. Perhaps I should remind you that I do not always follow the rules when it comes to high stakes."

Cemal swallowed. A hint of defiance gleamed in his eyes, and then he relented. "We were told to return within two days."

Ivan turned Cemal over to Matthias and grabbed the Turkish horses. He led them and his own back to Danilo. "Are you all right?"

"I hear ringing. We haven't wandered near a church bell, have we?"

"No."

"I didn't think we had." Danilo rubbed his head.

"Can you ride?"

"I can ride in my sleep. Of course I can ride with a little headache."

Ivan motioned for Danilo to remove his helmet, and then he circled his cousin, looking for blood in his hair or bulges to indicate bruising. Danilo wasn't one to complain, so Ivan examined him closely.

"I'm fine, Ivan."

"In that case, choose which horse you'd like." He offered both captured mounts to Danilo. They were good horses, which brought a smile to Danilo's face.

Cemal's friend was dead by the time Ivan went to check him. He let Cemal bury him in a shallow grave. Their religion was strict about burial, and Ivan didn't want another set of Turkish raiders to find one of their own killed with a Serbian arrow.

Danilo tended to his wounded horse. "I think we can save him." Danilo tied a lead rope to the injured animal and mounted the larger of the two horses they'd taken from the Ottoman scouts. They placed Cemal, still tied, on the other.

They rode for Lazar's camp, more cautious now after Cemal's ambush. Darkness covered the sky when they arrived. Ivan took one of Cemal's arms and Danilo the other as they approached Knez Lazar's tent.

Allies and members of the war council stood outside, consulting each other in small groups. Konstantin wove his way through the crowd with Miloš Obilić at his elbow.

"A prisoner?" Konstantin asked.

"Yes."

Obilić studied Cemal. "Have you questioned him?"

Ivan nodded. "He and a friend were out seeking a worthy village to sack. As is a good portion of the Ottoman camp."

"Do you think he's telling the truth?" Obilić asked.

"I do. I've had dealings with him before, and I don't believe him a liar. And what he told us matches what we saw."

Obilić called two men over. "Take this prisoner and secure him. Give him something to eat, and keep him under guard." As Cemal was led off, Obilić turned to Ivan. "Come. You are the last scouts to report. Knez Lazar is waiting."

The inside of the tent was warm and well-lit, with terra-cotta oil lamps set on tables around the edges. Knez Lazar stood as they entered. Gray lined his temples and streaked his beard, but he walked toward them with a steady warrior's gait.

"Our last scouts, lord." Obilić stood to the side, and Konstantin stood next to him, giving Ivan and Danilo the center of the tent. "They seem to have gotten closer to the camp than the others."

Knez Lazar appraised Ivan the way a collector might scrutinize a new painting. "So, you are the grandson of Župan Đurad Lukarević?"

"Yes, lord."

Lazar turned to Danilo and gave him the same careful study. "And you are the cousin?"

Danilo bowed. "Yes, lord."

"And you spent the last two years in Edirne?"

"In Adrianople, yes, lord." As soon as the words left Ivan's mouth, Konstantin caught his gaze, warning him not to correct the knez.

Lazar chuckled. "You prefer to call the city by its Christian name?"

"Yes, lord."

"Very well. What did you learn of our enemy while you dwelled in their city? And what did you see today?"

Ivan and Danilo gave their report. When they finished, Knez Lazar thanked and dismissed them. Konstantin came with them. "Adrianople?" Konstantin asked. "You should have left it."

"He didn't seem to mind."

"No, but if you hadn't also told him the exact information he's been waiting for, you wouldn't have left a good impression. You've been too long a hostage or a prisoner of men you owe no loyalty to. Respect, Ivan. The knez has earned the right to your respect. He's our only hope of staying free of the Turks."

"I'm sorry." Ivan took his horse's reins from one of Lazar's grooms but didn't mount. "Should I go back and apologize?"

Konstantin shook his head. "No. We should prepare our men. I have a feeling we'll attack tomorrow." Two of Konstantin's warriors waited nearby. He motioned them over, and all mounted their horses.

The night brought a cool breeze, a welcome respite from the day's heat. The clear sky revealed stars sprinkled like glittering gems from horizon to horizon. As they rode back, Konstantin pulled his horse alongside Ivan's. "I'm sorry. I was too hard on you."

"No. You were right. I'm used to being subject to a sultan or kephale. Men I must obey by force, not by choice. Knez Lazar is different, if Grandfather is to be believed." Ivan wanted his grandfather to be right, because they needed someone like Lazar to unite them if they were to have any chance against Ottoman might.

They rode in silence until they reached Ivan's camp. Ivan, Danilo, and Matthias dismounted.

"Do you know what Grandfather told me before we marched?" Konstantin smiled as he spoke, a soft hint of emotion from a man who was normally stoic.

"No."

"He said Fate is often like a woman you've been married to for decades. Sometimes she delights you, sometimes she taxes you, but there are few surprises. There's a give and a take, and overall, it is comfortable." He glanced at Philippos as he came and took the other horses. "Other times, Fate is like a songbird. If you get too close and try to capture it, you scare it away, and you're left with silence. Or Fate is like a wolf, and it will destroy you the first chance it gets." Then he locked eyes with Ivan. "And sometimes, Fate is like a corpse. It must be dug from the earth, wrestled back to life, tamed to your will, and made your servant."

"He gave me no such advice."

"That's not all he said." Konstantin glanced at the sky, then back at Ivan. "He said you would either take Fate and tame it, or it would be a wolf to you."

"Why didn't he tell me that himself?"

"Because he thought it might seem harsh coming from him. Coming from me, you'd know my hope without question. Fate has long howled at you, Ivan. I think of how sickly you were as a child and how much family we've lost. Then your time as a prisoner and your time as a hostage. But the future is yours to create. You've never been ordinary, and now, my brother, it is time to be great. Take Fate and make it your servant."

CHAPTER THIRTY-THREE
THE BATTLE OF PLOČNIK

A DRY BREEZE RUFFLED THE mane of Ivan's destrier. He waited at the head of his fifty-five cavalrymen. Beside him were Danilo, Konstantin, and Konstantin's cavalry. Their mounted bowmen were under Župan Dragomir's command. Ivan's satnik from Sivi Gora waited with the infantry, to be held in reserve until they were needed.

Based on Ivan's scouting trip, the information from Cemal, and the stream of villagers fleeing the pasha's army, it seemed most of the ghazis were spending their stored-up frustration on Pločnik and nearby villages. Unless the pasha was hiding the majority of his army, now was the opportune time to attack those who remained. Once the main force was defeated, they could focus on the other units and save the villagers from the ravaging ghazi raiders.

Miloš Obilić rode toward them and pulled his splendid horse to a stop beside Konstantin and Ivan. "The Turks are assembling. We attack soon."

Obilić trotted down the line to the next group of soldiers, the Bulgarian cavalry.

Konstantin turned to Ivan and Danilo. "I hope we've made the right choice. Because we're unlikely to be forgiven now."

"I've been to Adrianople," Ivan said. "Trust me, we've made the right choice. And that will be true regardless of the outcome."

It would be an open battle, and that made them nervous. Anything could happen. Entire armies were lost in open battles, two very different fates balanced on the edge of a knife. Ivan checked that his sword was loose in its sheath and glanced at his men. A few compulsively sharpened daggers or fiddled with their armor. Others sat completely still on their horses. Some seemed uneasy, but they all looked ready. Their chain mail had been scrubbed until it shone, and their open-faced helmets reflected light like mirrors.

"I can't think of better men to go into battle with." Konstantin's face softened into a smile as his destrier whinnied. He turned to address the cavalrymen. "The time will soon come, my brave men. If you wish to keep your children free, do it today, by the sword. If you wish to retain the sanctity of our churches, do it today, by the sword. If you wish to preserve your homes and fields, do it today, by the sword. Fight boldly. If we fail, we will be little better than slaves. If we succeed, we can look forward to a future bright with freedom. We are but pilgrims here on earth. All must die eventually. As for me, I would rather die armed, in battle, saving my family and defending my faith, than submit to slavery. By the sword, my brothers! Today, we live by the sword!"

A cheer rose through the ranks as men lifted their swords and repeated Konstantin's refrain.

Ivan joined them. "By the sword!" He had nothing left, no other purpose in life than to serve his people. If he was required to give his life, here, outside Pločnik, he was ready.

Knez Lazar, mounted on his dappled courser, would direct the battle from the center, where most of the Serb forces waited. The Bosnian cavalry waited to the right, the Bulgarian cavalry to the left, with archers on the flanks.

A horn sounded, signaling the attack. Konstantin led, and Ivan urged his horse to keep pace with him. Across the field, Ottoman horsemen rode out to meet them with mace and scimitar glinting in the sun. Ivan forgot his worries, focusing only on the task ahead: reach the enemy and slice through them.

A swarm of Turkish arrows zipped past him, barely heard over the thunder of galloping horses. Ivan blocked the arrows with his shield and used his other hand to hold his lance. When they met the Ottomans, Ivan's momentum carried him past the first line and into the second. He skewered a Turk atop a bay stallion, ripped his lance free, and thrust it into the next enemy, then the next. Around him, Danilo, Konstantin, and the others did the same, meeting their enemies amid the ring of clashing blades and neighing horses.

The Ottoman line didn't crumble despite being outnumbered. Lala Şahin Pasha must have kept his best, most disciplined troops in camp and allowed the rabble out to plunder. The Turks stood their ground. Ivan blocked a jab from a Turkish javelin and stabbed his opponent with his lance. The lance stuck, so Ivan drew out his sword. One of the Turks—a leader, if the pennant waving nearby was any indication—raised his scimitar into the air, calling the sipahis back to him. That was how the Ottomans fought, how they were trained: charge, retreat, reorganize. Charge, retreat, reorganize. And then destroy.

"Keep our line steady!" Ivan shouted. He had listened to account after account of Ottoman victories that had come because the Turks had kept their organization, and eventually, their enemies had descended into disorder. That would not be the case today, not if Ivan could keep his men together. Danilo, Matthias, and Niketas waited beside him beneath a blazing sun, preparing for the next Ottoman attack.

The Turks retreated until they were out of bow range, then formed for another charge. They set out again, making the earth beneath them vibrate with the coordinated canter of their mounts. When the Turkish riders crashed into the Serb line for the second time, the Serbs held. Ivan dueled with a fat man on a bay horse, striking him in the neck with his sword, then with a hairy man on a gray horse, striking him in the thigh. Ivan chopped off the head of his third opponent, a man galloping toward him so fast that Ivan never saw anything beyond the red of his cap.

Eventually, the Ottomans retreated again. It wasn't the end, but Ivan was glad for the respite. Niketas's left arm dripped blood.

"Fall back," Ivan told him. "Get it bandaged." Niketas handed his lance to Ivan and obeyed. Goran took his place. In the pause, Ivan glanced at his brother and cousin. Weariness and determination marked their faces. They were covered in dust and gore, but they held ready for the next wave. Ivan's chain-mail hauberk extended to his elbows. In the lull, he used the cotton sleeve of his exposed tunic to wipe at his skin. Sweat and spurts of enemy blood had made his brow sticky.

The third Ottoman assault was much the same. Serb and Turk met in a ferocious struggle. But this time, the Ottoman tide broke more swiftly, at least in front of Konstantin and Ivan's section of the line. Farther toward the center, the Ottomans held strong and threatened havoc.

Ivan scanned the battlefield. Nearby enemies were all defeated, but he saw a chance to flank the Turks attacking Knez Lazar's men. "Kostya!" Ivan shouted over the sound of wounded men, charging horses, and clanging weapons.

His brother turned. "What?"

"Their flanks are exposed."

Konstantin nodded. "I'll rally my men."

"No. I'll go." Ivan's men were closer. "They'll regroup and attack again. We can't leave a hole in the line. You hold here. I'll take my men, and we can end their rally in the center."

"Agreed." Konstantin began shouting orders to his men.

Ivan did the same. "Danilo, Matthias, we're swinging into the center to crush their rally. Organize the men into two groups. One to smash into their backs, the other to lay waste their withdrawal. Danilo, take your group and form a screen. Cut off their retreat. You'll get them before they reorganize, so they'll be in small groups."

"We'll chop them to pieces," Danilo said as he gathered the men.

"Matthias, come. Let us barrel into the back of them and see how quickly they fall when surrounded."

Ivan's group included twenty of his men. They formed a wedge, with Ivan at the point, and the others riding knee to knee to his left and his right. Even over the noise of the field, their horses' hooves made a steady beat as they approached, closer and closer to the enemy. They plunged into the back of the Ottoman line with a mix of speed and sharp iron. Ivan's lance bit into first one, then another of his enemy. He recognized one of his opponents, but memory of training together wasn't enough to justify mercy. He slew him, then turned to the next sipahi.

The Ottoman group had been making headway, but as more and more of them turned to skirmish with Ivan's group, the Turks could no longer continue forward. Bit by bit, they dispersed. And as they scattered, they fell back into Danilo's group, where their numbers were further reduced.

The battlefield cleared for a few moments. The Serb line had been saved, the Ottoman rally driven back, but Ivan didn't believe the enemy was defeated, not completely, not yet.

"Back to our positions!" he ordered. If the Ottomans regrouped and attacked again, he wanted to be ready.

Konstantin maneuvered his horse next to Ivan as Ivan returned, and Konstantin handed him a waterskin so he could quench his thirst. "You might not have seen it from the middle of the action, but that was magnificent."

In the distance, Ivan could see Ottoman infantry. "Perhaps. But it didn't break them. They're charging again, on foot."

"Horses behind," Danilo said.

It took Ivan a few seconds longer to see them through the thick smear of dust.

"I'll send word to the infantry. It might be time to draw in our reserves." Konstantin called his runner, and the message was sent.

"It's best if we meet the infantry in a charge." Ivan looked along the line of his men. "But we must stay together, or we'll be vulnerable. It's a favorite Ottoman strategy to wear their opponents out with infantry, then strike with their cavalry."

Word spread along the line, a warning to stay together and watch for an attack by the horsemen. Konstantin gave the command, and the group charged at a steady pace, moving as a unit. The battle had spread their forces so they were only one man thick, but Ivan had confidence in their thin, well-disciplined line. It included some of his closest friends and a cohort carefully trained by his grandfather. He'd drilled with them and watched them prove themselves on the field over the past hour.

He used his sword to slice down on the Ottoman infantry. One, whom Matthias had wounded, swung his mace into Ivan's leg, but there was little power behind the blow. Ivan didn't think it would cause anything more than a bruise. The mounted Turks beyond the infantry came up quickly, before the infantry was finished off, and the horsemen proved more of a challenge. Their group was surrounded by enemy underfoot and enemy ahead, but for the most part, Ivan's men outfought their rivals.

Ivan stabbed his sword into the chest of a Turkish warrior, yanked it out, and sliced at another enemy. The sun beat down with oppressive heat, and weariness nibbled at his muscles. Above the cries of the wounded men, he heard a shout from a familiar voice. He turned to see Matthias fall from his saddle. Ivan fought off another pair of Turks and urged his horse back to where he'd last seen his friend. He dismounted next to the still body, keeping the reins to his horse gripped tightly in one hand.

"Matthias?" Ivan removed his friend's helmet so he could better see his face. Matthias squinted back. Blood streamed from his shoulder, so Ivan grabbed a cloth from his saddle bag and wrapped it around the wound. Not for the first time, he wished Helena were near. She could repair something like this with needle, thread, and a little wine. "Are you wounded anywhere else?"

Matthias nodded and brought Ivan's hand to his ribs. Ivan hadn't noticed it before because it was broken off level with the skin, but an arrow had plowed into Matthias's side. If it had gone deep, that was something not even Helena could fix.

Matthias coughed, and blood trickled from his lips, joining the dried layers already splattered on his skin. "Will you see that my wife is taken care of? And my sons?"

"Your family will be provided for. I swear it."

"Tell them . . . Tell them I died free."

"Free. And valiant."

Matthias drew in another shuddering breath, and then he exhaled his last. Ivan choked back his emotion. He had to return and finish the battle, no matter what it cost. But there was a new burden now. Matthias had trusted him, followed him. And Ivan had led him to his death. No matter what else happened, Ivan had to ensure that this battle ended in something that Matthias would have been proud of.

The fighting had moved farther from Matthias's body. Ivan mounted and urged his horse back into the fray. Rage and grief gave Ivan added strength as he drove into the enemy. Why couldn't the Turks leave them in peace? They were stronger and better organized than the Serbs or their allies, but that was not adequate claim for Christian lands.

A Turkish rider roared as he galloped toward Ivan. His scimitar glimmered in the crisp sunlight and sped toward Ivan's helmet. Ivan threw up his shield and swung his horse around as the man rode by. Ivan swayed with the blow, but before the man was out of reach, Ivan swung his own sword into the enemy's back. The man arched and toppled from his saddle with a guttural cry.

As the enemy fell, Ivan saw something that made him pause. Kasim rode twenty paces away, and his eyes were fixed on Ivan. Kasim lifted his sword in challenge. Ivan smote two of the Turkish cavalry between them, but as he advanced, Kasim withdrew.

Three years ago, Gregoras had drawn Ivan away from the rest of Konstantin's army into the middle of the Greek lines. Now Ivan was more experienced; he wouldn't make the same mistake again. Few things would give him more pleasure than slaying Kasim, but the day was not about pleasure. The day's duty called him to defeat a dangerous enemy while they were vulnerable.

"Did you see him?" Danilo slid his sword into the neck of a nearby sipahi, and the man fell from his stallion to be trampled by a Serb horseman.

"Yes. But what if it's a trap?"

"Their left flank is crumbling. We can't let him get away."

Ivan had been so focused on the nearby enemy that he hadn't seen what was happening farther afield. If the Ottoman left was collapsing, that changed things. Ivan signaled for six of his men-at-arms to follow him while Danilo asked for spare arrows because his quiver was empty. Given enough time, they could find more arrows among the dead, either in their quivers or in their bodies, but Kasim was riding farther and farther away.

"Kostya!" Ivan called.

With a grunt and a mighty swing, Ivan's brother sliced off the head of a Turkish warrior. "What?"

"We're going in pursuit of an old enemy."

"Shall I come?"

"No. You're needed here."

Konstantin nodded, then engaged another Turkish sipahi. Their blades clashed thrice before Konstantin disabled the man in the arm.

Ivan swung his sword and forced an opening for him and his group. His other cavalrymen followed, engaging with the Turkish men Ivan had pushed through and forcing a larger hole in the Ottoman line. Though he'd hesitated before, Ivan now saw a double benefit in pursuing Kasim. With every leader they defeated, the enemy lost some of its ability to organize and plan, and the newly exploited gap in the Ottoman line would split and scatter those Turks still fighting.

Ivan and his entourage slashed their way through more of the enemy troops. The smell of blood assaulted his nostrils as weary men fought a weakening enemy. Finally, Ivan led them through the last of the sipahis.

There, in a meadow of calm, sat Kasim astride a white horse. Ten warriors in tall red hats flanked him. Their uniform appearance and iron faces suggested discipline and skill. Kasim had indeed set a trap, but enough of Ivan's men had followed him that this would be an even contest, not a massacre.

Ivan expected the Turks to fan out to meet them, but Kasim spoke several sharp commands, and his men stayed beside him, acting as bodyguards. Ivan would have to go through them in order to meet Kasim. He glanced at Danilo, who nodded. Together, they urged their horses forward.

A score of Ottoman infantry appeared through Kasim's guard, shouting as they rushed at the Serb horsemen. Ivan killed three, but a fourth stabbed his spear into Ivan's horse. The destrier collapsed, Ivan with it. He was on his feet again a moment later, sword in one hand and broken lance in the other. He beat off another set of infantrymen, and then the charge came. Five of Kasim's mounted warriors converged on him. Ivan was outnumbered, and Kasim's men had the advantage, swinging their scimitars from high in their saddles.

Ivan held one Turk off with his sword and pierced another with the end of his lance, but the lance stuck in the man's body and was gone. A third attacked. Danilo's arrow pierced the man's neck before he could complete the swing of his saber. Ivan ducked away from another of his opponents, grabbed a mace from beneath a Turkish corpse, and smashed the new weapon into the other man's leg. The man bellowed in agony and retreated. Ivan couldn't pursue because he was on foot, and more of Kasim's men were coming for him.

Goran drew one away, and Danilo killed another. A Turk with a long, smooth mustache swung his curved blade toward Ivan. Ivan's ears rang as his blade blocked the strike. He pinned the scimitar to the flesh of the horse, and pummeled the mace into his opponent's back. The Turk dropped his blade with a grunt, and Ivan punctured the man's ribs with his sword.

The way to Kasim was now clear. Ivan didn't hesitate. "It seems that if you want me dead, you will have to kill me yourself."

Kasim let a low, menacing chuckle escape his throat. "I always intended to. But it is only fair that you should tire yourself first. I am weary. I was up all night flaying Serb scouts and beating my wife."

Ivan's jaw hardened in rage. But Kasim couldn't be telling the truth. Ivan, Danilo, and Matthias had been the last to return the night before. All of Knez Lazar's scouts had made it back, so Kasim couldn't have been torturing them. And he'd said himself that he had more pleasurable things to do with his wives than beat them. Ivan would keep his wits about him, regardless of how Kasim provoked him. "Will you dismount and face me on equal ground?"

"Only a fool gives up an advantage." Kasim jabbed his heels into his horse's flanks and charged at Ivan.

Danilo loosed an arrow, his last, but Kasim blocked it with his round shield of cane and iron. Ivan prepared to defend against a mounted foe, but Danilo spurred his horse into Kasim's path and blocked him.

"Ivan!" Goran called. "Take my horse!"

Everyone seemed to understand that it had to be Ivan who faced Kasim, but Danilo and Goran wanted it to be on equal terms. Ivan used Goran's offered knee to mount the horse, accepted a shield, and rode to where Danilo and Kasim sparred with their blades. Danilo backed off and engaged another Turkish horsemen with his sword.

"On foot or on horse, you will fall to me." Kasim adjusted one of his wrist guards. "Not even the loyalty of your friends will save you—I will sever your head from your neck and leave your body for the vultures."

The two had never fought before, but Ivan had heard rumors of Kasim's skill. He was one of the sultan's finest warriors, but he was overconfident, and that might give Ivan an edge. Their horses circled each other at a distance. How would Kasim fight? Would he go directly for Ivan's head, or would he toy with him first?

Kasim forced his horse closer and swung at Ivan with a scimitar. Ivan blocked it with his shield and used his knees to nudge his horse into a better position. He swung his sword at Kasim's shoulder, trying to hack through the Turkish armor, but Kasim met the blow with his own blade. Ivan swung again, and Kasim blocked and changed positions.

A drum sounded, calling the Ottomans to retreat.

Kasim looked around. Danilo slew the last of his companions within sight. Kasim grunted, then turned his horse and galloped off.

Ivan pursued in the next moment. Kasim had cost Ivan and those he loved far too much; Ivan wouldn't let him get away without a fight. Ivan's eyes focused on Kasim, but his ears noted the sound of Danilo and the others following.

Ivan spurred his horse and crashed into Kasim's side, swinging his sword and almost unseating the formidable Turk. Kasim blocked but had trouble keeping his balance. The two traded blows as their horses raced toward the Ottoman lines of retreat. Ivan gripped his horse with his legs, feigned a strike with his sword, and brought his shield around, chopping it into Kasim's elbow.

Kasim grunted and transferred his scimitar to his other hand. Then he leaped from his saddle, grabbing Ivan and dragging him down into the dirt with him. A hoof struck Ivan's shoulder, and something sharp pierced his arm. Ivan swung at Kasim with his fist, forcing him off his chest and off his sword arm.

Ivan gripped his sword and struggled to his feet to face Kasim. His shoulder ached, and his upper arm streamed blood. He'd been fighting for hours, and his armor was heavy, but he did his best to catch his breath and gather his strength. Around the two, the Turks retreated and the Serbs pursued in a loud, dusty mass, but Kasim and Ivan were concerned only with each other.

Ivan hewed with his sword. Kasim's injured elbow hung limply at his side, but he calmly deflected Ivan's blow with the weapon held in his healthy hand. The blades came together, then apart, then together again. A dying horse writhed nearby, its hooves thrashing in panic. Kasim's strikes still held force, and Ivan had to step with care over ground littered with broken weapons and broken men.

Exhaustion gripped Ivan with crushing strength. Each Ottoman charge had worn him down. His hands ached, his muscles burned, and the cut in his arm continued to bleed. He struck and countered, parried and riposted, but could find no weakness in his enemy. Kasim seemed to see Ivan's fatigue, and his haughtiness grew.

Ivan feigned and flicked his sword into Kasim's chin, but Kasim's block kept it from doing much damage.

Kasim sneered. "You may have drawn blood, but I'll take your head and carry it from the field in my horse's oat bag." Kasim attacked with such alacrity that Ivan was forced backward. Ivan nearly stumbled over a fallen corpse and barely brought his sword up to block Kasim's next thrust. The tip of Kasim's scimitar nicked Ivan's forehead. The cut stung, and blood ran into Ivan's eyes.

Ivan's body ached with weariness, but he would not give up. Kasim was skilled, but Ivan had a store of stubbornness, and it would not let him fall to a Turk so loathed and despised. He met Kasim's next blow with more strength, then blocked the one after, then got in a thrust of his own.

Ivan hewed again, forcing Kasim back over the same corpse the two had been sparring around. He blocked Kasim's blows and smashed his sword into his again and again. Ivan let his anger consume him, and each thrust, lunge, and slash drove his enemy back. For the first time, Kasim's eyes showed a hint of fear.

"You are a fool," Kasim said. "No matter how this ends, you are a fool, and Sultan Murad will defeat you."

"Perhaps." Ivan blocked Kasim's saber and shoved him back. "But that defeat will not come today."

With his free hand, Ivan gripped a broken lance protruding from a corpse. As Kasim attacked again, Ivan beat the scimitar away with the lance and swung his sword at Kasim's neck. It bit into the skin, and Kasim fell to the blood-soaked battlefield. He twitched and gurgled as his eyes lifted skyward in surprise.

And then, finally, Kasim fell still.

Chapter Thirty-Four
PILLAGE

ISKANDAR GAVE THE SIGNAL, AND his men attacked the village. Some of the inhabitants resisted. The ghazis slew them. As his horse stepped along the main road, Iskandar saw the rabble, mostly men, lying on the ground with their eyes open, fixated on a world they no longer saw. The pattern of screams reminded him of a wave, rising as the alarm spread, then falling as ghazis silenced those who fought and as the cries of ravaged women faded into sobs.

"Gather the boys and take them to the north end," Iskandar told two of his men. The sultan would pay a good price for the boys. If they were healthy, he would have them trained up as janissaries. If they were weak or stubborn, they could be put to a different use or sold to someone else.

Iskandar kept his scimitar out, ready to use if any of the villagers put up more than token resistance, but there were no warriors here. Craftsmen and farmers, that was all. A pity there weren't more merchants—they might have had more valuable plunder. The people here measured their wealth in animals and fruit trees, not in jewelry or fine cloth or precious goblets.

Perhaps this village hadn't been the best target after all. Yet the village had been easy to take, and his men would feast tonight. That would raise their spirits. An easy sack today and another like it tomorrow—they'd be rich men if it continued.

As resistance crumbled, his men gathered goats and chickens, cooking pots and candles, cloaks and blankets. Two came from the small church with patens, chalices, and a pair of candlesticks. Iskandar motioned one of them over to examine their finds. They were silver.

Perhaps the church contained other items of value. Tapestries? Incense containers? Iskandar went to investigate. He didn't bother to dismount, and once inside, the horseshoes echoed loudly on the stone floor. His eyes were immediately drawn to a half-finished mosaic depicting Jesus on a throne, with a golden halo about his head. Light from the windows made the pieces of the halo shimmer like the sun. Could they be made of real gold? Iskandar would send some of his ghazis to pry the tesserae off and find out. The artist's tools lay on the ground nearby, beside the slain man.

Outside again, Iskandar urged his horse toward his five men who were tying the boys into a line so they could be marched off. They'd made a good haul. A dozen lads of varying ages were already bound. As he approached, an older boy, perhaps ten years of age, swung an elbow into one of the ghazis' faces. It drew blood. The ghazi knocked the boy to the ground and held a scimitar at his throat. Iskandar waited to see if he would run the boy through. Taking someone who wouldn't show the proper meekness carried risk, but children could usually be beaten into submission, eventually, and they were too young to escape without help.

The ghazi restrained himself. Two of the others drew the fair-headed boy to his feet and pushed him toward the line.

As they tied the boy's hands in front of him, a young woman charged them with a spear. She ran from the woods, yelling in Slavonic. And her spear pierced one of Iskandar's men.

It seemed to surprise the girl as much as it surprised her victim. The boy broke free, but only for a moment before another ghazi captured him again. Iskandar dismounted and reached the woman as one of his ghazis took her weapon. Iskandar gripped her arm so she couldn't escape.

"Shall we slay them?" Ahmed asked.

The boy looked at the ground as two of Iskandar's men held him. The young woman stared at Iskandar, her eyes drawn into angry slits. There was a resemblance between them. Siblings? The woman was perhaps fifteen. Her uncovered golden hair was unlike anything he had ever seen before. He touched it with his free hand to make sure it was real. The woman turned away. Her lips trembled as Iskandar moved his fingers to the smooth skin of her jaw and neck.

When they'd marched against Byzia, Kasim had told Iskandar of the first time he'd seen Helena. He'd known he had to have her. Iskandar hadn't understood then, but he understood now. The golden-haired girl was more than beautiful. She was bewitching. "Secure the boy. The girl is mine." Even if he took no other booty from this village, he was content with his prize.

The time had come to take a bride, and if she resisted, Iskandar would find pleasure in the required taming.

Shouts sounded from the other end of the village. Iskandar glanced at the captured boys and at the Serb dead lining the streets. If there were more villagers, surely they would have attacked by now, but the calls sounded like war cries. Iskandar shoved the woman toward Ahmed. "Tie her with the others."

Iskandar led his horse toward the disturbance. The pleasant summer breeze suddenly turned harsh as a group of horsemen turned the corner, galloping toward him. Armed Serbs. How had they made it through the ghazis on the other side of the village?

"Mount up!" Iskandar yelled. He stood alone in the center of the village against the advancing Serbs, but he quickly mounted his horse and retreated to his men. He didn't want to face the band of Serbs alone.

The men by the captives drew scimitars and javelins. Ahmed shoved the boys and the golden-haired girl into the dirt next to the injured ghazi.

"Form a line!" Iskandar ordered.

The approaching Serbs were more numerous than Iskandar's group, but some of them had stopped to examine the fallen villagers. As they drew closer, Iskandar recognized the leaders: Ivan and Danilo. Not a day had passed since Kırkpınar that Iskandar hadn't wished their bodies impaled outside Edirne. He recognized another of the men who rode with them, a Greek soldier captured and then freed during the siege.

Anger burned through Iskandar's veins. He wasn't sure which of them he hated more. Ivan, who had killed his father and vanquished his forces during the siege, or Danilo, who had almost thwarted Iskandar's work as a spy, then made good their escape from Kırkpınar, injuring Iskandar in the process. Perhaps today would be his chance for vengeance on both.

Three of his men rode to join him. Now there were four horsemen to face the enemy vanguard, and the ghazis still on foot to meet the other Serbs.

"Ready!" Iskandar called out. "Advance!"

Their horses lurched forward. There wasn't time to match the Serbs for speed, but at least they wouldn't be standing still, waiting for attack.

Iskandar rode right for Ivan. Their blades connected, and their bodies twisted from the force of their charge. Iskandar rode through the line and had to straighten himself in the saddle. He'd nearly been unhorsed.

Ivan, Danilo, and the Greek were now behind him. Ahead of him, a score of Serb soldiers fought with Iskandar's men, though many of them had already defeated their opponents and were gathering together into a force Iskandar dared not attack. Nor could he flee. Ivan's forces had Iskandar's band surrounded. Iskandar had lost half his line of horsemen in the first clash. One lay on the ground, unmoving—Danilo's doing. The other was on foot, battling a dismounted Serb.

Iskandar turned his mount around and prepared for another charge at Ivan and Danilo. "The one on the black horse," Iskandar ordered his last ghazi. "We focus on him first." If he could destroy Ivan, perhaps the Serbs would be less organized. He caught sight of Danilo. Maybe not—the half-blood was a capable leader. Allah willing, Iskandar would slay Danilo immediately after he slew Ivan. Then the Serb group, effectively decapitated, would be easy prey.

They smashed into the small group of enemy horsemen with even more force the second time. Iskandar blocked the Greek with his shield and thrust his scimitar at Ivan. The Serb knocked it away and blocked the other ghazi with a mace. Between Ivan's mace and Danilo's sword, the man on Iskandar's right was now gone.

Ivan swung his heavy mace at Iskandar. Iskandar blocked the worst of it with his shield, but the momentum carried him backward, and he tumbled from the saddle. The bruising would be awful. Iskandar gasped for breath and struggled to his feet. But now it seemed there were two Serbs for every ghazi, and all Iskandar's men were dead or fighting desperately. Perhaps the pasha had been right. It would have been better not to disperse the army.

Ivan leaped from his horse and tackled Iskandar to the ground in a burst of speed and fury. Ivan had grown stronger since their last battle, two years before. Iskandar tried to yank his scimitar free, but Ivan grabbed Iskandar's wrist and pounded it repeatedly into the ground until Iskandar lost his grip.

Then he felt the blade on his neck.

Iskandar's entire world had imploded like a watchtower upended by a mine. The dead faces of his fallen ghazis met his eyes no matter which direction he looked. And Ivan's sword pressed into his flesh.

"You don't want to kill me," Iskandar blurted in desperation.

"Oh, I think I do." Ivan's voice was a low growl. "I should have finished you off outside the kastron in Byzia. You may think you owe me vengeance for slaying your father, but believe me, you have caused me grief far deeper than what comes from losing a parent."

Was Ivan referring to the two years he had been a hostage in Edirne, all because Iskandar had spied out Župan Konstantin's initial plans to ally with Knez Lazar? Or was he referring to what Iskandar and Kasim had accomplished together at Byzia? If that was the case, Iskandar might have a chance. "If you speak of the Greek lady, she is nearby."

Ivan's whole face changed, the fury replaced with fixation. "Helena?"

"Kasim brought her." Iskandar pushed his head into the ground, hoping to ease the pain where the tip of Ivan's sword broke the skin of his neck. "Spare me, and I'll show you where she is."

"We know the location of the Turkish camp."

"But can you reach her before Kasim does?"

"Kasim is dead." The words were spoken with certainty.

"But what of Kasim's men? They've heard rumor of her beauty. I doubt they'll leave her behind."

"Most of Kasim's men are dead as well."

What could Iskandar say to convince his enemy to spare him? He would do anything, *anything* to stay alive. "Even if they don't take her, others might. Do you trust every man in the pasha's army to treat her with respect? And what of your army? Will they see a Greek lady? Or will she be another item to plunder from the enemy? Ravished at will until their violence it satiated?"

Ivan eased the blade slightly so Iskandar no longer felt its sharp prick. "You would trade death to be a prisoner?"

"Yes."

"If you're not ransomed, you'll be sold. You would risk slavery?"

"Yes." Perhaps Bayezid would pay the ransom. Or perhaps Iskandar could escape, if he could just live long enough to make the attempt. Regardless, all his work here had fallen apart. Danilo was cutting the golden-haired girl and the captive boys free. "Slavery isn't always permanent. Kyria Helena, for example." Iskandar brought the conversation back to his strongest point of leverage. "She is little better than a slave now. But you could help her escape her fate."

"Danilo?" Ivan called his cousin over and repeated what Iskandar had said of Helena.

"He could lead us into an ambush," Danilo said.

Iskandar wished that were the case. But he'd set no trap because he hadn't known Serb forces were so near.

Danilo ripped Iskandar to his feet and bound his arms tightly behind his back. "Since it might be a trap, we had better find her quickly and go in force. Don't try anything, Ghazi Iskandar. If you go back on your word, it will take more than a fallen horse to save you from my next arrow."

Iskandar tested the ropes around his wrists. They bit into his skin. He almost complained, but he didn't think Ivan or Danilo would ease the bands. Blood stained their skin, dust clung to their armor, and rage highlighted their faces. They had seen hard battle, and they would show him no mercy if he tried anything now.

So, he would bide his time. The Serbs may have won the battle, won the day, but Sultan Murad would return in greater force and wrest power from them. And Iskandar intended to be at Murad's side when that happened.

Allah willing, Iskandar would have his turn as victor.

CHAPTER THIRTY-FIVE
THE OTTOMAN CAMP

Helena had never seen such chaos. Hundreds of Ottoman warriors trotted into camp, trailing sweat and dust and blood. Some rode through; others stopped to take what they could before galloping off again. Some walked or ran instead of rode. Helena peered from Kasim's tent. What would her husband expect her to do? Pack? Wait? Flee?

If Kasim didn't hold the safety of Leo's people in his hands, she might try to escape, despite the danger. But the men riding through camp had a wild look about them, and Byzia would pay a terrible price for her desertion. It was best to stay hidden and wait.

Thinking of her people brought an ache to her heart. She missed them, especially her sister and niece. Euphrosyne had beautiful handwriting, but Helena had received no word from anyone since she'd been forced to Edirne. Helena would have cherished a letter, but it seemed she had been not only exiled but also forgotten.

A Turkish warrior barged inside and leered at her. Helena grabbed a knife and held it in front of her as she stepped away. The man turned his attention to Kasim's silver plates, and Helena relaxed with relief. Another man joined the first in pillaging the tent. Helena fastened her veil and crept beneath the back of the tent into the open. She was immediately surrounded by four ghazis. She screamed as one of them grabbed her arm and squeezed her wrist so hard that she dropped the knife. She couldn't remember the Turkish words that would tell him whose wife she was.

A horn sounded nearby. Not an Ottoman signal. Her captor dragged her for a few steps, but she squirmed and flung her elbow into his side. He shoved her to the ground and ran to catch up with his friends. Scores of tents blocked her view, but she could guess what the signal meant. The pasha's army had lost, and the Serbs were pursuing their defeated foe. She wasn't sorrowful over an Ottoman loss, but she was scared. Most soldiers, regardless of religion, saw pillage as a right of victory. She wore Turkish garments and spoke almost no Slavonic. How many of them would understand Greek? Even if she told them she was the wife of their enemy against her will, would they care, or would they carry her off?

Helena crept to the front of Kasim's tent. She saw the two pillagers a tent away now, carrying one of Kasim's chests between them. A Serb warrior rode around a tent and speared one with his long lance. Helena ducked back inside the canvas. The inside of the tent might not be safe, but danger swirled without. If one of the soldiers rushing past took her, what would Kasim do to Byzia?

Kasim had several chests and trunks large enough that she could hide inside, but she quickly dismissed that plan. A pillaging army would search anything that might contain valuables, and she didn't want to surprise someone holding a weapon. Nor did she want to be trapped if they set the camp afire.

Waiting and worrying would accomplish nothing. She straightened her shoulders and gathered her sewing supplies. Then she searched through the food stores until she found an unbroken amphora of olive oil. Kasim's devotion to Islam meant he had no wine, but perhaps she could find some elsewhere. There would be wounded men, Serb and Turk. There was no reason not to tend them. Perhaps one of the more educated Serbs would speak Greek or Latin, and she could offer her services as healer.

She grabbed Kasim's bedding and hesitated. She wanted to tear it into bandages, but she feared his wrath if she ruined his quilts. Would he return? If she were captured, would he want her back enough to ransom her? She closed her eyes as the uncertainty of her future swirled around her. Would she be carried off just like the silver? And would that be better or worse than life with Kasim?

Helena had lost a knife when the ghazi had grabbed her outside the tent, and all the others had been pillaged. She lifted a panel and saw the one she'd dropped still lying on the ground. She waited for a pair of Serb riders to pass by, and then she grabbed it and set to work on one of Kasim's blankets. As she cut bandages, she ignored the men shouting, swords clashing, and horses charging about the camp. Her headdress got in the way, so she tore it off and flung it onto a wooden chest.

The flap of the tent burst open, and an Ottoman soldier charged in. The moment had come. Would he see her as a person or as a prize of war?

She didn't have long to wait for the answer. He lunged at her. She dodged, grabbed her knife, and held it in front of her. In response, he drew out a long curved sword. Helena backed away. Her turbaned assailant swung his scimitar into her knife, knocking it from her grip. Her hand stung from the vibration, but his aim had been true enough not to injure her skin. She turned her head to the left, hoping to distract him. He followed her gaze, and she darted to the right, toward the tent entrance.

She didn't make it. Just as her fingers reached the flap, he grabbed her roughly about the waist. In another moment, he'd thrown her over his shoulder despite her screams. She pounded his back with her fists and would have pummeled his front with her legs, if only he weren't holding them so tightly.

"Let me go!" she shouted at him.

He ignored her. Perhaps she hadn't said it correctly, but more likely, he didn't care. Not far from the tent was a sturdy dappled mare. He dropped Helena to the ground and bound her hands in front of her, then pushed her onto the horse. A chill wind tugged at her loose hair as he climbed on behind her. She told herself that her captor couldn't be worse than her husband, but in truth, she was terrified. Commotion filled the camp and sounded in her ears. Horror swirled in her chest. With Kasim, she had at least been valued as property. A pillaging soldier might use her and then discard her. Death didn't scare her, but torture did.

Her captor urged his horse forward in a canter. So many riders raced through the camp—occasionally stopping to duel with an enemy or loot a tent—that Helena didn't pay much attention to any of them, not until one rode beside her assailant and skewered him with a long cavalry lance. He tumbled to the ground, writhing in agony. Surprise and fear battled in her chest, but she caught the reins and brought the frightened mare to a halt.

She turned to look at whoever had struck her assailant. There were four, but the sun shone behind them, and their faces were in shadow. Were they rescuers, or were they simply stealing her for themselves? She glanced at their horses. Could the dappled mare outrun them, and could she control a horse well enough for a chase when her hands were bound?

The one who'd slain her assailant dismounted and rushed over to her. "Helena, are you all right?"

Helena gripped the saddle horn in astonishment. She'd assumed he would be with the Serb army, but she had never thought to see him again. "Ivan?"

He helped her from the saddle and used his dagger to free her hands. "Are you hurt?" Dried, dusty blood clung to his hair, his armor, and his skin. She'd never been happier to see anyone. The pasha's army had been massive, but Ivan had not only survived; he'd also won.

"Thanks to you, I am safe." The emotions she had felt that day threatened to overwhelm her, but her body was uninjured. She tried to push aside the horror and worry and clung instead to the joy that came with seeing Ivan safe.

He knelt on the ground before her. "I must beg your forgiveness. I met your husband in battle and slew him."

Kasim had been defeated and killed? It had been a possibility when he'd ridden off to fight, but she hadn't allowed herself to hope that his control over her might end. She put one hand on the horse to steady herself and clasped the other over her mouth. Her eyes teared with overwhelming relief. Surely it was a sin to feel gratitude for the death of a husband, but if so, she was guilty wholeheartedly. "Kasim is dead?"

Bewilderment crossed Ivan's face, then sadness. "I'm sorry, Helena. He sought me out."

Helena shook her head, not wanting him to misunderstand. "I've never heard better news. That means I am free." Her hands trembled with shock as she wiped at her tears. If Kasim was dead, then she would no longer have to serve him, no longer have to submit to him, no longer have to live among foreigners. Her life was once again her own.

The others removed their open-faced helmets, and she recognized them: Ivan's cousin and Niketas. The fourth was bound in ropes and wore Turkish armor: Iskandar. She turned to Ivan again, intending to ask him why Niketas rode with him and how they'd taken Iskandar prisoner, but first, she let her eyes drink in the sight of Ivan standing before her once more. The last time she had seen him, it been dark. She'd noticed the increased breadth of his shoulders and the neatly trimmed beard, but she hadn't been able to scrutinize his face. She did that now. Under the thick grime of battle, she suspected he had grown more handsome in the last few years. His body had certainly become more muscled, though a bandage wrapped his arm.

"Are you wounded?" she asked.

Ivan's gaze went to his injury, then back to her. "It's not deep."

"I assumed there would be wounded for me to treat, so I gathered supplies." She motioned toward Kasim's tent. "I'll begin with you."

"If you are willing, there are others who need your help more urgently than I do."

"I'll be glad to help as many as I can. I still need wine, if you have any."

Ivan took her hand to help her to the tent. His touch was warm and strong and gentle, and she had to pull her thoughts back to the task before her. She was a widow now, but that didn't make her a good match for a župan. She was glad to see him, grateful to him for freeing her from an oppressive husband and a violent pillager, but their earlier dreams were still irreparably broken. It would be better not to admire the line of his jaw or the curve of his lips.

Ivan issued a few orders to the others, and soon, her patients arrived along with some wine. Niketas told her of what had happened to the pronoia as she cleaned and stitched a wound in his arm. She was heartbroken to learn of Leo's death, but she would grieve later. At the moment, a leg pierced with a spear awaited her attention, and when that patient was cared for, she had an arrow to pull from a man's shoulder.

She lost track of time, seeing to the Serb wounded. Yet after the first few cases, most of the wounds were minor. She assumed other healers, nearer the battlefield, helped those who had been wounded early in the day. Most of her care involved washing with wine, anointing with oil, and bandaging with fresh cloths. A few of the patients required stitches.

And then only Ivan remained in the tent with her. He'd removed part of his armor, and at some point between finding her more water and wine, he must have washed his face. His hair was still damp, dripping onto his tunic. Her original impression had been true—without the dust and the spattered blood, he was handsome. A cut on his forehead still oozed blood. She fingered the skin around it. "It's not deep. I don't think it needs stitches. May I see your other wound?"

He held his arm out, and she unwrapped the soiled bandage and tossed it into the pile for burning. She studied the jagged wound along his upper arm. "It's not awful, but it will need to be sewn together. You should have let me see it earlier—it's more serious than the last ten I saw."

"I wanted the men cared for first. Thank you for helping them."

"You're welcome." She met his eyes. They still had that intent look, so penetrating that she was sure he could peer through the walls of Constantinople if he tried. Gazing into her soul would be easy in comparison. She focused on the gore on his arm and washed his wound. "There's enough wine if you wish to drink some to dull the pain." She hadn't offered it to the earlier patients for fear of running out, but there were no more patients to save it for, and Ivan was a župan.

He shook his head. Helena stitched. He took it well, but she hadn't expected any different. He'd always been stoic when it came to physical pain. Some things hadn't changed all that much since he'd been a young, wounded enemy. She tied her last stitch and carefully wrapped the arm. He caught her hand as she pulled it away and held it earnestly.

She almost withdrew it, and yet her hand fit so perfectly in his. And she had missed him.

"I also waited until the end because I wanted to be alone with you."

"Oh?" Heat rose in her chest and traveled to her face.

"Since the moment I heard you were here, a hope has been growing inside me. You once agreed to be my bride. Now that Kasim is dead and he no longer holds the fate of Byzia in his hands, will you marry me?" The corners of his lips turned up in supplication, and his eyes softened in a plea. He was still everything she had fallen in love with—brave and strong and determined and utterly vulnerable when it came to his heart.

"Things have changed, Ivan. It was a good match at the time, but the reasons for it no longer exist."

"I still love you. Is that not reason enough?"

"Marriages are rarely about love."

"Ours could be. As a widow, you are free to make your own decisions. You've already done everything you can for your people. Now you're free to do something for yourself."

Helena looked away. "In the eyes of the church, it would be my third marriage." First, she had been betrothed to Callinicus, then married to Kasim. "Third marriages are frowned upon."

"But they're not forbidden. Few priests would stand against it. Your first was merely a betrothal, and your intended died in war. Either of those circumstances alone would argue for allowing another marriage. Together it's a certainty. And your second marriage was entered under threat—and to an unbeliever—so it can also be dismissed. And you're still young. No priest would tell a childless woman of twenty and one that she must stay a widow the rest of her life. There will be a waiting period, and perhaps a penance, but in my lands, we follow the requirements set by St. John the Penitent, and he is more merciful than St. Basil. Will you not think on it?"

"Ivan . . ." She blinked away tears. "I am changed since you last saw me."

"Did you come to love Kasim?"

Helena shook her head. "No. I feared him and cowered at his touch. But you cannot want me now. The marriage was consummated."

"I did not expect to find matters otherwise." Ivan was silent for a moment, then he pointed to the bandage on his arm. "It will scar, don't you think?"

"Yes." She expected it to form a jagged red line that would never fade completely.

"I, too, am changed. A new scar, something I had to suffer to help my people. Was not your marriage to Kasim the same, in a way? A scar, suffered to help your people?"

"It's no mere scar . . . I carried his child for a time. I lost it . . . But that was long enough ago that I may be with child again." She would know for certain in a fortnight. Even if she were not with child, she was the widowed fourth wife of a defeated Ottoman warrior. She was barely more than a slave. Her former life, if it mattered, was little better. The blood of Greek nobility ran in her veins, but she was poorer than a paroikos. A victorious župan with a prosperous mine and dreams of a city so great it would rival Thessaloniki deserved better than someone like her. Ivan had to think not just of himself when he selected a bride, but also of his people. "I'm a widow now. Widows often take vows and enter convents. That is what I must do. I will live a life of service."

"Your life can include service outside a convent. Is that what you really wish? To take vows while you're young?"

"It will be better than what my life was in Edirne."

"Helena . . ." Ivan looked down, sadness lining his eyes and disappointment bending his lips for a moment before he met her gaze, the earnest determination back. "I've finally found you again. Don't make me lose you a second time because of a past you couldn't control. Nothing that has happened has changed my love for you." He reached for her face and held her cheek for a moment.

Tears rolled down her face as she thought of her time in Edirne. "You cannot still want me."

"Indeed, I still do."

She pulled away and stood. She wanted to believe him so badly, but even if a priest agreed to it, surely Ivan's brother or grandfather would protest. "It wouldn't be an advantageous marriage for you. Before, when we first planned a betrothal, it was a wise match. We cared for each other, but beyond that, it benefited our people because it sealed the peace. But now I have nothing. I am nothing."

Ivan stood and followed her. "You are not nothing, Helena. You are the most extraordinary person I have ever known. I love you, and that is reason enough to marry you. If others need more cause, I have it ready. Your skills as a midwife will add to Sivi Gora's prosperity. And by marrying the widow of an enemy defeated in battle, I give my people confidence in my ability to defend them. Who else could I marry who would add so much to my lands? And to my heart?" He stepped closer, and when she didn't back away, he wrapped his arms around her. She didn't have the will to resist. "Please, give me a chance to win your heart again. Let me show you that marriage can be better than whatever it is you've been through."

Helena sobbed and leaned her face into his chest. "Is he really dead? Kasim?"

"Yes."

"And this is not a cruel dream? You are really here to rescue me? And you would take me as your wife . . . Even after . . . Even after everything?"

"Yes, Helena. I love you more than I love my own soul." He looked at her with the same admiration and compassion she remembered from their time together in Leo's lands, before the Turks had robbed them of their future together. Her time with Kasim had battered her confidence until she'd thought of herself as little more than a slave. But Ivan's esteem for her seemed unaffected.

She had tried to think of Ivan as only a friend, had tried to forget her love for him while she'd been married to another. But there, in his arms, she knew those feelings had never fully gone away. Falling in love with Ivan again would be like learning to walk after a period of illness. Simple. Natural. And appreciated all the more because it had been missed so very much.

She had planned to follow Esther's example and live a life of sacrifice. But perhaps that was not her fate after all. There were women in the scriptures who had lived different roles—happy roles—married to men they loved. She'd lost sight of that hope, that desire. Now it seemed that her four moons with Kasim had been a sufficient sacrifice, and God was handing her something far better than what she'd expected as her reward.

Helena searched her memory, trying to recall the Slavonic words she wanted to say. She stumbled over them. Ivan tilted his head slightly, as if he didn't understand. She must have said them wrong, or his reaction would have been different, she was sure of it. "Never mind, I'll use Greek." She looked right into his hazel eyes. "I love you, Ivan, and I want you to kiss me."

Ivan ran a finger along her jaw and up to her mouth. That one simple movement held more tenderness than anything she'd experienced during her time in Edirne. It was as if with one caress, he had bound up all the wounds of her heart and set them on the path to healing. Then he pulled her close and met her lips. For a moment, she remembered the other men who had kissed her, and Ivan's mouth was far better for the comparison. Then she forgot the others and thought only of Ivan.

His kiss was warm, like the first days of spring when the bitter snow finally disappeared and the sun brought the wildflowers to life once more. Then his kiss grew heated as he poured in two years' worth of bottled-up passion. It consumed her like Greek fire, and she responded fiercely. She didn't know how long the kiss lasted, and she didn't care, for time no longer seemed to matter. Her dark night of Ottoman captivity was over, and the new day dawning beyond the crescent sky was brighter than she'd ever imagined.

A gentle breeze blew past her cheek as Ivan ended the kiss and yanked his sword back into his hand. Helena felt dazed from the kiss, but she recognized the face peering at them from the tent opening. It was Ivan's cousin.

"Unless there is an emergency, I would prefer no interruptions," Ivan said.

Danilo murmured something, bowed, and left. He spoke to the men outside, and laughter followed. A hint of mirth crossed Ivan's face as he turned back to her.

"What did he say?" she asked.

"He said, 'Ivan is once more a captive, this time held by a woman.'"

Helena smiled up at him. She couldn't remember the last time she had smiled for joy. "You have been captured, and I have been rescued."

EPILOGUE

1387

IVAN STOOD ON THE BALCONY of his bedchamber, overlooking Sivi Gora. He closed his eyes briefly, letting the soft morning breeze caress his face, confirming he was awake and not wrapped up in a pleasant dream.

New stone walls passed along the east of his citadel and continued on to the south. He still planned to build more towers, but the town was secure and strong. A quarter mile away, the walls of a new church rose in the town center. His grandfather had begun construction about the time Ivan had become a hostage in Adrianople. The workers had made steady progress, and the church would be glorious when completed.

The sun had been up only an hour, and already, people filled the streets. There were more than usual. Everyone from the mining settlement and most of the nearby villages had come for the ceremony yesterday, and some had stayed overnight at inns or with relatives. Petals still clung to the cobblestone streets. They had filled the air the day before, like snow in August, but they had perfumed the air instead of chilling it.

Then he turned to look at his bed, and his bride still sleeping there.

A year and two days had passed since he'd found Helena again. Before Pločnik, Ivan had been filled with anger, and his duty to his people had been a heavy burden for him. Now, anger against the Turks had softened into determined defiance, and his duty no longer weighed him down but instead gave him purpose. What he felt most, however, was joy.

He'd married Helena the day before. He had argued that since Helena had been one of four wives, the traditional mourning period should be cut to three moons instead of twelve. The priest hadn't agreed. When Konstantin and his family had come for the wedding, Suzana had laughed at Ivan's complaint. *The waiting period is so that when she bears you a strong son, there will be no question as to who the father is.* Helena had told him within a week of arriving in Sivi Gora that she was not carrying Kasim's child. Her word had been good enough for him, but now it would be clear to everyone, from the men of Knez Lazar's court to the miners just outside the city to the gossipy keepers of Sivi Gora's taverns.

He watched a family walk by below, a toddler holding on to his father's hand. He and Helena might have had a child that age had they married when they'd first planned to, before their time as exiles in Adrianople. But they were married now, and perhaps a child would come soon. The family followed the road that would lead past the new church and the home Ivan had given to Matthias's widow and children. Ivan had kept his promise to his friend, ensuring his family was taken care of, and he intended to make his city worthy of the sacrifices made by Matthias and so many others that day on the battlefield.

The family below disappeared around a corner, taking the same route to the city gate that Ivan had taken numerous times the past year when called to defend the villages from raiders. The Ottomans had been quiet lately. The Hungarians had not. Iskandar bin Abdullah had also taken that road. When no ransom had come for him, he'd been bought by a Venetian merchant.

The Battle of Pločnik had altered the fates of many. Kasim bin Yazid killed. Lala Şahin Pasha defeated. Iskandar enslaved. Helena freed. Ivan raised to Knez Lazar's war council. More and more lords were flocking to Lazar—Wallachians, Albanians, Bosnians, Bulgarians, and, of course, Serbs. Sultan Murad would have a challenge before him when he came for his revenge. Ivan didn't consider Fate his servant, but he had done his best to seize it at Pločnik, and for the moment, Fate was more songbird than wolf. He would enjoy the sweetness of the music while it lasted.

Helena's voice drifted out to him, humming the same song she'd sung so often when he'd been wounded in Byzia. She strolled toward him, more intoxicating than Homer's Helen of legend. Over the last year, she'd healed his heart as thoroughly as she'd once healed his body. He opened his arms, and she leaned into him, fitting next to his skin. They were like pieces of a bow, layered together, complete only when united. He kissed the top of her head and held her waist.

"That song. It's always been sad before. Do you feel like a wanderer here?" he asked. Women often left their families when they married, but Helena had traveled a longer distance than most. She had healed Sivi Gora's wounded and delivered Sivi Gora's infants for almost a year. She was loved and admired. But that didn't mean she felt at home.

"There are new lyrics now. Happier ones." Softly, she sang them. "'Now I'm dwelling very near to Eden. Finding goodness, after all went wrong. Once a stranger, now beloved family. In the Sivi Gora I belong.'"

"I like the new version." Ivan bent to kiss her more thoroughly. Malleable lips, scented hair, and warm skin filled his senses. He ran his fingers along her cheek, down her neck, across her shoulders.

Helena chuckled and stepped away. "I'm not sure it's proper for a župan to be seen kissing his wife on his balcony."

"Then, we'll go back into the bedchamber and draw the curtains. And stay there for a year."

"A year?"

"At least." Ivan pulled her back toward him and played with the curls of her hair.

"Perhaps you should send a proclamation out, ordering all brigands to cease raiding your lands and all women to cease having babies until we emerge again."

Ivan ran a finger along Helena's lips. He spent a significant amount of time chasing off bands of Hungarian robbers and Turkoman pirates. He doubted they would give him the luxury of seclusion for an entire year. Nor did he want to deprive Sivi Gora's women of their midwife. Danilo's bride would need Helena's assistance before the winter solstice, and plenty of others with her. The Ottomans were expanding, not into Sivi Gora but into other realms, and refugees flooded his lands. There was work to do, for both him and Helena.

"Did I say a year? How about a morning?"

"The morning would be lovely." She took his hand and led him back inside.

The path Ivan's life had taken wasn't what he would have chosen for himself. But the destination was. Helena was by his side, and now, whether he had twenty days or twenty years of peace, he would make the most of what God had given him.

AUTHOR'S NOTES AND ACKNOWLEDGMENTS

THIS STORY IS ONE I'VE wanted to tell since before my first novel was published back in 2012, and I'm so grateful it can now be available as part of a series. I've loved these characters, their journeys, and their adventures for a long time now, and I'm grateful to readers who are willing to try a novel with a setting that is unfamiliar to most. Thank you for reading my book!

As for the history behind Ivan and Helena's story, most historians believe the Battle of Pločnik took place sometime between 1385 and 1388, though at least one Turkish historian claims the battle never happened. I've attempted to stay as close to history as possible, given the limited information available in English. Unfortunately, going back to this time period sees a blending of history and legend. The battle almost certainly did take place, but whether it took place in 1386, as portrayed in this novel, is a matter of debate.

The 1371 Battle of Maritsa (also spelled Marica, or called the Battle of Cernomen/Chernomen) is more well-known, if still shrouded in legend. Some historians argue that though less famous than the 1389 Battle of Kosovo, Maritsa was more devastating to the Serb warrior class. As portrayed in this novel (and detailed in the series prequel novella, *After the Crescent Strike*), the Turks attacked the Serbs while they were camped and soundly defeated them. Radomir's role, like his character, is fictional. Betrayal is a strong theme in Serb legends, but its inclusion in the Battle of Maritsa is added for storytelling purposes.

In writing a novel about civilizations that used Cyrillic, Greek, Turkish, Arabic, and Persian alphabets, I ran into multiple spellings of various names and places. I tried to use the spelling that would be most familiar to modern readers. I chose not to use the term *Byzantine* to describe members of the Byzantine Empire because it wasn't used in the fourteenth century, though *Byzia* is a not-so-subtle historical nod to the name now used for that civilization. The Byzantines referred to themselves as Romans, but in the manuscript, I generally used *Greek* because that was what most of their European neighbors would have used. On the other hand, I went with Latinized Serbian spelling for many names and places, which often uses a *j* instead of a *y*, even though the letter *j* was added to the Latin alphabet after the time of this novel. Serbs in the late fourteenth century spoke a language that originated as Old Church Slavonic but was changing into Early South Slavic. Contemporaries wouldn't have been familiar with either name; they would have called their language Slavonic or Slavic.

At the time of the story, the Ottomans would have been reluctant to refer to themselves as Turks, considering that term more appropriate for rival, less-civilized Turkish tribes in Anatolia. Their Christian opponents wouldn't have placed much of a distinction between Turk and Ottoman.

The devşirme system, or child tax, which took Christian children from their families and forced them into service for the sultan, often as janissaries, was one of the most bitterly remembered elements of the Ottoman Empire. There is some debate about when this practice originated. Some sources suggested it began under Orhan, Murad I's father. Other sources placed it after the time of this novel.

I tried to depict the overall political atmosphere as accurately as possible. The Serbian and Byzantine Empires were in decline during the late fourteenth century and the Ottoman Empire on the rise, though still some distance from its apex of power. Contemporary Byzantines left written records of their history. Most accounts of Serbian and Turkish history were recorded some generations after the events. As might be expected, many of my sources contradicted each other. In my research for this series, I took notes from over sixty books and read many of them cover to cover, but that doesn't mean I got everything right. If I made any errors, I offer my most sincere apologies.

Most of the characters portrayed in this story are fictional, but some are real. Sultan Murad and his sons Bayezid, Yakub, and Savcı are real people, as are Lala Şahin Pasha (known in some sources as Şahin Bey) and Çandarlı Halil Pasha. John V Palaiologos (also spelled Palaeologus) and his son Manuel are real, as are their respective attitudes toward Ottoman suzerainty. Knez Lazar (or Prince Lazar) is also a real figure, though later legends refer to him most often as Tsar Lazar rather than prince or knez. Miloš Obilić's status is more ambiguous. He may not be real, but he played a large role in legend. In either case, he is not a product of my imagination.

Places like Edirne/Adrianople, Thessaloniki, and Kırkpınar are real. The Turks still have a Kırkpınar wrestling tournament every year, and the event is considered the world's longest-running sports competition and a UNESCO Intangible Cultural Heritage. Rivak, Sivi Gora, and Byzia are fictional but are based on Serb and Byzantine culture and governance.

Quotes from the Bible are based on the King James Version. Though the King James Version was not yet created at the time of this story, most of my readers are not Greek speakers, so contemporary versions would do them little good. I felt the King James Version was the best choice (and the most convenient for me, since it is the version I use).

I've done my best to describe clothing, weapons, and buildings as they are most likely to have been at the time. I have also tried to portray the religious beliefs and attitudes with accuracy to the time period. Firearms and cannon were both invented by the time of this story, but they were not yet reliable or widespread, so I'm saving them for Danilo's story.

Most medical practices shown in this book come from texts that would have been available to someone living near Thessaloniki in the late fourteenth century. The use of cesarean sections by Jewish midwives in the late fourteenth century is more a matter of conjecture than proven fact. Several researchers, looking at numerous reports from rabbis, concluded that Jewish mothers were expected to survive cesarean sections from about the second century on. In the Medieval Islamic world, the practice was forbidden. In the Christian world, Beatrice of Bourbon survived a cesarean in 1337 (roughly fifty years before this story), though that seems to have been more luck than studied techniques applied by her attendants.

In closing, I wish to express tremendous gratitude to my test readers: Bev Walkling, Linda White, Charissa Stastny, Kathi Oram Peterson, Jaime Theler, Bradley Grant, Ron Machado, Terri Ferran, and Dr. Carrie Sloan, ob-gyn. Each of them offered advice that made this book better.

I'm also incredibly grateful to the teams at both Covenant and Shadow Mountain for helping me get this book to readers. Special mention goes to my editor, Samantha Millburn, to whom this book is dedicated.

Few things are more helpful to an author than recommendations from one reader to another. If you enjoyed this novel, I would greatly appreciate your telling others about it in person or online wherever books are sold or discussed.

Enjoy this sneak peek of

AGAINST A
CRESCENT
STORM
THE BALKAN LEGENDS

CHAPTER ONE
OMENS OF WAR

The Balkans, 1389

DANILO DARRASEVIĆ HAD SCARCELY HAD a chance to exchange greetings with Konstantin when his cousin swung his fist at a crass Frankish mercenary in the Bosnian tavern. Konstantin's aim, as usual, was right on target.

"Kostya!" Danilo grabbed his cousin's arm before he swung again.

"Did you hear what he said?" Konstantin's expression was controlled, but indignation colored his voice.

Danilo glanced at the mercenary. Blood streamed from the man's nose, and rage showed in his eyes. "Yes. But we're supposed to be making friends, remember?" Konstantin had been sticking up for Danilo since he'd been a boy, but they weren't children anymore, and the Frankish warrior wasn't the first to cast insults at Danilo because he was only half Serbian. "Let him say what he wants. I stopped caring about things like that a long time ago."

"I care." Konstantin glared at the man, who backed away as he wiped the blood from his face, smearing it. Two of Konstantin's men, Miladin and Bojan, stood nearby, both with hands on sword hilts, ready to defend their župan—and Konstantin's kinsman—with their lives.

The injured man looked around the drafty tavern that smelled of onion, bread, and dampness as if looking for allies, but the few locals turned away, and everyone else had either traveled with Konstantin from Rivak or with Danilo's group from Kruševac and Sivi Gora. A few moments more and the injured man retreated to the street outside.

Danilo tugged on the sleeve of his cousin's tunic. "Come on, let's eat before we have to ride again." Danilo hadn't had a hot meal in days, and they had more road ahead of them on their journey west to meet with Kral Trvtko. They sat on a bench before a rough-hewn table.

"What was that all about?" Miloš Obilić joined them, sitting across from Konstantin. Miloš was middle-aged and muscled, perceptive, and prestigious among the Serb nobility. Danilo had traveled with him for most of the last fortnight, though they'd first met years ago.

"That man insulted my cousin." Konstantin glanced at the doorway, as if to make certain the man hadn't returned.

"Rather foolish of him." Miloš accepted a cup of cheap wine and a bowl of stew when the tavern's owner brought food. "But I suppose he hasn't seen either of you in battle. Can't have, or he would have known not to pick a fight with a family as skilled as yours."

Danilo waited for Miloš to remind Konstantin of the importance of their mission and the need for diplomacy, but instead, their companion spoke to Danilo. "Your cousins are protective of you. I'm not sure which one shows it more fiercely." Miloš seemed amused.

Konstantin glanced at Danilo. "Has Ivan had need to protect you lately?"

Danilo accepted his food. He would rather leave that particular incident in the past, where it belonged, but Konstantin would give him no peace if he stayed silent. Either Konstantin would pry, or Miloš would give his version of the events. Danilo had spent enough nights around a fire with him to know any story he told was likely to include a few exaggerations. Better for Konstantin to hear Danilo's account, without any added dramatics. "Ivan hired German mercenaries. Sivi Gora's garrison is strong, but if the Hungarians or the Turks decide to stir up trouble—and especially if they do it at the same time—we can use the extra manpower. One of them claims he saw an ill omen that means I will be the cause of Sivi Gora's destruction. Rumors also circulate that I'm cursed and Tatjana's death was punishment for marrying a Turk."

Konstantin frowned. "That's utter nonsense. Ivan could search to the ends of the earth and not find anyone as loyal as you. And your father may have been an Ottoman, but you've proven that you have a Serbian soul again and again, as did he, regardless of where he was born."

Danilo tasted the stew. It was warm, but that was the best that could be said for it. "Ivan threatened to cut out the man's tongue when he found him, but I told him it was better to let the matter drop. Punishing whoever started it wouldn't stop the gossip. Besides, I expect we'll need those mercenaries come summer. Mutilating one of them won't exactly encourage devotion."

"Ivan let it drop?" Konstantin didn't seem pleased.

"Not at first. But once I convinced his wife that it was the wisest course, he relented."

Konstantin chuckled. "I don't suppose he would want to argue with both of you at once." He tried the stew and made a face.

Miloš finished his meal and stood. "Now that we've met, as scheduled, and Župan Konstantin has frightened off all the riffraff, I'll go check with the others. I want us on the road within an hour." He lowered his voice. "Perhaps Kral Trvtko's cook can give us something decent to eat if we make it there by sunset."

As Miloš left, Konstantin frowned at the stew.

"It's better than the biscuits I've been living on for the last week," Danilo said. "Hurry and finish it because I want to show you something."

Konstantin ate, albeit without enthusiasm. Danilo had spent the first nineteen years of his life in the land his older cousin led as župan before following his younger cousin, Ivan, to his inheritance in Sivi Gora. He was well acquainted with the fine skill of the kitchen staffs in both župas. The tavern fare fell far short, and Konstantin had always had a finicky palate. They'd planned to meet at the tavern for its location along the crossroads, not for the quality of meals. Konstantin had traveled from the southeast; Danilo and Miloš from the northeast.

"How is Suzana?" Danilo asked.

A smile lit Konstantin's face. "She is recovering well, and we are both pleased that our daughter came before I needed to make this journey."

"And the boys?"

"Marko wants to be as good an archer as you." Konstantin finished his stew, and the two men stood. "Spends all his spare time on the archery range. Reminds me of you and Ivan when you were still boys. Pavle doesn't show much interest in weapons yet, but he does well on his pony."

They stepped outside, and Danilo led Konstantin to where his own horse was tied next to Miloš's powerfully built stallion.

"That's a fine animal." Konstantin admired Miloš's horse. "Do you suppose Miloš would sell him to me?"

"Not a chance. Miloš values Ždralin almost as much as he values his own mother."

Konstantin smiled wistfully. "How is your mother? She is missed."

"My mother is in good health. She sends her love and letters. Ivan sent a slightly more ostentatious sign of his affection." Danilo gestured to an unsaddled Hungarian destrier tied near his own warhorse.

Konstantin walked over to the big chestnut stallion. "He didn't."

"He did."

Konstantin moved to his new horse and examined it. "Well, whatever he's asking me to do, the answer is undoubtedly yes."

Danilo smiled. "It's a gift, not a bribe."

"I hope that means things are well in Sivi Gora?"

"For the time being." Danilo looked around the mostly empty yard. One of Miloš's men had stayed to watch the animals. He lay in a pile of hay with his eyes closed and his face relaxed.

"And in the days ahead? Will Ivan have needs then?" Konstantin asked.

"As long as Murad reigns, he is a threat. For now, the sultan is busy subjugating the Bulgarians, but he intends to make us pay for beating his generals at Pločnik. We'll all be in need then." Danilo had lived as a hostage among the Turks for two years. He knew what they were capable of, and that knowledge sometimes frightened him. Victory at Pločnik had freed them, but sometimes, their liberty felt fragile and fleeting.

"Rivak will stand with Knez Lazar. That's why I met you here. You know that. "

"I do. And Miloš and I are grateful to count you a firm ally." Danilo patted his own horse, Dazhbog. Like Konstantin's, it was a gift from Ivan. "We hope Trvtko will fall into the alliance with as much ease. But Bosnia is farther from the Turks, so the danger is not as great for him. And if the Turks distract Knez Lazar, Kral Trvtko might be tempted to snatch up some of Lazar's lands."

"Or Ivan's lands. My brother lies between three giants."

Danilo well knew the precarious geography of Sivi Gora, but not all neighbors gave him cause for concern. "Knez Lazar won't turn on Ivan, not after Ivan's role at Pločnik. Kral Trvtko is more of an unknown, which is why Ivan and Lazar send gifts for him as well."

Konstantin ran his hand along his new destrier. "That sounds diplomatic. Not a skill I would normally credit to my brother."

"The first time Ivan picked up a sword, he could barely wield it, and the first time he climbed on a pony, he fell off. He mastered those skills. He will master diplomacy as well."

"Good. Because even if he is safe from Knez Lazar and Kral Trvtko, the Hungarians aren't to be trusted."

Danilo grunted his agreement. He had accompanied Ivan on patrols time after time to stop Hungarian brigands from attacking Sivi Gora's outlying villages and mining community. Hungarian nobles didn't send the raiders, but nor did they stop them. If Ivan made too strong of a protest, it might provoke war. But too weak a response could embolden the enemy. A delicate balance with Király Sigismund and his Hungarian nobles, combined with concern over the Ottomans, shadowed Ivan's rule. "Miloš and I may approach them on our way back from Bosnia."

Konstantin frowned slightly. "Make an alliance with the Latin half-believers?"

"If Murad attacks, we can't be picky about whose support we accept. We met with an ispán, Janos Bokori, over the winter. He didn't agree to an alliance, but he didn't outright reject it either. Knez Lazar wants us to try again, as does Ivan." Miloš and Danilo carried thoughtfully selected gifts for Trvtko and more general gifts for Bokori because they knew so little of him.

"Surely Knez Lazar has his own emissaries without stealing Ivan's. It sounds as though you've been traveling all winter and all spring."

Ivan had said roughly the same thing to Danilo, asking him if he was sure he wanted to leave again so soon after returning from his last trip. "I volunteered for this journey. And for the previous ones. I'm more useful to our people out here than I am in Sivi Gora."

Konstantin turned his attention from the horse and focused only on his cousin. "Does Ivan never let you rest?"

"I am in good health. There is little need for me to mope about in Sivi Gora when Ivan can handle everything there himself." Župan Ivan couldn't be in two places at once, but Danilo knew his cousin's goals and needs well enough to act with confidence on Sivi Gora's behalf.

Konstantin folded his arms across his chest. "Danilo, ever since you were little, you and Ivan have been inseparable. Have you quarreled?"

"Of course not." There was no one on earth Danilo admired and loved more than his cousin Ivan.

"A quarrel with Helena?"

Danilo shook his head. His relationship with Ivan's wife had seen more than one strain. He'd frightened her on their first meeting, and it had taken him a long time to understand how Ivan could trust her so completely when she'd once broken a promise to him and crushed his heart. Yet they had come to respect each other, especially after Helena had befriended Danilo's timid wife. Helena had been the attending midwife when the time had come to deliver Tatjana. Neither Danilo's wife nor his child had survived. "What happened with the baby wasn't Helena's fault."

The delivery had been a difficult one, and Tatjana had been so delicate. But the double loss still felt raw. In Sivi Gora, Danilo slept at the barracks instead of in his empty home. And when emissaries were needed for diplomatic tasks all across the Balkans, he used the missions as a chance to escape.

"Are you unhappy in Sivi Gora?" Konstantin's gray eyes studied Danilo carefully. "There will always be a place for you in Rivak, should you desire it."

Danilo glanced at Miloš's man in the haystack. Tihomir looked to be asleep. "Sivi Gora is prosperous, and Ivan is a good župan and a good friend, but sometimes I think my presence is difficult for him."

"How? You've been his best friend since he was old enough to toddle along after you."

"I think he feels guilty that his wife and daughter are alive and healthy and my wife and daughter are dead."

Konstantin bit his lip. "I am sorry for your loss, Danilo." It wasn't the first time Konstantin had expressed his condolences, and Danilo knew he meant it. Konstantin had lost three infants but not his wife. He could understand part of the pain but not all of it. And Konstantin would never have the guilt Danilo carried, the ever-present worry that the rumor started by the mercenaries was true, and the deaths were somehow Danilo's fault.

Danilo nodded his acknowledgment. His daughter had been born too early, and something inside Tatjana had perished with the infant. The fever had been but the final blow to someone who had already given up on life.

Konstantin was quiet for a few moments before changing the subject. "Does Ivan still obsess over defenses?"

Danilo smiled. "Until the walls of Sivi Gora resemble the Theodosian walls of Constantinople, he will keep building."

"Ivan's never been to Constantinople. How would he know what the walls look like?"

"His wife was born there. And it's not just walls. He's been buying cannon."

Konstantin nodded. "If Trvtko won't help us, I'm afraid we'll need more than cannon. We need him as an ally, not an enemy."

Danilo worried about Trvtko, too, but the past gave him hope that their mission would prove successful. "He came to Pločnik and fought well."

"Yes. But many things can change in three years."

Danilo thought back to Pločnik, when the Serbs had thrown off their vassalage and won their freedom from the Ottomans. The battle had been hard-fought, but they'd been lucky. They had caught the Turks while they were scattered, and they'd inflicted heavy losses on their enemy while suffering relatively light casualties themselves. Danilo had followed his best friend into battle, and he had seen Ivan rise to greatness. They had been triumphant, and that exhilaration had made it seem as if Sivi Gora would stand unthreatened for a hundred years. Danilo had married, and then Ivan had. And they had both been delighted with their brides, confident that their hard-earned happiness would last. But it took only one difficult delivery to take a wife, and it would take but one failed battle to take their freedom.

Konstantin was right. Many things could change in three years.

CHAPTER TWO
THE SMUGGLER'S SLAVE

THE ADRIATIC SEA SHIMMERED LIKE polished copper in the light of the setting sun, but it offered little beauty for a slave. Iskandar bin Abdullah shouldered another barrel of salted fish and carried it down the ramp of his Venetian master's ship currently docked in the port of Durazzo.

"Quickly now. I want the unloading finished before the light disappears," Signor Grato called to his workers and slaves.

Iskandar picked up his pace, at least while Grato could see him. The rotund man with whiskered jowls and ridiculous curled-toe shoes had owned Iskandar for two-and-a-half years. In contrast to his master's red hose and thick doublet, Iskandar's clothing was stained and tattered. He still wore the robes he'd been captured in after the Battle of Pločnik. He'd made numerous mistakes then, when he'd been a leader among the Ottoman raiders, choices he had regretted ever since. He shouldn't have been so sure of himself, shouldn't have underestimated his Serbian foes, shouldn't have given in to pressure from his men to ease their restlessness through pillage. At times, he also regretted begging for mercy when he'd been captured by his enemies. Ivan and Danilo had spared him, but there had been moments—so many of them—when Iskandar had been certain death would have been a better option than slavery.

But he would not remain a slave forever. He had learned from his past mistakes. He would wait for the right moment, and then he would have his vengeance and escape his wretched condition. Allah willing, the moment would come soon. He had imagined up twenty-seven ways to kill Grato, one for every scar his master's whip had left on his back.

When they'd first docked in Durazzo, Iskandar had deemed the port a poor choice for his escape. None of the other ships looked like they belonged to Muslims, and anyway, his destination wasn't along the coast. But as he put the heavy barrel in the back of a cart and went for another, he reevaluated his options. Durazzo was far from his old home in Edirne, but from Durazzo, the Via Egnatia led all the way to Constantinople. The road would take him through Thrace and Macedonia and into Ottoman lands, where he would be safe. As long as he was among Christians, he was vulnerable, but joining a caravan would offer him a measure of protection while in hostile lands, and he spoke enough Christian languages to blend in. Yet no caravan would take a beggar, so Iskandar needed not only his freedom but also coin.

As he unloaded barrels, he kept an eye on Grato negotiating with a merchant. A purse exchanged hands, and Grato put it inside his doublet next to his black heart. Then he turned to one of his employees, d'Artusio. "Bring the trunk. Use the Turk and the heretic."

D'Artusio waited until Iskandar unloaded another barrel, then motioned for him to follow. On their way back up the ramp to the ship, d'Artusio motioned over the Bogomil slave with a branded face. Iskandar didn't know what was in the trunk, but it was heavily guarded, so it had to be valuable. He took one end, and the Bogomil took the other, and they walked it down the ramp and set it in the back of an otherwise empty cart.

"Climb in. We'll want you for the delivery." D'Artusio sat in the back with Iskandar and the Bogomil and kept his hand on the dagger at his waist. Grato called out a few instructions to the ship's crew and then climbed onto the cart, took the reins, and urged the horses forward.

Iskandar leaned into the planks of the cart as it jostled along. He'd sailed into Durazzo before. He'd been a new slave then, chained on the ship until they'd sailed again. As they moved away from the waterfront now, he admired the red-tile roofs and the tall houses. It wasn't as splendid as Edirne or Venice, but Durazzo was certainly more impressive than most of the villages he'd raided as a ghazi.

Grato stopped the cart at a wide double-door gate. He gestured to Iskandar. "Go knock."

Iskandar obeyed, something he had learned well over the last few years. As a slave, all his choices had been taken away save one: he could obey, or he could suffer a beating. But now curiosity mixed with his resigned subservience. Grato owned his ship and transported goods for a profit, but normally, his business was with other merchants. This was a private residence, and it lay far from the waterfront.

One side of the gate swung open, and an armed guard examined Iskandar through narrowed eyes. Then he looked past Iskandar to Grato and d'Artusio. He expression changed from hostile to neutral, and then he opened the other half of the gate.

Iskandar climbed back into the cart as Grato shook the reins. The guard closed the gate after they passed through, then walked ahead of the horses to guide them.

The clip of horses' hooves echoed through the courtyard, past what Iskandar assumed were the home's more public rooms, to a small, dark door in the back of the courtyard. The guard's knock was met by a narrow-faced man in rich robes.

He glanced at Grato. "Come."

D'Artusio motioned for Iskandar and the Bogomil to follow him with the trunk. Four torches lit the room they entered, but it was otherwise empty.

Grato took a key from a chain on his neck and unlocked the trunk. The man with the expensive clothing gestured for his guard to open the lid. At first, all Iskandar saw was pale linen, but it had to hide something else. Grato wouldn't have locked a trunk of ordinary cloth, nor would a load like that have weighed so much. The guard turned back the fabric, revealing five metal tubes. Hand bombards? Iskandar stepped closer, drawn to the weapons he'd heard of but had never before seen.

Grato cleared his throat, and d'Artusio took Iskandar and the Bogomil outside. But d'Artusio's curiosity must have been nearly as strong as Iskandar's because he went back in.

The Bogomil looked around the courtyard, and Iskandar followed his example. The fading twilight showed it to be empty other than the two of them. The Bogomil started for the gate.

"If you want to escape, it would be best to wait," Iskandar said.

"Why?"

"If you leave now, Grato will begin the search as soon as he comes out. If you wait, I'll help, and I'll make sure no one starts looking for us until daybreak." If the Bogomil left now, Grato and d'Artusio would be far more vigilant, ruining Iskandar's chances of escaping later, after he'd had the chance to take Grato's coin.

"Why wait? This may be my only opportunity."

"You're a marked man. How will you hide the brand on your face when there's a reward for your capture?"

The Bogomil stopped. Iskandar picked up a fist-sized rock and hid it in the folds of his robes. Then he leaned against the side of the cart, playing the part of a tired slave at the end of a long day. If the Bogomil left, Iskandar would follow, but he still hoped the man would return to the cart and wait for better timing.

The Bogomil came back eventually. "You have a plan?"

Iskandar nodded.

"One you can accomplish?"

"I am a slave only because I was captured in battle. I know how to kill men, and I know how to blend in. I expect to use both skills tonight. Follow my lead, and we'll both earn our freedom."

Grato and d'Artusio came back outside before the Bogomil could ask for details. D'Artusio held a leather satchel. Iskandar expected grand payment for a trunk of hand bombards. Perhaps the satchel contained gold. He would find out soon enough.

Iskandar feigned slumber as Grato drove the cart toward the wharf, believable after all the work Grato had given him that day. The muscles of his arms were sore whenever he moved them, despite his long acquaintance with the labor demands of a slave. The skin of his hands was scratched, despite the calluses he'd long ago developed from hauling around heavy cargo. He would have liked a real weapon, but a quiet confidence settled on him, not unlike when he had gone into battle.

The night grew dark, and though the hour was not late, most people were off the streets, especially as the cart returned to the waterfront. Iskandar gazed around with half-closed eyes. Grato's ship was still a hundred paces away. D'Artusio stared across the water, and Grato guided the horses.

Iskandar caught the Bogomil's eye and nodded. The other slave tensed. Iskandar gripped the rock and swung it into the side of d'Artusio's head. The foreman slumped to the side immediately, and Iskandar leaped toward Grato. His master turned. Iskandar saw the terror on his face just before he smashed the rock into Grato's throat. Iskandar would have rather smashed his aquiline nose, but he didn't want to give Grato a chance to call for help. Grato wouldn't suffer the same way he had made Iskandar suffer, but the punishment would be enough to satisfy Iskandar's thirst for justice. With his free hand, Iskandar grabbed Grato's throat and squeezed. Grato fought back, clawing at Iskandar's hand and gouging it with his heavy rings, but then Iskandar struck Grato's head again, and the master's resistance ended.

"Are you mad?" the Bogomil asked. "We'll be wanted for murder now."

Neither d'Artusio nor Grato was dead yet, but their deaths would be necessary. "Help me dump them in the harbor."

The Bogomil shook his head and climbed from the cart. Then he darted away, moving toward the buildings of Durazzo. Iskandar let him go. He wasn't running for the authorities. He was running away, but he wouldn't get far. Heretics weren't welcome in Durazzo, and with neither friend nor money, the Bogomil would have few options. Iskandar would have helped him, pretended to be his master until they passed through Bosnia, but he didn't need the heretic's assistance.

Iskandar took d'Artusio's cloak, tunic, boots, dagger, and satchel. Then he dragged him to the harbor and slipped him into the water. He did the same with Grato, only he took fewer pieces of clothing from him. He'd never cared for Grato's ostentatious fashion. Iskandar did, however, take the man's hat and the pouch of gold.

The horses stamped and grunted as Iskandar unfastened them from the cart. He wasn't sure he could find a saddle to purchase overnight, but he would try. He fastened the dagger to his belt, wrapped d'Artusio's cloak about him, and donned Grato's hat, then led the animals from the waterfront as quickly as he could. He would wait and change into d'Artusio's serviceable tunic when he was farther away. Thus far, no one had noticed the two bodies dumped into the dark harbor, but that could change at any moment. He checked the scratches across his hands and wrists. They stung, but they bled only a little.

He slowed his pace when the smell of the harbor faded and forced his stride and posture to match that of an average man, one who had no master. He followed the main road, assuming that would give him the best chance of finding a caravan.

By the time the sun rose the next day, he had bought a saddle and provisions. At first light, he left with a group of twenty travelers. He'd heard no talk of runaway slaves or murdered merchants. No one in the caravan seemed to doubt his tale that he carried a message from a Venetian senator.

As the morning grew warm and Durazzo faded in the distance, the feeling that he was again master of his own destiny slowly began to sink in. Grato and his whip were no more, and vengeance against his other enemies—including the Serbs—was now within Iskandar's reach.

For more books in this series,
visit https://shdwmtn.com/alsowards,
or scan the QR code below:

Photo by VaLynn Woolley

ABOUT THE AUTHOR

A. L. SOWARDS IS THE AUTHOR of over a dozen historical fiction novels, with settings spanning the globe from the fourteenth to twentieth centuries. Her stories have earned multiple awards, including a Whitney Award and a Readers' Favorite gold medal. Sowards grew up in Washington State, spent a few decades in Utah, and now resides in Alaska with her husband, three children, and ever-growing library. She enjoys hiking and swimming, usually manages to keep up with the laundry, and loves it when someone else cooks dinner.

Sowards enjoys connecting with readers and can be found online at ALSowards.com or on Facebook, Goodreads, and Instagram. Readers can sign up for her newsletter at ALSowards.com/newsletter.